# MAYE'S REQUEST

Visit us at www.boldstrokesbooks.com

# What Reviewers Say About Clifford Henderson

## The Middle of Somewhere

"The characters in this book are easy to relate to, I found myself caring about their struggles, and celebrating their triumphs... Clifford Henderson writes with depth and ease. Her writing gives you the sense that her muse was not only visiting, but had moved in."—*Out In Jersey*

"...Henderson grabs her readers in a firm grip and never lets go. *The Middle of Somewhere* is a wonderful laugh-out-loud read filled with pathos, hope, and new beginnings...a very good read."—*Just About Write*

"I read this book as the required reading for a book club. What a great pick it was! I loved this book. I was laughing from the first paragraph all the way to the end, and in the meantime fell in love with all the characters. Although this is Henderson's first published novel her writing is replete with complex characters and a full-bodied plot, sort of like a well-rounded Merlot. I can't help but give this book a hearty two-thumbs up review and hope that you'll read it. I know you'll enjoy it just as much as I did."—*Kissed by Venus*

## Spanking New

"Clifford Henderson has written a masterpiece in *Spanking New*. ... Henderson's clever exploration of her protagonists' feelings leads the reader into a world where gender and identity are fluid. *Spanking New* should be a required reading for all gender and queer study courses. While the author addresses serious issues, her book is fun, fun, fun! The playfulness, curiosity and fresh naivety as portrayed through the eyes of the story teller is refreshing and often humorous. It is pure genius on Henderson's part to write from this perspective. The protagonists are endearing and very human as you follow their struggles to navigate through life. The reader is able to sympathize with the antagonist's feelings as well, in this richly developed exploration of human beings' struggles to make sense of their worlds."—*Anita Kelly, LGBT Coordinator, Muhlenberg College*

"Spanky, the narrator of this delicious novel, is an unborn baby who can flit from one character's thoughts and emotions to another's—a storytelling perspective that, from a less able author, might have come off as a diaper-load of a gimmick. But Henderson, in only her second book, handles the unorthodox point of view with inventive style and charm. ...Already a "best" of 2010."—*Richard Labonte, Book Marks*

"*Spanking New* is a book that brings the fantasy of what happened before I was born, to life. If you have ever wondered what you were, or where you came from, Clifford Henderson gives you an interesting, oft times hilarious answer. The gender benders in this book are lovable characters, the most memorable being "Spanky" the "floating soul" that is looking to attach to his parents. When Spanky finally does manage to finagle a meeting of his soon to be parents Nina and Rick, the sparks fly, and all seems right with the world that he is about to enter, until Spanky finds out he is a girl! Other than being hilarious, this is a poignant point of view, and makes for a fun and interesting read."—*Out In Jersey*

"Clifford Henderson took a warm look at people in her first novel, *The Middle of Somewhere.* She continues her warm looks in *Spanking New.* Spanking New is told through the viewpoint of Spanky. As a floating soul, he is able to get into the minds of his chosen parents, their friends, and their families. The viewpoint is that of someone new to our world and all of its nuances. What emerges is a funny commentary on the foibles of humans. ...*Spanking New* is a book I found myself talking about with others, and one which I won't soon forget. This is a wise and funny book."—*Just About Write*

# By the Author

The Middle of Somewhere

Spanking New

Maye's Request

# MAYE'S REQUEST

*by*

## Clifford Henderson

2011

**MAYE'S REQUEST**
© 2011 BY CLIFFORD HENDERSON. ALL RIGHTS RESERVED.

ISBN 10: 1-60282-199-2
ISBN 13: 978-1-60282-199-6

THIS TRADE PAPERBACK ORIGINAL IS PUBLISHED BY
BOLD STROKES BOOKS, INC.
P.O. BOX 249
VALLEY FALLS, NY 12185

FIRST EDITION: JANUARY 2011

**CREDITS**
EDITOR: CINDY CRESAP
PRODUCTION DESIGN: SUSAN RAMUNDO
COVER DESIGN BY SHERI (GRAPHICARTIST2020@HOTMAIL.COM)

# Acknowledgments

My partner, Dixie Cox, for her keen plot and character insights. (And for putting up with me when the going gets rough.)

My writing group, Sallie Johnson, Gino Danna, and Philip Slater, for keeping me on track and being willing to sit around and discuss the proper placement of a semicolon.

Bookshop Santa Cruz for letting my writing group meet there.

My father, Lee Henderson, and his wife, Mary Henderson, for getting me to think about Guillain-Barré syndrome.

My editor, Cindy Cresap, for making this tale a better one.

Stacia Seaman, for answering my many punctuation questions.

My cover artist, Sheri, for a cover I absolutely love.

Captain of the Good Ship Bold Strokes, Len Barot, for her tireless efforts to get lesbian fiction on your bookshelf.

Connie, Lori, Lee, Paula, and all the other women and men of Bold Strokes, for making us authors look good.

And most importantly, you, the reader, for completing the circle.

A heartfelt thanks to you all.

# Dedication

For my sister, Biz, who always helps me
get through the hard parts.

# CHAPTER ONE

Trapped. Row twenty-two, center seat, Mexicana airbus roaring thirty thousand feet above the earth. Occupying the window seat to my left is Joe Dude Laptop Junkie returning from his "vacay in Me-hi-co." He's blowing up digital aliens while rocking out to some heavy metal blasting from his earbuds, his elbow occasionally ramming my ribs. On the aisle: Miss Dorito-Smacking-Everything's-So-Cheap-I-Couldn't-Stop-Myself who's crammed the surrounding overhead compartments so full with her "deals" there's no room for my backpack. She's gabbing with her BFF sitting across the aisle. I offered to switch seats with one of them, but apparently they like their conversation spewing out for everyone to hear. I lift my face to the spray of cool air shooting from my vent. Miss Dorito Breath has mentioned to her BFF several times (for my benefit I'm sure) how chilly she is. But if she gets the aisle and the overhead compartment, and Laptop Junkie gets the window and the armrest, I get my vent.

I should be honest. If I weren't afraid of being apprehended as a terrorist, I'd leap from my seat and start shrieking in tongues, or screaming nonsensical obscenities. Anything to relieve this pressure. But it's not due to my current neighbors. They aren't making a dent in the tornado of emotions whirling inside me.

I'm about to see my family.

I slip my itinerary from between the *Sky Mall* magazine and puke bag to check my arrival time. An hour and seventeen minutes left. I stare at my legal name at the top of the document—Brianna Cleo Bell. But nobody will be calling me that for a while. Oh no. Once this plane touches ground, I'll be back to being Bean. Please, God, if you even exist, don't let me revert along with the name change. Let me retain some shred of maturity.

I touch my fingers to my tongue. I can still taste Serena.

I sure didn't see that coming.

We took off for Mexico as friends. Not even good friends. Our relationship consisted mostly of pulling weeds and hosing off aphids. We both just graduated the apprenticeship program at UCSC's garden, land of organic farming and agroecology studies. And sure, I liked her all right, but she seemed, I don't know, too emotionally stable for me? Then, at our graduation potluck, she mentioned she was looking for someone to share the rent of the palapa she'd lined up in a place called Sayulita, and seeing as the three thousand dollars my dad gave me as a graduation present was burning a hole in my pocket, I thought, why not? My life was going nowhere.

When I told Mom that a friend and I were going to the small town of Sayulita, Mexico, for an undetermined amount of time, she was not enthused. She accused me of squandering my graduation money, of tagging along on Serena's trip. Which of course was true. Not only had Serena already secured a job serving up "Real Fish Tacos" and "Tilapia Mexicanos" at one of Sayulita's prime tourist restaurants, she'd also enrolled in a local yoga class.

We were only five days into the trip when I got the call to come home. Serena was asleep, her soft cheek resting on my shoulder. I was thinking about how crazy it was that we'd made love. It was so out of the blue; we weren't drunk or anything.

She was teaching me to play cribbage at the sturdy wooden table in our palapa. I was resistant. My mom loves to play games, and I'm not talking about the Hasbro kind. I'm talking the mess with your head kind, where a person thinks they know what's good for you and goes about manipulating it to happen. Suffice it to say, my childhood left me with a decided dislike of any kind of scheming. I crave truth, transparency.

Serena was wearing a green and blue sarong and had her curly black hair knotted on her head and huge gold hoop earrings in her ears. She's exotic looking, her skin the color of toasted almonds, her eyes, accentuated by bold black eyebrows, are a brilliant green. Her lips are full and love to smile. As for me, I had on brick-red cargo shorts, a white bikini top, and my new favorite leather-strand choker with a small shell. Both of us were glowing from days at the beach and swimming in the warm, warm water. On the table next to the cribbage board was a brightly painted clay plate holding mango slices and jicama sprinkled with lime and chili powder. A balmy breeze was picking up on the ocean and blowing through the faded paisley cotton curtains over the sink. For some reason, we started cracking up about what you say when your hand contains a jack with the same suit as the start card: "One for his nob." It's stupid in retrospect, but at the time it was hilarious. The next thing I know, she leaned across the table and kissed me on the lips. It was an awkward kiss because I didn't expect it. I was reaching forward to move my peg and her lips brushed against mine just as I was settling back in my chair. But that brushing of lips ignited in me a blaze so strong that my body jumped into action before my mind had a chance to consider if it was prudent to have sex with someone with whom I'd signed a month's lease.

I dropped my cards, pushed the mango and jicama out of my way, and crawled up over the table for more. Then everything went crazy. We started pulling off each other's clothes, stumbling from the table to my bed by the wall. I was kissing her eyes, her neck, her small breasts. She had her legs locked around my waist and was tugging at my hair, nipping and sucking my ears.

I've had sex with friends before. A lot, actually. Some friendships survive it. Some don't. But one thing is always true. It leaves me feeling unsatisfied, like a dry, tasteless carob bar, making the next morning, if I even spend the night, rather awkward. This was different. It was rich, sweet, creamy, dark chocolate sex that left me simultaneously buzzed and wasted. Serena was amazing—*is* amazing—and as I lay there listening to the ocean waves slapping against the sand, Serena sleeping cuddled in my arms, I thought I might love her.

At some point, I must have fallen asleep because I woke to the sound of my phone's ring tone. I pried myself out of bed and padded across our small palapa, hoping to turn off the phone before it woke Serena. I fumbled around until I found the phone in the pocket of my cargo shorts. When I glanced at the readout, I knew I had to pick up.

"I'm sorry to be calling so early," Aunt Jen said, her voice all business. "But it's about your mom."

I was immediately suspicious. Mom loves drama, and if there's one thing I've learned in my twenty-three years of life, it's to hold out jumping onto her drama mobile until I've heard all the facts.

Serena sat up in bed, her mango-scented breasts exposed. "Everything okay?"

"Don't know," I mouthed then turned my back to her. What can I say? I'm not good at multitasking.

"She's come down with something serious and it seems to be getting worse," Aunt Jen continued.

A gecko dropped from the wall onto the kitchen counter.

"Tell me…"

"You need to come."

❖

I pull my backpack from beneath the seat in front of me and rummage through it for the slip of paper where I wrote down what Mom's got. It's got some weird French name that I keep forgetting. Guillain-Barré syndrome. I've never even heard of it. Which is just like Mom to get something no one's ever heard of. In the airport I did a little research on the Web and learned that it causes temporary paralysis for up to two weeks and that it can kill a person if the paralysis moves into the respiratory system. Which is the worry with Mom. She's on day four and supposedly can't move her arms and legs at all. Aunt Jen said it all started with Mom getting one of her sinus infections. Now she's in the ICU.

I swear, if this turns out to be one of Mom's fake-outs, I'm going to kill her myself.

Aunt Jen made the six-hour drive from Santa Cruz to Shasta two days ago.

Of course she would. She's still in love with Mom. That's my opinion. For all I know, Dad's still in love with her too. He's dated other people. So has Aunt Jen. So has Mom, for that matter. But somehow, none of their dates ever lives up.

No wonder my love life has such a disappointing history. It's in my genes.

I rub my tired face. Did I remember to brush my teeth? Everything this morning happened so fast—getting the call, barely catching the bus to the airport in Puerto Vallarta, getting on the standby list, a seat, and now flying thousands of feet above the earth and breathing fake air.

Dad and I are meeting up at the airport in Redding, California. His flight from Philly arrives about the same time as mine. This is going to be so weird. Mom must have made Aunt Jen call him. Actually, knowing Aunt Jen, she e-mailed. But the fact that Dad agreed to come is mind-blowing. He hasn't been in the same room with Aunt Jen for fifteen years. They despise each other.

It's the family geometry. Begin with a love triangle. Not the kind you usually hear about, because those aren't true. Those are love Vs, because two of the points never connect. Maybe the lover and the betrayed one stand awkwardly across the room from each other at a party or pass each other on the street, but the thing that draws them together is hate, not love. Mom, Dad, and Aunt Jen make a true love triangle. That final line between lover and betrayed one is connected by blood. Mom's lover, Aunt Jen, is Dad's twin sister.

Mom says there was a time when the Bell twins were freakishly close. Indeed, Jake and Jen Bell look so similar it leads one to wonder if a boy and a girl can't be genetically identical. They are both tall and angular with walnut-colored hair and penetrating hazel eyes. Mom loves them both. She also feels guilty that she came between them.

Aunt Jen will say she isn't the one who came between Mom and Dad; it was Dad's drinking, but I know she feels guilty too.

Which brings me to the next geometric shape—the square. This is where I come in. I'm situated in the corner between Mom and Aunt Jen with Dad clear across on the other side. True, I'm genetically closer to Dad, but Mom and I moved from Philly to live with Aunt Jen in Santa Cruz, California, when I was only eight, so I have only vague memories of him as a father. I never get the feeling that Mom wants to get back with him, but there's some deep connection between Mom and Dad that makes Aunt Jen a little crazy.

At least Mom and Aunt Jen aren't together anymore. That should make a difference to Dad. Right after I graduated from high school, their relationship blew apart. Mom moved six long hours up the state of California to Shasta. Aunt Jen stayed in Santa Cruz, as did I, only I moved up the hill to the UC Santa Cruz campus and stayed so busy I didn't have much time for any of them.

I turn toward Miss Dorito and tap her on the arm as she's chatting it up with her BFF across the aisle. "Excuse me."

She twists around in her seat and takes me in through her beady, overly made-up eyes.

"I have to go to the bathroom."

She sighs at the imposition then heaves herself up out of row twenty-two. Now the only obstacle is the seat directly in front of me, which is fully reclined. After a bit of contortion, I extricate myself and head down the aisle.

Once inside the claustrophobic wash station, I go through the motions of peeing, even though barely anything comes out, then I sit there a few seconds imagining my pee falling to earth in one of those blue ice balls and crashing into someone's living room. I get up, splash water on my face, and stare at myself in the mirror. I definitely resemble Mom's side of the family, the Parfreys—small but strong, kind of scrappy-looking actually, with wavy blond hair, and a mouth almost too big for my face when I smile. Mom's and my looks differ when it comes to our eyes. We both have the same color, gray-blue, but hers have this perpetual soft focus as if she's gazing at auras instead of concrete matter. Which may be true. When she remembers an event, she never has a clue what anyone was wearing or where the event took place, but she can recount, accurately, everyone's emotional state. Whereas my eyes fix on their target. I've been told I could stare down a skyscraper.

I lean over the sink and shake my head hoping to free some of yesterday's sand. The seawater gluing my short curls together makes it look like I'm trying for dreadlocks. (Yah, mahn.) My favorite turquoise "Question Reality" T-shirt, which gives me that extra-tan sheen and brings out the blue in my eyes, is rumpled, but I don't care. I wore it to remind myself of yesterday. Anything to help me hold on to the life I've created for myself.

Walking down the caterpillar tube that connects the plane to the terminal, my anxiety hits epic proportions. Seeing Dad is always so difficult. The last time was when he flew out for my graduation a few weeks ago. Of course, he didn't actually attend the event. He couldn't do *that;* Aunt Jen was going to be there. He just flew in, took me to dinner, gave me three thousand dollars, and flew home.

I took him to my favorite Greek restaurant, and over lamb souvlaki, freshly baked pita bread dipped in tzatziki, and a massive Greek salad with feta and olives, we talked politics—a subject normal families avoid. He liked Obama all right, but he loved the blue-collar Joe Biden. We also talked briefly about my future, a topic that makes me want to break out in hives. He was curious what a person did with a degree in environmental studies. Eager to avoid the discussion of my employment plans (I had none), I told him about my work in agroecology and sustainable farming, how this was the wave of the future. "It has to be," I said. "We're running out of resources." But even as I said this, I knew Dad would be just as happy eating at MacSquander's or Waste King. To his credit, he tried to look enthusiastic and wished me luck and then we moved on to movies we'd seen.

The three thousand bucks was shocking. He's always given me money for birthdays and such, but usually just fifty bucks. Mom said the money was because he feels guilty for not being more a part of my life and that he's trying to make amends. Then again, she gave me an IOU for "something special" she's making me. What does *that* mean? Aunt Jen's was the only gift from my family that didn't need deciphering—a newly refurbished iBook. It was a great gift and so her. She can't imagine anyone getting through life without a state-of-the-art computer. It's in my backpack right now as I walk through the crowded terminal.

I can't stop imagining this place from a bird's-eye view. It's as if we're all on a game board—one with multiple paths we must negotiate, each one leading to a different fate. Do you follow the flock? Strike out on your own? Or go charging down the hall waving your arms like a chicken?

Great. I haven't even seen Dad yet and already I'm jumping out of my skin.

I head past the security checkpoint into the un-secure area of the airport. (Or should I call it insecure?) I spot Dad. As usual, he's towering over everybody. He's dressed in his casuals—khaki trousers and a crisp, light blue, short-sleeved button-down.

He sees me and waves.

I wave.

There's no going back now. Like it or not, I'm heading into the complicated jigsaw puzzle of my family. The problem is there's no box with a picture on the front, so there's no telling what it's supposed to look like. What's more, there are pieces missing. They've been swept under rugs, kicked under the sofa, caught in the cuff of a pant leg and transported to who knows where.

I take a deep breath and break away from the crowd. "Hey, Dad."

\*

Ten-and-a-half-year-old Jake sat at the small stained table across from his twin sister Jen. Their dad sat catty-cornered between them. They were at Rizzo's and the square table rocked whenever one of them leaned on it. Jake watched his 7UP slosh over the edge of his glass. He'd ordered his favorite pizza steak sandwich while

Jen had ordered her favorite—a cheesesteak with grilled onions and mushrooms.

He bit into the chewy crust of his sandwich. Pizza sauce dripped down his chin. Something weird was going on. Their dad hadn't been home for five nights in a row and then just showed up at the house and announced he was taking Jake and Jen out for cheesesteaks. "You'd like that, wouldn't you, kids?" he said. Their mom had raced up the stairs to her bedroom and slammed the door making it clear *she* wouldn't.

It wasn't the first time their dad hadn't come home at night, but all the other times he'd stayed away for just one night. And he'd never taken stuff with him before. This time he'd taken a bunch of his clothes; everything off his dresser including the bowl where he emptied his pockets at the end of the day so it was always full of coins, paperclips, finish nails, pocket knife, and what have you; his pile of *Hotrod* magazines; and the mantle clock that had been his father's.

Jen said he was gone for good. That their mom's episodes had finally scared him off. Jake thought she was probably right. Then, when their dad came to take them to lunch, he hoped she wasn't.

"So everything's going okay?" their dad asked.

Jake looked at Jen for how they were going to answer. Were they going to tell him that Mom had had one of her episodes? Then for sure he wouldn't come back. But maybe if they told him…

"It's going good," Jen said. "At school they made recess ten minutes longer."

Their dad took a bite of his hoagie then spoke with his mouth full. "Wow."

Their mom hated how he did that. She'd say the flies were going to swoop in and then he'd be filled with maggots.

One of their dad's friends from plumbing came up to the table. The two of them started talking about work stuff so Jake and Jen focused on their sandwiches. Their dad had lots of friends, both from work and from Ye Olde Tavern, where he often stopped after work.

Jake knew what his sister was thinking. He was thinking it too. Their dad had brought them here to break some bad news. The bravado in his voice and the way his eyes kept darting around told them he was nervous. Jake looked at Jen. She was staring at him. *We're in trouble,* her eyes said. *I know,* his said back.

By the time their dad's friend left, they'd finished their sandwiches. Their dad stepped over to the counter to buy them each a candy bar. Once back at the table he rewrapped what was left of his hoagie. It wasn't like him not to finish. He had a huge appetite. He took a deep breath. "So you've probably noticed I haven't been at home."

Once again, Jake's eyes met Jen's. "Yeah," he said cautiously.

Their dad ran his fingers through his thick brown hair, which he'd let get a little longer than usual. It was brushing the tops of his ears. "What am I saying? Of course you've noticed. You two aren't stupid."

Jake stared at a loose button on his dad's work shirt. It was hanging on by a thread.

Their dad glanced at the door. "I guess what I need to do is just come out and say this." Another deep breath. "I'm leaving your mom."

Jen coughed up a little soda. "Getting a divorce?" A girl in their class had parents who'd divorced and she'd lost a lot of weight and started sucking her thumb when she thought no one was looking.

"Uh, yeah. We haven't worked out all the details, but that's the direction we're moving."

Jake fiddled with the wrapper of his Heath Bar. Jen glared into space.

"Your mom hasn't said anything to you?"

Jake shook his head. When they'd asked her where he was all she'd said was, "That's between him and God."

"As you know, your mother isn't always easy."

"Where are you going?" Jake asked.

"Well, at the moment I'm staying with a friend from work."

Jake glanced at Jen to see what she was feeling. Just as he thought, their dad was lying.

He put his hand on Jake's shoulder. "That leaves you to be the head of the family now, bucko. I need you to take care of your sister and your mom."

Dread shot through Jake's bones. Then he heard Jen's thoughts. *I will help you,* she said. *You are not alone.*

"Do you have a phone number?" Jen asked.

Their dad shifted in his chair. "Probably best if you don't call me till I get my own place. I'll give you that number when I have it."

*Another lie.*

Their dad stared at his folded hands as if he were praying. "I'm sorry, kids. I really am."

Jake's throat tightened. He willed himself not to cry.

Jen stood. "Can we go now?"

I pray the drive from the airport to the hospital is short. Dad and I have nothing to talk about. We covered my future when I saw him last time. We can't talk about anything involving Aunt Jen because he hates her. We can't talk about me and Serena because he hates my being gay, and we're both pretty clueless about what's going on with Mom.

I slip into the passenger side of the rental. "Nice car."

"Thanks. I would have preferred something not quite so…"

He doesn't finish his sentence, but I know what he's thinking. The car is a purple PT Cruiser, aka a rolling eggplant.

"You didn't get a choice?" I ask.

"Not unless I wanted to upgrade. They have a whole fleet of these." He starts the engine.

Dad likes to blend in. Whether casually dressed or in his business wear, his color choices are always muted, his style somewhere between Sears and Lands' End. He wears his hair cut short and parted on the side, always the same side, and when standing in a group, he'll choose a spot where he can see everyone. He doesn't like his back to people. But for all his attempts to blend in, he rarely does. He's strikingly handsome, and tall (six-three and a half), and his attempts to go unnoticed only make you want to take a closer look.

I turn on the GPS. The electronic female suggests we go left once we've exited the garage. She predicts we can make it to the hospital in nineteen minutes.

"So," he says. "Did my sister tell you any more than she told me?"

Here we go. We're starting in on the game where he asks me about Aunt Jen while pretending he's not. Trying to keep my voice neutral, I ask, "What did she tell you?"

"Not much. She shot me an e-mail, actually, with a link about this thing that Maye's got."

"Guillain-Barré."

He cracks his window, taps his finger on the steering wheel, then backs out of the parking space. "So…Jen has been here awhile."

"Two days."

We cruise out of the parking lot and into the street. "Wonder why she didn't call you before now."

"Mom told her not to."

I know what he really wants to ask. Why did Mom want *him* to come? Personally, I'm wondering the same thing. They haven't seen each other since they broke up fifteen years ago.

*Left turn in two miles,* our electronic guide chirps.

I pop open the glove compartment and pull out the rental agreement as if it holds some interest for me.

"So did she?" he asks.

"What?"

"Tell you any more than she told me."

"Not really. Just that Mom is losing her ability to move. And that usually people get better, but sometimes they don't. Sometimes they…" I start to choke up.

He gives my leg two little pats.

I stare out the window. People at a shopping center are going about their business as if it's a regular day.

"How was Mexico?" Dad asks.

"What little time I spent there? Great."

"I bet."

I think about Serena, the softness of her skin, the way she cried out and grabbed the bedpost when she climaxed.

"I've never been to Mexico."

"It's nice."

*Left turn in point five miles.*

Dad flicks on his blinker.

"How's work?" I ask.

"The usual. Doing a job out on the Main Line. We're widening a millionaire's escape route. Wouldn't want all those rich folks having to sit in traffic on their way back from Philly."

I smile as if I care.

The GPS goes *Ding Dong!*

We take the turnoff.

What if Mom dies and I'm left with only the Bell twins?

## CHAPTER TWO

D ad and I approach the nurses' station at the ICU. I can't stop worrying about what it's going to be like to see Mom. I'm also freaking out about how Dad and Aunt Jen are going to get along.

A nurse in crisp rose-colored scrubs looks up from her computer. Her silky black hair is pulled back in a silver clip at the nape of her neck. Her name tag reads Samantha. "How can I help you?" she asks. Her tone is no-nonsense but kind.

I take a deep breath and say, "We're here to see Maye Bell." Such a simple sentence, yet I can barely get it out.

"She mentioned you were coming." Her eyes linger an extra millisecond on Dad. "Her room is down the hall on the right. Room twenty-five."

"Thanks."

Dad lets me lead the way.

I brace myself for a showdown—Aunt Jen storming out when she sees Dad, or Dad greeting her with some cutting "home wrecker" remark, catapulting the two of them into an enormous scream out. Then I see Mom. She's lying on the hospital bed with the IVs sticking in her arm. She looks pale, fragile, terrified. I drop my backpack and rush to her side. "Mom..." My touch makes her wince. "Sorry, Mom. I just..."

Her eyes swell with tears. "Bean."

I try not to reveal how freaked I am. She looks like a mummy. Her face muscles move while her arms and legs lie there dead. This is so not Mom. She's the epitome of health and *joie de vivre*, strong from chopping wood and capable—graciously defiant. Not this frail, scared waif lying in a bed. "What happened? How did you get this?"

She rolls her eyes, one of the few parts of her body she can move.

"Do you hurt?"

She blows a soundless whistle. "My skin's on fire."

"Her immune system is attacking her nervous system," Aunt Jen says. "Her nerves are screaming."

Aunt Jen is standing by the long, narrow window. Her Musson Theatrical T-shirt and carpenter jeans droop from her slender frame. The multi-colored cheaters she has pushed up on her head have hooked a strand of hair from her long braid, causing it to stick up. She's a striking woman. Her eyes, like Dad's, are a piercing mix of amber and hazel, and she has the same high cheekbones and long limbs.

"Hey, Aunt Jen." I go over to hug her. Dad is still standing in the doorway, the Tin Man from *The Wizard of Oz*.

"Maye," he says tentatively.

Mom's eyes flick over to him. "Jake. You're here." Her speech is labored so she chooses her words carefully. She's clearly moved to see him. "Flight okay?"

"Uneventful," he says, then looks over his shoulder as if mapping out an escape. "Which is good, I guess."

She smiles. "Yes. Good."

Neither Dad nor Aunt Jen greets the other. Instead, Aunt Jen keeps a proprietary arm around my shoulders, which I'm sure makes Dad feel even more out of place, standing there in the doorway, outside our little coven of women, the family we became after him. It doesn't help that there's only one chair. He clears his throat. "I figure I'll park myself in a motel. Any recommendations?"

"My house," Mom says before Aunt Jen can get a word in.

Flabbergasted, Aunt Jen lets her arm drop from my shoulder. "Maye…" But what can she say? Mom has set down the law. Dad, Aunt Jen, and I are all going to be staying under the same roof.

Dad rocks back on his heels then steps into the room and pulls the covered metal trashcan over to Mom's bedside to use as a chair. "How long is this supposed to last?"

"They don't know," Aunt Jen says to the room, not Dad. "It's different for everyone."

"Might lose my talking," Mom says.

"Temporarily," Aunt Jen adds.

Try as I might, I can't get out of my head an account I read on the Internet about a guy who not only lost his ability to speak but even his ability to blink. They had to weigh his eyelids down so his eyes didn't dry out. He did survive, but at his worst moments, he said it was like being "buried alive."

Aunt Jen takes the chair on the other side of the bed, staking out her territory. "We're believing she's hit her plateau," she says to me. "That this is going to turn around any second now." She rests her hand on Mom's. I noticed someone has removed Mom's rings. She usually wears at least three chunky silvery things with stones and bold settings.

"You're here," Mom says. "That's what matters."

Samantha comes in. "How's everybody doing?"

Dad, Aunt Jen, and I bobble our heads like dashboard ornaments. Dad stands and returns the trashcan to its spot by the wall.

"How about you, Maye?" Samantha says.

"Been better."

"I need to do a few more tests. Okay?"

Mom nods.

Samantha checks the IVs, makes Mom breathe into this weird beaker thingy, and takes some of her blood.

The sight of Mom's blood makes me go weak in the knees.

"She's checking arterial blood gas," Aunt Jen says, not for my benefit, but for Dad's. He's peering over Samantha's shoulder as if he might need to take over.

Why did Mom want him here?

"Thanks for letting us stay in the room," Aunt Jen says to Samantha, her meaning clearly aimed at Dad: *Behave. Or we're going to get kicked out.*

Samantha looks up from the clipboard. "I think it's great Maye has such a loving family."

I have to bite down on my lip. Loving family? The Bells? You've got to be kidding. Then again, Dad and Aunt Jen were spawned from insanity. "Your Grandma Evelyn was a piece of work," Dad always says. "Nuts" is what Aunt Jen calls her.

\*

Jen sat next to Jake in the backseat of the family Dodge Dart while their mom, Evelyn Bell, practiced driving. It wasn't something their mom had done much, relying instead on their dad, but since he'd abandoned them a month earlier, she had no choice.

She picked a vacant warehouse parking lot for her "final driving challenge." Parking. It was a Saturday afternoon and Jen wished she were home, or with friends—anywhere but in the backseat of the lurching car. Most kids' moms already knew how to drive. Not theirs. She was intimidated by anything mechanical and would go to great lengths to avoid plugging something in or turning a key to engage a motor. Some days she even avoided light switches.

Jen stuck her head out the window to get a taste of sun. It was stupid they had to do this. Just because their mom was scared of everything. It wasn't fair. Why couldn't they have a normal mom? Jen pulled her head back inside and gave Jake a pathetic look. He rolled his eyes.

Their mom glanced over her shoulder as if a police officer or someone who worked in the building might come out and scold them, then she ground the gears into first. The car jolted forward. "The trick is," she said, "to keep it inside the lines." She was clearly feeling confident, having already gone up and down the painted aisles a few times flawlessly. She aimed the car between two parallel lines and glided the car into a parking spot. "This isn't so hard," she said. "Look. Here we are, all parked."

"Then can we go home now?" Jen moaned. "Please?"

"No we cannot go home. Mommy has to learn how to back up." Again, she glanced around nervously.

"Would you mellow out?" Jake said. "We're not doing anything illegal."

"I just don't know what their policy is."

Jake threw his head back and rested his knees on the front seat. "About driving in their *public* parking lot when *no one's here?*"

Jen's stomach bunched up. She shot Jake a look. *Don't egg her on.*

But it was too late. Their mom twisted around in her seat. "You think this is easy? You think you could drive this car?"

"Sure. It's not that hard."

"All right, then, let's see you try, Mr. Smarty Pants." She put the emergency brake on, swung the car door open, and stepped out. "Well, come on. What are you so afraid of?"

Jen glared at him. *Now you've done it.*

Jake knew she was right. He'd gone too far. "Mom, I'm only eleven," he said. "It's against the law."

"So?" she said. "Nobody's out here. Isn't that what you said?"

Jen could tell that he wasn't going to let this one go. She covered her face with her hands as he flung the car door open and got into the driver's seat. Their mom came around to the passenger side, climbed in, and slammed the door behind her. "Go on then. Go on! Show your stupid mother how easy it is."

Jen had to stop this. It was insane. She leaned over the front seat. "Can we just go home? He's too young to drive. His feet don't even reach the pedals."

But Jake was eager to prove his mother stupid. "Yes, they can," he said and slid down the seat until he could barely see over the dashboard.

Emitting a little snort, their mom crossed her arms and legs and turned toward the window next to her.

Even though she knew there was no point, Jen said, "Jake, don't do this." Once he had something to prove, there was no stopping him.

Jake released the brake, revved the motor, ground the car into gear, and pressed down on the accelerator. The car lurched forward then stalled. Their mom laughed. He tried again, pressing the accelerator to the floor. The car fishtailed forward through the parking lot, whining to be shifted into the second gear.

"Stop! Stop!" their mom screamed, bracing her high-heeled sandals against the floorboards and her perfectly manicured hands against the dash.

Jake slammed the brake. Jen pitched forward. The car stalled.

Jen slapped him on the back. "Moron!"

Jake smiled. "I *told* you I could do it."

Their mom adjusted her stylish knee-length skirt over her knees. "Sorry, Charlie. You went over the lines; you ran over the other cars."

Jake's expression crinkled into disgust. "Mom. There are no cars. The parking lot is empty."

"You think I don't know that?" She began fussing with her collar. "You think I'm just a stupid woman who doesn't know what's going on?"

Jake looked as if he were going to say something. Jen willed him not to.

Their mom's voice shifted into her eerie singsong tone, the one that meant *Other Mother* was on her way. "You're sounding an awful lot like your father," she said. "Thinking you know so much. Thinking the whole world revolves around you."

Jen felt nauseated. Why had Jake provoked her?

Their mom thrust her milk-white finger with the blood-red polished nail at Jake's face. "The world doesn't revolve around you, mister. And for your information, there are lines that can't be crossed, just like in this parking lot. But the lines I'm talking about are invisible. Everywhere. And if you cross them, you get punished. Big time. But they'll tempt you. Yes, they will. And once you cross over, you're going to have to pay. Do you hear me? Hot flames licking at you for eternity. How would you like that, huh? To have your skin burning and blistering forever?" Other Mother flipped her hand so her palm faced up. "Give me the keys. Now."

An act of mutiny, Jake left the keys in the ignition and backed away from Other Mother. Jen watched as he unlatched the door and slid out of the car, praying he wouldn't do what he was silently threatening. *I'm getting the hell out of here.*

*You can't leave me,* she shot to him.

He shot her a look, assessing, then, mercifully, opened the back door. "Move over," he said gruffly.

She knew what he was thinking. She was thinking it too. *There's no longer an adult around to protect us.*

"Roll up your windows," Other Mother snapped. "Now."

✳

Mom drifted off to sleep about a half an hour ago. A blessing. Except now Aunt Jen, Dad, and I are left without the binding that holds together this crumbly batter of my family.

Dad is back on his trashcan and Aunt Jen across the bed from him in the only chair. I'm on a stool I dragged in from the waiting room. I've got my feet on my backpack and am leaning against the wall. The adrenaline has worn off and I'm exhausted. Whatever this is, it's going to take a while.

I watch Mom breathe *In. Out. In. Out. In. Out. In. Out.* Keep on breathing, Mom. Keep on breathing.

The gargoyles still haven't said two words to each other. To amuse myself I think up this little poem. I pull a scrap paper from my backpack and write it down.

> *Jake and Jen Bell*
> *Born ten minutes apart*
> *Sitting six feet apart*
> *Wishing they were miles apart*

Both Dad and Aunt Jen have a fear of going crazy like Grandma Evelyn. It never occurs to either one of them that the crazy gene could continue over generations. Or if it does, they never mention it to me.

Dad leans forward and rubs his lower spine. Aunt Jen slides down in her chair and rests her head on the chair back. A nurse rolls a squeaky cart past the room. We all go on alert. Will Mom wake up? She doesn't. We all relax again.

This sucks. I need caffeine.

"Anyone want coffee?" I whisper.

"I don't think they want us bringing coffee in here," Dad says softly.

"They let me yesterday," Aunt Jen says.

A few seconds of silence follows before Dad says, "Well, okay then."

What do you know? They're deigning to talk to each other.

I tiptoe toward the door.

Aunt Jen's phone vibrates. She scrambles to answer it on the off chance its muted sound might wake Mom. She shimmies past me to the door. "This is Jen," she whispers, creeping into the hall. Dad scowls after her, shaking his head.

The timing of Mom's illness could not be worse. Aunt Jen's got a play loading into the Encore Theater, a non-profit community theater she manages, Dad's got that Main Line road gig, and me, shit, I might have found love.

Then again, no one would ever accuse Mom of being convenient. Living with her is like living in a world of constant surprise parties. One loves her for her inconsistencies, her unpredictability, her undying optimism.

I slip out of the room in search of the cafeteria, passing Aunt Jen in the hall. "Call Mike," she says into her phone. Her voice is tense. "He's run lights once before and was pretty good…Mike Asher…Check the database. Oh, and did you get those changes I made to the program?"

I follow the signs to the elevator. All the hallways look the same. After a couple wrong turns, I locate the elevator and take it down to the cafeteria. I pour three cups of coffee, grab a few packs of sugar, snag a small carton of milk so we don't have to ingest the carcinogenic whitener, and get in the short line at the cashier with my tray.

The last time I saw Mom was right before taking off for Mexico. I came up for the weekend. She was on the far side of the garden weeding around the peas—in the rain. Her favorite straw gardening hat was dripping onto her oversized gardening shirt; her feet were bare. She was squatting. I was inside keeping dry and waiting for my ride, a friend of hers who was making a run down the mountain. We'd already said our good-byes, but I still felt a little miffed that she wasn't waiting with me in the house. But that's Mom. She hates good-byes.

"Don't you have the sense to get out of the rain?" I yelled.

She laughed. "Guess not!"

Her friend pulled up in front of the house. "My ride's here!" I figured I might as well give her one last chance to walk over and, well, not hug me because she was so wet, but at least look me in the eyes meaningfully.

She stood and blew me a kiss. "Call me when you get there!" Then she took off her hat and waved it back and forth like a person might do to someone departing on an ocean liner.

She grows way more vegetables than she can eat. She has this idea she's going to start a small business where folks pick up a weekly bag of veggies. She just never gets it together. Winds up either giving the veggies away or composting them. Right after I graduated, she begged me to move home for the summer to help her set it up.

I said no.

❖

The cashier gives me one of those foldout cup carriers, for which I'm grateful. My world feels suddenly unsteady, and balancing the three cups could be dangerous. When I get back to the ICU, I find Aunt Jen sitting in the waiting room checking her phone for e-mails. My backpack is on the short couch next to her. "Shift change," she says. "The new nurse isn't nice."

"Where's Dad?"

"Still in there. She says just one at a time." Aunt Jen runs her fingers through her hair, sending her cheaters clattering to the floor. She bends to retrieve them. I hand her a coffee then put the cardboard carrier on the small table between her and the couch.

I settle onto the couch, slip off my shoes, and cross my legs. I flip the plastic top off my coffee and add plenty of milk. It's a far cry from a soy latte, my leading vice, but it will do.

Aunt Jen shuts her phone. "So how's it going, Bean?"

Under the circumstances, this seems an odd question. I shrug. "Okay, I guess."

"I like your new look." She gestures to my sea-matted hair.

"Unintentional. I didn't have time to shower."

Her phone rings again. She checks to see who's calling, then flips it shut. "I'm glad you're here."

I can't resist. "How about that Dad's here?"

She attempts to ward off my accusation with a raised palm. "Hey. You know better than anyone how many times I've tried. But until he's ready—"

"More like when you're *both* ready."

She laughs, but I can tell I've gotten to her because she starts going on about them being born on the Aries Taurus cusp. I've heard this a million times. "We each have two sets of horns," she says, holding up her fists with a pinky and forefinger extended on each. This is supposed to represent a little Aries ram and a little Taurus bull. "And they're either fighting something or someone outside of themselves…" She faces the little bull and ram toward me. "Or fighting internally with each other." She faces the little bull and ram at each other and clashes their horns. "That's why we're so driven; we have an intense inner life."

I stifle a yawn. "Wow. That's heavy."

"Hitler has our same birthday," she says casually.

"Thanks for the demo. I now have a much better understanding of my dysfunctional family."

"You should take my car and go to the house and get some rest."

"I can rest here." I adjust myself on the couch, using my backpack for a pillow. The worn passport in the front pocket bends comfortably around my cheek. "Wake me if anything changes."

"You got it."

Closing my eyes feels good. I can shut everything out. In a weird way, I'm glad they won't let us in the room with Mom. There's nothing we can do.

Aunt Jen takes another call. "What now?...Did you check the prop room?"

Listening to her conduct business while I try to sleep reminds me of growing up. Right after Mom and I moved to California, Mom signed up for a dance class, something she'd always wanted to do. Which was fine for her. The only problem was, I could never sleep when she was gone. Aunt Jen would have to let me bring a blanket and pillow onto the couch in the living room. I've fallen asleep to the sound of her folding laundry, repairing light fixtures, washing dishes, talking on the phone, having production meetings in the kitchen. I remember the first time she let me.

*"I don't get why she had to take a stupid dance class anyway!"*

Aunt Jen was in the middle of fixing a desk lamp with the broken plug. She put it onto the upturned milk crate she was using as a table. "I'll take that as a no."

I rubbed my eyes. "I'm not even sleepy."

"I see."

"What? I'm not."

She picked up her wire clippers and snipped the faulty plug off the wire. "It must be hard sleeping in a new place."

I donned my superior eight-year-old tone. "It's not that. I'm just not tired." Outside the window, it was dark. Zombie dark.

She placed the wire clippers on the floor. "Tell you what. I'm going to bring your pillow and a blanket in here. You can lie on the couch and sort of pretend to sleep until your mom gets home then, when she gets here, you can pretend to wake up. That way I won't get in trouble for not putting you to bed."

Unsure what to make of this new adult in my life, I eyed her suspiciously. "What if I want to keep my eyes open until she gets here?"

"That's fine. Just so long as you lie on the couch with your head on the pillow."

"What are you going to do?"

"Fix this lamp."

I pulled the blanket up to my chin, my bones sinking into the worn cushions on the couch. Everything about Santa Cruz was strange. People drove around with surfboards on the roofs of their cars. There were trees so big that ten people with their arms stretched wide couldn't reach around them.

"Aunt Jen?" I said through a yawn.

"Yeah?"

"Are you ever going to have kids?"

She looked up from her project, clearly amused. "Never thought I'd be any good at it."

*Before drifting off to sleep, I decided to let her practice on me.*

I wake to Dad's voice. "A Dr. Reneaux came in to do some tests."

"She wouldn't let you stay?" Aunt Jen asks.

The sounds of the hospital waiting room creep into my consciousness. I keep my eyes shut and listen.

"This coffee mine?" Dad says.

"Yeah. Probably cold by now. Did Maye wake up?"

"Only when the doc came in."

"How'd she look?"

"Scared."

I hear Dad settle into the chair by my feet, putting me between him and her. He opens his coffee.

"You okay?" Aunt Jen asks.

I get this weird feeling that the only reason she asks is because I might be listening.

Dad takes a sip of coffee. A few seconds later, I hear Jen sigh and flip open her phone. Dad grabs a magazine.

Progress, I suppose.

## CHAPTER THREE

Forget trying to sleep. A guy and his teenage daughter have just joined our happy crew in the waiting room. The girl has a bandaged forehead and cheeks streaked with dried tears. The dad looks like a zombie. From their whispered conversation, I gather they were in a car wreck. He was driving. They're waiting to see how the mom makes out.

I have no room for other people's problems. I pull my iPod from my pack and hit my mellow playlist. It's got everything from KT Tunstall to Deep Forest, Miles Davis to the Bulgarian Women's Choir. If I can't sleep, at least I can attempt to relax.

Aunt Jen stands up and stretches. "Think I'll take a walk. Call me if anything changes."

Dad clears his throat and flips through a *Newsweek*.

Aunt Jen collects our empty coffee cups into a bag to throw away.

My soundtrack turns the scene into a movie.

A pudgy nurse's assistant pokes her head in and says, "Somebody needs to feed the chickens and Mrs. Simpkins."

"Is Maye awake?" Aunt Jen asks.

"Who's Mrs. Simpkins?" Dad asks.

"The cat," Aunt Jen says. "So is Maye okay?"

"She's worrying about Mrs. Simpkins and the chickens," the nurse says.

So much for me watching from the outside. Dad, Aunt Jen, and I exchange glances. Who's going to go? It's a good one-hour drive up the mountain. So much could happen in one hour. My brain surges into action—the neighbor kid Mom has quasi-adopted. "We should call Ari. He could do it."

"I left him a bunch of messages, but haven't heard back," Aunt Jen says.

"Maybe there's another neighbor we could try."

"You have any of their numbers?"

"We could ask Mom."

"She doesn't need to be thinking about phone numbers," Aunt Jen says. "We should just take care of it."

"I concur," Dad says.

So it's up to one of us. And they're both looking at me.

"Well, I could use a shower," I say.

"I could use a break," Aunt Jen says. "I'll come with you." Which is a crock; she doesn't want to be alone with Dad.

"Want us to bring back dinner?" I ask Dad.

"That would be great." He reaches into his back pocket. "Let me give you some money."

Aunt Jen waves off his intention. "I've got it."

Dad pulls out a couple of twenties. "I insist. Dinner's on me."

"I said I've *got* it, Jake. Christ."

I take the cash. "Thanks, Dad. You want anything in particular?"

He glances at the bandaged daughter and her father, but they couldn't care less about our squabbling; they're in the middle of their own nightmare. "You choose. Just no peppers."

I step forward to hug him. Our hugs are generally stiff, formal. This one is no exception.

Aunt Jen exhales loudly.

So much for the happy family façade.

Dad walks us out to the parking lot so I can get my suitcase from the eggplant rental. We take the halls, the stairs, the sidewalks in total silence. Aunt Jen grumbles something unintelligible under her breath as Dad unlocks the car. I don't ask her to repeat it, just drag my bags over to her Subaru Outback, wedge them in the back between a box of old gel frames and a few broken lighting instruments, and get in. Aunt Jen, already in, switches on the ignition. Hank Williams yodels about having the lovesick blues. She flicks off the CD player.

I glance out the window. Dad is still standing by his rental eggplant. He's got his hands in his pockets, his eyes turned inward, as if he's trying to work out a complicated freeway cloverleaf.

"Your mom is going to get through this," Aunt Jen says as we pull out of the parking lot.

A nice thought, but come on. How can anyone know what's going to happen? "How does it feel to see your twin?"

"He's the same old Jake. An enigma even to himself."

"I feel kind of sorry for him. He seems so lost."

She lets out a little snort, which I ignore.

"Why do you think Mom wanted him here?"

"Who knows? But she was adamant about it. You know how she can get."

As always, Aunt Jen steers with the crook of her left wrist wrapped over the top of the wheel and her right hand gripping the bottom. I notice a black leather and bead wristband I've never seen before.

I gesture to it. "You make that?"

She looks at it briefly. "Yeah. One of those sleepless night projects."

Aunt Jen and Dad both struggle with insomnia. At night you could hear them wandering around like untethered souls.

I pull my legs back and my foot hits something under the seat. I lean over and pick up a Bible. It's got a soft black cover and the pages are trimmed in gold. "Finding Jesus at this late date in your life?"

She laughs. "It was your Dad's. I thought he might want it back."

I flip it open. Inside the cover is a note.

*To Jake*
*There's room for you at the cross!*
*Your friend, Ernest*

"Reverend Bates gave him this?"

Aunt Jen nods.

"Did he give you one too?"

"Are you kidding? He wouldn't have wasted his money on me."

"You sound jealous."

"I don't know about that. I resented all the special treatment Jake got, if that's what you're getting at. Bates was the closest thing we had to a father."

Dad and Aunt Jen's childhood was a total nightmare. Or so I'm told. They had a dad who walked out on the family when they were kids—never turned back, didn't even send child support—and a nutso mother who fell in with a crazy fire-and-brimstone minister.

"You ever wonder if your real dad is still alive?"

She clears her throat. "Sometimes. And then sometimes I don't care."

"It just seems like—"

"It is what it is, Bean. I've come to terms with it. Can we talk about something else now?"

Doesn't sound to me like she's come to terms with it. But then nobody asked me. Nobody ever asks me. I turn the Bible over. The back cover is slightly mildewed. "Dad always talks like he hated Bates."

"He would say that. But trust me, in the early days, he and Bates were tight. They'd go to ball games together, special youth events, while I had to stay home with crazy Evelyn."

"The Church of Redemption," I say. I can't help myself. The stories are always so rich.

Predictably, she groans. "God, I hated that place. Every sermon was about fornication, adultery, and sins of the flesh, which, believe me, he knew *all* about. He took total advantage of Mom's instability. "

She's sure that Evelyn and Bates were doing the nasty. Dad doesn't agree, or he's never mentioned it. Either way, the Reverend Ernest Bates hung around their house a lot.

We approach the huge sparkling expanse of Lake Shasta. Houseboats and other water toys look tiny floating on its fingered stretch of turquoise water. It's beautiful. Even on a day like today.

I set the Bible on the back floorboard.

I suppose I should be thankful that neither Aunt Jen nor Dad turned out to be a chainsaw murderer or a Bible thumper.

\*

Eleven-year-old Jake eyed the guest pastor in the front passenger seat of their car. He looked a lot like their dad, tall and lanky, a big smile, short hair with a spiraling cowlick at the top, only Reverend Bates's hair was sandy colored, not black, and he wore a suit and polished shoes, while their dad wore Ben Davis work pants and Red Wings. When the Reverend preached at the church a few weeks back, he stared the congregation down with his blue eyes, did a lot of pointing, and used the words "vex my soul" and "eternal damnation." The elders didn't seem to like him much; the congregation was squirming in their seats, but Jake thought he was entertaining. Way better than the regular dry, pot-bellied pastor with the comb-over. Jake hadn't a clue why their mom invited him to lunch, but he was glad. She seemed happy for the first time in days.

They were returning from Sunday services. Their mom, all gussied up in her red dress and shiny black belt, was maneuvering the car like she'd been driving for years. She was in her public mode—charming, talkative, "kittenish" as their dad used to say. Jake tried to push Other Mother out of his mind, but it was hard. She'd been showing up a lot more since their dad had left. The last couple of days were really bad. She'd sat at the kitchen table with all the blinds down, drinking cup after cup of coffee, and clutching her Bible, afraid to walk by the windows. Never once did she shower or change her robe or comb her hair.

She stopped at a red light and looked at Jen in the rearview. "Jennifer, why don't you tell Reverend Bates about your science project?"

Jen squinted at the vinyl back of the front seat. She was wearing the light blue, puffy-sleeved dress that she hated—part of one of the "twin outfits" that their mom always made them wear to church—dress for Jen, and matching tie and coordinated suit for Jake. Today his suit was navy blue and his tie the same light blue as Jen's dress. "It was on surface tension," was all Jen said.

"She got an honorable mention," their mom boasted, checking her crimson lipstick in the rearview mirror. "It was the most ingenious thing. She had these little cups of water with needles floating on them. Only some of them had detergent in them so they wouldn't float, and some of them…well, you tell him, honey. I'm really not too up on science."

Reverend Bates turned around and fixed his eyes on Jen. Their mom hadn't made him wear his seatbelt the way she always did with them. "So you're a little scientist, are you?"

"Not really," she said. "I've never won before."

Jake, sitting directly behind the pastor, felt Jen's annoyance at being put on the spot. Couldn't she tell he was just trying to be nice?

Reverend Bates flashed a smile. "Well, this surface tension sounds neato." One of his front teeth had a small chip in the corner, which Jake thought gave him character.

Jen fiddled with the buttons on the front of her skirt. "Jake did his on pulleys."

Reverend Bates twisted around further to get a good look at Jake. "Now that sounds more up my alley. I grew up on a farm, and we were always using pulleys for this or that."

Jake snuck out a smile. *He grew up on a farm. Cool.*

"Isn't that something," their mom said, pulling into the intersection. "I don't remember ever using a pulley in my whole entire life."

Reverend Bates winked conspiratorially at the twins then faced forward again, only he left his arm draped across the seat. He wore a gold pinky ring with a cross on it. Jen signaled with her eyes for Jake to take a closer look. *The ring is chipped. It's not real gold.*

*So?* thought Jake.

"Well now, Evelyn," Reverend Bates said, "I just bet you have seen a pulley. You have curtains in your house, don't you?"

"Well, of course I do."

"What do you think pulls them back and forth?"

Their mom stepped on the accelerator to catch the tail end of a yellow light. "Pulleys!"

"That's right. I bet Jake knew that too, didn't you, son?"

"Yeah, I did." Jake liked somebody taking up for him in front of his mother. It made him sit up a little straighter. What was it going to be like to have Reverend Bates at their house? Would their mom keep acting normal?

Jen picked at her cuticles and chewed her lower lip.

They pulled up in front of the brick row house.

"Would you look at this," Reverend Bates said, standing out on the street sizing up the place. "Such a nice place. Perfect." Jake was relieved the pastor didn't mention how the garden needed weeding or how the porch chair had a broken rung.

"Jen?" their mom said. "Be a good girl and go set the table."

Jen gave Jake the dirty look she always gave him when their mom made her do the girly chores. Jake rolled his eyes. What did she expect? She *was* the girl.

At lunch, Reverend Bates said a long grace, which included a blessing of the Velveeta and ham on toast and lime Jell-O with fruit cocktail. "...for I was hungry and you gave me food; I was thirsty and you gave me drink; I was a stranger and you took me in; I was naked and you clothed me..."

Jake peeked at Jen to see if she thought the naked part was as funny as he did, but she was focused on her tightly clasped hands.

During the meal, Reverend Bates asked about their school and friends. Jen was shy with her answers and played with her food, but Jake liked having someone to talk to besides his mom and sister. He told the Reverend about the baseball team at school and how they were on a winning streak.

"Sounds like lots of fun," he said. "Maybe you'll take me to a game sometime."

Once they were done eating, the adults moved on to talking about their church.

"They lack the moral backbone to steer our young people away from the many temptations that lure them," Reverend Bates said.

Their mom lapped it up, fluttering her hands at her chest, her cheeks. "I've felt that myself. I've just never had the sense to put it into words."

"Can I be excused?" Jen asked, pushing her chair out just a bit.

"You both may," their mom said, and smiled like it was no big deal, "but don't forget to change out of your church clothes before doing the dishes."

❖

In the basement, Jake screwed the wheels from one of Jen's roller skates onto a piece of one-by-four while Jen got the paint ready to decorate the top of their homemade skateboard. Since their mom didn't allow them to close doors, they had to listen to her and Reverend Bates's conversation. They heard stuff about a confrontation between Reverend Bates and the church elders, something about being too evangelical, and that he was going to start his own church. Jake didn't know what evangelical was, nor did he care. What mattered was their mom was acting normal.

Jake finished painting a long forked tongue on the red and yellow snake and went on to paint the eye. "Maybe him being here is good."

Jen, who was working on the fiery tail, dipped her paintbrush into the jar of murky water. "We'll see."

✳

"You think Bates was in love with Grandma Evelyn or just taking advantage of her?"

"Who knows?" Aunt Jen readjusts the vents on the dashboard. "But I'm sure he was nailing her. They'd stay up until the wee hours on the pretext of working on church stuff. He'd 'drop by' right at dinner. He loved her meatloaf. 'Evelyn,' he'd say, 'I'll know I've reached heaven when they tell me it's Evelyn Bell's meatloaf every night for dinner.' One night when he was going on and on about 'meatloafs in heaven,' Jake and I laughed so hard milk shot out our noses. Boy, did we get in trouble after he left."

"You've told me that story."

"Did I tell you how this little snotty kid at school asked if Reverend Bates was our new dad? Jake beat the crap out of him for that."

I set my seat into its fully reclined position. "No. I don't think you told me that one." I'm hoping that Aunt Jen will launch into a story long enough that I can listen with my eyes shut. Mount Shasta has come into view, its beautiful volcanic tips laced with snow, but my eyelids feel like sandbags. "So this kid thought Bates was your dad?" I stifle a yawn and give in to my eyelids.

The car cuts sharply to the right. I jerk up, eyelids peeled back.

We're headed into a scenic pullout. Aunt Jen cuts the engine and starts whacking the steering wheel, muttering, "Fuck fuck fuck fuck."

"Are you okay?"

Her eyes fill with tears. She flings the door open and slams it behind her.

Should I follow? See if she's okay? But Aunt Jen hates for people to see her cry. Just like Dad. Only Dad's solution is never to cry.

I stare at the mountain. Solid and unmoving. It's always reminded me of Hokusai's rendering of Mt. Fuji. It has a similar shape and majesty. A lone mountain standing—

Aunt Jen's cell phone rings. I check the number in case it's Dad. It's not. Would he even call if something changed with Mom?

I shut my eyes. My family is so messed up.

Aunt Jen returns to the car. Her eyes are rimmed in red. "Sorry, kid."

"No problemo. We're *all* tense."

She turns the key in the ignition and pulls back onto the road. "Between the opening of *Doubt*, and Maye's illness, and now my fucking brother...I haven't seen him in how many years? Fifteen? And he doesn't even hug me. Did you notice? When you guys arrived?"

"Well, you didn't exactly—"

"What will it take for him to get over this? It's not like I snatched Maye away from him. He killed their relationship all by himself. And contrary to what I'm sure he's told you, I did *not* get intimate with Maye until *after* he accused me—hell, *convicted* me.

I made a point not to, and it wasn't easy. When the two of you came out to Santa Cruz, Maye needed comfort. And I loved her, sure, but I told myself: Keep your hands off, Jen. They need to work things out. But then he started calling. Fuck, do you remember those phone calls? How he'd be all soused and then have the nerve to accuse me of turning your Mom into a 'lesbo'? His word. I'd tell him he was wrong, that she just needed a place to be until he could get his shit together. But he wouldn't believe me, so I'd hang up. He'd call back. I'd hang up. This went on for weeks—"

"Aunt Jen?"

"Yeah?"

"I really don't want to hear this."

For reasons I can't explain, I always feel defensive when Aunt Jen starts badmouthing Dad. It's weird because I badmouth him all the time to my friends.

Aunt Jen squints at the road. "Sorry."

"If it's any consolation, you were a great father figure."

She laughs. "Thanks, Bean. For all we put you through, you sure turned out good."

We pass an eighteen-wheeler crawling up the steep incline.

"At least Dad's not drinking anymore."

"So I hear. He's got some kind of group."

"Straight Pool. It's like AA, only they shoot pool instead of talking to a higher power."

We ride in silence for a while before I remember her missed phone call. "Oh, you got a call while you were having your little breakdown." I hasten to add, "It wasn't Dad."

She cuffs my head. "'Little breakdown. Aren't you the cheeky one?" She dials in to retrieve her messages.

"You know that's against the law. Using a cell phone while driving."

She looks up from her phone, a single brow arched. "Who's gonna stop me?"

I pinch back a smile. Aunt Jen is so easy. I can say anything.

She shakes her head while listening to her messages. "Brain-dead actors. They've locked themselves out of the dressing room."

She dials in the call and I listen to her describe where to find an extra set of keys. She tosses her phone back on the seat. "It's so like Maye to come down with this during hell week."

I slip out of my flip-flops and put my tanned feet up on the dashboard. "Do you think I should call Dad? See what's up?" Serena likes my feet. Says they look sturdy, like two little tractors.

"Let's call him from the house. That way he can assure Maye we're taking care of Mrs. Simpkins and the damn chickens."

The spires of Castle Crags State Park pass by the window. My ears pop from the altitude change.

"When was the last time you saw Dad?"

"Evelyn's funeral. Actually, he never made it to the funeral. Maye and I had to go find him."

I remember the day well. "You made me stay with the Razowskys and Eva Razowsky kept making fun of me because you wouldn't let me stay by myself."

"You were just a kid."

"Hel-*lo*. I was in ninth grade. People let ninth graders stay by themselves all the time."

She adjusts the lumbar support pillow behind her. "If it's any consolation, in retrospect, I think it was a mistake not to bring you. You should have been at your grandmother's funeral."

"Thank you." Of course, there's more to them just babying me and we both know it. The circumstances of my grandmother's death are pretty ghoulish. "It is pretty creepy that she burned to death."

"I prefer to believe she died of smoke inhalation."

"Did they ever find out what started the fire?"

"They found thirteen points of origin. Who knows what she was doing."

Grandma Evelyn's death is one of those subjects the Bells don't like to talk about, which means my knowledge of the event is spotty. I keep trying, though. "So Dad didn't make it to her funeral?"

Aunt Jen rotates her neck to get the kinks out. "In fairness, he helped set it up, and paid for the urn and stuff. I wasn't making shit back then. But come the day, he didn't show. There we were sitting through the lame-o service—the preacher we hired didn't even know

Mom, and she had no friends by then. Bates didn't even have the decency to make an appearance. He'd given up on her years before, but still, you'd think he would have at least stopped in. Anyway, all I could think was, *Where the fuck is Jake?* We're the only two people on this planet who care that she's dead. He should be here.

"Right after the service, Maye and I took off to find him. We'd started to worry. I mean, what if something had happened to him? Then we got to his house, banged on the door. Nothing. By now, I was totally freaked. Fortunately, Maye still had a key. In some ways, I wish she hadn't. I'll never be able to get that picture out of my head—him snoring on the living room floor, plates of half-eaten food everywhere, old newspapers and dirty clothes scattered around. It was disgusting. He had an empty bottle of Jack Daniel's pressed to his chest like a teddy bear.

"We hauled his fucked-up ass off the living room floor and onto his bed. He just kept going on about the fires of hell and how we're all going to burn for our sins. Your mom made us clean up before we left. He stayed passed out while we washed the dishes and picked up. It was pathetic."

"You just left him there?" No matter how estranged I felt to my brother, I think I'd want to at least stick around until he was sober. Then again, I've never had a brother, or any sibling, for that matter.

"Maye made him a sandwich and a cup of coffee and forced me to sit there while she coaxed him to eat. The whole scene was so disturbing. I didn't trust him at all. And with good reason. Once we got him semi-sobered up, he got abusive and told us to get the hell out of his house, that we were no longer family. It was awful."

"And you haven't talked to him since?"

"Nope."

"That's pretty sad."

"That's life. Sometimes it sucks."

Outside, pine trees form an impenetrable wall on either side of the road, blocking out the mountain.

## CHAPTER FOUR

Aunt Jen pulls over at the entrance of Mom's driveway. I jump out to pick up the mail. Mom's mailbox is decorated with shooting stars and flowers. It also has the words NO JUNK MAIL! IT'S WASTE! painted on the front. You've got to admire her pluck.

The Scotch broom is in full bloom, its yellow flowers lining the driveway and meandering throughout her twenty acres. Mom's always begging me to help her pull it out. Using a superhero-like voice she'll say, "Join the fight against the Invasion of the Scotch broom! Its insidious nature is wreaking havoc on the land. But you, yes *you,* can make the difference." She's even offered to pay me.

"Anything interesting?" Aunt Jen asks when I get back in the car.

I toss the pile of circulars and bills on the seat. "Under the circumstances, I can't imagine any mail being interesting."

"Point taken."

We proceed up the quarter-mile driveway and stop in front of the house. Mrs. Simpkins comes out to greet us. She's a black kitty with white spats, ascot, and tip of tail. Mom likes to say Mrs. Simpkins keeps her in line.

Aunt Jen runs her hand down Mrs. Simpkins's back and up her tail. "You feeling abandoned?" Mrs. Simpkins rubs against her leg, purring so loudly I can hear her from where I'm standing. Then she swats at Aunt Jen's hand.

"Watch out for her. She knows how to get what she wants."

"So I noticed when I stopped by the other day." Aunt Jen checks her hand for scratches. "She literally corralled me into the kitchen."

I yank my suitcase from the trunk, but my legs refuse to propel me toward the house. They want me back in Sayulita walking down its rutted dirt roads where lazy iguanas nap in the trees, it's hot, and the sandy beaches are full of people that aren't my family. My brain tells my legs to get over it.

I stare at the house—an old, lavender, two-story clapboard with a porch and decorative shutters. Charming. But Mom didn't buy the place for the house. It was the land she wanted. Mom likes to spread out.

Her projects are scattered everywhere, some close to finished, some just started, some just an idea and a few strewn tools. A stack of empty planters, several bags of potting soil, and a shovel in need of a new handle are over by the greenhouse. Fifteen or so second-hand solar panels stand against the side of the house. Leaning next to an arbor of twisted wood is a bicycle with silk flowers woven through its spokes and basket. Pathways of colorful stepping-stones wind through unruly flowerbeds.

And then there are her women. Larger than life, these sentries sculpted from stone and wood are scattered across her property. Strong and curvaceous, each one looks like she's trying to break free from whatever log or slab of rock Mom found her in. There's one by the porch, one by her sundial, one by the woodpile, and more out back.

"She's done well for herself," Aunt Jen says.

It can't be easy for her to be here. "Yeah. Mom loves it."

Aunt Jen walks over to the clump of Shasta daisies by the porch to smell them. They're odorless, of course, but it seems cruel to say so. She's making such an effort. She steps back, trying to mask her disappointment. "She always wanted a garden."

I pull up the handle on my suitcase and wheel it toward the house. "We should water the veggies while we're here."

"Whatever you say. Gardening isn't really my—"

"—thing, I know. You killed the potted cactus I gave you for your birthday." I bump my suitcase up the porch stairs and find the key under the small Guan Yin figurine. "I'll check the soil after I shower. You can feed the chickens. There should be a bucket of scraps under the sink. If they're too gross, or if it's empty, just root through the fridge for some old produce or bread. Anything in Tupperware."

"I did this the other day, remember?"

"Then you're an expert."

"Not exactly." She pauses at the bottom of the steps. "I didn't check for eggs." She grabs her crotch, all macho man, and speaks in a gruff voice. "Wasn't scared or nothin'."

"Yeah, right." I make a few squawking noises and flap my arms like a chicken.

"Punk!" She takes the steps two at a time, her intention clearly to cuff me.

I slam the door open, yank my bag in after me, then stop dead. Aunt Jen barrels into me. The house smells like Mom. Incense, cooking spices, and dried roses.

Aunt Jen rests her hand on my shoulder. "You okay?"

"Sort of."

We stand that way for a few seconds, the two of us seeing, smelling, feeling Mom's world. *What if Mom...*

Mrs. Simpkins head butts my leg.

Grateful to be brought back to the mundane, I say, "Okay, okay," and head for the sack of cat food in the pantry. There's not much left, so I pour it all into Mrs. Simpkins's bowl, an asymmetrical, mud-colored item I crafted in a pottery class, and which Mom refuses to throw away.

I return to the living room to grab my bags. Aunt Jen is standing by the wood-burner looking at the mantle. It's covered with candles, smudge sticks, feathers, crystals, rattles, small figurines of Buddha, Kali, Guan Yin, Shiva, the Virgin of Guadalupe, Wonder Woman. There are also photos, small slips of paper with prayers, glass hearts, and other trinkets. On the wall, a pair of barn owl wings spread wide. Aunt Jen picks up a blue marble painted to look like Earth. "I gave this to her."

I wish I knew what to say to make her feel better, but I don't. "You all settled in the guest room?"

She balances the marble on a cluster of amethysts. "I haven't spent more than five minutes in it. I pretty much came up here, showered, fed the cat and chickens, and headed back down the mountain, but yeah."

"Well...I'm going to hop in the shower upstairs."

She clears her throat and tries to hide the fact that she's feeling all emotional. "Where are we going to put Jake?"

Her question is a good one. Putting him in Mom's room, the only available one besides mine, would be weird. "Maybe we can get him to sleep with the chickens," I say, and head up the creaky stairway.

She yells up after me. "Maye doesn't happen to have wireless, does she?"

"You're kidding, right?" My legs are heavy and unresponsive as they negotiate the steps. Plunk. Plunk. Plunk. Behind me, my suitcase goes. Bump. Bump. Bump. Where *is* Dad going to sleep? I suppose I could use her bed and he could use mine...It's such a joke calling it my room. I never lived here, just like I've never lived with Aunt Jen or Dad. But they all keep rooms for me. Three rooms, three house keys, but no home. That about sums it up.

The inside of "my" room is a cluttered mess. Boxes spill their contents all over the place. Mom must have been in the middle of one of her projects when she got hit with this...thing. I push in the handle of my suitcase and drop my backpack to the floor. I'm so tired I can barely stand, but the bed has to be cleared before I can collapse on it. I start tossing photo albums, postcards, old sketchpads, pictures I drew when I was a kid, back into their cardboard boxes so I can stack them by the door. What was she up to, anyway? I pick up a Plexiglas photo cube I haven't seen in years. It's full of Polaroids of Mom and Dad when they were young, all from the same day. Mom's holding the camera at arm's length. Their faces, off-center, are both framed by winter hats—hers a colorful knit, his a leather and fur bomber hat. Snow dots their collars. They're beaming. I notice something sticking out of the cube, a folded-up piece of lined notebook paper. I pull it out. It's a letter in Dad's handwriting dated March 16, 1985. I would have been four years old.

*Dear Maye,*
*I am sorry about last night. I shouldn't have yelled. It*
*wasn't your fault! It was MINE! I don't know ~~whtt~~ what's*
*been happening to me. I think you're beautiful. Beautiful!*
*It's all me. Something is wrong with me. Please forgive*
*me. Please! I don't know what I'd do without you.*
> *Love,*
> *your husband*

Definitely a case of TMI.

I tuck it back behind the photo, put the cube on the nightstand, and collapse on the only part of the bed that's free of crap. But I can't stop thinking about the letter. What wasn't her fault? And what does he mean when he says something's wrong with him? He wouldn't have started drinking yet, so that's not it. An awkward thought passes through my brain. Maybe he hadn't been able to "perform."

I squeeze my eyes shut and try to hear the sound of the ocean lapping against the rocks, see lazy iguanas lounging in trees, taste Serena.

*

Jen stared at the underdone bacon and runny eggs that their mom slapped onto her plate. It was a Sunday morning and their mom had just announced to Jen and Jake that they were going to begin attending a new church. Reverend Bates's church.

"He's a very holy man," she said, pulling a chair up to the table. "And he feels the way I do, that our old church isn't doing enough to keep us safe."

Jen, dressed in her itchy mint-green church dress with the too-tight white sash, picked up her fork and began swirling the runny egg to make it more tolerable. The Reverend hadn't been in their lives three weeks, and already he was starting to take over. "I like our church," she said. "Mrs. Clover, our Sunday school teacher, is nice. Plus, we have to finish our palm leaf crosses. We can't quit now."

"Nonsense." Their mom sat at the table with her cup of coffee. She never ate breakfast. "A palm leaf cross won't be worth beans if the devil comes knocking."

Jen glanced at Jake. He didn't seem the least bit concerned by this announcement. This worried her. She scooped up a forkful of egg and stuck it in her mouth. Ever since their dad left, Jake had been like an abandoned dog howling for its master. Jen took a swig of watered-down orange juice, their mom's money-saving recipe. *Be careful,* she sent to her brother, *we don't know this guy.* But he acted like he didn't get it, which had been happening a lot lately.

On the hour-long ride to the church, Jake argued with their mom about why he couldn't have one of the doughnuts she'd bought for after the service.

"I want to make sure we have enough," she said.

"But if you don't know how many people are going to be there, how do you know how many you'll need?"

"I don't."

"Then why can't I have one?"

Jen adjusted the penny in the slot on her penny loafer so it was dead center. Why was he trying to win with their mom? It never worked.

They pulled up to a grimy storefront building in a part of town they had never been. There were three businesses in the Tri-Square Plaza, a one-story, flat-roofed, brick box. On the left was a discount pharmacy, on the right a second-hand record store, and in the middle a depressing-looking place with a large piece of paper taped in the window that said, REVEREND BATES TO PREACH TODAY. ALL ARE WELCOME! The window was covered in condensation, so you couldn't see inside. One corner of the sign was starting to come loose.

Jen stepped out of the car and tugged at the back of her tights. *"This* is the new church?" Even Jake looked concerned.

Their mom gingerly lifted the pink box of doughnuts from the front seat, placed it on the roof, and smoothed out the creases in her white sleeveless shirtdress. "We're just going to start out here until we can get a real church."

"We?" Jake said snottily.

"If you must know, Mr. Smarty Pants, Ernest has asked me to help run the business part of the church. I have experience you know. Before your father and I met, I did all the paperwork at a dentist's office. Now, come on, or we'll be late."

Jen had never heard their mom refer to Reverend Bates as Ernest. She didn't even know it was his name.

"I don't think we'll have a hard time getting a seat," Jake said.

"And how would you know that?" their mom snapped.

He gestured toward the empty parking lot. "Just look."

She glanced around, noticing for the first time that there were only three other cars in the lot, one of which was sitting on blocks. "It's still early," she said.

"*You* said we were going to be late," Jake shot back.

She looked momentarily confused then picked up her doughnuts and strode toward the church, her high heels going *clip clip clip*. Jake shook his head in disgust and followed. Jen took up the rear. What had their mom gotten them into now?

The shallow foyer had a folding table along the back wall. It was covered in a paper tablecloth and held a bouquet of daisies, a coffee pot, and a stack of paper cups. Next to it were a few folding chairs. Above it on the wall, a scary hooked rug of Jesus.

"Wait here." Their mom strode toward a room off to the right of the lobby. "I've got to put the doughnuts in the office." But before she could abscond with them, Reverend Bates stuck his head out the double doors by the table, which Jen assumed led to the chapel.

"Hey, you guys. Welcome." He was dressed in the same suit he'd worn when he'd come for lunch—black with thin lapels. His tie was black too, and his shirt crisp white, making his sandy hair and blues eyes gleam more than ever.

Their mom held up the doughnuts. "I think we should keep these in the office so people don't eat them before the service," she said glancing at Jake. "We want people to stick around afterwards."

Reverend Bates kicked the doorstop down so it held the double doors open. "Don't tell me you made the kids ride all the way over here without giving them a doughnut."

"Well, we need enough for—"

"Evelyn," he said in a scolding tone. "That's cruel and unusual punishment." He stepped over to Jake and clapped a hand on his shoulder. "Isn't it, kids?"

Jake rocked smugly back on his heels. "I'll say."

"What do you think, Jen?" the Reverend asked. "Do you want a doughnut before service?"

Jen looked him in the eyes. "Sure."

"Well then?" the Reverend said to their mom.

Jen glanced at her mom. Would she be mad? She didn't seem to be. She was shaking her head like she was mad, but she was smiling. "You'll spoil them."

"What could it hurt?" he said.

Sighing, she handed the box to Jen. "Say thank you."

Jen reconsidered her dislike of the Reverend. Maybe he was okay after all.

"Thank you," Jen said.

"Thank you," Jake echoed.

"Now take them into the office so other people won't get any ideas," the Reverend said gesturing to a door off the lobby. "I'm going to get your mom set up with the programs."

Jen and Jake charged toward the door.

"Just one!" Evelyn shouted after them. "You each just get one!"

Jen threw the box onto a metal desk and pried the tape with her fingers. She didn't want Jake getting the chocolate-covered one with colored sprinkles.

She plucked it from the box. "Mine!"

"No fair!" he said.

"Yes fair. I got to it first."

"But you knew I wanted it."

"So did I."

Jake surveyed what was left and chose another chocolate covered one, no sprinkles.

There was only one chair in the office and Jake took it.

Jen hiked herself up onto the empty desk. It was a lot like Miss Carter's desk at school only it didn't have the dinosaur-shaped pencil holder and the stack of papers and books. In fact, it looked like it didn't have anything in it. She leaned over and opened a drawer. There were some envelopes, a tablet of paper, some pens, and some paperclips. She slammed the drawer shut. "This is a weird church."

Jake shrugged. "All churches are weird."

"Yeah, but this one isn't even really a church. It's a store."

Jake shoved a huge bite of doughnut into his mouth, chewed a little, and said, "Do you like see-food?"

"No," Jen said.

But he opened his mouth anyway. It looked like poop.

Jen rolled onto her back laughing.

About ten people showed up for the service, half of whom Jen recognized from their old church. The other half looked like drunks who came for the doughnuts. And there was no Sunday school. But that made sense. She and Jake were the only kids.

Jen looked at the Xeroxed program she'd been unconsciously mangling. It reminded her of the handouts that Miss Carter passed out. Miss Carter was beautiful. She looked a lot like her mom only she had chocolate skin and coarse black hair, and her hands were perfect, each finger had a deep nail bed and a little white crescent on the tip. Her teeth were super white. Jen had even dreamed of what it would be like to kiss her. Just thinking about it made her feel warm. Jen crossed her legs at the ankles. She would never tell anyone. Not even Jake. Girls weren't supposed to kiss other girls. She squinted at the makeshift wooden cross behind the podium. The chapel sure didn't look like a real one. It was more like a classroom without any decorations. There was just the ugly podium, the cross, and a bunch of chairs taped together at the legs to make pews.

"I once felt dirty," Reverend Bates preached, "And thought I could *never* feel clean. I was terrified. I was weak. I was prime for the devil. Prime for his evil to slip into my heart, my *soul.* And then one day when I was about as low as I could go—I was in the gutter, my friends, in the filthy rotten gutter—Jesus came to me. And you want to know what he said? You want to hear his words? He said, 'Backslider? There is room for you at the cross!' Well, I picked my sorry head up, unable to believe what I'd heard. He couldn't be talking to me, could he? I was nothing. I was a slob in the gutter. And I was about to go back to my slothful ways, when Jesus said, 'Yes, you, sinner. God wants you to turn your life around. He wants to set you free!' You see, Jesus doesn't give up. It's we who give up…"

Jen listened to the sermon with her arms crossed. It kept his words from shooting in and giving her a stomachache. She wished there were more singing. She noticed a shaft of light coming in from a small skylight and strained to see why it was pouring into the room in the shape of a triangle. Was something blocking it? Again, she thought of Miss Carter and the pictures of triangles and other shapes decorating the walls of her classroom.

Reverend Bates moved on from the sermon to talk about his plans for the Church of Redemption. He asked the people on the benches to help him make this space worthy of the Lord, to bring buckets and sponges, paint and brushes. Next Saturday, he said, was going to be a workday.

\*

"I didn't think I heard the shower," Aunt Jen says from the doorway.

I blink a couple of times. My head feels like fuzz. I must have conked out. "I'm sorry…I'll jump in the shower right now."

"My GPS found a Thai place pretty close to the hospital. Does that sound all right?"

"Perfect."

She picks up the photo cube from the nightstand. "Wow. I haven't seen this in years."

I snatch the cube from her. "Yeah. I found it when I was cleaning off the bed."

She gives me a questioning look then decides to drop it. "So I fed the chickens. And I *considered* heading into the pen to look for eggs, but this one big hen gave me the evil eye."

I force a laugh. "Give me a few minutes to shower and I'll be down."

"Right."

Once I hear her padding downstairs, I wonder who it is I'm trying to protect. Mom? Dad? Aunt Jen? Me? I tell myself to get up and shower, but I don't feel like washing off Mexico. I pull out my phone and dial Serena. She answers on the first ring.

"You made it."

It's so good to hear her voice I can barely speak. "Uh…Yeah. It all went pretty smooth."

"How's your mom?"

"Pretty freaked. She can't move. Only her face."

"Wow. Do they have any idea how long—"

"Could be weeks, could turn around today. It's different for everybody." A tiny spider drops down on its web from the ceiling. If the light weren't just so, I'd have never seen it. "I'm at my mom's now, but we're heading back to the hospital soon."

The next obvious topic is trickier. I try to formulate the words to ask how she feels about what happened between us. "So…uh… where are you right now?"

"I'm at work. I really can't talk. An order for a ranchero salad and two fish taco plates just came up."

"Oh…well…maybe I'll call you later?"

"I would love that. And I miss you. But it's good you're there. Your mom needs you. And in a way, it's an amazing opportunity. To get to be with her at such a critical time in her life."

Clearly, she doesn't want to talk about us. I'm about to feel sorry for myself when I remember that her mom committed suicide when Serena was at summer camp. "Yeah. I guess."

"Brianna, if she's facing her death she's also facing her life. She's going to need someone to talk to. Someone she loves."

I take a deep breath. What she's saying is right. "My family is just so dysfunctional."

"All families are dysfunctional. And now I've really *got* to go deliver this order."

"Okay. But…well…I miss you."

"Me too. Especially the you I got to know last night. I can barely work my thighs are so raw."

A blush shoots up my neck. "I'm sorry, I didn't mean to—"

"It's a *nice* raw, Brianna. Now call me later."

"Okay bye."

"Bye."

I let her hang up first then do the same. I think I almost said, "I love you."

## CHAPTER FIVE

After a long, hot shower and collecting eggs, I head back to the veggie garden to see if it needs watering. The land works wonders on my nerves. The giant ponderosa pines surrounding Mom's property make it so private, like some Buddhist sanctuary or a nature preserve. Above, a red-tail circles in the cloudless sky.

Aunt Jen is sitting on the deck off the back of the house facing the vegetable garden. Showered and in a fresh T-shirt and jeans, she's in the final loops of braiding her hair. "Sunlight is such a relief after all that fluorescent shit at the hospital," she says.

I breathe in a lungful of clean air and exhale a long, "Yeeaaaaaah."

She wraps a rubber band around the tail of her long braid. "We ought to head back." I notice she doesn't stand up, just kicks the ground lightly to keep the sway going on the glider.

The lettuce and beet tops are wilting. It's been unseasonably warm, which causes plants to draw water from their leaves into their roots and look as if they're dying. Mom immobile on the hospital bed flashes through my mind. I stick my finger in the soil. It's dry. This is no fake out. "I need to water before we go."

Aunt Jen stretches. "Can't it wait?"

"Mom loves her vegetables." I walk over to the hose. "She'd want us to do this."

"You still need to call your dad."

"Why don't you call him? You're just sitting there."

"He doesn't want to talk to me."

"How do you know what he wants? You haven't talked to him in fifteen years."

"I talked to him at the hospital."

"Oh, please."

She doesn't budge.

I hold out my hand. "Toss me your phone."

She lobs it right to me and I catch it easily. I point to the red spray nozzle attached to the hose. "But if I call, you've got to water."

She salutes, says, "Yes, ma'am," and hauls herself up off the glider and takes the hose.

"Try not to get water on the leaves."

"How do I do that?"

"Aim."

I hate to say it, but if I had to choose one person to be stuck with on a desert island, it wouldn't be Aunt Jen, much as I love her. She'd be a disaster if you had to forage or hunt.

Dad picks up on the first ring.

"Hey, Dad. Just checking in."

"That nurse still won't let me in with Maye, but assures me she'll let me know if anything changes." He sounds tired. "I've a mind to report her."

"She's just doing her job, Dad." I listen while he grumbles a bit more about the nurse then say, "We're just now watering Mom's garden. After that, we'll head on back. Thai food all right with you?"

"Anything," he says. "Just no—"

"Peppers. I know. We'll be there in a little over an hour."

I shut the phone off. Aunt Jen has the hose so close to the stem of the peas that the spray is washing away the dirt. "Give me that," I say, taking it from her.

"I was just trying to keep the water off the leaves."

"It's no wonder you killed that—" I hear a vehicle pull up out front. The crappy muffler tells me it's Ari. The car door slams shut. "Back here!" I yell.

"Who is it?" Aunt Jen asks.

"Mom's latest waif." Mom always has at least one. She quasi-adopts them—teenagers with good hearts and rotten circumstances. In Ari's case, his parents, a biker and his bitch, have no idea what to do with the flamboyant fairy they spawned.

Ari strolls around the side of the house. He's wearing cutoff overalls, very short, with hiking boots, a tie-dyed, wifebeater tee, and lots of beaded jewelry around his wrists and neck. His short, spiky hair, which had turquoise streaks the last time I saw him, is now jet-black.

"Where have you been?" I ask in a tone more testy than intended. "We've been trying to get a hold of you."

He glances at Aunt Jen then ups his teenager act, groaning like the world is too stupid to exist. "My parents had one of those *rare* surges of responsibility, which resulted in them grounding me and taking my phone away for a *week*. It was soooo stupid. All I did was cut school for a gay marriage rally, but Mom went all emo on me, like she never cut school when she was a kid." He does a double take. "What are you doing here, anyway? You're supposed to be in Mexico."

"I take it you haven't listened to your messages yet."

"Mom let the battery die on my phone. I've got it charging in the truck."

I'm going to have to be careful how I tell him about Mom. Tough as he likes to act, he's a vulnerable kid. I set the nozzle on the hose to drip and lay it on the carrots.

"Ari, this is my Aunt Jen."

Aunt Jen looks up from a stalk of deep green kale leaves as if she's just now noticing Ari. "Oh. Hi."

"Hey," Ari says back, but he knows something's up. "Where's Maye?"

"She got sick," I reply, "and had to go to the hospital."

His brow furrows. "How sick?"

I hesitate. "Pretty sick."

He looks at me with withering contempt. "Are we going to keep on, Miss Cryptic, or are you going to tell me what's going on?"

"Well, she's got this thing…" Telling him turns out to be harder than I expected. My words sputter and stammer. I hear myself utter "rare disorder" and "her immune system is attacking her nervous system" and "paralyzed."

"Are you talking about Guillain-Barré?"

"You've heard of it?"

"I did a paper on immune disorders for school. Extra credit."

Aunt Jen, like most people, has underestimated Ari, and lets out a small snort-like chuckle.

Ari narrows his eyes. "Who's with Maye now?"

"My dad," I say. "But as soon as I finish watering, we're going to head back down to Redding."

"I'll take care of the garden," he says. "You should be with her." As an afterthought, he picks out a string of beads from around his neck. There's a little jade goddess at the center. "Give her this from me?"

I take the beads. A sweet gesture. "Will do."

Aunt Jen and I gather up our stuff from the deck.

Ari walks us to the car. We swap cell numbers. "It's good to know we can call you," I say.

Ari is staring at Aunt Jen. "You're one of the twins."

She's thrown by Ari's bluntness. "What of it?"

"You and your brother are Maye's favorite examples of good people who came from a supremely fucked-up family."

Aunt Jen laughs defensively. "Thanks…I guess."

*

It was going to be a bad day for the Bell household. Jake knew it the second he came downstairs for breakfast and saw the window shades still down, and Other Mother, her hair and robe a disheveled mess, standing by the stove stirring a saucepan with a metal spoon.

"What are you making?" he asked cautiously.

She spoke without looking up. "Coffee pot doesn't work."

Jake popped a piece of bread into the toaster, but when he lowered the lever it wouldn't stay down. Hoping Other Mother hadn't noticed, he went for the cereal. His stomach sank when she said, "That's *two* things."

"Well, they *were* both kind of old."

She yelled, "You think that's what this is about?" and stormed out of the kitchen.

Jake turned off the burner before pouring his Special K. He was trying not to freak out too much when he heard her coming back downstairs. He peeked out the kitchen door and saw she had the small wooden cross that usually hung on her bedpost. She cracked the front door open to hang it on the doorknob like a Do Not Disturb sign.

By the time Jen entered the kitchen, the burner was back on and Other Mother was back stirring her coffee, the spoon scraping the bottom of the saucepan. *Scrip. Scrip. Scrip.* "Two things," she murmured.

Jen glanced at Jake. He shook his head. *Don't ask.*

Jen started gathering up her schoolbooks.

Other Mother pointed the stirring spoon at Jen as if it were a wand. "Don't think you're going anywhere, missy."

Jake and Jen locked eyes. This was new. Other Mother had never forbidden them to leave the house.

Jake noticed the jar by the door was gone. "Where are our bus tokens?"

"Someplace you'll never find them," Other Mother spat.

"Mom, we've got to go to school," Jake said.

"You think the devil cares about your stupid little school?"

"But we have a history test!" Jen said.

Other Mother glanced over her shoulder and muttered, "You *bet* you have a test. But it's not just numbers or spelling or geography. This is a *big* test—the biggest. And you don't want to fail this one, missy."

Jake stood so abruptly his chair clattered to the floor behind him. "This is stupid! Things breaking is not a sign of—"

Other Mother whirled around and slapped him. "Watch your mouth, young man. I will not have you tempting the devil into this house. He's listening, you know. He can tell you're weak."

Jake's eyes filled with tears causing his world to go blurry. His mom had never hit him.

"Mom..." Jen was saying, but Jake didn't stick around to hear the rest; he just peeled out of the kitchen and up to his bedroom, swept everything off his desk, then fell to the floor crying.

A few minutes later, Jen knocked softly on his door. "Jake? It's me." She cracked the door. "Can I come in?"

Even though Other Mother was two floors below in the claustrophobic row house, Jen moved quietly and was careful not to let the door latch click behind her.

Jake used his sleeve to wipe his face to hide that he was crying. "I hate her."

Jen picked up his baseball trophy and returned it to his desk so she could sit next to him on the floor. "Are you okay?"

"What do *you* think?"

Jen leaned against the bed and pulled her knees up to her chest. "That test is forty percent of our grade."

"Would you quit harping about the stupid history test?"

Jen squinted her eyes, something she did when she was mad. "What are we going to do?"

"We should run away," he said.

"To where?"

"We can find Dad."

She kicked off her loafers. "Right."

"Or we could—"

"Just forget it, okay?"

Jake tipped his head back against the bed and looked at the ceiling. Jen bit her cuticles. They'd been through this before, and the best they'd ever been able to come up with was hiding out in Tony Lambardo's garage.

They sat in silence for a long time.

"Want to play Battleship?" Jake finally asked.

"Sure."

Jen won the first round, Jake the second. On their third tiebreaker game, the doorbell rang. Jake bolted to the window. "It's Ernest."

Jen groaned. "Great."

But Jake was relieved. Ernest would know what to do. He headed for the door.

"Where are you going?"

"I'm going to let him in."

Jake tore out into the hallway, down the stairs, and flung the door open.

Ernest was holding a box of church paperwork. "What are you doing home from school, Jake?"

"Mom won't let us go."

"Jake? Who's that at the door?" Other Mother yelled.

"Ernest."

Ernest laid his box of paperwork on the table by the door. "Everything okay here?"

"Mom's having one of her episodes," Jake whispered.

Ernest's eyebrows drew together. "Episodes?"

He cared. He was going to help them! "Uh huh. She gets kind of...scared and won't go out."

"Shall I go talk to her?"

Jake nodded.

"She in the kitchen?"

"Yeah."

"Okay. I'll go see what's up."

"Don't worry if she gets kind of mad. That's just how she is."

Ernest squatted so he could look Jake right in the eye. "Hey, everything's going to be fine. What's more," he said putting his hand on Jake's shoulder, "I'm going to take you and your sister out for doughnuts once we get this all sorted out."

Jake bobbed his head up and down. He would not let Ernest see him cry.

Ernest walked tentatively through the dining room toward the kitchen. "Evelyn? It's me. Ernest."

Jake stayed in the living room, picked up a comic book, and settled onto the couch waiting for who knew what. By the time Jen tiptoed down the stairs, he'd given up trying to overhear the conversation. He watched her position herself in the dining room trying to eavesdrop.

"He said he'd take us out for doughnuts once he gets things sorted out with Mom," he whispered loudly.

Jen put her finger to her lips to shush him, but Jake knew there was no way to make out their hushed tones. Ernest and their mom were huddled at the kitchen table, their foreheads almost touching.

Finally giving up, Jen returned to the living room and sank down into the worn rocker by the window. "What about school? And our test?" she whispered. "Has he mentioned anything about that?"

Jake craned his neck to see into the kitchen. "Would you shut up about school?" Other Mother was looking directly at Bates, a good sign. Other Mother never looked directly at anyone. Jake closed his eyes and tried to pretend it was a Saturday, that school wasn't going on, and that his mom hadn't slapped him.

After what seemed like an hour, Ernest entered the living room with his arm around their mom's shoulders. Her eyes were puffy and her skin super pasty, but she did manage to look at both Jake and Jen. "Ernest is a good man," she said, making a feeble attempt to pat her hair into shape. "He's going to help us."

Ernest smiled. "Evelyn, you go get yourself prettied up and we'll all go out for some doughnuts."

Their mom ran her hands over her robe, blinked a couple of times, then shuffled up the stairs.

Ernest sat on the couch next to Jake. "This has got to be hard on you guys."

"She's a nutbag!" Jake said angrily.

"Don't say that about your mother," Ernest said. "She's an extraordinary woman; her burdens are just bigger than most, and she needs our prayers." He held out his hands. "Would you pray with me?"

Jake took his hand right away and was annoyed when Jen wouldn't get up from the rocker. But Ernest kept his hand out and finally Jen rose, walked over, and took the outstretched hand. Jake took her other hand, completing the circle. They bowed their heads.

"Dear God, we ask that you help Evelyn cast out the demons that afflict her soul. Free her of the evilness that tortures her and those around her..."

The prayer went on for a long time, but Jake didn't care. He believed. Ernest was going to make everything okay.

✻

The ride down the mountain is subdued. The sun hangs low in the sky and there are barely any cars on the road. It's beautiful. I allow my thoughts to drift to Mexico. To the magic I experienced those two days.

*Serena and I swam out past the break.* I was floating on my back staring at the prehistoric-looking frigate birds riding the currents in the sky; she was treading water, her hair slicked back, her crystal stud earrings sparkling. I heard an eerie sound coming from the ocean floor. I started to tread water. "Did you hear that?"

"I think it was a whale."

A whale so close was thrilling. Terrifying. "Should we..."

Serena dove down. I tried not to panic. She resurfaced. "I think there's two."

We floated in the water listening. It sounded like a mother and calf's call and response. *Their songs drifted slowly out to sea.*

A Mustang convertible with the top down rockets past.

"So I think I like Serena," I say to Aunt Jen before I have a chance to censor myself.

Aunt Jen takes her eyes off the road for a split second. "As in *like* like?"

I nod.

"I thought you two were just friends."

"Yeah, well..."

"Yeah, well what?"

"Yeah, well, we're not just friends anymore. I think I might love her."

Aunt Jen lets this piece of information simmer for a few seconds. "That's a first."

"Uh huh."

"How do you feel about it?"

"Not sure. It could be risky. She's really nice."

"And?"

"And I don't want to hurt her," I say definitively then add in a much wimpier tone, "Or get hurt myself."

Hurt. The common denominator for us Bells.

"Take it slow," Aunt Jen says.

I nod, wondering how I'm going to do that. "It's hard to go slow."

"But it can save a lot of heartache."

We're passing Lake Shasta. The houseboats all appeared to be moored for the night. I imagine the happy families settling in after a day of adventure. Parents pulling out the deck chairs and pouring drinks while children, eager to make the most of the ebbing sunlight, take a last kayak paddle into the nearby cove.

"Then again, what do I know about love?" Aunt Jen says.

What indeed? She keeps herself so busy she doesn't have time for anyone. She does have friends, lots actually, through the theater, but she never lets anyone get too close. Not since Mom.

A flatbed piled high with recently live trees rumbles by.

"That's a lot of wood," Aunt Jen says.

"They're always logging up here. It's amazing there's any trees left."

"Too damn many people on the planet."

She and Dad are so similar. Both opinionated, both perfectionists, both kinda sad underneath their gruff exterior. "Why do you think Dad started drinking and you never did?"

She purses her lips for a millisecond. "Well, of course we're two different people." She glances at me. "But you know that."

I nod. Duh. "It just seems like with you being twins and having the same fucked-up upbringing, you'd deal with it in the same way."

She adjusts the seat so it tilts back a little. "In fairness, I've asked myself that same question. More than once. And here's what I think. It's a gender thing."

This makes no sense to me whatsoever. "Gender?"

"Yeah. We were treated differently from day one. By Mom, Dad, Bates—the whole world. While Jake was being told he was going to be something, do something, I was getting the message that the most important things I needed to learn were to clean, do laundry, and wash the dishes. It made me expect less from my life."

I'm about to ask her to expound when she clicks on the radio signaling End of Discussion.

# CHAPTER SIX

Dad's snoozing in the waiting room, his head resting on the back of the couch, his feet stretched out in front of him, and a *Time* magazine lying open on his chest. He's snoring. I debate whether or not to wake him. I'm sure he needs the sleep, but the Pad Thai and Kang Ka Ree are hot now. Besides, I don't think he'd want Aunt Jen and me to sit here watching him saw logs.

I step in so close I can see his nose hairs. Waking a person is awkward. It's such an intimate act. I plop the bag of food on the table next to him, hoping that will do it. It doesn't.

"He's always been a sound sleeper," Aunt Jen says. "When he actually manages to nod off."

I nudge his shoulder, once, twice. "Dad."

He sucks in a mouthful of air, opens his eyes, and stares at me with the disoriented gaze of one trying to mesh the dream world with reality.

"Dinner has arrived."

He blinks a few times, straightens up, and emits a gruff, "Great. Good. That's good."

"Any news on Mom?"

"Not last I asked, which was"—he glances at his watch—"about forty-five minutes ago." He clears his throat and runs his fingers through his hair.

"I'm going to see if I can rustle up some plates from the nurses' station," Aunt Jen says and disappears down the hall.

"How were the chickens?" Dad asks. "And...uh..."

I settle onto the chair catty-corner to his. "Mrs. Simpkins. They're fine. We watered the garden too." I try to think of something to say that will get him to drop his guard, like how weird dreams are or how scary Mom's illness is, but all my ideas short-circuit before finding their way to my mouth. I pick up the bag of food and pull out the cardboard take-out containers. "We got yellow curry, rice noodles in peanut sauce, green papaya salad, and rice."

"Sounds good."

Dad and I have never done too well with personal topics. We pretty much stick to what's concrete.

Aunt Jen returns with three plastic kidney shaped bowls.

"Tell me those aren't bedpans," I say.

Dad and Aunt Jen laugh, and I'm filled with a quiet pride at having caused this brief ceasefire.

Aunt Jen hands one to each of us. "Maybe they use them for drool."

Chuckling, Dad spoons rice into his. "Or surgery. For the spare parts."

"Eew," I say, though secretly I'm thrilled. We're acting like a normal family. Then my mind kicks out: Yeah, because one of us might be dying. I gesture to the cardboard carton Aunt Jen's about to set on the table. "Pass the Kang Ka Ree."

Dad, who's already put some of the curry on his rice, asks, "Is that what this yellow stuff is?"

"Yes, Dad." I scoop some on my rice. "Believe it or not, there are some delicious dinner foods that aren't nestled between buns."

More laughing and mindless chatter.

Dr. Reneaux steps into the room and the merriment stops dead. She's a big-boned woman with jet-black hair and a deep French accent. I like her immediately. She scans the three of us with our kidney bowls full of food. "We've had a new development."

I momentarily forget how to chew.

"New development?" Dad sets his bowl on the table and stands.

"Maye has lost mobility in her face and can no longer speak. We need to monitor her very closely at this time. As I said, we need to react quickly if this moves into her respiratory system."

Aunt Jen also sets her food aside and stands, positioning herself not three feet away from Dr. Reneaux. She widens her stance, all macho-like. "We should be with her." It's rare to see her talking to a woman as tall as she is.

Dad steps up next to Aunt Jen, flanking her right shoulder. "Yes, we should."

Dr. Reneaux nods. "I understand your wishes. I'll talk to the nurses on duty."

"She must be scared shitless," Aunt Jen says.

Dr. Reneaux nods again. "Very likely. I'll have a word with Barbara, our head nurse. In the meantime, why don't you finish your dinner?"

I don't swallow until she's gone. Is this it? Is Mom dying?

Aunt Jen collapses into the couch. "This is bullshit. Maye shouldn't be alone."

Dad sits ramrod straight, his hands gripping his knees.

"She said she was going to talk to the nurse," I say. "We don't know that they're going to keep us out."

"If it's the nurse I've been dealing with," Dad says, "don't get your hopes up."

A stern, gray-haired nurse with the body of a linebacker and the face of a bullfrog enters the room. Her nametag reads Barbara. Dad and I glance at each other. He tips his head slightly, indicating it's her. She runs her beady eyes over the three of us trying to figure out who's the leader of the pack. Predictably, she speaks to Dad. "She's asked to see her daughter."

Before I have a chance to process this information, I've bolted to standing. Is Mom dying? Is that why she asked to see me? But how could she have asked to see me if she can't speak? Maybe it's a mistake. I so want to believe this.

Bullfrog Barbara sizes me up. I'm clearly not the sweet young femme thing she was hoping for. But I don't care what the hell she thinks of me. I look right through her. "Shall we?"

I follow her through the double swinging doors to the ICU, my heart slamming in my chest. *Baboom. Baboom. Baboom.* I hear hearts pounding all around me. Bullfrog Barbara's heart as she strides in front of me. *Baboom. Baboom.* The patients' hearts in the rooms we pass. *Baboom. Baboom.* The orderly's heart as he pushes past us with a tray of dirty dishes. *Baboom. Baboom. Baboom.* A stray thought passes through my mind—the heart is the strongest muscle. I'm pondering the possible significance of this brain burp when Barbara stops dead.

What's she up to? We're not there yet.

I notice a little gold cross hanging around her thick neck. It's stuck to her skin. "The only reason I'm letting you in here," she whispers through tight lips, "is that your mother indicated there's something important she needs to say to you."

Oh God. She is dying. "I understand," I say, though I don't. None of this makes any sense. Didn't Dr. Reneaux say she couldn't talk?

We make the turn into Mom's room. Like before, she's on her back, only now her eyes are bulging like a panicky fish lying on the bottom of a boat—helpless, terrified, trapped. I sit on the chair next to the bed and take her hand. "Hey, Mom."

Her eyes strain to the side. Before I have a chance to reposition myself, Barbara motions for me to get up. Damn, she's annoying. I rise from the chair so Mom can see me face-to-face.

Bullfrog Barbara hands me a board with the alphabet on it. "She can communicate using this," she says. "One blink for 'Yes,' two blinks for 'No.'"

I can't figure out what she means. How is Mom going to point?

Bullfrog Barbara gives me an exasperated look. "*You* point. She'll blink to let you know if you're on track."

"Oh. Okay. I get it."

"Will you be all right then?"

What do I do if I'm not?

Bullfrog Barbara reads my mind and points to the button above the bed. "Push this if you need me." A diamond wedding ring digs into her chubby finger.

"Okay."

She pivots on the heel of her sensible shoe and bustles out of the room.

I look back at Mom. What if she stops breathing? Or her heart stops…"I'm here," I say.

She blinks once.

Shoot. I can't remember if one blink is yes or no. I step over to the door and glance into the hallway. Bullfrog Barbara is talking to an orderly. I return to Mom and hold the board where she can easily see it. I point to the YES. "How do you say this?" She blinks once. "This?" I say pointing to the NO. She blinks twice.

I take a deep breath. Okay. Easy. "How are you feeling?"

She swirls her eyes around in an effort to communicate.

Good one, Brianna. "Let me rephrase. Are you still having that burning feeling?" She blinks once. *Yes.* "Has it gotten worse?" She blinks once. *Yes.* "You're going to get through this, you know." No blinks this time, just a hard stare. The knot in my stomach tightens.

"Um…There's something you want to say to me?"

She blinks once, the urgency this time, unmistakable.

"Okay, then. I'll just start going through the alphabet." My arms feel heavy, resistant. I don't want to talk to my mother through a stupid board! My mind flashes to the whale and her calf in Mexico, their effortless communication wafting through the water. I return my attention to the alphabet board. The letters are out of order, which makes no sense. I point to the first letter. "Q?" Two blinks. "W?" Two blinks. This is going to take forever. Finally, in the middle of the third line we get to a one-blinker: B. "Okay the word starts with B." She blinks once.

This is excruciating. For both of us. There's got to be an easier way.

I point to the first line. "Is your letter in this line?" She blinks twice, and I can tell she's relieved I've found a new method. I point to the second line. "This one?" She blinks once. Now we're talking. "How about I slide my finger really slowly underneath the letters and you blink when I hit the one you want?" She blinks once. She likes the idea. Good. I start sliding my finger. She blinks on A. "Cool. BA." One blink. Yes. Much better. "Next line." Two blinks. "This one?" One blink. Slide finger. Blink on D. Is that the end of your word? BAD? She blinks once. "Awesome. We have our first word. Bad." I gloss over the ominous nature of the word. "Do you feel bad? Is that it?" She blinks twice. "You think this place is bad?" Two blinks. "You think I'm bad?" Tenderness passes through her eyes, but still only two blinks.

"Okay," I say, like this is a normal way to carry on with one's mother. "Back to the board." This time we spell out the word BLOOD.

"Is this about your blood?" Two impatient blinks. "The hospital's? Have they given you bad blood?" Two more impatient blinks.

"I think we should do more words." She blinks once, a real slow one, like she's trying to say, *Duh!*

We start with the letter J. The next one I get is A.

"Is this about Dad?" She blinks once. "Dad has bad blood?" Two blinks.

I want to rip my hair out, but go back to the board again. Another J. "Oh. You're talking about the bad blood between Aunt Jen and Dad." She blinks once.

To put her mind at ease, I start telling her how well they're getting along—I want her to focus on healing, not on their bullshit—but right in the middle of my blathering, she interrupts me with two staccato blinks.

"What? That's not what you're talking about?" She blinks once. "It's not about Dad and Aunt Jen?" Two blinks. "It *is* about Dad and Aunt Jen." One blink. Resigned, I go back to the board. We spell out the word SECRET.

An uneasy feeling passes through me. "Whose secret?" I ask. We spell out the name JAKE. I begin to question if I even want to continue with this, but the look on her face is desperate, forceful. "Secret from Aunt Jen?" I ask. She blinks once.

"Do you want to tell me the secret?" Two definitive blinks. No. Of course not. Here she might be dying and all she can think to do is

play one of her games—manipulating people "for their own good."
I could scream.

We go back to the board and spell out, TELL JAKE I NEVER
TOLD.

I try to keep the impatience from my voice. "You want *me* to
tell *Dad* that *you* never told his secret to *Aunt Jen*?" She blinks once.
"Will he even know what secret I'm talking about?" She pauses, then
blinks once. "Maybe you should give me a key word or something
to jumpstart my conversation with him. I mean, you know Dad. He's
not exactly forthcoming." She thinks for a minute then blinks once.
We spell out the name BATES.

Shit. I feel like I'm doing a crossword puzzle where the
consequence for missing a word is death.

"The secret's between him and Bates?" I ask. One blink. "You
want to tell me what it is?" Two blinks. No. That would be too easy.
Too healthy. We spell out the words. ASK DAD. I feel like pulling
out my hair. Ask Dad? Right. Like he'd tell me anything.

She senses my reluctance and makes me spell out PROMISE.

I nod my head, but don't actually say the words, "Yes, I
promise." I'm not committing to anything.

She glares at me.

I ask again how she's feeling. We spell LIKE HELL.

If her intention is to make me feel guilty, it works. Seeing her
suffer this way is killing me. "How about I play some harmonica?"

She gives me a final look that says, *Tell him*, which I ignore,
then she blinks once and shuts her eyes. I'm thinking she wants me
to play. Or she's given up on me. I mean, surely she's not thinking
I'm going to rush out and do this now?

I pull my harp from the pocket of my cargo shorts and start out
with Bob Marley's, "No Woman No Cry." I play quietly, so as not
to disturb other patients. My eyes are filling with tears. I move on
to "Michael Row the Boat Ashore" keeping my eyes trained on the
gentle rise and fall of her chest. Please keep breathing. Please.

✳

It was raining, so their mom picked Jen and Jake up from school. "There are some things I have to take care of at the church," she said. "Plan on doing your homework."

"Can't you drop us off at home?" Jen whined, climbing in the backseat. "I hate hanging out there. There's nothing to do."

"Well, next time you talk to your father, tell him to send some money so I don't have to work."

Jen gave their mom a withering stare. She knew darn well that they hadn't had any contact with their dad since he'd taken them out for cheesesteaks that day. They didn't even know where he was.

Their mom checked her lipstick in the rearview mirror. "Just be thankful I didn't make you walk home in the rain. We've got a newsletter to get out."

Jen glanced at Jake hoping he'd take up her cause, but the oaf just threw his backpack on the shotgun side of the seat and settled in.

Twenty minutes later, they were pulling into the Tri Square Plaza parking lot.

Jen gazed despondently at the church store. The words CHURCH OF REDEMPTION were now painted in a gothic font on the front window, and there were potted plants out front, but the car propped up on blocks was still at the end of the parking lot. A week ago, she'd been next door at the used record store flipping through albums and overheard the hippie owner call the church "weird-assed," the parishioners "a cult," and Bates a "zealot." Later, when she told Jake what she'd heard, he shrugged her off. "At least we don't have to memorize stupid scriptures in Sunday school anymore."

Jen opened the car door and prepared to dash through the rain. She hated Bates and considered him responsible for Jake's new behavior, and for the fact that she and her brother could no longer do mind-talking. Bates had filled Jake's mind with all this stuff about being "the man of the family," and how he had to take care of "the womenfolk," and the more Jake bought into it, the further he grew away from her. It was stupid. Jen could take care of herself just fine.

The lights were on in Bates's office and Jen tried to scuttle through the lobby into the main office before he could come out to greet them. She didn't make it.

"Hello, hello," he said spreading his arms wide. "Nothing like some rays of sunshine on this dreary day."

Their mom, as usual, barely contained her adoration of the Reverend, and got all flustered. "I told the kids they could do their homework while I finished up with the newsletter and the deposit."

Bates leaned down to Jen's eye level. "Your hair looks very nice in a ponytail, Jennifer. You should wear it that way more often. It really shows off your features."

"Yeah, Jen." Jake flipped her ponytail. "Nice features."

Jen kicked him in the shin.

"Ow!"

Bates wagged his finger at Jen. "Is that any way for a lady to act?"

"Thank you, Ernest." Their mom slipped off her dripping green raincoat and hung it on a chair by the door. "They've been squabbling since I picked them up from school."

Jen looked at her in disbelief. They'd barely said two words on the ride over!

"Hey." Bates clapped a hand on Jake's shoulder. "Before you start on your homework, there's something in my office I think you're going to want to see. You might enjoy it too, Jennifer."

Jen followed the two of them into Bates's office. She knew she'd only been invited out of courtesy, but she was tired of being left out.

"Don't forget they have homework," their mom called after them.

Bates gestured to the low table in the back of his office. It housed his train set—the one thing besides Jesus and their mom that seemed to interest him. Since they'd already seen his train set a bunch of times, Jen didn't know what the big deal was. Jake did though. "A new engine!" he said, dropping his book bag. He crouched to get a better look. "And you've added a bridge."

Bates squatted next to Jake, blocking out Jen's view of the new additions. She listened to Jake and Bates talk about the new engine for a while, hoping one of them might remember she was standing there. When they didn't, she headed back to their mom's office to do homework.

"Not interested?" her mom asked, looking up from her Corolla.

Jen let her book bag tumble to the floor then dropped down cross-legged next to it. "Just trains." But she might as well have said, *Just boys.* More and more, she was being excluded from Jake's life because she was a girl.

She pulled out the Galileo books she'd picked up at the school library and began working on science. The office was stuffy and hot, and the sound of the train chugging around its track in the other room, the two-fingered tap tap tapping of her mom plunking out letters, and the rain splat splat splatting against the flat roof of the building made her eyelids start to droop. She pushed her schoolbooks aside and curled up on the floor using her folded arms for a pillow.

The next thing she knew, the phone was ringing. She could still hear the train going around on its tracks. She watched her mom through her eyelashes, pretending to still be asleep so she wouldn't have to go back to her homework. Jen missed the crimson tips of her mom's fingers and the lipstick to match, but ever since Reverend Bates had come into their lives, their mom had started painting her nails and lips a chaste pink. Her clothing had changed as well; her blouses were plainer and her skirts now covered her knees.

*Bates has stolen my entire family,* Jen thought.

Her mom finished answering questions about the church's hours and location and then began working on the deposit. She seemed nervous while counting the offering money. She kept glancing toward the door and was kind of panting. Jen worried she might be on the verge of one of her episodes. She hadn't had one in two whole weeks, and Jen wanted to believe they were over for good. Then she saw her mom tuck a few bills of the offering in her blouse.

Jen tried to convince herself that she was mistaken, that her mom was fixing a bra strap, but in her gut, she knew she'd just seen her steal from the church. *I have to tell Jake,* she thought, and was just about to get up to find him when he stepped into the office. "Um. Ernest wants to take us out for fish and chips."

Jen crinkled up her nose and yawned trying to give the impression she was just waking up. "We don't like fish."

Their mom's finger shot to her lips to shush her. "Maybe you can order something else when we get there," she whispered with a wink.

Jen closed her textbook and rolled onto her knees. "I don't get why we can't tell him the truth."

Their mom shut the desk drawer. "Because he's saving your mama's soul, that's why." Then she locked the drawer.

Jen's eyes flew to Jake. She had to tell him what she'd seen. She tugged at his sleeve. "Wanna see if it's still raining?"

Jake pulled away. "It is. All right? What do you want to know for anyway? What difference would it make?" His tone was harsh, mean.

The corners of Jen's eyes started to sting. What was going on with her family? They were all acting so messed up.

"Everybody ready?" Bates said, strolling into the room.

✳

Bullfrog Barbara pokes her head in the room and whispers, "Has she gone back to sleep?'

I put my harmonica down and say quietly, "Mom? You awake?"

Mom doesn't open her eyes.

Barbara gives me the once-over (she obviously thinks I'm a deviant) then walks over and checks Mom's IVs. "We need to check her arterial blood gas."

The idea of waking Mom seems so wrong. "She just fell asleep."

Bullfrog Barbara glares at me. Clearly, I have no business having an opinion. "This won't take a minute." She takes a syringe from the cabinet, prepares it, then jiggles Mom's arm. "Maye? Maye?"

Mom's eyes flutter open. She's alarmed.

I step in so she can see me. "Welcome back."

Mom looks confused for a few seconds. Then frustrated. Then panicky.

"Time to check your arterial blood gas," Bullfrog Barbara says in a singsong voice, like Mom's a fucking three-year-old. She sticks a needle into Mom's wrist. I turn toward the window. The last thing any of us needs is for me to faint.

Outside, it's grown dark and a half moon hangs in the sky. Where does Bullfrog Barbara get off judging me? Her and her little gold cross.

I slip my hands in my pockets and come across the beaded necklace with the little goddess that Ari gave me to give to Mom.

The Bullfrog chats with Mom, trying to put her at ease. She tells her about some family reunion, something about her son, Dirk. Classic that she should have a son named Dirk. The only other Dirk I've ever known made me feel like a deviant too.

*Fourth grade.* I was playing handball with Dirk Weiner.

He whacked the ball into the wall. "My dad says our teacher is a lezzy,"

"What's a lezzy?"

"A girl who does it with girls."

The ball whizzed right past me. There are girls who do that?

"Dad says one of 'em acts like the girl and one acts like the boy. How perv is that?"

Dirk's words catapulted me into an ultra freakout. Was I a lezzy? A perv? I thought about Rochelle with the cool pop beads who sat two desks in front of me. How I imagined us kissing.

For the next few years, I tortured myself every time I fantasized about kissing a girl. I even went so far as to wish for an inner electric chair that would shock unnatural impulses out of me. Why it took me so long to figure out about Mom and Aunt Jen is beyond me. I guess somewhere I was still harboring hopes that Mom and Dad were going to get back together. And Aunt Jen, well, she couldn't be Mom's girlfriend. *She was my aunt.*

"All done," Barbara says.

I turn away from the moon and the shadowy world below. "Thanks."

The Bullfrog writes on the clipboard. "Don't you go wearing her out now."

"Not to worry." I'm dying to point out that she's the one who woke Mom.

She gives me one last disapproving look and leaves.

I turn to Mom. "You okay?" Which is *such* a stupid question. Mom, bless her, blinks once. But how could she possibly feel okay?

She directs her eyes to the alphabet board. Reluctantly, I pick it up.

We spell out TELL DAD and NOW. Like I might have forgotten her earlier request.

"Mom, whatever this secret is, it's not your fault that they don't get along. They made their choices."

Her eyes bore into the alphabet board. I begin sliding my finger under the first line then the second then the third. We stop on M. After many more passes we spell out MAKE HIM TELL HER.

"How? I can't make him do anything. He's a brick wall when it comes to anything having to do with feelings."

The weird thing is, I want her to fight back, to cuff my head and call me a selfish brat. Not that she'd ever do it, even if she were well. But I can't stand her looking at me with those scared eyes.

Tears start streaming down my face. I'm not ready for this. I don't want my mom to die. "Mom…" I sputter. Then I remember the beaded necklace. I pull it from my pocket. "Ari wanted me to give you this."

A look of tenderness floats across her face.

I hang the necklace on the cabinet knob. "He's worried about you. We all are."

Her eyes flick to the board. We spell out LOVE.

"Me too," I say because what if she *is* dying? What if this is the moment that you always hear about when you better say your feelings or else?

I'm about to sit down when she looks to the board again. We spell out. GO. NOW.

"Now? You want me to deal with this now?"

She blinks once.

Great. My mother, on her deathbed, kicks me out of the room.

I kiss her on the cheek then head out to the lobby so angry, so hurt, so confused that I can barely think. I'm a pawn in a game where I don't even know the rules.

## CHAPTER SEVEN

Dad's reading a copy of *USA Today*, his cheaters perched low on his nose; Aunt Jen is on her computer, no doubt checking e-mail, her cheaters similarly positioned. They both look over their glasses at me when I enter the waiting room, two owls scrutinizing a rodent.

"Did they kick you out again?" Aunt Jen asks.

I stare at the fake bromeliad hanging on the wall above Dad's head. How do I explain that it was Mom who kicked me out?

Dad notices my hesitation. He lets the paper drop to his lap. "Is she okay?"

I bobble my head up and down, deciding right then to do as Mom asked. It might be the last thing I ever do for her. But how to get Dad alone?

I spot the Thai food containers and stroll over. "Would one of you go hang with her while I scarf some food? I'm starving." I lay my hand on Dad's shoulder and fix my eyes on Aunt Jen. "I haven't had much time with my dad here." Neither one responds right away, and I'm sure they're on to me, then I realize they're just exhausted.

Aunt Jen shuts down her computer. "Sure. I'll sit with her."

I tell her about the alphabet board.

She nods, eyes glazed, dull. "Got it." She drifts down the hall.

"Call my cell if anything changes," I call after her. "Dad and I might take a walk."

"I thought you were hungry," Dad says.

"I was—am. But this place is starting to get to me. Wanna go find a bench outside? Some fresh air? I'll bring my dinner with me."

Dad folds his paper. "Are you okay, Bean?"

"I'm fine. I—we—just need to talk." How could Mom have put me up to this? I don't know how to talk to Dad, let alone broach a sensitive topic like a secret he's been keeping for years and years. He must have his reasons.

"What's going on, Bean?"

I glance at the bandaged girl and her father who are still waiting on the outcome of the mom. The girl acts like she wasn't watching. "Can we go outside?" I lean in and whisper to Dad. "Please? Mom asked me to talk to you about something and I don't want to do it here." Now I've done it. Any chance of gently easing into the topic is totally obliterated.

He places the newspaper on the table and stands. "Lead the way." I hate that he's so much taller. I start walking, my feet encased in cement.

"Bean?"

"Yeah?"

"Don't you want your dinner?"

I do an about-face and sweep up the containers. Where am I taking us?

"I noticed a sign for a courtyard when we came in," he says.

What? He's a mind reader now?

Dad has this uncanny way of negotiating through the world. He never asks directions, not because he's a man, but because he doesn't have to. He always knows the shortest route, the most scenic route, like he's got a built-in GPS.

"Which way?" I ask.

He points down the hall. "Go straight."

*In your dreams,* I think, and continue walking forward. I wish I didn't feel so defensive. It's going to make this conversation painful.

He guides me out of the ICU, down the stairs, and out to a dimly lit courtyard. It's empty and the air is balmy. I sit on a bench next to a planter. Dad sits on a bench at right angles to mine. There's a topiary at the corner where the two benches meet, a couple of small shrubs cut to look like stacked balls. The outside lights buzz.

"Go ahead," he says, "I'm all ears."

While his words encourage me, his body does everything but. He crosses his arms, stretches out his long legs, and crosses them at the ankles. I'm locked out. "Dad..." I say, my voice way pathetic-sounding.

"Just spit it out, Bean. Whatever it is Maye wants you to say to me."

I set the take-out container on the bench. "It isn't so much something she wants me to say to you. Well, in a way it is. I mean, sort of." I run my fingers through my hair. Look up at the moths crashing into the buzzing lights. "I think Mom wants you and Aunt Jen to make up."

He doesn't say anything, just breaks eye contact to study his feet. If I didn't know better, I'd think he was mentally conversing with his size eleven Top-Siders.

"Well, that's what I think anyway, not what she said. Not exactly. See, she asked me, rather, *told* me—you know how Mom is. You should see her now that she has to pass her ultimatums down through an alphabet board, wow, talk about persuasive. Anyway, she *told* me that you, um, have...some secret? At least I think that's what she said. I might have gotten it wrong. The alphabet board leaves lots of room for...interpretation. But it seems to really matter to her. Whatever it is..." As I listen to myself spew (I've truly leapt out of my body) I see myself trying to execute a U-turn in this narrow alley I've ventured into. Only the more I try to angle around, the stucker I get. "Well, I told her..."

"Bean?"

"Yeah?"

"Did she give you any clues as to what this 'secret' was about?"

"Um. Yeah."

"And?"

"She spelled out BATES."

Trying to act nonchalant, he unknots his arms to lean back and prop himself up. But I can see he's rattled. He's doing his steely-face thing where all his facial muscles freeze into a mask. The next thing he says sounds as if it has to squeeze past his larynx to get out. "Did she tell you what it was?"

"No."

He nods perfunctorily, then continues to converse with his Topsiders. "I suppose you want me to tell you what it is."

"No! I mean, only if you want to." My words fly out so fast they trample each other. "I'm just supposed to tell you that she never told Aunt Jen." I mentally slap my hand over my mouth to keep more from spewing.

He gives another curt nod, waggles his ankles, and claps his hands together. "That's it? We're done?"

If only. "Actually, there's one more bit."

Sighing heavily, he goes back to his previous position, talking to his feet. "Lay it on me." But he's pissed. His jaw is shuddering.

I can't wimp out now. "She wants you to tell Aunt Jen your secret."

He purses his lips. Some old resentment is pressing against them.

Whatever game Mom is playing is dangerous, cruel, and I momentarily hate her for putting Dad through this. For putting *me* through this. Why couldn't she have told him herself? Why couldn't she have spelled it out on her little board to *him*?

"And she put you in charge of making this happen," Dad finally says. His tone is flat, dead.

"Yup." I pick up my cold Thai food and poke at it with my fork. "You know Mom," I say, trying to lighten the mood. "She always wants everything on the table, everybody to get along." The mixture of gelatinous Kang Ka Ree and raw emotion makes me want to throw up. I glance at him. Even in this dim light, I can see that he's battling some horrific demon.

"I need to walk," he says.

"Want company?"

For a second he looks surprised to see me here, like he's coming out of some bad dream, then he stands and brushes imaginary dust from his trousers. "Sure."

＊

Jake loved the miniature town with its tiny trees and houses, its tiny railroad track and tunnel, its tiny people. It was old timey and organized. Everything made sense. There was a family outside the train depot that he especially loved, even if they never did get on the train. Week after week, they waited in their tiny world where the only thing that moved was the train. He liked to think about where they might be going.

He ran his fingers over the new engine. It even had a tiny engineer. "Jen. Check this out."

"She's not here anymore," Ernest said. "I guess she doesn't like trains the way you do."

Jake reached out to touch the grass by the station. It looked soft.

"You and I need to have a little talk," Ernest said, shutting the door.

Jake drew his hand back from the grass. Was he in trouble?

Ernest dragged his chair to the side of his desk and sat. His expression was sad, as if he was disappointed in something…or someone.

Jake stared at the buttons on Ernest's shirt. The top one was unbuttoned.

Ernest pulled a worn magazine from his top desk drawer. "Your mother said she found this under your bed."

Jake's heart quickened. It was the dirty magazine that Tony Lambardo had loaned him, the one with the lady with the really big tits who was licking a cherry Popsicle. Tony's dad had a whole stack of dirty magazines in the back of his closet. "It's not mine." His legs felt like flimsy pipe cleaners.

"Now, Jake. Let's not add lying to our list of sins."

"It's true."

Ernest shook his head and sighed. "Do you remember last week in church when I talked about the many faces of temptation?"

Jake wound his fingers into a tight knot behind his back and placed one sneakered foot on top of the other. He wanted Ernest to put the magazine down. It was humiliating to have to look at it in front of a grown-up. Not only that, he was starting to feel "that way" down below.

"Do you?" Ernest prodded.

Jake nodded.

Ernest opened the magazine to show Jake the folded-out page. A woman with her legs spread gaped out at him. "Pull up that stool," Ernest said.

Jake glanced toward the closed door. What if someone came in?

"The stool, Jake."

"Um…"

Ernest made as if he were about to stand. "Should we go get your mother? Would you rather have this talk with her?"

Jake did as he was told and pulled the short stool in front of Ernest—and the magazine—and perched on its seat. The woman's beaver was right in his face. He crossed his legs to hide his stiffy.

"You like this, don't you?" Ernest said.

"Not really."

"Of course you do. I can see it. You're erect."

"No, I'm not."

"Then open your legs."

Jake glanced toward the door again.

"What are you afraid of, Jake? That your mother will find out what a sinner you are?"

"No."

"Have you ever thought about her naked?" Ernest waited a second then repeated. "Have you?"

"No!"

"I'm just trying to help you, Jake. Now look at the picture."

Jake pressed his folded hands down on his penis, trying to get it to go back down. "I don't want to."

Ernest stood and held the magazine at waist height. His own penis was bulging in his black trousers. "We're all sinners, Jake, every one of us."

Jake squeezed his eyes shut. He wanted to go home.

Ernest rested a hand on Jake's head. "I've promised your mother I'm going to help you with this, Jake."

Jake could barely make out Ernest's words. The sight of the woman's beaver and Ernest's touch were getting mixed up inside him.

"Look at me, Jake."

Jake squeezed his eyes shut even tighter.

Ernest brushed his thumb across Jake's forehead. "Look at me."

Jake peeled open his eyes. The magazine was gone and Ernest was looking at him with a peculiar expression.

Ernest reached down to take Jake's hand. Jake flinched. "Relax, Jake." He gave Jake's hand a tug to get him up off the stool. "You and I are going to cast out the devil together."

Ernest wasn't mad? Curious, Jake followed him into the private bathroom, a room not much bigger than a closet—sink and toilet freshly cleaned by his mother. There was a silver cross on the wall above the toilet.

"Are you ready to face the devil?" Ernest asked.

Jake didn't know what Ernest meant. Then Ernest undid his own belt and unzipped his pants.

"Go ahead, boy," he said motioning to Jake's pants. "Don't be afraid."

Jake hesitated, a mixture of anxiety and arousal shooting through him.

"Do as I say."

Jake's robotic hands fumbled with his fly. His too-big jeans dropped to the floor.

"Take the devil in your hand, Jake. Like this."

Jake glanced at Ernest's erect penis. It was huge. And his long fingers were wrapped around it like a hotdog. Jake swallowed. Ernest didn't expect him to touch that big penis, did he? That would be creepy weird. But that's not what he was saying. He was talking about jacking off, which Jake had done a bunch, even a couple of times with Tony and their friend Roger. The three of them pawing through Mr. Lambardo's pile of magazines had shot off like rockets together. It was funny. Stupid.

But Ernest was a grown-up. This was different.

"Go on, boy. Take the devil in your hand."

Jake couldn't get his mother out of his mind. What would she think? Her perfect Reverend Bates in here jacking off. Wanting Jake to jack off with him. The thought was sickening. Thrilling. He felt his penis begin to swell.

Ernest began stroking himself. "Do as I say. We must make you clean."

Jake took his stiffening penis in his hand.

A fat tear rolled down Ernest's face and clung to his chin. He was looking at Jake's penis. "Forgive us, Lord, for our lasciviousness. We are filthy and dirty and full of sin."

Jake closed his eyes and thought about the lady with the big tits and the Popsicle.

Outside the bathroom, the tiny train chugged around the track.

＊

I practically have to trot to keep up with Dad as he strides the perimeter of the hospital.

"Your mother," he says, "always thinks she knows what's best for everyone."

I almost laugh at his attempt to distance himself from Mom, calling her "your mother." But there is no arguing this point. I do a few skips to catch up.

"Not only that," he says, "but she always thinks everything can be fixed by talking."

Another truism. In Mom's defense I add, "She's scared, Dad. Give her a break."

"I've half a mind to wonder if this isn't why she…"

"You can't blame her for getting sick, Dad."

He abruptly stops walking; I nearly barrel into him. "Of course not," he says. I wait for him to say something more, but he's looking at the sky. Nighthawks, lit by the sodium parking lot lights, swoop on sharp wings scooping up bugs.

I walk over to a trashcan and toss my dinner box. "Should we head back?"

He looks at me. "You go ahead. I have some thinking to do."

I take a few steps.

"Bean?"

"Yeah?"

"Are you going to mention this to Jen?"

"Do you want me to?"

"I'd rather you didn't."

"Okay. I won't." Again, I wait hoping he'll say more. Thank you, perhaps? But he's already gone back to whatever hell is haunting him. I start walking back to the building, deliberately placing one foot in front of the next. Inside, I take the stairs slowly, pausing at a window that looks out onto the parking lot. Dad hasn't budged. He's just standing there with his head tipped back looking at those frantic nighthawks scaling and plunging, scaling and plunging.

## CHAPTER EIGHT

Great. Dad's acting all mad—like him having a secret is *my* fault. He got back from his walk four hours ago and since then the three of us have been doing nothing but hanging out in this oversized fish bowl and basically ignoring each other. We watch the doctors, nurses, and orderlies come in and out of the ICU, but we're stuck out here. Even the bandaged daughter and her worried-sick dad have left, making it just us and some dude who keeps talking business on his cell. It's one in the fucking morning.

I attempt to fluff my bunched-up hoodie to make a more comfortable pillow, but sleeping is pointless. Can't someone at least dim the florescent lights?

A few minutes ago, I tried to convince the night nurse that I should be with Mom. I said nothing would make her heal faster than love. But the nurse—a new one who looks like she came out of that freaky Mormon compound in Eldorado, especially her sculpted forties hairdo—says Mom has entered a critical stage and needs constant monitoring. They've got her hooked up to oxygen and have started feeding her intravenously.

Mom must be so scared.

If I could just tell her that I told Dad, that would make her feel better. Shit, if Nurse Eldorado would let me be with her, I'd stoop so low as to tell Mom that Dad confessed his secret to Aunt Jen. "He even cried," I'd say. She'd love that. "And then *she* cried," I'd say. "And then they both promised to cherish each other forever and ever."

That would heal her more than feeding her through tubes.

I glance over at Aunt Jen. She's frowning at her laptop. And good old Dad is sitting ramrod straight, staring at the ICU entrance like he has the power to will someone to come out and give us an update. He's barely looked at me once since our little talk. Aunt Jen knows something's up. She keeps peeking over her cheaters at Dad. Or maybe that's just the way she is around him. Who knows? Who *cares*? I want this whole nightmare over. I want Mom to get better and Dad to go on being the jerk he's always been.

Aunt Jen catches me staring at her. We hold eye contact. Does she think I know what's going on with Dad? Is that what she's trying to communicate through her eyes? Damn, I hate this whole secret thing—Mom's game.

Aunt Jen sets her computer aside and stands. "This is ridiculous. I'm going to see if I can find something out."

Dad springs to his feet. "I'll take care of it."

Aunt Jen flicks her eyes to Cell Phone Dude who appears to be texting someone and lowers her voice. "I don't know if it matters which one of us goes, Jake."

"Then I will," he says. "She was *my* wife."

That does it. Now Aunt Jen is pissed. "Don't go there, Jake."

"Go where?" Dad acts like he hasn't just slammed Aunt Jen. "I was just saying, they'll respond better if they understand who I am."

"Her ex?" Aunt Jen says. "I don't see that as much collateral."

"Better than her ex-lesbian lover."

There's a tense silence. Cell Phone Dude, showing excellent judgment, looks at his Rolex, clears his throat, and exits the scene. I'd join him if I could get my legs to move.

"Jesus, Jake," Aunt Jen half-whispers. "Do you have to be such an asshole?"

"It's the truth," he says. "People understand husbands better than lesbian lovers."

"*Ex*-husbands."

"Whatever."

"No. Not whatever. You had her. You fucked up and lost her. I'm not to blame for that."

"Look, I know I wasn't a perfect husband." He steals a quick look at me. "Or the perfect father. But that was no excuse for you to—"

"What was I supposed to do, Jake? Turn my back on Maye. On Bean?"

I glare at the acoustic tiles on the ceiling. Leave me out of it.

"You were drunk," Aunt Jen says, "twenty-four-fucking-seven."

"Bullshit," he says. "I was holding down a job. I was providing."

"Barely."

Dad starts pacing the small room. "You stole her away from me. She was my wife." He looks like he wants to punch a wall.

Aunt Jen drops her head to her chest in disgust then looks right at him. "You don't get it, do you?"

Dad whirls around and jabs his finger at her chest. "No, *you* don't get it! You never *have*. You don't *know* what I was up against. You don't *know*—"

"Jake! I was there! Remember?"

"No, you weren't, Jen. No. You. Fucking. Were. Not."

They stare at each other like two bulls.

Eldorado pokes her head in. "Everything okay in here?"

Cell Phone Dude must have narked on us. I wait for Aunt Jen or Dad to say something, but they're stuck in this showdown and don't even look at her. "Fine," I sputter. "What's the news on Mom?"

"We're not out of the woods yet, but we'll let you know if—"

"Anything changes," I say, "Thank you." Now take the hint and leave.

She doesn't. "Is there something I can help you with?" she asks, though her meaning is clear: *Do I need to call security?*

Aunt Jen turns away and drops back into her seat. "Nope. Everything is fine. Isn't it, Jake?"

Dad just stands there, a firecracker that can't explode.

\*

It was Jen's thirteenth birthday and she was sitting with the rest of the girls in her class listening to Miss Nash, the health teacher, talk about "The Miracle of Reproduction." Jen stared at the diagram at the front of the classroom—a uterus with wing-like fallopian tubes. It was weird to think that anything like that was inside her— let alone shooting out eggs. She wondered when she would start bleeding. Most of her classmates already had. She knew because they got excused from swim practice.

Miss Nash began describing how babies were made. Jen cringed. Doing that with a boy seemed wrong. Unnatural. She thought about the slumber party she'd been to the weekend before and how Beth Stein was scared and wanted to sleep close to someone. Jen volunteered and Beth fell asleep with her head tucked into the crook of Jen's neck. Jen imagined she was Beth's husband. It was nice.

Miss Nash flipped to the next picture—a squinched-up baby inside the womb. Jen's mind began to wander.

It was the first time ever she and Jake weren't going to spend their birthday together. Ernest had taken Jake out of school for the day to watch the Flyers practice in New Jersey. They wouldn't be back in time for cake.

Her mom had offered to do something special with Jen after school. "Maybe a movie," she'd said, sitting at the table in pink capris and a white eyelet blouse that morning. "Or we could drive out to the mall and find you something pretty." Jen knew she meant well, but the two of them hanging out together sounded awful. Other Mother hadn't been around for a while, but still…you never knew.

Jake clomped downstairs after hogging the bathroom all morning. Lately, he took forever to do anything.

"I want to go see the Flyers practice too," she said.

"Well, you can't," he said.

"It's not fair. I'm the one who turned you on to ice hockey to begin with."

Jake shrugged on his jacket. "Nuh uh."

"Uh huh."

"Pour yourself some cereal," their mom said to Jake.

"I'm not hungry."

"You should still—"

"I *said* I'm not hungry," Jake spat and stomped to the living room.

Their mom drummed her fingers on the side of her coffee mug. "He sure has been in a nasty mood lately."

"I'm not in a mood!" he shouted from the living room.

Jen pushed her cereal aside. Their mom was right. Even the kids at school were starting to notice. He'd gotten aggressive, quick to go on the offensive, and was getting into fistfights after school.

"Well, I wouldn't want to have to hang out with Ernest all day anyway," she hollered. "Even if I did get to go to a Flyers practice!"

"Jen," their mom said. "What a thing to say."

Jen jumped up from her chair, almost knocking it over. "It's true. I think he's creeeeeeepy."

Their mom slammed her coffee mug onto the table. "That man is taking care of our family."

"Just because you love him doesn't mean we have to." Jen tore into the living room to be with Jake.

"That is no way to talk to your mother," their mom yelled.

Jen's heart was beating so fast she could hear it in her ears. "Why? It's obvious you have the hots for each other!" She shot a look at Jake who was standing by the window waiting for Ernest. "Don't you think Ernest has the hots for Mom?"

Jake shook his head slowly like she was deluded.

"Jennifer, you come in here right now and apologize!"

"Jennifer?"

Jen snapped out of her daydream. Miss Nash was walking down the aisle toward her desk. "Would you care to repeat back to the class what I just said about the function of the cervix during labor?"

The whole class was looking at her. This was the worst birthday of her entire life.

\*

I must have slept. My neck is all kinked. I push up from the scratchy waiting room couch and look around. No one's here except Cell Phone Guy, only now he's reading a magazine. Adrenaline courses through me. "Did you see my dad or aunt?"

He clears his throat and adjusts his designer wire rims. "They left with the nurse about half an hour ago."

I jam through the double doors and to the nurse's station, nearly crashing into Samantha. "What's going on with Mom?"

"I just got here," she says. "Let's see what we can find out."

"I know what room's she's in."

"Yes," she says, missing my gist. I meant let's just go. Now.

I stand there while she and another nurse talk quietly with their backs to me. When she finally turns around, she's smiling. "Let's go visit her." Her tone is obviously meant to put me at ease, but it doesn't. And she walks way too slowly so I have to bolt past. When I'm about to turn into Mom's room, I hear Dad and Aunt Jen burst into laughter.

Dad and Aunt Jen, who, last I remember, were at each other's throats. Weird.

I step into the room.

The two of them are at their usual posts on either side of Mom. She's just finished spelling something on the alphabet board in Aunt Jen's hand. She's still flat on her back with tubes stuck down her, but her eyes are twinkling like she'd be laughing if she could.

"What's so funny?" I ask.

"When we asked if she needed anything," Aunt Jen says, wiping the mirth from her eyes, "she spelled out knitting needles."

Hardly the laugh riot they're making it out to be.

I glance at Mom. She actually looks like herself. Nothing's changed really, but I can tell she's back.

"She moved a finger," Dad says proudly.

Suddenly it all makes sense. Mom's turned a corner. She's getting better.

Dad takes my hand—a total shocker. His palm is clammy and his fingers are so long that they could wrap around my hand twice. I feel like a two-year-old. Are we just going to go on standing like this, hand in hand? I get the feeling Dad's wondering the same thing. His move was impulsive and now he can't figure out what to do next.

Samantha enters. "Hey, Bells."

"Hi," Aunt Jen and Dad say in unison.

Her entrance gives Dad and me the excuse we need to unclasp hands. I step back so Samantha can get closer to Mom. Dad pulls his trashcan seat back with him.

Samantha wipes a bit of perspiration from Mom's forehead. "How you doing, Maye? You hanging with us?"

Mom blinks once. Sure enough, her index finger twitches slightly.

"I saw it move," I say.

Aunt Jen nods.

"She's quite a fighter." Samantha checks the dials and tubes and records the numbers on the clipboard.

"How long before she'll be able to…" Dad doesn't finish his sentence, but we all know what he means.

"I'll get Dr. Reneaux in here to talk to you. In the meantime, let's not over-stimulate her. She needs to rest."

And so Dad, Aunt Jen, and I sit around and tell Mom how exceptionally good the weather's been, how gross the cafeteria food is, and how hard it was to sleep in the waiting room with Cell Phone Guy blabbing the whole time. We know we should sit here quietly so as not to tax her, but we can't. Mom's coming back to us.

Dr. Reneaux steps into the room. She greets us with that commanding presence of hers then looks over Mom's chart. She tells us that Mom is doing amazingly well, and that usually people with Guillain-Barré plateau for a week or two before there's any improvement. "I'm quite encouraged," she says directly to Mom. "It's only been four days."

Dad rocks back on his heels, his hands dug down in his pockets. "She's always been a tough one." I worry that Aunt Jen's going to take offense at his proprietary show. Remarkably, she doesn't. She just smiles and shakes her head

"Any questions?" Dr. Reneaux asks.

Aunt Jen is the only one who has the clarity of mind to come up with any, so we let her do the talking. Dr. Reneaux listens politely, answers everything, then excuses herself to see other patients. Once she's gone we talk at Mom a while longer. Finally, she says, via her alphabet board, GO. When we protest, she blinks three times, signaling that she wants to say something else.

Aunt Jen lifts the board.

Several minutes later, we get to: HAVE A GOOD BREAKFAST FOR ME. Her true meaning, as usual, remains a mystery.

## CHAPTER NINE

I'm pretty sure Mom wouldn't consider an IHOP breakfast to be a "good" breakfast. She'd want us to be at some mom-and-pop place with free-range chicken eggs and organic home fries, but we couldn't find the "someplace nice, but not too expensive, and locally owned" that Aunt Jen was angling for, which caused Dad to start leaning toward Burger King, and there was no way either of us was going to do that. A place near the hospital called the Anarchy Joint looked totally cool to me. It had these crazy metal sculptures hanging from the ceiling, and posters for open mikes and other events tacked to the graffitied walls, but Aunt Jen said she made it a point never to eat in an establishment where she was the oldest person by twenty years. Said it hampered her digestion. Dad just walked out mumbling something about "liking to be able to *see* his food." Since I wasn't going to be footing the bill, the discussion kind of ended there. Then Aunt Jen's GPS found us this IHOP, and, what can I say? Here we are.

Before being seated, Dad says he's going to slip into the restroom to wash up. Aunt Jen and I decide to go too. After our night at the hospital, we all look pretty thrashed.

The ladies' room is ultra-sanitized—strawberry-scented antibacterial chemicals that make my eyes water, and disposable seat covers available in each of the squeaky-clean toilet stalls in case a germ happens to survive the strawberries. Mindboggling. We're cutting down tropical rainforests to protect us from our poop.

Once I've done my business, I step up to the gleaming white sink and bathe my hands in what I'm sure is also an antibacterial cleanser, then use another piece of rainforest to dry them. Aunt Jen does the same.

We meet up with Dad by the hostess station. A frighteningly chipper hostess in her crisply pressed red, white, and blue uniform leads us to our table overlooking the parking lot. I slide into the booth. Aunt Jen slides in next to me and Dad slides in across from us.

Trapped.

A perky young waitress, Cathy, approaches us on the heels of Miss Chipper Hostess. She takes in our rumpled clothes and messy hair, smiles a super fake IHOP smile, and says, "I'll bet you'd like to start off with coffee." We all nod. I amuse myself by imagining a giant autoclave in back where they disinfect all their employees before work. "I'll get right on that," she says and prances off.

I open the multi-paged menu—plastic-coated pages, of course—and am completely overwhelmed. Should I go eggs? Pancakes? Eggs and pancakes? French toast? International crepes? Dad and Aunt Jen seem equally perplexed, flipping back and forth in the menu like they're studying for an exam.

"Wow," Dad says.

"I'll say," Aunt Jen says.

We study a few minutes longer.

Cathy returns with the coffee. "You guys ready to order? Or do you need another minute?"

We look at each other blankly. "I guess I'm ready," I say.

"Go for it," Aunt Jen says and goes back to flipping through the menu.

"I'll have the Double Blueberry pancakes with warm blueberry compote, but no whipped topping." Who knows what they put in that shit?

"Good choice," Cathy says, her dimples framing her fake-o smile like two cheery exclamation points.

Aunt Jen orders the Quick Two-Egg Breakfast and asks to substitute fruit for the bacon. Dad orders the Colorado Omelet, billed as "a meat-lover's delight."

Once Cathy has scampered off, Dad says to Aunt Jen, "You're still a vegetarian."

Aunt Jen fiddles with the saltshaker. "Nope. Just don't like them breakfast meats."

He looks at me. "You?"

"No. But I don't eat much meat."

Having done his bit for the conversation, he rests his folded hands on the table. It's our turn. I notice a scar by his thumb. "How'd you get that?" I ask pointing to the jagged red line.

He opens his hand and studies the scar. A slight smile creeps across his face. "Gutting the biggest trout I ever caught."

"You still fish," Aunt Jen says.

"Not much these days," he says. "It's getting harder and harder to make the time."

She nods. "I know what you mean. We get awfully important as we get older."

After this bit of adult wisdom, the two of them just sit there gazing at the snappy décor and pondering their busy lives while I wonder why I ever agreed to this outing. I should have let them come by themselves. Then again, without me, they never would have. I pick up the small pitcher of maple syrup and drop a dab onto my finger.

"Sounds like her recovery's going to take a while," Aunt Jen finally says.

Dad nods. "I worry about her being all alone up there…"

"She's not really alone." I suck the syrup off my finger. "She has lots of friends…"

"I worry too," Aunt Jen says completely ignoring me. "I'm thinking I'll take some time off so I can be with her."

"You shouldn't have to do that," Dad says. "I'm due some vacation time—and it's paid—so I'll just notify them that I've had a family emergency—"

"Now would be a really good time for me," Aunt Jen says. "My show's just about to open, then I don't have another one for six weeks."

"It's a good time for me too," Dad says. "And I'd be happy to do it."

I butt in. "You know I'm not *totally* incompetent."

The two of them look at me as if I've just said, *I'll have snakes for breakfast.*

"But you've just graduated from college," Aunt Jen says.

"So?"

Dad takes his napkin from his lap and places it on the table. "Jen is right, Bean. This is an important time in your life. You shouldn't have to spend it taking care of someone." He fishes out his cell phone. "I'm going to step outside to make a phone call. Give them a heads up that I need some time off."

Aunt Jen gets up to leave. "Me too."

I watch the two of them through the window. They walk in separate directions squinting at their phones. Classic. The only thing they've been able to agree on since we got here is that I'm useless.

I pull out my phone and dial Serena.

She picks up on the third ring.

"I needed to talk to someone sane. Is this an okay time?"

"Perfect. I'm just walking out of yoga." I listen as she says good-bye to someone. I try to feel happy that she's making new friends while I'm stuck here with Dad and Aunt Jen at IHOP. "How's your mom?"

"Getting some mobility back."

"That's fantastic."

"How was yoga?"

"Amazing. We did some pranayama that made me feel so alive."

"Pranayama?"

"Breathing exercises. Jim, the teacher, focused the whole class on the connection of breath to the body. It was very enlightening. I was amazed how often I hold my breath when I don't even realize it."

I think about Mom and how close she was to losing the ability to breathe at all. My eyes start to sting.

"Brianna? Are you still there?"

"Yeah." My voice comes out like a whimper.

"Oh, Brianna. I'm sorry. Here I am going on and on about all this, and you're—"

"It's okay." I squeeze the bridge of my nose. "It's just been stressful." Talking to someone who isn't family feels *so* good. "Dad and Aunt Jen are driving me crazy. They act like I'm still ten years old."

"Don't forget they're scared too."

"Yeah. I know." I see Dad making his way back to the table. "Can I call you later?"

"Is everything okay?"

Aunt Jen's on her way back too. "Could be better. My world's about to be re-invaded by parents."

She laughs. "Don't forget to breathe."

I flip my phone shut and take in a lungful of air.

"It's all set up," Dad says slipping into the booth. "I'm a free man—for a week or so."

I hope he's not planning on staying at Mom's too. Where are we all going to sleep?

Aunt Jen slides in next to me. "As usual, they're acting like they can't live without me. But I'm good to go, for a least a couple of weeks."

I take a swig of coffee. No matter what, I'm not giving up my room.

Cathy appears with our food. "Prepare for some yummy eatin'!"

\*

Jake slumped down in the front makeshift pew while Ernest preached to the congregation about temptation. He was wedged between his mom and Jen.

The Church of Redemption, in operation for over a year, had become the focus of his mom's world. She typed up the programs, made the coffee, did the books, cleaned up after the service, and took out the trash. She was also Reverend Bates's strongest supporter.

She liked to sum up her position by saying, "I'm the first to get here and the last to leave." Unfortunately, so were Jake and Jen.

"My friends," Ernest said gripping the edges of his podium, "temptation is not just a word we preachers like to throw around to scare you. Temptation is the real deal. It's the itch in the middle of your back that's hard to scratch. It's the hunger that won't be satisfied. It's the song you can't get out of your head. And *I* know *you* know what I'm talking about."

Jake didn't have to turn around to know that the room was only half full. He and Jen had passed out programs to only about twenty-five people. There was the strange older couple who always wore matching sweaters, a young family that lived down the street and often arrived a little late, some guys who were down on their luck and came for the free coffee and doughnuts, Mrs. Porter who always pinched their cheeks and said what a blessing twins were, Celia Conway who wore black wool no matter what time of year it was, and the fat guy who breathed really loud…And then there was that new boy with his mom. He was a little younger than Jake, and he didn't seem to have a dad either.

Jake picked at a scab on his knuckle. Their mom had arranged for him to stay after the service to help Ernest move in some used office furniture. Some guy had closed his insurance office and told Ernest if he was willing to load it off the pickup, the church could have it. Jake had tried to get out of helping by telling their mom that he had a paper due at school, but that hadn't held any water with her. "You never seem to care about your homework when there's fun things to do," she said. "Besides, it's good for you to be around a strong male. Every boy needs that."

Jake stared at a crack in the wall behind the podium. Ernest would want to "test" him with a *Playboy* or *Penthouse* magazine again, he was sure of that. Why else would he have told the other guys who'd offered to help that he "had it under control"? Jake sucked on his scab, now bleeding. *If only Mom knew,* he thought, scarcely listening to Ernest beseech the paltry crowd to "wage war with temptation." Jake began to get aroused. He opened his hymnal to hide the pup tent that was forming in the front of his trousers.

Jen nudged him in the ribs. Had she seen? Or was she just goofing around? He glanced at her. She *seemed* oblivious, but you could never tell with Jen.

He'd thought about telling her, about begging her to stay with him when Ernest was around. He'd leave his reasons sort of undefined, say he didn't like hanging out with Ernest by himself, that he thought Ernest was a geek. But was he really ready to give up on the magazines? They were great, always new and always Jake's favorite kind. They didn't show too much and looked like the woman was oblivious to the fact that she didn't have any clothes on. She was just washing her car, or baking a pie, or sitting on a car hood. She just happened to be naked. Or partially naked. If too much showed, it made Jake nervous, made him not like the woman. And so what if Ernest was—but Jake didn't like to think about that part. That part was gay, something even Ernest, in his sermons, said was bad. Sinful. Disgusting. But Ernest never touched him, so it was okay.

Jake tried to redirect his mind to things that would gross him out so he'd lose the pup tent. He thought of a dead rat covered in maggots, an old woman with a huge boil on her neck, a pail of bloody body parts. Before he knew it, church was being dismissed.

"You sure were fidgety today," his mom said to him as they walked out to the lobby.

Jake tugged at his belt. "These pants are too tight."

"Well, hopefully you can wear them a few more months. I'm still trying to pay off getting the car fixed."

Jake dug his hands into his pockets. "I'll be fine."

During coffee and doughnuts, he and Jen were supposed to mingle and pick up unwanted cups and napkins. Jake slipped into the main office, collapsed into his mom's chair, and rested his head on the desk.

Jen stuck her head in the door. "What are you doing?"

"What does it look like I'm doing?"

Jen walked over to the little half-fridge and pulled out a carton of milk. "Leaving all the work to me?"

Jake sat up straight. "So you have to fill up the milk pitcher. So what?"

"That's not all. Mrs. Porter knocked her coffee off the table and I had to clean it up."

"At least you don't have to stay after and move furniture."

"Well, Mom's making *me* mend some of Ernest's clothes. What if I have to do his underwear? I'll bet he wears hair underwear."

"Hair underwear?"

"You know, like those hair shirts the monks used to wear to help them 'resist temptation,'" Jen sniggered.

"No, he doesn't," slipped out of Jake's mouth before he knew what he was saying.

Jen glanced over her shoulder and said teasingly, "And how would *you* know? Are the two of you *that* close?"

"Shut up!"

Their mom poked her head in the door. "Jen. Where's that milk? And what are you doing in here, mister? I thought I told you to keep an eye on the doughnuts. Make sure old Louie leaves some for everybody else." She had lost weight over the last year, making her face angular, severe.

Jake dropped his feet to the floor. "Coming." He was glad to be interrupted. He didn't want to have to explain how he knew about Ernest's underwear.

"It's probably too late to save the doughnuts now," their mom said grabbing a handful of brochures, "so go collect programs off the floor, and make sure every chair has a hymnal. Oh, and sweep around the doorway too. Someone was tracking mud. And, Jen, give me that milk. Poor Mrs. Porter is just standing there waiting."

As Jen and Jake passed through the lobby, Jake overheard Celia Conway praising Ernest on his sermon. "What you said was so true. Temptations are landmines! One has to creep so carefully through life to avoid them."

Jen punched him in the arm and whispered, "Be careful where you step."

Jake followed her into Praise Hall, leaping this way and that to avoid the deadly exploding temptations.

By the time they'd finished their chores, Ernest and their mom were standing by the coffee pot discussing the logistics of the afternoon. Everyone else was gone. "We had a big breakfast this morning," she said, "so he shouldn't be hungry, but if he is, there's some egg salad in the fridge. And I put his work clothes in the office."

"I'm right here," Jake said testily. "You can talk to me directly."

"Oh. Good. Well, call when you're done."

Ernest rested his hand on Jake's shoulder. "Not to worry. I'll give him a ride home."

Jake wanted to smack off Ernest's hand, but he knew he'd get in trouble.

"I don't know what we did to deserve you," their mom said, looking at Ernest adoringly.

"Can we go home now?" Jen whined from the doorway. "Please?"

Their mom picked up a bag of trash to be tossed into the Dumpster. "All right, Miss Complainer, we're off."

Jake walked to the plate glass window in the lobby and watched his mom and Jen get into the car and drive off. He stood there watching until the car turned the corner at the end of the block.

"You ready to move some furniture?" Ernest asked.

"I guess." Jake dragged his body into the public bathroom to change into his T-shirt and shorts. He locked the door behind him.

❖

Sleeves rolled to the elbows, sweat bloomed in the armpits of Ernest's white button-down. He and Jake had just carried in the last bookshelf and placed it by the window. "What do you think?" he asked, his blond hair disheveled, his face glowing. "Pretty snazzy, huh?"

Jake looked around and shrugged. "I guess." But he liked the wooden desk that had been there before. It was the right size for the room. This new big metal one made the ceiling seem lower and the walls closer together. The towering bookshelf, so wide it covered half of the window, made the room dark.

Ernest dug his hands into his hips and laughed. "What do you mean 'I guess'? It looks like a real office now. The church is moving up, Jake, just like I knew it would. And wait until you see what I've got in here." Ernest reached for a paper bag next to the train set.

Jake felt his pulse quicken.

"Chocolate chip cookies!" Ernest pulled out a lumpy roll of tinfoil. "Baked by our very own Miss Wiggins."

A snort-like chuckle burst from Jake's lips.

Ernest began unrolling the tinfoil. "It's one of the perks of the ministry, my boy. Little old ladies are always baking you things."

*And they never think you do anything bad,* Jake thought. *They trust you.*

"Why don't you go get us some milk from the fridge," Ernest said. "I think we deserve a treat."

Jake took his time crossing the lobby to the main office. When he returned with the milk, he noticed the *Penthouse* next to the cookies on Ernest's desk. "Roll up a chair," Ernest said. The new office chairs had wheels, something Ernest was very happy about. He gestured for Jake to take a cookie. "So what did you think of my sermon?"

Jake had to reach across the *Penthouse* to get a cookie. The woman on the front was straddling a motorcycle in her underwear. You could see most of her butt because her panties were so small, and the way her breasts bulged out, you could tell her bra was too small too.

"How are you doing with *your* temptations, Jake?"

Jake took a bite of the cookie.

Ernest flipped open the magazine. The same woman as on the front was washing the motorcycle, only now she was dressed in short shorts that were unzipped and no top. There were soapsuds all over her, making her gigantic breasts all shiny. A little tuft of blond hair could be seen at the bottom of her zipper.

Jake felt his penis begin to swell.

"I asked you a question, Jake." Ernest opened to the centerfold where the woman was bending over a picnic table with no panties at all. You could see her snatch, which made Jake uncomfortable. But his penis stayed erect.

He reached for the carton of milk and took a swig so he could swallow the cookie.

"Do you need to seek forgiveness?" Ernest was peering over the desk to Jake's crotch.

Jake wanted to say no, that he was done with these weirdo sessions, but he was so aroused it was beginning to hurt. Disgusted with himself, he nodded and followed Ernest into the bathroom where the two of them unzipped their pants and let them drop to the floor. Ernest began praying. Jake closed his eyes and thought about the lady washing her motorcycle. He imagined her being so hot that she peeled off her shirt, unzipped her shorts, and began rubbing bubbles all over her breasts and down her pants. Her head was tipped back. She had no idea he was watching...

Something brushed his penis.

He whacked it away then looked to see what it was. Ernest's hand was pulling back. Jake stepped backward, bumping against the wall. He glanced at Ernest who looked briefly confused then crazy mad. He raised his palm like he was going to slap Jake. Jake prepared himself to take the blow, but Ernest just stood that way for a few seconds then let his hand drop.

Jake willed his knees not to buckle.

Ernest yanked up his pants, grumbled a fierce, "Amen," then walked out of the bathroom, slamming the door behind him.

Jake stood a moment with his pants around his ankles, his penis now limp. What was he supposed to do? He tugged his pants up, buckled his belt, and put his ear to the door. Was Ernest planning to come back? He peered through the keyhole but couldn't see anything but the bookshelf. Maybe he'd left. Jake cracked the door. Ernest was sitting at his desk, glowering at his tightly folded hands. "Get out of here," he growled.

Jake hesitated. Ernest was supposed to take him home.

Ernest thrust his finger toward the door. "GET OUT!"

Jake shot into the lobby and out onto the street. He had no money and no bus pass. How was he going to get home? He had a feeling he'd forgotten something. Then he remembered his church clothes in a pile in the main office. He'd catch hell for it, but there was no returning.

He started walking, his legs rubbery and unsure. The air was thick with humidity, the sky gray.

The neighborhoods he traveled through were different on foot than they were in a car. People sat out on their steps and porches, sometimes acknowledging him with a nod, sometimes not. He passed a corner market where a bunch of older boys asked, "What his little honky-ass was staring at?" He tried not to show how scared he was and walked on. Then the humidity turned into thunder and lightning and driving rain, which in a way was better because the people went inside. He started crying, his tears mixing with the raindrops and snot. By the time he got home it was dark and he was soaked.

"It's about time," his mom said when he pushed through the door. "Ernest said you left hours ago."

Jake searched his mother's face for an indication as to what Ernest had told her, but all she looked was angry. "What got into you?" she barked. "Just walking out on him like that? Leaving him to do all that work by himself?"

Jake stared at her, hating her. "I didn't just walk out."

"Then what happened?"

He could tell by her tone that she wasn't really asking. She was accusing. "Nothing, okay? Nothing happened! I just felt like walking."

"When I think of all that man does for this family—"

"Can I change now?" he spat.

Her eyes crinkled in contempt. "I'm ashamed of you, Jake. I truly am."

"Are you done?"

She never answered his question, just turned away.

The pancake-eating family at the table across from us is super chatty. They keep laughing and saying things like "Atta boy!" and "You're kidding!"

Dad looks up from his plate of meat and eggs. "How are those blueberries?"

"Fine." But they're way too sweet, like they've been simmered in corn syrup.

"Mine's good too," Aunt Jen says.

We go back to eating.

Aunt Jen makes another stab at conversation. "Any thoughts on what's next for you?"

I know what she's getting at, but say, "You mean after breakfast?"

"In general. Now that you've graduated."

Dad takes a sip of orange juice. "Yeah. How's that going?"

So bogus. Just because they can't talk to each other, they're ganging up on me. I shove a huge bite in my mouth, smile, and gesture that I'm chewing. They go back to their breakfasts satisfied that it's not *their* turn to talk. Which suits Dad just fine. As long as he can keep me talking, he doesn't have to think about his big secret. Maybe I should bring it up now? Say: *Dad, what was that thing that Mom wanted you to say to Aunt Jen?* See how *he* likes being on the hotspot.

"I made a good connection at this organic farm in Watsonville," I finally manage. I don't mention to them that she asked if I speak Spanish.

"That's great," Dad says.

"Yeah," Aunt Jen says. "Anyone I know?"

"I doubt it."

We go back to eating.

The table next to us has moved on to embarrassing sports moments. They're hooting and hollering, having a grand old time.

"I Googled Guillain-Barré," Aunt Jen says.

"And?" I say.

"I found a Yahoo group for people and their loved ones who've had it."

Dad shakes his head. "There's a group for everything these days."

Aunt Jen chooses to ignore Dad's cynicism. "She's not going to have a lot of strength at first, and she's going to need extensive physical therapy."

"For how long?" I ask.

"It varies, but we should count on at least three months. And from what I read, some people retain permanent disabilities."

The thought of Mom with any physical disability curdles the too-sweet blueberries in my stomach. "But not all."

Aunt Jen smiles. "No. Not all."

Dad pushes his plate aside. He's eaten every bit except the orange slice and decorative kale. "We should make a plan."

"That's what I was thinking," Aunt Jen says. "Seems like we should take turns at the hospital."

The moment to act has arrived. "I'll go first," I say. Now Dad won't have an excuse not to talk to Aunt Jen. It'll be just the three of them—him, Aunt Jen, and his secret.

Dad leans back in the booth. "I don't mind taking the first shift."

"But I want to," I say.

"Why not me?" Aunt Jen interjects. "The two of you have traveled the farthest and could use the rest."

"You haven't gotten any more sleep than the rest of us," I say. "Besides, you and Dad haven't seen each other in *such* a long time; it would be good for you to visit."

Dad looks panicky. "Let's draw straws."

"Sounds fair," Aunt Jen says, "I'll get some toothpicks." She gets up from the table.

Dad, desperate to avoid eye contact with me, flags down Cathy and hands her a credit card. "This should take care of it."

Aunt Jen steps up to the table with the toothpicks. "I thought we were going Dutch."

"I've got it," Dad says.

They squabble a bit, finally settling on Dad paying and Aunt Jen leaving the tip and promising to "pick up the next one." Having no intention of paying myself, I stay out of it.

Once Cathy is gone, we focus on the toothpicks. Aunt Jen snaps one in half, arranges them under the table so we can't tell which is short, then holds them out. "Go for it, Bean. Short does the first shift."

*Short, short, short,* thrums through my head as I reach out to take one, but the second I start pulling, I know it's long.

Dad's next. I will his to be short so he and I won't have to hang out together, but he gets the other long one.

"First shift is mine," Aunt Jen says puffing up like a hen on steroids. "Fair and square."

Dad takes a final slug of coffee. "Looks like it's you and me, kid."

I nod. "So it is."

"What say you we drop Jen at the hospital then drive up to Maye's for a shower and a nap?"

"Okay." My mind is on the logistics of the three of us under one roof. Who's going to sleep in Mom's bed?

Cathy comes back with the receipt for Dad to sign. Then before scurrying off to her next customers, she just has to say it. "Have a great day!"

## CHAPTER TEN

We swing by Mom's room before splitting up. Samantha is massaging Mom's hand. Their hands look beautiful together, both are squarish with blunt fingers, but Samantha's are the color of milky hot cocoa while Mom's are golden and freckled from the sun.

"You all have a good breakfast?" she asks.

"Great," I say. "We found an IHOP."

Samantha places Mom's hand on the bed, palm up. "I was just boring Maye with my personal movie reviews." She adds with a wink. "She's a good listener."

Mom's eyes are laughing. She obviously likes Samantha.

Aunt Jen sets her satchel on the floor. "Well, Maye, we made some decisions over breakfast."

Samantha checks the settings on some of the tubes stuck in Mom, then stands. "How about I give you folks some time alone?"

"Thanks, Samantha," Dad says, and steps into the hall so she can get out.

Aunt Jen walks around the bed and takes the chair. "It looks like we're all going to stick around for a while."

Mom looks surprised and momentarily flips her eyes to Dad and me by the door.

"I cashed in my vacation time," Dad says.

"So did I," Aunt Jen says.

I feel like saying, *me three,* but we're all fully aware that my life is nothing but a sea of vacation until I get a job, so I keep my mouth shut.

"We're going to take shifts here at the hospital," Aunt Jen continues, "until you come home."

I walk around to Aunt Jen's side of the bed so Mom doesn't have to strain her eyes, flipping back and forth between us. "We drew straws at breakfast. Aunt Jen is up first."

Mom does three deliberate blinks. She wants to use the alphabet board.

Aunt Jen picks it up. Dad pulls his trashcan chair up to the other side of the bed, understanding that this could take a while.

Aunt Jen points at the top line. Mom blinks once. She points at Q. Mom blinks twice. She points at W. Mom blinks once. We're off and running. WHAT is her first word, the beginning of a question. BEAN the second. A question about me. I shift my weight from one foot to the other. Mom looks at me reassuringly then spells. JAKE TO DO.

"You want to know what Dad and I are going to do?" I ask.

She blinks once, but I know what she's up to. She's trying to figure out if Dad and I have had our little talk. And if he's told Aunt Jen.

"I dunno," I say. "Shower? Rest up? It's been really nice for the two of us to *catch up.* Just like I'm sure it will be for"—I give Dad a look—"*him* and *Aunt Jen,* when I do *my* shift."

Dad clears his throat. "Yes. Bean has been sharing *all kinds* of things with me."

Aunt Jen gives me the evil eye. She's about to ask what we're scheming.

Mom blinks three times. Aunt Jen sighs and holds the board back up. But I know she knows something is up.

Mom spells out the word REQUEST.

What will it be this time? Will she ask us to hold hands and bare our souls to one another? Break out in song? Break *her* out? But what she spells is SCOTCH BROOM.

I sigh with relief.

Aunt Jen furrows her brow. "Scotch broom?"

Dad looks equally perplexed.

"I think what she wants," I say, "is for us to clear the Scotch broom from her land." What I don't say is that she's been trying to get me to help her with this since she first moved.

Mom blinks once.

"Gardening?" Dad says.

"More like landscaping," I say.

Dad repositions himself on the trashcan. "That sounds easy enough."

Mom's obviously planning on milking this illness for all it's worth. She knows neither one of them has ever gardened a day in their lives and don't have a clue what they're in for.

"It might not be as easy as you think," I say.

"How hard can digging out a few plants be?" Aunt Jen asks. "Count me in."

"Me too," Dad says.

I can't decide whether, under the circumstances, it's forgivable that Mom is taking advantage of them—us. She has this thing about "leaving things better than you found them." It's like her mantra, her mission in life. But getting us to do what she's been putting off for years seems a tad manipulative.

"Bean?" Dad says. "Your mother has asked you a question. Are you going to help us with this plant?"

Him using the fatherly tone on me is almost laughable. But apparently, I'm the only one who thinks so because Aunt Jen and Mom both have these inquiring looks on their faces, as if to say: *Yes, Bean, are you going to help with your dying mother's request?*

"Okay. I'll help," I mutter. "But when you guys are complaining about how sore your backs are, just remember I tried to warn you." Who cares if Aunt Jen and Dad think I'm totally unfeeling? I'm good with Mom. She knows I'm on to her.

Dad and I say our good-byes and take off. I'm dreading the ride up as much as anything.

We climb into the eggplant. I wonder if it would be tacky to throw on my iPod and tune him out?

*Right turn in point five miles,* the GPS informs us.

It's hard not to compare these two trips up the mountain, one with Aunt Jen and now one with Dad. I'm so relaxed around Aunt Jen; I can tell her anything. But Dad, he's got a wall of impenetrability around him. I watch as he negotiates his way through the Redding traffic. He's one of those overly cautious drivers who won't pass a moving vehicle—no matter how slow.

"You still dating that pharmacist?" I ask.

"Didn't work out."

"I thought you liked her."

He adjusts his rearview mirror.

Whoops.

"Sorry to hear it didn't work out."

"Thanks," he says.

We ride a while longer in silence, not saying much. Then we get that first glimpse of the lake. Crystal blue water surrounded by giant red rocks. "Wow," he says.

I'm not sure why, but him liking Mom's neck of the woods makes me proud. "You can rent boats," I say. "Maybe you'll want to check out the fishing while you're here."

He points to a barge-looking water vehicle. "Is that a houseboat?"

"Looks like it."

He rolls his window all the way down and breathes in the fresh air. "Don't know why, but I've always thought that would be the perfect family vacation. Out there on the water, you could fish, swim, hang out on deck reading, play cards, or just talk to each other…"

Talk to each other? Since when does he consider talking to each other a fun way to pass the time? "I hear you can get to some excellent secret coves."

"Neat."

While his use of the word "neat" is nerdy, it's not nearly as nerdy as him dreaming of a family vacationing on a houseboat. Which family does he picture doing this with? Surely not ours.

He's drumming his fingers on the wheel and smiling. What's he got to be so happy about? At least with Aunt Jen, I always know where I stand. She can get in your face, sure, but you're not mired in guessing games. You don't sit there wondering why the hell she's drumming her damn fingers.

Just as I'm thinking about how different Dad and Aunt Jen are, Dad swerves into the same pullout Aunt Jen did.

"You'll excuse me for a moment?" he says. "All that coffee is catching up with me."

I stay in the car and watch him walk out to an overlook of the lake, Mount Shasta looming behind. He takes the classic male-peeing stance, legs spread, hands out of sight, and, I assume, goes about his business. It's so easy for men. They get to look dignified when they pee, whereas for us, we have to squat behind a bush or rock, our pants sagging at our ankles.

I divert my attention to the mountain, but it can only hold my attention so long. What's taking him so long? Prostate problems? I risk a peek. His back is still to me but his hands are on his hips. Maybe he's done. Then again, he could be waiting for action. Either way about it, sitting in a car on this glorious day is pathetic. I crack open the door. "Safe?"

Dad turns around. "Sorry. I was just taking in this spectacular view." He waves me over. "Check out these kayakers. There are like twenty of them."

I join him on the cliff. Below, a kayak class appears to be taking place. They're poking around the calm inlet, practicing paddling, backing up, and turning. "Shasta's own Keystone Kops."

Dad laughs. "Looks like fun."

A slight breeze makes the leaves on the cottonwoods tremble. I think of something I've been meaning to say. "Thanks for the graduation money."

He skims over me with his eyes then sits on a big rock outcropping. "I'm sorry your trip got cut so short."

"Yeah, well, what are you gonna do?"

He rests his elbows on his knees and clasps his hands. Apparently, we're not leaving anytime soon. I sit on the trunk of a downed tree, pull a leaf off a nearby shrub, and begin shredding it.

I don't know if I blocked out my early childhood or what, but I barely remember living in the stone duplex in Mt. Airy where Dad now rattles around by himself. And the visits were always so weird. The first time I went, I had such high expectations. It was going to be me and Dad having fun. But then he had to work most of the time so I just watched TV. When he did come home, I felt like I couldn't talk about Mom or Aunt Jen, or anything else in my life. It made him too uneasy. I remember telling Mom I wouldn't go back. She made me though.

It took me until I was eighteen to tell him I was gay. That went over well. He accused me of being brainwashed. I never went back. Not once through college.

"I know I've been a disappointment to you, Bean."

My first impulse is to say, *No you haven't,* which is totally bizarre. Why would I want to protect him? Still, I can't quite say, *Yeah, all through my teens I referred to you as the sperm donor.* "You know…" I finally get the nerve to say, "Aunt Jen didn't make me gay."

He stiffens and squints back at the water. "So you say."

"She didn't. Being with girls came totally naturally to me."

"It would, wouldn't it? If that's all you'd been exposed to."

"Dad, I was at a school full of heterosexuals. Every TV show I ever watched was full of heterosexuals, every movie, every book, every news item. If anything, I'd say I was *over*-exposed to heterosexuality."

"It's not the same," he says quietly, "when it's a parent. Or pseudo-parent."

I grip my lips to keep from saying something stupid. Should I tell him about that article we read in school that said our peers have more influence over us than our parents? Or that I didn't even figure out that Mom and Aunt Jen were lovers until I was twelve? I decide to postpone the conversation until we've both had more sleep and rack my brain for topic changes. Mexico? Mom? The big secret?

"You know, I'm really proud of you," he says.

"How so?" slips out before I have a chance to bite it back.

"You seem so sure of yourself."

"I do?"

He laughs. "Aren't you?"

I lean over to tighten the lace on my sneaker. "I guess." My ears are getting hot, and I pray I'm not blushing on the outside too. Why should his opinion of me matter so much? "You know one of my best memories with you?"

"What's that?"

"We went to some beach and flew a kite, and you made this parachute out of a napkin and a paperclip that you sent shooting up the string. Once the parachute hit the kite it released and came floating back to earth."

He looks at me for a moment with those clear hazel eyes of his, the flecks of gold glinting in the sun. "I can't believe you remember that. You were so little."

"What was I? Six? Seven?"

"Something like that. We were at the Jersey shore, by Asbury Park."

"How did you do it?"

"A simple trick." He leans back and crosses his ankles, his legs out straight in front of him. "Besides the napkin and the paperclip, you need dental floss and a stick. A skewer works. That's probably what I used at the time. Wasn't it a barbeque?"

I shrug, unable to remember much about the event other than the parachute zipping up the line and then magically releasing when it reached the tiny kite in the sky. Its slow descent to earth reminded me of a little angel coming home.

"Tell you what. When Maye is able to come home, I'll pick up a kite and we'll make one."

We sit in an easy silence, the sun on the water making a shimmering path aimed right at us.

"I never meant for our family to fall apart," he says softly.

My dad has sad eyes. I've never noticed that before.

✳

It was past bedtime on a Sunday night. Jen lay on her bed reading *The Grapes of Wrath*. Her book report wasn't due for another few weeks, but she figured she'd get a head start. She glanced at the

Mickey Mouse alarm clock on her bedside table. Ten fifteen and Jake still wasn't home. So unfair. If she tried to pull a stunt like this, she'd be grounded for weeks. Jake hadn't gone to church either. He'd slept right through it. He didn't get in trouble for that either. Just like he hadn't for the last few months.

Whenever Jen confronted her mom about it, she said not to worry, that Ernest assured her Jake would get through this "difficult phase," all they needed to do was "give him time" as he faced his "struggle with the devil." Ernest had her convinced that he was counseling Jake on a regular basis, but when Jen asked Jake point-blank how his talks with Ernest were going, he'd looked at her like she was crazy. "What talks?" he said. "I hate that motherfucker."

Jen glanced at her clock again. Ten twenty-five.

If her mom weren't acting so messed up, Jen wouldn't care where Jake was.

Even before they went to church, Jen could tell her mom was having one of her bad days. She kept looking over her shoulder as if someone were talking to her. She mellowed out in church, though, so Jen thought they were through the worst of it. Then, when they got home, she shut all the curtains and turned off the lights.

Jen went upstairs to see if Jake was awake yet. He was in his pajama pants, brushing his teeth. She wasn't in the mood to pick a fight. "Mom's having one of her days," she said.

Jake spat into the sink. "So?"

Over the last six months, his body had changed. He'd gotten taller, more filled out, and his face was breaking out.

"You know, you can use my Stridex," she said. "It really does make a difference if you do it every day."

Jake didn't respond. As far as Jen could tell, he didn't care what he looked like. He wore rumpled clothes and barely ever washed his hair. One day their mom had gone so far as to accuse him of *trying* to look unattractive and all he'd said was, "You want me looking all gay?"

Jen hated the way he used "gay" for everything bad, but she went back to the larger issue. "Anyway, about Mom, I just thought you should know."

"Why? What can I do about it?"

Jen shrugged. He had a point. "So what are you up to today?"

"Thought I'd hang with Lenny. His brother's in town and said he'd drive us around in his Mustang." Lenny was the kid around the corner whose mom had lots of boyfriends.

Jen rested her head on the doorframe. "Jake, please don't leave me alone with Mom."

Jake ran his fingers through his stringy hair. "You don't have to stay. Go do something fun. Hang out with some of your nerdy friends."

"Have you written your history paper yet?"

Jake looked at her with disdain. "No. But I have a study hall tomorrow."

"Jake, this is supposed to be the culmination of everything we've done all semester."

"I've got it covered! Now do you mind if I take a dump?" Jake slammed the door in her face.

Jen retreated to her room to change out of her church clothes. Jake always made her feel like such a goody-two-shoes. Was it a crime that she liked good grades?

Once changed into jeans and her favorite Flyers sweatshirt, she spread out her books on her bed and stared at them blankly. She was hungry. She listened to Jake tramp down the stairs with those over-sized feet of his and wondered if he was going to eat breakfast before leaving. If so, she'd go downstairs too. Then she heard the front door slam. She went to her window and watched Jake saunter down the sidewalk. When he reached halfway down the block, he stopped to light a cigarette then continued walking.

Jen flopped back onto her bed, her body suddenly heavy with a wave of exhaustion. She pulled the pillow from beneath her bedspread and held it over her face for a few minutes, wondering what it would be like to suffocate, then she put it under her head and slid into a deep, dreamless sleep.

A loud clanking sound woke her. When she tiptoed downstairs, she found Other Mother in the kitchen wearing rubber gloves, with a yellow bandana around her nose and mouth. Pots and pans surrounded her. Against Jen's better judgment, she asked, "Mom, what are you doing?"

"I smell gas." The bandana puffed in and out as she spoke.

Jen sniffed the air but didn't smell anything. "So why are you emptying the cabinets?"

"Got to find the source."

Jen popped a piece of toast into the toaster. In the time it took the bread to go from soft fluffy white to crispy and golden, Other Mother had put the pots back in the cabinet and then taken them back out again.

Jen began slathering honey on her toast.

Other Mother unloaded the coffee mugs from the shelf and set them on the floor in perfect lines.

Jen poured herself a glass of milk.

Other Mother murmured to some invisible entity, "You won't win. I won't let you."

Jen took her toast and milk back up to her room and knuckled down on her paper. She'd get an A if it killed her.

Now it was past ten thirty, her paper was done—and good, if she did say so herself—and Other Mother was still at it, judging by the sounds emanating from the stairwell. She hadn't dared go down for dinner, just hoped her mother would snap out of it, as she usually did, or simply wear herself out. Where was Jake?

A super loud crash shook the house. Jen sat up. Should she go downstairs? Another crash. Then another. Jen slid into her slippers and darted down the two flights of stairs.

Other Mother, still in rubber gloves and bandana, had on her winter coat and Jake's knitted hat. She was smashing a hammer into the dining room wall.

"Mom! Stop!"

Other Mother glanced at her briefly and mumbled, "Poison," then went back to smashing the wall.

Jen rushed toward her. "Mom! There's no gas. It's all in your mind."

Other Mother snorted like a bull. "You can't see it, but it's there. They never lie." This time when she swung at the wall she clipped the ceramic lamp and sent it crashing to the floor. She dropped to her knees and began rooting through the shards. "It's here. I just have to find it." She got back up and smashed at the wall again. "You won't win. I won't let you!"

Jen wondered whom she could call. The neighbors? But one was a really old deaf lady, and the folks on the other side were out of town. Her teacher at school? She didn't know her number. The police? They'd throw her Mom in the loony bin.

Other Mother took a strong swing at the wall causing a picture to drop to the floor and the glass to shatter.

Jen picked up the phone and dialed Ernest's number.

He picked up on the first ring. "Reverend Bates."

Jen was so breathless, so scared, she could barely get her words out. "Mom's freaking out."

"Jennifer?"

Other Mother smashed the wall again, sending a shelf of framed photos clattering to the floor.

"Yes. You need to come over here."

"What's that racket?"

"Mom is smashing up the house."

After a bit more back and forth, Ernest finally got the gist of the nightmare and said he'd be right over. "Just make her stay there," he said before hanging up.

Jen wasn't sure she could make her mom do anything, but for the time being, it seemed Other Mother was content to stay where she was until she found the "gas," so Jen unlocked the door and scrambled up the stairs to sit on the landing. From there she could see the front door.

By the time Ernest arrived, Other Mother had moved on to the living room and was slashing open throw pillows with a knife. "Evelyn." His voice was stern, like a schoolteacher's. "What in heck are you doing?"

Other Mother stood, kitchen knife in hand, and blinked a few times. "Ernest?"

"Put the knife down, Evelyn."

"But the gas—"

"I'm going to help you find the gas, Evelyn. But first put down the knife."

Other Mother let the knife drop to the floor. How was Ernest able to rationalize with Other Mother? What was it about him?

"Do you smell it?" Other Mother asked. "The gas?"

Ernest walked toward her with one hand raised, like she was a spooked horse. He paused briefly to sniff the air. "I think Jesus fixed it. It's all gone."

"No." Other Mother scuttled over to the couch and pulled off a cushion. "Smell. Smell!"

Ernest strode to her and put his hand on her shoulder. "Evelyn, I tell you it's all gone. Jesus has taken care of it."

"But—"

"You don't believe Jesus has the power to save you from a little gas?"

"But it's poison!"

"He knows that, Evelyn. And that's why he made it go away. He was taking care of you, like he always takes care of you." He glanced up at Jen on the landing. "Isn't that right Jennifer?"

Jen, unsure her voice would work, nodded.

"See, even your daughter, Jennifer, knows that Jesus can protect you. Look at your daughter, Evelyn."

Other Mother jerked her head away, but Jen could see she was starting to snap out of it.

"Look at your daughter, Evelyn. She's sitting at the top of the stairs and she knows Jesus is in control." He beckoned for Jen to come toward them.

Jen willed her legs to stand and began descending the stairs, one by one, very slowly.

"If you'd look up, Evelyn, you'd see your beautiful daughter coming toward you, and she's as full of Jesus' love as I am."

Her mom hunched into herself then lifted her head slightly and peeked out through her disheveled hair.

"See that, Evelyn? That's your beautiful daughter, Jennifer. Can't you see how Jesus' love is wrapping around her? It can do the same for you. You just have to let it in. Let Jesus heal you."

Jen was just a few steps away from the two of them. She glanced at the kitchen knife on the floor to be sure it was out of her mom's reach.

"Show your daughter how you're full of light, Evelyn. Look her in the eyes and let Jesus' love pass between you."

Her mom raised her head.

Ernest untied her bandana and put it in his pocket. "Can you feel it, Evelyn? Can you feel Jesus' love?"

Jen looked into her mom's tear-filled eyes and felt a wave of nausea. Why couldn't she have a normal mother?

Ernest put a protective arm around her mom's shoulders. "Feeling better?"

She nodded.

"No more gas," he said.

She tried to pat her hair into place, her hands trembling beneath the rubber gloves. "I'm sorry," she whispered. "I'm so so sorry."

Ernest held out his other arm, indicating that Jen should join the fold.

Jen didn't want to do it; she wanted to run as far away from this scene as she could. But Ernest had chased off Other Mother and she was grateful for that. She slipped under Ernest's arm.

The front door swung open, and Jake stood there staring at the mess. "What the hell?"

Jen didn't know what to say. The last thing they needed was to stir their mom back up.

"Your mom has had a difficult evening," Ernest said.

Jake snorted in disgust then jerked his head at Ernest. "So what are *you* doing here?"

"I called him," Jen said, aware that their mom was growing agitated. "We needed *Jesus to help us*." She knew how it must look, her and their mom in the arms of the pastor, her talking about Jesus like she believed.

Jake's eyes narrowed. "Jesus?"

"That's right, Jake," Ernest said. "Jesus."

Jen racked her brain for a way to let Jake know that it wasn't really Jesus, but that they needed to say that it was to keep her calm.

She tried sending it to him, *I'm just saying this so Other Mother won't come back,* but of course he didn't hear. It had been forever since they did mind-talking.

Jake scanned the smashed walls and the sliced pillows. "Looks like Jesus was real helpful."

Jen fixed her eyes on his, trying to make him get what was going on. "You don't know what you're talking about, Jake."

He laughed bitterly. "No, Jen. You don't know what *you're* talking about." Then he stormed back out into the night.

✳

Driving up the mountain, Dad talks about my childhood as if it were yesterday, recalling how we worked on a bike in the basement. "I'd picked it up at a rummage sale," he says. "For next to nothing. It was green, but you wanted blue."

"I remember," I say, but don't.

"I *bet* you do. You used to scream up and down the block on that puppy."

He seems so happy, like he's talking about the best years of his life. Which is so delusional. He was gone a lot. And when he was home, he was often sleeping off a drunk or tearing up the house trying to figure out where Mom had hidden the car keys—a far cry from the Dad off *Father Know Best* that he's trying to portray now. How he held on to his job is a mystery.

I notice a lull and realize I should contribute something. "You still playing pool with your buddies?" I feel like a shit for bringing up the not-so-rosy part of life, but this game he's playing is too weird.

He squints his eyes for a moment like he's trying to solve some mental puzzle. "Still sober if that's what you're asking. Had my ten year anniversary a month ago."

"Dad, that's not what I meant…" But of course I did. "I just…"

"It's okay, Bean. I know my drinking was hard on the family."

This is my opening to talk about my feelings, but I point out the beautiful scenery instead; from there we move on to weather, politics. He asks about Mexico and the organic food industry. I ask about his work.

We stay off the gay topic.

When we reach Mom's driveway, he starts nervously drumming on the steering wheel and doing his odd tuneless humming.

"Watch out on the left," I say. "It washed out last winter."

His overcorrection squashes me into the car door. "Somebody should fix that."

I turn away, tears pricking the corners of my eyes. I know we're talking about the road, and his business is roads, but is he going to come up here and start criticizing every little thing?

We pull up to the house.

He gets out of the car. I follow suit, expecting him to head for the trunk for his bags, but he just stands there with his hands on his hips gawking at Mom's spread.

My heart starts to race. I need to defend Mom. But it's hard. Her creative clutter is a mess. The flowerbeds need weeding. The solar panels stacked by the side of the house are covered in cobwebs. The upstairs shutter is halfway missing. Why haven't I noticed this before? Mom never finishes anything. She starts projects with the best intentions, but she's someone who lives in the moment. Only in her case, the moments don't always connect.

I saunter back to the trunk to unload Dad's bags. I know what he's thinking: *She could use a man to help her clean this up.* Or maybe he's not. After our little bonding session by the lake, I don't know who he is anymore.

Mrs. Simpkins steps out from beneath a tangle of Cosmos and begins rolling on her back. Dad bends down to give her belly a rub. "Who are you?"

"That's Mrs. Simpkins. And be careful. She's not big on her belly being—"

But it's too late. Mrs. Simpkins has already dug her claws into Dad's hand. Dad laughs as he rescues his hand from her grip. "Okay, Mrs. Simpkins. I get the message." He notices me unloading his bags. "Here. Let me get that." He reaches for the carryon and grabs it by the side handle.

I hang on to the top handle. "That's all right. I've got it."

He gives the side handle a yank. "Bean, they're *my* bags."

I give the top handle a yank. "It's okay. I've *got* it!"

There's an awkward moment as we both realize how asinine we're acting, then, wordlessly, he lets go of the bag and pulls the heavier bag out of the trunk.

"You can either use my room," I say. "Or…I guess…Mom's. Aunt Jen's already laid claim to the guest room."

He carries his bag without bothering to pull the handle for rolling. "Let's check it out."

We head toward the house. The idea of his sleeping in Mom's bed is disturbing. Why did I offer it? He doesn't belong there, and it would be a bad omen, like we're giving up on her.

The lock on the door sticks and I have to jiggle the key to get it to work. Once inside, Mrs. Simpkins starts herding us toward the kitchen. "Hang on." I place Dad's bag on the floor. "Let me see if Ari fed her yet."

Dad puts his bag down. "Anything I can do?"

"Nope. I got it. Uh…make yourself at home."

I head for the kitchen, just to the right of the foyer. Mrs. Simpkins's bowl is by the pantry, and it's covered in ants. Mrs. Simpkins gives me a look that says she does not approve. I dump the food into the trash outside the kitchen door and run a paper towel under the faucet to swipe the ants up from the floor. They've made a line from the side door to her bowl. "The two rooms are upstairs," I say loud enough so Dad can hear me—wherever it is he's wandered off to. "Mom's is the big one overlooking the garden. Mine's on the left by the bathroom. It's got a bunch of boxes in it, but we can move those. I don't mind sleeping in her room if you want to take mine. She and I could always share the bed when she gets home."

"Why don't I just sleep out here?" he says from the screened-in porch just off the deck, a rickety contraption Mom hired a couple of not-too-skilled day laborers to build for her.

I begin the ant massacre. "On that old couch? Are you sure?"

"It'll be fine. Just throw me a blanket and a pillow. I'll be in heaven."

I toss the paper towel covered with ant carcasses into the trashcan then refill her bowl with kibble. "I hope this is up to your standards," I say to her. She sniffs the kibble and takes a taste. I shout to Dad, "Suit yourself." I don't mention that on the other side of the wall is the guest room where Aunt Jen has set herself up, or that they'll be sharing a bathroom; I just head back to the foyer, grab the carryon, and join him on the porch. "It'll be nice and cool at night. Plenty of ventilation."

"It'll be like camping," he says. "Remember?"

I nod, although my memories of camping are blurry at best.

He stows his bags next to the couch. "So what do you say we knock out that…what was it called?"

It takes me a second. "Are you talking about the Scotch broom?"

"Yeah. What do you say we bang it out before napping?"

His naïveté physically hurts me, right in the gut. "It's going to take a bit more than a few hours, Dad."

He claps his hands together. "That's okay. Just point me to it."

I push the screen door open and we step outside. "See that yellow stuff over there, and over there, and over there?"

He nods.

"That's Scotch broom. Her twenty acres is covered in it."

He scans the blankets of yellow. "Holy cow."

"I tried to warn you."

He shakes his head and chuckles. "Maye hasn't changed one bit."

But of course she has. She can't move anymore.

"So if you don't mind," I say, "I think I'll take a nap before we start on the heavy landscaping."

## CHAPTER ELEVEN

I wake to the sound of crunching bones. It's coming from over by the doorway. I keep my eyes shut and listen. Mrs. Simpkins, who acts like she'd starve if you didn't give her organic kibble, is eviscerating whatever critter was unlucky enough to cross her path. Her feral cat breathing is ravenous and greedy, untamed and wild. I guess we all have a shadow, a dark underbelly that needs to let loose sometimes.

I let my eyes float open. The last of the late afternoon sun is streaming through my window. I've slept for hours. My body feels heavy, dense; my head muddy. I stare at the familiar wood-slat ceiling, fighting the creepy feeling that the whole of civilization has vanished, that Mrs. Simpkins and I are the only ones left on the planet, and we're battling to survive.

She gnaws at what sounds like raw gristle and makes a low, growling sound.

I push myself up to sitting and shake my head. Civilization returns. Mom's stuff is everywhere. Boxes of it all over the floor. Some boxes are opened and spilling over with clothes, books, and shoeboxes of what looks like letters. My old jewelry box, a small desk lamp, a teacup and saucer sit on a pile of boxes that are still taped shut.

She must have been cleaning out. Which for Mom is historic. She borders on being a hoarder.

A yawn slips out.

I wonder what Dad is up to? No doubt something meaningful, "banging out" the Scotch broom, or, if I'm lucky, fixing us something to eat. Then again, he could be sleeping. I doubt it, though. On the rare occasion that he does manage to nod off, it's fitful and brief.

I glance at Mrs. Simpkins. She's next to a pile of empty picture frames working on the hind end of a mouse.

"That's gross."

She doesn't bother to look up, just tears out more entrails.

It's weird being back in this room, supposedly *my* room, even though I've never lived here.

I survey my past attempts to make the room feel like mine—the glow-in-the-dark stars on the ceiling, the Tibetan prayer flags over the window, the Edward Hopper print—all done on various visits. It never worked.

I swing my legs off the bed and grab a tissue to swipe up what's left of the mouse. "Snack time's over, Mrs. Simpkins." She glares at me for a second then turns into lovey-dovey domestic kitty, rubbing on my leg and purring.

Is she playing me?

"Hope it was a good day to die." I say to the carcass before tossing it in the trash.

I pick up a half-full photo album swimming in a sea of loose and rubber-banded photos. Another of Mom's 'round-to-its. I flip through some pages. It's full of Mom and Dad when they first got together and some early snaps of her before she knew him. She even tucked in some of Dad before he knew her, ones he must have given her. It's like she was trying to merge their two histories together.

I come across a totally Eighties photo of Mom, Dad, and Aunt Jen posing in front of the giant clothespin in downtown Philadelphia. Their outfits are hilarious. Mom's in an oversized *Flashdance* sweatshirt with the collar cut out, leg warmers, and her blond hair is not only permed, it's pulled into a ponytail on the side of her head. Dad's very stylin' with his sweater tied over his shoulders and khaki pants. Is that product in his hair? And Aunt Jen's wearing plaid peg legs and a jean jacket rolled at the sleeves with her long braid hanging over her shoulder. Mom's got an arm around each of their shoulders. They're all laughing at something.

I slip the album under my arm to take downstairs. Maybe if I leave it open to this page Aunt Jen and Dad will remember they used to like each other.

I head for the kitchen. There's a note on the table.

> *Bean,*
> *Hope you slept well. I've gone back to Redding to pick up some work boots. I'll connect up with Jen to take over the next shift. Call if you need me.*
> *Dad*
> *PS. I haven't forgotten what we talked about.*

I flip the note over as if there might be an explanation for the postscript on the other side. Of course there isn't. Dad, the King of Cryptic. He could be talking about the secret Mom wants him to tell Aunt Jen, our talk about me being gay, or the kite parachute and all the fun we used to have. Who knows? Dad is so unpredictable; his mood can make a sixty-mile-an-hour U-turn.

I remember one time I was visiting him. I was fifteen and it was summer vacation. Dad spent the whole time I was there at work, coming home each day dirty and tired.

It was the third day of a five-day visit. I hated being back in Philadelphia. It was hot, humid, and it had been so long since I'd lived there, I no longer had any friends.

*"Bean! I'm home."*

"In here," I yelled from the living room then added, "Watching TV." Like there was something else to do. I slipped out of the wing-backed chair onto the floor so he wouldn't catch me in it. Not that he'd ever said I couldn't sit there, but it was obviously his favorite chair, all the dimples and hollows to prove it.

He stepped into the living room and held up a Burger King bag. "Dinner." He seemed really happy until he looked at the TV screen. "Why are you watching *that*?"

"I like trains," I said. "A lot." Which was a lie. I could have cared less about the antique show and their model trains putting around their "realistic" looking track, but his accusing tone pissed me off.

He walked over to the TV and clicked it off.

"Hey! I was watching that!"

He tossed the bag of burgers onto the coffee table. "Not anymore you're not."

"Says who?" I picked up the remote and flicked it back on to a close-up of a model train going under a bridge.

"Says me. It's time for dinner. Now turn it off." He slipped off his jacket.

"No."

He turned toward me, his eyes icy and hard. "I said, turn it *off*."

I didn't.

He slammed out of the living room, leaving the Burger King bag on the coffee table.

We barely said two words to each other that night, and neither of us ate. *The burgers just stayed on the coffee table getting cold.*

I wad up the note and toss it into the trash, angry that he left without telling me—which I know is irrational. I wouldn't have wanted him to wake me either.

I dial Serena.

She picks up on the second ring. "Brianna?"

"I just wanted to hear a friendly voice." My voice sounds sputtery and thin. She's going to think I'm a total basket case.

"Are you okay?"

"Just tired."

"I wish I could hold you."

I sniff. "Me too."

She mumbles something to someone.

"Oh. Is this a bad time?"

"No," she says. "I'm just sitting here at the beach with Chrissy. You remember her from the restaurant? The bartender?"

"Oh yeah," I say. How could I forget Chrissy of the sculpted thighs and abs? How could anyone? The satiny blond Amazon has a black belt in jujitsu *and* Tae Kwon Do. Plus, the chick's a champion surfer. And she does *amazing* tarot readings, or so says Serena…

"Brianna? You still there?"

"Yeah."

"You don't sound too good."

"Well, um," I stammer as I try and think of some lie to get me out of this. "I think I just heard someone drive up. I should see who it is."

"Oh. Okay. Call me later?"

"Yeah. Probably," I say in a cool voice. "I'm not sure really. I'll have to see how things go." I feel like such an asshole coming off so brusque, but I can't stop myself. "So, bye." I hang up before I can fuck things up even further. Could I be more pathetic?

What is Serena doing hanging out with Chrissy? Chrissy's a shark. I knew it the moment I laid eyes on her. And she definitely had the hots for Serena.

I feel an ache in my chest. Has Mexico moved on without me?

I drag myself out onto the back deck, stopping to nab the yoga mat that Mom keeps by the door. The sun is close to disappearing behind the pines. I sit in Hero's pose and try to clear my mind, but thoughts buzz around my brain like hornets. Buddhists call it "monkey mind." The moment I think this, the hornets turn to miniature monkeys swinging from lobe to lobe.

I release each thought with breath.

Why did Mom have to get sick?

Breathe.

What if Serena falls for Chrissy?

Breathe.

What if Mom never gets all the way better? And I have to take care of her for the rest of her life?

Breathe.

Once centered—and it takes a while—I begin a modified sun salutation.

Mountain pose. My body is my true home. Hands up. My true home is my body. Head to knee. I have only myself. Lunge. I am enough. Plank. I am strong. Stick. I can handle what comes at me.

Upward dog. I am aware. Downward dog. I am humble. Lunge. I am ready. Knee to head. I am grateful. Hands up. Always grateful. Warrior III. But I don't take shit. Mountain. My true home is my body.

I repeat this sequence until the sun is well behind the trees, do a brief corpse pose, then go inside to find something to eat. It feels great to have the kinks out. And while I still feel uneasy about Chrissy and Serena, I get it that I have no control. What will be will be. But I hope she and I are meant to be. Please, please, please.

There's a can of lentil soup in the pantry. I open the can, dump it in a pot, and click on the flame. While it's heating, I flip to the last photo in the half-filled album. It's a picture of Mom and Dad holding a tiny me between their faces. My face is red and squinched and I'm bald. But Mom and Dad are glowing, as if they expect the best of life is ahead of them.

Monkey mind flashes to the day Mom told me we were moving. I was playing with a rope outside on the front lawn of our townhouse. I was eight years old.

*Mom rushed out from the house, letting the screen door slap shut behind her.* "Bean! What are you doing?"

"Hanging Robbie's sister's Barbie."

"Why?"

"When Robbie gets back from his piano lesson, we're going to put it in her room."

She squatted next to me and put her hand on my shoulder, her face kinked with concern. "Are you unhappy, sweetie?"

"No."

"You sure?"

"Yeah."

I knew she wanted to talk to me about the fight she and Dad had the night before, because she always wanted to talk to me after they had a fight. Last night's had been bad. They'd slammed doors and something big, like a lamp or a picture, had been thrown across the room.

"Mind if I hang out with you a little?"

She took my shrug to mean I wanted her there, and swept her colorful skirt beneath her to settle crossed-legged on the grass. She tucked a blond curl behind her ear. "Are you mad at Mommy?"

"No."

"Are you sure?"

"Yes."

"Were you scared by me and Daddy fighting last night?"

"Mo-*om*."

She rested her elbows on her knees and dropped her face into her hands. As usual, her fingers were covered in multiple silver rings.

I focused on my knot until I realized she was crying. I'd seen her cry before, but only when she was watching a sad movie. "Mom, are you okay?"

She lifted her head and wiped away the tears. "Can you keep a secret?"

"What?"

She thought for a moment, her eyes watery and red. "How would you like to visit Aunt Jen?"

"By myself?"

"With me."

"Not Dad?"

"No. Not Dad. And we need to keep it a secret from him, because Mommy hasn't told him yet."

"I just started at my new school."

"I know, sweetie, but we might need to do this."

A few days later, we were waiting on the porch for a cab to take us to the airport. I was wearing my favorite shorts with the zipper pockets.

"Isn't Dad going to say good-bye?"

Mom hugged herself. "He had to go to work."

"You should have told him not to."

The cab rounded the corner. *"Grab your backpack, Bean. We have to go."*

I had no idea when we left that day that we weren't coming back.

I stick my finger in the soup. It's lukewarm and looks unappealing, all brown and lumpy.

I open the cabinet in search of salt. Healthy soups never have enough salt.

"Anybody home?"

It surprises me that I didn't hear Ari drive up. "In here," I yell.

He flounces into the kitchen. His rainbow tie-dyed wifebeater and short-shorts make him look even scrawnier than usual. "I just saw the cutest guy at the gas station. And he was like totally checking me out until his cavemen friends showed up."

"Want some soup?"

He peers into the pot then scowls. "*That* looks appetizing."

"It's all I could find."

"Then you didn't check the freezer," he says walking over to it. "Maye and I made pizzas last Saturday."

I join him at the freezer. Sure enough, it's filled with Mom's homemade pizzas. "There is a God."

"Goddess," he says.

"Whatever. I'm going to preheat the oven. You staying?"

"Sure."

I choose a pizza that looks like it has sausage, summer squash, spinach, and heirloom tomatoes smothered in an array of tasty cheeses.

He sits at the table and starts flipping through the photo album. "How's she doing?"

"Not getting worse, which they say is good."

"Mom says she knew someone who had the same thing, and they're like totally fine now."

"Hang on to that thought."

He points at a picture in the album. "Oh my goddess. Who's this hottie? And *what* is he wearing?"

I finish pulling the plastic wrap off the pizza and take a look. "That's my dad."

"That's your *dad*?"

"Well, years ago."

The picture looks like Dad's prom photo. He and some girl are standing in front of a hideous waterfall mural. Dad's wearing a black double-breasted tuxedo jacket with wide satin lapels, and a ruffled shirt. He's looking off to the side.

"I wonder how he got stuck going to the prom with the school ho?" Ari says.

I pinch his arm.

"What? Look at her. She's like totally skanky, falling out of her dress and covered in ho makeup."

He's right. The heavyset girl definitely has too much makeup and too little dress. The red sequined number has only one strap, which is hardly enough to hold in her rather substantial bosom. What's more, if you look past the high school posturing of Cool Dude and His Date, the two of them are doing that thing I remember oh so well from high school—looking cool on the outside when you're freaking on the inside.

*

Jake was sitting alone in the school cafeteria staring down a plate of greasy meatloaf and potatoes when he overheard a group of girls sniggering about the fact that Rhonda Babinski didn't have a date for the prom.

"Just because she puts out doesn't mean the guys actually *like* her," one of them said.

"I overheard her telling Shauna that Grant *loved* her," another said. The girls erupted into malicious giggles, which after a few seconds subsided into self-satisfied sniffs and coughs.

The school's very own Farrah Fawcett wannabe finished the conversation with a neat bow. "As far as I'm concerned, she's getting what she asked for."

Jake took a bite of meatloaf. The prom. He had no idea who he was going to invite, or if he was even going to go. He wasn't exactly popular. Had only a couple of encounters with girls that could have been considered dates and both of them got weird when it got to the kissing part. He came on too strong. Or so he'd heard one of them say the next day when she thought he was beyond earshot. "He just kinda came at me out of nowhere," she'd said.

Later, after physics, he lingered by the lockers where he often saw Rhonda switching out textbooks between sixth and seventh period. Her locker was three down from his. He made a deal with himself. If she was alone, he'd go up to her; if she wasn't, he'd forget all about the prom.

As fate would have it, she was alone and squeezed into leggings so tight you could see the dimples in the flesh of her behind. As she bent over to work the combination, Jake peered down her hot pink top to the lacy black bra beneath. It was no fluke she was regularly written up for "inappropriate attire."

A group of guys from the football team strolled past. "Hey, look. It's Fondle Rhonda," one of them said.

"Rho the Ho," another shot back. They laughed and slapped each other five.

She gave them the finger, the tip of which was covered in chipped pink nail polish. "Fucking hypocrites."

He waited for the football guys to pass, then took a few deep breaths, willing himself the courage to speak, and walked up to her. "They probably don't even know what that word means."

Rhonda shot him a disgusted look. "Are you talking to me?"

"Um. Yeah. I was just saying they probably don't know what the word hypocrite means."

"You got that right." She patted one of her wings of hair into place. "Anyway, who cares? The world is full of hypocrites."

Jake dug his hands into his pockets then removed them. Why was he so nervous?

She dug her hands into her hips making her gazillion silver bracelets clink. "Do you want something, Jakey Wakey? Or do you just want to stand there with your tongue hanging out?"

"I was just wondering…um…if you'd like to go with me to… um…the prom. That is if you're not…um…going with someone else already."

A mild look of revulsion passed over her face. "*You're* asking *me* to the prom?"

He cleared his throat. "If you're available, yeah."

"If I'm *available*?"

Her mocking tone was getting to him. "Look. If you don't want—"

"I didn't say that. I just think it's kinda crazy that a guy I've barely said two words to wants to take me to the prom."

"We've said more than two words. I was your chemistry partner. Remember?"

"That was you?"

"Fuck off. If you don't want to go—"

She grabbed his sleeve. "Can't take a joke?"

He challenged her with his eyes. "You want to go or don't you?"

"Sure, I'll be your *date*. Do you have a car?"

"I can get one."

"Okay then. Pick me up at six."

"Where do you live?"

She grabbed a sticker-covered spiral-bound notebook from her locker, ripped out a piece of paper, and wrote down her address in big loopy letters, dotting each "i" with a tiny circle.

He stood there and wondered where he was going to get a car. His mom's had thrown a rod a month earlier and there was no way she'd get a new one before the prom.

He brought the problem up with her when he got home later that day. She acted thrilled that he'd managed to get a date at all, which pissed him off, then suggested he hitch a ride with Jen and her friends.

"What, and pick up my date in a car filled with girls?"

"How about Ernest's car? I'm sure he'd loan it to you, if you'd ask nicely."

"No way," he'd said emphatically.

But as the prom grew closer and closer—without any other cars materializing—Ernest's car started to look better and better. He begged his mom to ask him for it.

"I don't know why you don't ask him yourself," she said as she folded laundry on her bed. "All he's ever wanted is to be your friend."

Jake had to keep from snorting in disgust. He flopped down next to a pile of neatly folded towels and looked up at her, his eyes pleading. "Please, Mom?"

She tousled his hair. "Oh, all right. I'll ask him tonight after church."

Jake rolled off the bed. "Thanks, Mom." So what if it was Ernest's puke green Pinto? He had wheels.

❖

Jake pulled up in front of a filthy three-story row house a few blocks from Chinatown. The bricks were black with grunge. There was a large dead plant on the porch. Taking a deep breath, he forced himself out of the Pinto and headed for the steps, the whole time fighting the urge to pivot on the heel of his polished wingtips and forget the whole thing. He and Rhonda had barely spoken since that day by the locker. They hardly knew each other. He shot up the three steps to the porch and rapped on the door then stared at the gray smudges around the doorknob.

A few painful seconds passed. He glanced back at the Pinto. How many times had he sat crammed in the back seat of that car listening to Ernest bullshit his mom? Once, right after he and Ernest had had one of their "cleansing" sessions, when his mom was going on and on about her struggle to "stay on the righteous path" and not succumb to "the sins of the flesh," he heard Ernest tell her that it was "once difficult for him too," but his "earthly desires had been quenched since he'd devoted his life to Jesus."

A bead of sweat trickled down Jake's temple. He raised his hand to wipe it away. The door flew open revealing a carbon copy of Rhonda, only older and fatter and with bigger hair and more makeup. She looked him over then spoke around the cigarette dangling from her lips. "You're even better looking than she said."

Jake shifted his weight from one foot to the next. "Uh, thanks." He could see a pot-bellied guy with a comb-over slouched on the couch with his feet on the coffee table. He was guzzling a Budweiser.

"Rhonda!" the guy bellowed. "Your prince has arrived!"

Rhonda, in a short red sequined dress with only one strap, sashayed into view, the flimsy fabric of her dress straining to contain her voluptuous milky breasts and doughy thighs. "I heard." When she reached the couch, the ribbon tie on her three-inch platform sandal came undone and she bent down to fix it.

The guy on the couch swatted her on the ass. "Don't do anything I wouldn't do."

She jolted up, letting the ribbon on her shoe hang undone. "Fuck you, Ray Ray."

"That's what I'm talking about, cupcake," he said, laughing. "That's what I'm talking about."

Rhonda's mom chuckled uneasily. "Leave her alone, Ray. It's her special night."

Rhonda glared at her mother then said to Jake, "Let's get out of here."

Jake held out an arm for her.

"Sweet," her mother said, tossing her smoke into a can on the porch. "A real gentleman."

"She'll let you have it anyway," Ray yelled from the couch. "No need to waste your energy."

As they walked out to the car—Rhonda hobbling due to her untied four-inch platform sandal—Jake couldn't rid himself of the notion that he and Rhonda were both somehow damaged goods. "Was that your dad?" he asked opening the car door for her.

"Hell no. Ray Ray's my mom's boyfriend."

Jake walked around the car, a righteous anger burning in his belly. Rhonda was right. The world was full of hypocrites. He slid into the driver's seat.

Rhonda snapped open her gold lamé purse. "Mind if I smoke?"

Jake sneered at the gold cross hanging from the rearview mirror. "Be my guest. And if you're in the mood, I've got half a bottle of tequila in the glove box."

She lit up her cigarette and blew smoke at the windshield. "I may have underestimated you, Jakey Wakey."

Jake smiled and clicked on the radio. From its tinny speakers came, "Yes, the lamb is meek, and yes, the lamb is mild..." He switched over to WMMR and Creedence Clearwater's "Proud Mary." "Not my car," he said.

"It is tonight," she said, flaunting her leg as she braced her right foot on the dashboard to tie her shoe.

❖

The moment they walked into the ballroom of the fancy hotel, it was obvious that elegant clothes, fancy corsages, and done-up hairdos weren't going to change a thing; it was still high school. The jocks and cheerleaders dominated the refreshment table like they owned it. The geeks huddled around a table in the corner shooting straw sleeves at each other, and the drama kids were dancing wildly on the dance floor. Jake spotted Jen in a circle of her goody-two-shoes girlfriends standing by one of the tall windows overlooking the courtyard. She towered over the other girls in her light blue ankle-length chiffon dress, her large hands and feet almost clown-like. And her waist-length braid was so out of place. All the other girls had highly coifed hairdos.

She glanced toward the door where he and Rhonda were standing, but she made no effort to act like she knew him. He reciprocated.

Rhonda fixated on Grant Houston. "I can't believe he gave Pam Whitman his ring. He told *me* he didn't believe in that."

Jake had a momentary flash of guilt. How many times in the locker room had he listened to Grant boast about his exploits with Rhonda? "Tits the size of cantaloupes," "a tight twat," and "gives killer blow jobs" were about all the feelings Grant had ever mentioned having for her.

"Come on," he said braving the long walk across the room. "Let's go find someplace to sit."

"What's the rush?" Rhonda said, tottering after him.

The idea of the two of them as damaged goods wouldn't quit buzzing around his inebriated mind. He took her hand and dragged her toward a far corner of the room. "Hey," she said. "You're pulling my arm off."

Once they'd reached the corner, Rhonda plopped down on an empty chair. "Did you see that gown Pam was wearing? God! You'd think she was Princess Diana or something. And she must be wearing a hairpiece because she sure doesn't have *that* much hair."

Jake ran his finger around the tight collar of the rented dress shirt with ruffles down the front. The guy at Ralph's Formal Wear had talked him into it, but now that he was actually wearing the damn thing, he felt like a fucking peacock. "Uh, no. I didn't notice." He glanced at the group of drama kids on the dance floor. They were dancing in a circle, doing the twist, the swim, and other old dances. No doubt Rhonda was going to expect him to dance. "Want some punch?" he asked to stave off the inevitable.

"Why not?" Rhonda stood and took his arm. "Fuck Grant and his little prom queen girlfriend."

Jake had intended to bring the punch to her, but now that he had a girl on his arm, he found that he liked the feeling. *So what if I'm not fucking Grant? She sure as hell ain't any Pam Whitman either.*

For the next hour Rhonda was all over him. She sat on his lap, taught him to slow dance, and placed fresh strawberries in his mouth. He knew it was all a show for Grant. Everybody did. But Jake didn't care. If Grant didn't want what Rhonda had to offer, he was happy to take it. *Sloppy seconds,* he thought to himself as she pressed her body against his in a stimulating slow dance.

"You should have brought a smaller bottle for the tequila," she said as they walked off the dance floor. "We could have snuck it in."

"Let's go out and fill our cups." *The perfect chance to see what she really has to offer.*

She glanced over at Grant. He was sitting at a table with his back to her and his arm around Pam. "Fine by me. The scenery here stinks."

They made their way out of the building and through the parking lot. Jake noticed that Rhonda stopped fawning on him the second Grant wasn't watching.

"What do you say we drink out here?" he said. "In the car."

She tugged at the neckline of her dress to keep her breasts from spilling out. "Okay by me. Just so long as we don't miss getting our photo taken."

Jake had almost forgotten about the photo. The photographer wasn't coming until nine thirty. "I'll get you back in time." He opened the door on the driver's side and unlocked the seat so she could slide past. If she wondered why they were cramming into the almost non-existent backseat, she didn't say so, just scooted across the seat to make room for him.

"We painted the mural for the photos in art class. That's how I knew to wear red. The corner, right next to the waterfall, has these red tropical flowers. I'm hoping it's the same red."

The car stunk of Ernest's aftershave. Jake leaned over the seat to shut the door. Once he was sitting, the seat flipped back and pinned them in. "You'll go perfect."

"You think?" she said, once again adjusting the neckline of her dress.

"Uh huh."

She lifted her arms to fiddle with her hair; her breasts rose with the motion. "I was so glad when I saw you went with the traditional black and white. I would have died if you showed up in a tux like Dean's."

He laughed. "What? You don't go for lavender?"

She gave him a playful push, making her cleavage more pronounced.

Now was his chance. All he had to do was lean over and—

"Aren't you going to get the tequila?" she asked.

"Oh. Right." He leaned over the seat, nearly bumping his head on the cross hanging from the rearview, popped the glove box, and nabbed the bottle. It was only a quarter full. He fell back into the seat, the bottle held high. "May I?"

She held up her plastic cup. "You know you're really not bad looking. You should comb your hair back more often."

He filled her cup then his own. Maybe she did like him.

"Is there a worm in that bottle?" she asked. "Cuz I'm not drinking any worm."

He wiggled his finger menacingly. "You scared of worms?"

She took a sip of her drink. "Can you believe I found this dress on sale?"

Jake downed his drink. "It's pretty."

"You think?"

He refilled his glass. The smell of Ernest's aftershave mixed with the tequila and the proximity of her large breasts was causing something inside him to rile up; it made him feel bold. He edged close to her and slipped his finger under the single strap. "Um...if you don't mind me asking, how do you wear a bra with it?"

Her painted eyebrows furrowed.

"Well?" he pressed.

"It has one built in."

He let the back of his hand brush her breast.

"Can I have some more?" she asked.

"Oh...sure." He refilled her cup, swallowed his own down, then refilled his too.

"You don't think it's nine thirty yet?"

"Why?"

"The *photo*."

"Oh right. No. There's no way." He downed his third glass.

"You might want to slow down. We drank quite a bit on the way over."

"I'm fine," he said, although his thoughts *were* getting blurry. Ray slapping Rhonda's ass...Grant bragging about fucking Rhonda so hard that she cried...Ernest calling him a dirty boy with dirty thoughts...What did they have to lose? He lunged forward to kiss her, his hand groping for her breast.

"Slow down," she said. "You're going to mess up my hair."

But he couldn't slow down. He was a dirty boy and she was a dirty girl. He slipped his fingers under the low neckline of her dress and pulled it down to reveal one very large, very white breast.

"God, you guys are all the same! All you think about is sucking tittie."

He squeezed the fleshy mound in his hand, took the nipple in his mouth.

Her tequila spilled on the back of his neck. "Don't suck it off, for Christ's sake."

He reached up under her short dress searching for a way past her panties.

Rhonda struggled to get out from under him. "Hey…wait…"

He yanked her panties down.

"Jake…"

Fighting to keep visions of Ernest's tiny bathroom, the magazines, Ernest's hungry eyes and swelling cock from his mind, he held her still with one hand while ripping at his cummerbund and unzipping his trousers with the other.

Rhonda tried to push him off. "Jake. Stop it!" But he was too strong for her, and reached down between his legs to take the devil in his hand. *Forgive me, Lord, for my lasciviousness. I am filthy and dirty and full of sin.*

Rhonda dug her fingers into his face, poking one of his eyes with her thumb. "Jake. I said stop it. *STOP* it!"

He reared back, his head spinning, eye throbbing.

She shoved her red platform sandal into his chest, bracing him back. Her eyes were fierce, scared, her mascara streaked like war paint.

He stared back at her. *What kind of monster am I?*

The interior of the car whirled frantically around him; his stomach churned. He smashed the seat forward, flung the door open, and puked all over the asphalt.

Rhonda kicked him the rest of the way out of the car and onto the ground. "Jesus, Jake."

He landed on his knees, face-to-face with his puke. "I'm sorry, Rhonda…" he stammered. "I'm—"

She pulled up her dress and stepped out past him. "You better not have ripped my dress."

He stared at her polished toenails now towering above the puke. "Want me to take you home?"

"Fuck no. I want you to clean yourself up and take me inside to get my picture taken—with *you*."

"But—"

"No buts about it. There is no way I'm going to go through life without a decent prom picture. Now get your sorry ass up."

✳

Having dusted off the pizza, I watch Ari clear my plate from the table. He's just told me the reason Mom's boxes are all over the place—my graduation present. Someone gave her a scanner and she was making me a digital family photo album.

"Sorry I ruined the surprise," he says, "but under the circumstances—"

"I would have done the same thing. Besides, who knows when she would have finished it? Graduation was over a month ago."

He stacks the dishes on the sideboard next to the sink. "God. She has photos tucked everywhere."

"Due to her cleaning methods. Periodically, she sweeps anything that needs dealing with into a box; her idea being she'll get to it later. Only she never does and the box gets shoved into the closet with the other boxes. Each one is a mini time capsule."

He begins filling the sink with hot water. "Well, she's got a lot of 'em."

"You don't have to do those."

"Chillax." He squirts in the dish soap. "I want to."

I rest my feet on the crossbeam under the table. "Thanks." Even though I've slept, I'm still tired—weary, really—so Ari's kindness is much appreciated. He's a good kid. It's a shame he was born into a family that doesn't treasure him. I would if he were mine. Not that I want kids. That's one complication I can do without. "So you were helping Mom sort through her shit."

He holds a plate up to check its cleanliness, the black spikes of his hair backlit from the window above the sink. "Yup. And was I getting the stories every time she'd come across one of her ginormous envelopes of pictures. She's all guilty about your dad and aunt not getting along. Like it's her fault. When her fingers started tingling she thought that was the reason."

"What?" My tone betrays my annoyance. "She thought her fingers were tingling from guilt?"

"Well, she kept talking about people and things she'd let slip away—those two in particular."

I drop my head to my chest and groan. "Mom…" She's always been a firm believer that illness stems from unresolved emotional issues. But this is ridiculous. Sighing, I pick up my bowling ball head and grab a toothpick from the ceramic tulip on the table. I begin working on my teeth, just like my dentist told me to do.

At least now I know why she wants me to get Dad and Aunt Jen talking. She believes she's responsible for their feud and it's making her sick. Of course, if she'd take the thought one step further, she'd figure out that the reason she's paralyzed is because there's nothing she can do about their bad blood. The next thought that careens through my head almost makes me laugh. Maybe her paralysis *is* psychosomatic, but it's working at a deeper, unconscious level, to keep her from meddling.

Ari puts the last of the dishes in the drainer, clinking one into another. "The more tingly she got, the more freaked she got." His voice is quivery. "I kept telling her she should go to a doctor, but she wouldn't listen…" Although he's finished with the dishes he doesn't turn around.

I walk over to him. "Hey. You did everything you could."

"I called her the next day and she told me she was fine. No more tingling."

"That sounds just like her."

"But if I'd known she was…"

I wrap him in my arms. "You did good."

"And then my stupid parents had to take my phone." He's now sobbing.

I squeeze him tight and let him cry, but my mind is wandering. Could guilt be paralyzing her? Is that possible?

Ari begins to fidget. I release him.

"Shall we call and see how she's doing?" I ask.

He rubs the tears from his eyes. "Could we?"

## CHAPTER TWELVE

A unt Jen tells me nothing much has changed with Mom.
"But your dad arrived an hour early. I told him to go do
something, that my time wasn't up yet, but he wouldn't budge."

For some celestial reason, our connection isn't that strong. I
press the phone to my ear. "Wasn't it kind of nice, him giving you
a break?"

"He was marking his territory."

"You don't know that for sure."

She grunts. "Anyway, I found myself this café with wireless.
I'll be heading up the mountain shortly." No doubt the reason for the
static; too many people horning in on the waves.

I snap my phone shut and relay the news about Mom to Ari.

His big blue eyes hang like a baby Boxer's. "We should be
doing *something* for her."

"There's not much *to* do."

"We could keep sorting her photos. She'd like that."

The thought of pawing through Mom's photos makes me want
to puke up my pizza. "Isn't this photo thing supposed to be a surprise
for me?"

He yanks at my arms trying to get me to stand. "Please? This
is important to her. And I know her system. We were sorting them
into four piles—Pre-you, Philadelphia, Santa Cruz, and Present."
He pulls with all his weight, nearly dislocating my shoulders, but
I resist. "And if you and I got working on it tonight, it would give

me something to do besides going home and facing the barbeque from hell. Last time Mom and Dad had one I got there during the wet T-shirt contest. Do you know how disturbing it is to see your mom—and grandmother—in wet T-shirts?"

I laugh. "You just don't want to go home."

"Come on. It'll be fun. We could watch a movie while we do it."

"Shouldn't you at least call and tell them you're here?"

"Can I spend the night? I'll sleep on the couch."

"If they let you."

"Bodacious!"

He digs his phone from his pocket and heads for the living room. Mrs. Simpkins steps through her cat door and begins nagging me for dinner.

The ordinary marches on.

I walk over to Mrs. Simpkins's bowl. The ants are back. She yowls. "Hang on," I tell her and swipe them up again. This time I put her food bowl in a bigger bowl full of water creating a moat. "Let's see them get past that."

She rubs up against my leg once then starts daintily eating like she wasn't the cat I saw earlier ripping at raw meat.

I join Ari in the living room. From what I can make out, his parents' party is well underway. I can hear his mom screeching above blaring music on the other end of the line.

I met her once. She's the type who lets a child run wild until someone is watching, then begins loudly scolding so no one will think the child's bad behavior is her fault. Which sounds like her game now. I hear her say something about not staying up too late— like if he were home he'd be able to go to bed early.

Ari rolls his eyes for my benefit.

I collapse on the worn couch facing Mom's altar. Actually, her whole living room feels like an altar. Native American drums, crystal singing bowls from Tibet, large chunks of amethyst and smaller quartz geodes, prayer sticks, and rattles wrapped in beads and dangling feathers are scattered about the room.

I pry my exhausted body from the couch and light a star-shaped candle on the mantle. *Come on, Mom. Get through this.*

Ari flips his phone shut and flops onto the couch. "God, I wish I had your mom instead of mine."

I've heard this all my life. "Shall we?" I sit cross-legged on the floor next to the stacks of photos.

"Don't you want to watch a movie?"

What I want to do is climb into bed and stay there until this nightmare is over, but what I say is, "Go ahead. Pick something."

He kneels by Mom's very small, very outdated, very random collection of VHS tapes and pulls out one with episodes of *The Brady Bunch.* "Perfect."

"You're kidding."

"Nope." He whips the colorful scarf off Mom's TV and plops the tape into the VCR.

I pick up an envelope of photos. They're of a fundraising carwash my soccer team put on in high school. I toss the envelope in the shoebox labeled Santa Cruz.

Ari grabs a blanket and curls up on the couch, all interest in sorting pictures apparently gone.

I pick up another photo, a rare one, because it has the whole gang—me, Mom, Dad, and Aunt Jen. I look about five years old. We're sitting on a blanket by a river. Paper plates with bagels, macaroni salad, and sliced apples are strewn around. Mom has *Fourth of July Fun!* written on the back. I don't even remember the event, only what Mom has told me. I was afraid of the loud explosions so we watched the fireworks from a remote spot on the Schuylkill River. "You loved their reflections," she said. "Called them 'magical water bugs.'"

Ari chuckles. The Bradys are getting ready for a camping trip, all of them stuffed into a station wagon, Alice facing backward in the way-back and waving right to the camera. But before they pull out of the driveway, little Cindy whispers to her mother that she needs to pee, then Bobby has to, then Jan, then Peter. Pretty soon, they're all heading for the bathroom, leaving the dad alone in the car rolling his eyes.

Such simple problems they have. No wonder Ari loves it. He looks so young curled up on the couch in his blanket, grinning at the banality. All that's missing is his thumb in his mouth.

Of course nothing in life is ever Brady-simple. As actors, they're prancing around like everything is hunky-dory, but in real life the guy playing the dad is a closeted homosexual and the guy playing the oldest boy, not only has the hots for the actress playing the mom, he's also screwed the girl playing his sister.

I'm so sick of lies. I drop the photo and charge out to the back deck.

"You okay?" Ari yells after me.

"Fine!" I yell back. "Just need some air."

I sit on the glider and gaze out onto the moonlit garden. It's a beautiful night, warm, slightly humid. But I'm too livid to appreciate it.

Fuck Mom. Even if she is sick. And fuck Dad too. And Aunt Jen.

I spent my whole childhood with everyone thinking I had the perfect parents. But they were *so* far from perfect. Sure, Dad always managed to pull it together when it mattered, like for school plays and birthdays. But if he didn't, Mom always made up the perfect excuse. If he was passed out on the couch, she'd say he'd "hurt his back on the job," or if he didn't make it home—his empty place setting making it obvious that he was expected—she'd say "Now that I think of it, he *did* mention bowling tonight."

She was such a good liar even I didn't know how bad off he was.

I start flashing back on all the times I got mixed messages about his alcoholism.

One of the times, he surprised me at school. It was lunchtime and I was playing double Dutch in the schoolyard with some friends. All of a sudden, I heard him yelling, "Bean! Bean!" He was in one of his company trucks waving like a maniac. I asked the teacher doing yard duty if I had permission to leave the premises and she said yes, so I ran out to see why he was there, and he told me he was working on a road in the area and just wanted to give me this soft pretzel he'd picked up. His breath smelled of alcohol and his hair was kind of mussed up, but I didn't give it a second thought. I had a dad who would drive all the way to school to bring me a soft pretzel.

I skipped back into that yard, my pigtail flopping up down up down, my heart bursting with pride. When I bragged to Mom about it later, she grilled me. What time did he show up? What was he driving? Was anyone with him? I couldn't figure it out. Why was she turning my good thing into something bad?

And then there was the time the three of us went to the Christmas light show at Wanamaker's. It was fun at first and then we lost Dad and had to go home without him. I was hysterical. Mom was upset too, but not as upset. I told her we should call the police, that something terrible must have happened to him. She said if something happened to him it was his "own damn fault." I was so mad at her. How could she blame my perfect dad for getting kidnapped? Or worse?

She kept me in the dark about Aunt Jen too. I didn't know they were a couple until I was twelve. I just thought they were sharing a bed to save money. Then I walked in on them kissing. When she talked to me about it later, all she said was, "I love your Aunt Jen very much, and she loves me." The rest I had to figure out on my own.

I'm sure it was hard for her. She felt guilty she hadn't provided me with a more stable dad. And then she went and fell in love with his sister. But she should have at least *tried* to explain—

I hear Aunt Jen drive up out front. Great. I haul myself up and head inside. I need to explain Ari being here.

Aunt Jen looks tired but wired and doesn't seem the least bit fazed that Ari is spending the night. "*Brady Bunch*, huh?"

Ari clicks off the TV and sits up. He's unsure of Aunt Jen. "It was just something to do," he says, "while we sorted pictures."

Aunt Jen grabs Mom's meditation BackJack and settles onto the floor, her legs stretched out in front of her. "Sorting photos?" She picks up the *Fourth of July Fun!* photo. "I remember this."

I toss Ari's dirty socks off the couch and sit next to him. "Yeah. I was afraid of the fireworks so we watched them from a remote spot on the river."

Aunt Jen lifts an eyebrow. "Who told you that?"

"Mom."

Aunt Jen purses her lips.

"What? I wasn't?"

"Well, maybe you were, but that's not why we were on the river. Maye called me because she'd prepared this beautiful picnic, and your dad was having one of his...spells. She wanted some adult company."

Ari looks up from the photo. "Spells?"

I mime guzzling a bottle for Ari's benefit.

"Not that night," Aunt Jen says. "He was anxious. And didn't want to be in a crowd. He was like that sometimes."

"Then why's he in the picture?" I ask a tad defensively.

"She talked him into it. But at that point I was already there, and it was too late to make it to the park, so we wound up pulling over by the river. It was totally random that we wound up being able to see the fireworks from there. We talked some wino into taking this picture. Gave him a dollar."

*Fourth of July Fun!* Right. "Is the part about me calling the reflections of the fireworks magical water bugs bullshit too?"

She laughs. "Nope. That's true. You had us all in stitches."

I scooch down so my head rests on the back of the couch. I'm so sick of this Rashomon childhood. Why can't they keep their stories straight?

Ari clears his throat, therapist-like. "So you haven't always hated your brother?"

My eyes flick to Aunt Jen.

She squirms. "I wouldn't say I hate him." She places the picture in the wrong pile. "I'd say we have a history of getting along and then not."

A history? News to me.

*

Jen wandered the aisles of the A&P putting off going home. She was saving money by not having to move into the college dorms, but it wasn't worth it. Her mom, pretty stable the last few years, was getting weird again. The recent possibility that the church might lose its lease had her agitated. On several occasions when Jen got home from class, she found the cross hung on the front doorknob and her mom sitting inside with the curtains drawn. Ernest didn't come around as often either. For Jen, this was a blessing. His growing obsession with the devil and fires of hell creeped her out, but her mom was unhinged by his absence. She'd set an extra place at the table in case he came by; then when he didn't, she'd snatch the plate up, muttering to herself about the food being undercooked or too spicy, like it was her cooking that kept him away.

And Jake had moved out, or more like, he'd stopped coming home. It was a gradual process. He'd stay out a night here and there, then pretty soon be gone for weeks at a time. When Jen would ask where he'd been, he'd just shrug and say, "A friend's." Their mom never asked.

Jen missed him. It was almost a year since she'd seen him last. On one of his infrequent calls, he gave her a number to reach him, but when she tried using it the guy who answered said Jake had moved out, adding, "If you find him, call me. He owes me money." And there was the incident of the abandoned wrecked motorcycle. A cop had shown up at the house saying the bike, registered to Jake, was left in the gully by the side of the road for almost a week. Their mom wound up having to pay to have it hauled off. It was a worry.

Jen turned down the aisle of canned foods. Maybe if she got another job she could afford to move out. She'd almost saved up enough to get a place, but wasn't sure she could afford it on top of her school loan. Plus, looking for a place took time, something she had precious little of between going to classes and working the desk at the podiatrist's.

Canned ravioli was on sale. She put six in her cart. So was chicken noodle soup. Six of those too.

"Stocking up the bomb shelter?"

Jen whipped around to see Jake in a Phillies T-shirt and jeans. He looked so good, his collar-length hair tousled, his face tanned and healthy. Without a thought she threw her arms around him. "Jake."

He hugged her back. "Ah, sis," he said as they held each other. "It's good to see you too."

Once they released each other, she showered him with questions. "Where are you living? What have you been doing? Are you working? Going to school?"

He laughed. "You got time for a cup of tea?"

"Tea?"

"Yeah, I know this great little teahouse. So you got time?"

She didn't, not if she was going to write that paper. "You bet."

They left their baskets right there, full of groceries, and headed out to the street.

"It's so unusual that I was even shopping at this A&P," she blathered, "but I had a doctor's appointment, so it brought me out here."

His face filled with worry. "Everything okay?"

She took his arm. "Haven't gone nuts yet, if that's what you're asking."

He laughed.

"Seriously," she said. "It was just a checkup. I'm fine."

They wound up at a hole-in-the-wall called Sun's House of Tea. "Not much to look at," he said. "But Sun brews an oolong that'll knock your socks off."

Jen followed him into the tiny shop. This new tea-drinking Jake was intriguing.

"Ah. Jake. So early," a spry old man said. His face, Jen thought, looked like a peach pit.

The walls of the teahouse were covered in fine decorative teak and brightly painted masks. Big droopy plants hung by the window; an ornate screen filtered out most of the light. There were only two small round tables in the tiny room; both were empty. Jake motioned for Jen to sit at the one closer to the counter where shelves full of big jars of tea lined the wall. The counter was beautiful with scrolled and inlaid woodwork.

"Sun, this is my sister, Jen. Jen, my friend and landlord, Sun."

Sun clapped his gnarled hands together. "Your sister. You have not spoken of her before."

Jake smiled awkwardly at Jen. "We haven't seen each other in a while."

"Then this is a special occasion," Sun said. "Calls for litchi nuts and candied coconuts."

Jake started to protest. "Sun—"

Sun lifted his hand to silence him then directed his focus to Jen. "Your brother is most willful. Like ox."

Jen laughed. "We're both kind of like that."

"We're twins," Jake said.

Sun laughed. "Jake, you dog. You never told me you were a twin."

"Well, I—"

"No matter. I will brew you a smoky oolong on this fortunate afternoon." He retreated behind the counter shaking his head. "Twins. He never tells me this."

Jake and Jen spoke in hushed tones so as not to be overheard, for it was clear that Sun was doing his best to listen in.

"He's your landlord?" Jen whispered.

"I live upstairs. An apartment."

Jen was having difficulty figuring out how to phrase the questions that were buzzing around in her head. *What made you change? What in your life brought you here?* "Are you working?" she finally asked.

"Yeah. Road construction. It's just temporary, but it pays well. And I like being outside. What are you doing?"

"In school. Studying history with a minor in theater."

"Good for you. Still living—"

"At home, yeah."

"You don't look too happy about it."

Jen realized she still had her purse over her shoulder and dropped it on the floor. The back of her throat felt tight. "I just can't figure out how to move. And Mom…"

"How is Evelyn?"

"Not great."

Jake folded his arms. "And Ernest?"

"Still around, but not as much." Her stomach was beginning to knot up. She twisted the turquoise ring on her right middle finger round and round. "Why did you stop calling?"

He closed his eyes and inhaled through his nostrils as if summoning the strength to speak. "I don't know," he said. "I just couldn't."

She tried not to feel hurt. "I worried. Especially when they found your motorcycle—"

"Oh that. Yeah. That was stupid."

She nodded, not because it was stupid, but because she sensed he was beyond that kind of action now. He'd changed. But what had caused the change? She was about to ask when Sun approached their table with a teapot and two small cups.

"Let steep," he said to Jen. "Will be no good if you rush."

Jen couldn't get it out of her mind that Sun wasn't talking about the tea but about her desire to barrage Jake with questions. "Thank you."

Sun dipped his head slightly and once again retreated behind the counter, returning moments later with a small plate of litchi nuts and colorful strips of candied coconut. "On the house," he said.

Jake lifted an eyebrow and waited for Sun to go back behind the counter. "He must think you're pretty special. He never gives anything away."

Jen placed a strip of coconut on her tongue and sucked its sweetness. It was good to see Jake. "So what do you do exactly, when you're working on a road?"

Jake poured a bit of tea into his cup, looked at it, and decided it wasn't ready. "Most days I'm just directing traffic. But I like the guys I work with. Some of them have been laying roads for years."

"It must feel good to be financially independent."

"Heaven."

"I work part-time at a podiatrist," she said. "Mostly I fill out insurance forms and sweep up toenails. I've taken out a loan to go to school, but I also got some financial assistance."

"You always did get the good grades." He checked the tea again, this time deciding it was ready. He poured them each a cup. "You're kidding about the toenails, right?"

"Nope."

He shivered in disgust.

"Mostly old lady toenails."

"Stop."

She took a sip of her tea and could feel the edges of her smile peeking out on either side of the cup. "I envy you."

"Why?"

"You moved out."

"You could too."

"But—"

"But nothing. You could. You just have to do it."

She pulled her long braid over her shoulder and across her chest like a sash. "Every time I think about moving, it makes me tired."

"You need something to jolt you into it."

"Yeah, right."

"That's what did it for me. Well, not the moving thing. I was pretty unconscious when I did that. But I spent a night in jail, and it was the best thing that ever happened to me. It jolted me out of being an asshole."

She glanced briefly at Sun. He was polishing a figurine. "You were in jail?"

"For a night. They picked me up for being drunk and, like a jerk, I mouthed off to the officer." He chuckled. "Then again, you probably won't have to take the same path as me. Stuff always comes to you on a silver platter."

"Bullshit," she said, using the word for the first time ever. "It was no different for me than you. In fact, you had it better. Ernest was always taking you on those little trips. You never had to go to church." Jake began to fidget, but Jen couldn't stop herself. If they were going to be close again, it had to be based on the truth. "You got away with being irresponsible, and you were expected to be willful." She plucked a strip of pink coconut off the plate and let it dangle like a worm. "All because you were a boy."

Jake gripped his cup of tea, his eyes lowered. "Let's just drop it."

Jen placed the coconut stripe on her tongue. It wasn't as sweet as she'd expected. She poured herself another cup of tea. She hadn't meant to sound so confrontational. "Sorry. I guess I'm jealous."

Jake pulled out his wallet to pay the bill.

"Here, let me get that."

"No. I invited you."

Jen didn't want to leave on this awkward note. Why had she lashed out that way? "Could I see your apartment?"

Jake looked at her dubiously. "You want to?"

"Yeah. Maybe it'll motivate me to get my act together."

"She could help you with curtains," Sun said from behind the counter.

Jake laughed at Sun's obvious eavesdropping. "I told you I'd figure something out."

Sun shook his finger. "Better sleeping with curtains. More restful." He looked directly at Jen. "Your brother has no good sleep. I hear him walking in the night."

Jake dropped a few bucks on the table and stood to go. "Thanks for the treats."

Once they were outside, Jake said, "He's been on me about those curtains since I moved in. I keep telling him he's the landlord, that should be his job."

"He seems to care for you."

Jake pulled his keys from his pocket. "So don't get your hopes up. It's pretty much one room."

"More than I've got," she said. But following him up the dingy stairwell, she worried about what kind of place it was going to be. The hallway hadn't been painted in years, and the steps were worn and creaky.

The apartment turned out to be light and airy, and the few pieces of furniture were clean and well placed. A bed was on one side with a small kitchenette on the other. A round table with two chairs stood by the window.

"This is great," she said.

Jake opened the window and put a stick in to hold it up. "Thanks."

Jen walked over to the fridge where a few pictures were stuck on with magnets. It touched her to see one of them as kids. They were standing next to the entrance of the zoo. There was also a photo of Jake with his arm around an attractive woman she didn't recognize. "Who's this?"

Jake sat on the edge of his bed and kicked off his shoes. "Tina. We've been seeing each other on and off for a few months."

"I guess it's on now if her picture's on the fridge."

"Yeah, I guess. Come to think of it, she's moving out of the communal house where she lives in Mt. Airy. You want the number so you can check it out? It's kind of far from the Temple campus, but the rent is super cheap. And it's a cool house. All women."

The thought of moving out was both thrilling and daunting. Who would protect their mom if she had one of her spells? Then again, Jen wasn't expected to live at home forever, was she? She wasn't home that much anyway. And their mom had her church friends. And Ernest…when he was around. There was also the location to think about. Mt. Airy was kind of far from Temple University, but she could always transfer to their Ambler campus. "Sure, give me the number."

Jake reached for an address book on his end table and neatly wrote the number on a slip of paper. "It's worth checking out."

Jen took the paper and was oddly reassured to see his handwriting hadn't changed. She folded the paper and slipped it into her purse.

"Make sure you tell them you're my sister," he said.

Jen tackled him on the bed. *I have a brother again.*

The clock chimes eleven. Ari, blanket wrapped around him like a cape, parades back into the living room with a big glass of milk. "If I had a twin, I'd think it was the raddest thing in the world."

Aunt Jen pulls a thread from the fraying carpet and it turns out to be one of those that will unravel forever. "Sometimes life gets complicated." She digs a pocketknife from her pocket to clip the thread.

"Like when you both sleep with the same person?" Ari says.

I can't believe Ari just said this! Neither can Aunt Jen. She glowers at me briefly, like it's my fault, then clears her throat to say,

"Certainly, that's been a factor. And now if you don't mind, I think I'll head off to bed. Bean, you want me to wake you in the morning? I told Jake you'd take over around eight."

"No need. I'll just get up and go. Uh, can I borrow your car?"

"Actually, I have some errands to run. I'll drive you."

So much for a nice meditative morning drive down the mountain. "Okay. I'll be ready by six forty-five."

She heads to the guestroom. I glare at Ari.

"What?" he says.

I'm too tired to get into it and heave myself up off the floor. "I'm going to bed too."

On my way up the stairs, I hear *The Brady Bunch* click back on. "Dude. Turn it down."

"O*kay*," he says using a tone only a teenager can get away with.

## Chapter Thirteen

Being back at the hospital is depressing. I hate the vaguely Southwestern artwork that decorates the main lobby with its gift shop full of get-well teddy bears. I hate the maze of hallways devoid of sunlight and fresh air. I hate the smell of illness and disinfectants. How are people supposed to heal in a place like this?

I told Aunt Jen just to drop me off, but of course she wanted to say hi to Mom, so the two of us are trooping through the sterile hallways together. When we get to the ICU, I'm relieved to see that Samantha is on duty. Her genuine smile and kind eyes are a welcome contrast to the mind-numbing beige, light salmon, and milky green décor.

"How's she doing?" I ask.

She wiggles her clear-polished fingernails. "Still moving these."

Aunt Jen shuts down her phone. "Does that mean she's out of the woods?"

"You'll have to talk to Dr. Reneaux about that."

"Is my dad with her?"

"Jake? He's been here since I got here at five a.m. Says he stayed here all night." Just talking about Dad has got her pheromones humming. She briefly lowers her thick eyelashes. "He's one loyal guy."

Disgruntled, Aunt Jen gestures toward Mom's room. "Can we? We're changing the guard."

"Sure. But if she's sleeping, don't wake her. Rest is a real healer."

We head down the over-lit hallway, passing various hospital personnel, including an attendant pushing a cart of gray oatmeal and rubbery-looking eggs. Mom's door is open. Dad, the chick magnet, is in the chair next to her with a cup of coffee in his hands. His eyes are closed. Mom's are closed too, but as soon as she hears us they snap open. Dad clears his throat and blinks a few times. "Hey, Bean," he says. "Jen." He looks at his watch. "Talk about punctual."

"I'm just dropping off Bean," Aunt Jen says. "But I thought I'd pop in and see how things are going." She leans over Mom and places her hand on her cheek. "How're you feeling, Maye?"

Mom rolls her eyes. She's losing patience.

"You just missed Dr. Reneaux," Dad says. "She seems pleased. Says it's a good sign that Maye's still moving her fingers."

"Great," Aunt Jen says. "Maye, you're going to be up dancing in no time."

Mom gives her a skeptical look, but wiggles her fingers just the same.

"Ari sends his love," I say. "He spent the night. His parents were having one of their barbeques."

This gets a smile out of Mom's eyes. She loves Ari.

I glance at Dad and Aunt Jen. They're showing no signs of leaving. Which is ultra annoying. *I* didn't invade on *their* time.

Mom's eyes flick to the board.

Aunt Jen picks it up. "What is it, Maye?"

I squelch the urge to snatch the board from Aunt Jen.

Aunt Jen begins sliding her finger along the board until Mom blinks. The first letter we get is B, the second and third are EA.

"Me?" I say.

She blinks once. Yes.

The next word we get is NO followed by STAY.

BEAN NO STAY.

What? She doesn't want me to stay? "But it's my turn," I say sounding, even to myself, like a four-year-old.

"You don't want her to stay," Aunt Jen repeats, like maybe Dad and I don't have the intelligence to comprehend Mom's meaning. "Is that what you're saying, Maye?"

Mom blinks once.

"I get what she's saying," I say testily. "I just don't see why." And if the two of you would butt out and let me have some time alone with her I could figure it out.

I step up to the side of the bed. "If you want to rest, that's fine. I'll hang in the waiting room. I brought my iPod and the new Sarah Waters."

Her eyes blaze with meaning. What meaning I have no idea. Obviously something she can't, or won't, use the board for. She laser-beams this next thought into my head: *Make them talk. My life depends on it.*

I take a deep breath and remind myself that I'm a product of her mess, not the cause. I try to laser-beam back to her: *Stop worrying about the Bell twins and start healing.*

"Maye," Aunt Jen says. "You need someone here."

At least someone's on my side, even if she is clueless.

Mom blinks twice, no, then makes it clear she wants to spell out more words. Aunt Jen raises the board and begins.

NEED REST, they spell.

Dad, trying to respect her wishes, takes a last swig of coffee, crumples his paper cup, and tosses it into the trashcan, but I can tell he doesn't want to leave her alone either.

Aunt Jen, unwavering in her need to be Mom's protector, leans in so Mom can see her. "Maye, are you all right?"

"What kind of question is that?" Dad asks. "Of course she's not all right. She's living a nightmare."

"That's not what I was saying, Jake, and you know it."

"That's what you *said.*"

"Are you *deaf* to *inflection*?"

"No, I'm not *deaf* to *inflection*. But you're butting in where it's not needed."

"There's something she's not telling us."

"Yes. There is," I say before I have the intelligence to censor myself.

I instantly regret my words, but there's no retracting them now. I stepped right into it. I consider my options. I could simply walk out of the room, leaving them to ponder my obscurity. I could lie and say that I just wanted them to stop fighting. Or I could tell the truth.

Such a foreign concept to us Bells. Truth.

Even as Mom lies there—believing she's responsible for splitting up the once inseparable Bell twins—she can't speak it. Paralysis is apparently easier to deal with than truth.

I'm going to have to speak it for her.

"Mom thinks…" I begin then realize if I'm going to do this, I should do it all the way. "No. Mom *wants* you two to start getting along." I decide to go for the gold. "And she wants Dad to fess up to whatever secret he's hanging on to about Bates."

Aunt Jen is totally taken aback. "Secret? What secret?"

Dad's face is scarlet. But is it an angry scarlet or an embarrassed scarlet? Before I have a chance to find out, he charges out the door.

Shit! What have I done? "I'm so sorry, Mom, so sorry," I blubber, my mind wrestling with the question, should I go after him?

She answers with a flick of her eyes toward the door: *Find him.*

I bolt out to the hall. It's empty. I race past the nurses' station. Samantha, on the phone, lifts a concerned eyebrow. I ignore her and jog down the hall, then another and another. Dad has disappeared. I head out to the parking lot. I have no idea where he parked.

What did I have to open my stupid mouth for? Things are worse now than ever.

Eyes burning, I scan the main lobby and the gift shop, then head back toward Mom's room, glancing down each hallway I cross.

I find Aunt Jen in the waiting room of the ICU, her expression blank. She stands when she sees me. "Did you talk to him?"

"I couldn't find him."

She glances past me as if maybe she should go look.

"Why aren't you with Mom?"

"Nurse Nice kicked me out. She thinks we're upsetting Mom."

"Nurse Nice?"

"Samantha."

I notice Cell Phone Dude is back, only he's not on his cell phone. He's reading a *Sports Illustrated*. I turn my back to him.

"I totally screwed up, didn't I?"

Aunt Jen puts her hands on my shoulders. "Bean, I have no idea what this is about. All I know is your Mom wants the three of us to spend some time together, so I think we should go find Jake."

A ten-ton sandbag of despair presses down on my chest. Mom thinks we're the ones making her sick. "I don't know where he is."

"Then we should head back to the house. Sooner or later, he's bound to show."

"But what about Mom?"

"I made Nurse Nice promise to call if anything changes." She picks up her bag and starts walking. "I could kill Jake for this little stunt."

It shocks me that she's blaming him. I'm the one who opened my stupid mouth. Still, I don't rush to his defense, just tag along behind her. "Why are you calling her Nurse Nice?"

"Because she's too nice. I don't trust women who are that nice."

"Maybe she really is nice. It's possible, you know. There are nice people in the world."

She strides out of the building. "She kicked us out, Bean."

"I know, but…" I scan the parking lot for the rental eggplant; the lot is huge. "We were kind of…"

Ignoring me, she pulls out her phone and dials. I listen as she leaves Dad a message. "Jake, call me."

Way to be warm and fuzzy, I think to myself, but there's no way I'm saying what I think anymore. Or ever.

I slide into the passenger seat of Aunt Jen's Subaru. She gets into the driver's side, sticks the key into the ignition, and twists it. The engine rumbles but doesn't start. "Shit," she says. After a few more tries, she calls AAA.

The guy who shows up in the tow truck motor-mouths the whole way about how lucky he is to have a job, how he used to work in computers only he got laid off.

I want to deck him.

He tows us to Ernie's Garage where we find out the timing belt is broken and it's going to take at least forty-eight hours before Ernie can get to it. I try calling Dad again, this time leaving a message about Aunt Jen's car and could he please come pick us up.

Aunt Jen asks Ernie if there's a café nearby. He says there's a doughnut shop a few blocks away. My phone rings. It's Dad. He's on his way. I hang up. Aunt Jen asks, "How close is he?"

"I didn't ask."

"If he was on his way back to Maye's, it could be a while. Maybe we should head over to the doughnut shop."

"I'm not calling him again."

We settle into the white plastic deck chairs of the cramped garage waiting room. I pick up a greasy copy of *Popular Mechanics*.

"Bean, this is not your fault."

I glare at her.

"It has nothing to do with what happened in the hospital room."

I glare some more.

"And my car breaking down is an act of God. It has nothing to do with any of this."

Act of Mom, is more like it. She's finally getting what she wants—the three of us being forced to deal with one another.

Dad pulls up but doesn't shut off the motor. Aunt Jen says thanks to Ernie and follows me out. We vie for the backseat. I get there first.

The ride up the mountain is excruciating. All I can think about is how horrified Mom looked when I said what I said. I stare at the back of Aunt Jen's and Dad's heads. The space between them is pulsing with tension, yet neither one of them says a word. I almost tell Dad to pull over and let me out so I can hitch my way back to the hospital, but the inertia of my depression is too strong. I grab my iPod and tune in to Nona Hendryx. I'm lost in the Bermuda Triangle of my family; there's no way out.

\*

Jake lay curled in a quilt on his bed in the middle of the afternoon. There was no getting the temperature right in his apartment. His landlord Sun controlled the thermostat from downstairs and always had it turned to high. The night before, after getting home late, Jake had opened his windows to cool the apartment then fallen asleep. Now it was freezing.

He stared at the picture of his girlfriend Tina on his fridge. Should he remove it? They'd broken up. Again. Jake pulled the pillow over his head remembering what had sparked the fight. He kicked off her teacup poodle Minki when she started humping his socked foot. It was a reflex; he hadn't even realized it was Minki. But Tina went ballistic, and from there things escalated into the usual— Jake wasn't sensitive, a good communicator, and, most importantly, committed. At midnight, he stormed out of her place.

Now, lying on his bed, he tried to figure out why he was always being blamed for not being committed when she was the one who always broke things off. She'd call before the day was over; he was sure of that. She'd be full of remorse and wanting to try again. He'd counter, saying maybe she was right, maybe they did need some space, then she'd get silent and broody and he'd worry that she might cut herself like she had that one time.

He thought of her poetry, what had attracted him in the first place. He'd read an anthology with several of her poems in it. They were marvelous. He attended a reading. *She* was marvelous, reading with such passion, such intensity. Jake loved words. They were to him like roads, each string of them leading you in new directions. And Tina was a master. Her words filled the mundane with depth. She could make you choke up over a simple set of keys abandoned on an entry table. One of her poems, about a man choosing to stand alone on a subway car when all the seats around him were empty, had rattled Jake so profoundly it had disturbed his sleep for a whole week.

Jake groaned into his pillow. Wasn't love supposed to make things easier? He rolled off his bed, shut the window, and went to see what he could scrounge to eat. Half a hoagie (limp but still edible) sat on the middle shelf of the fridge. He plopped it on a plate, poured himself a glass of milk, and returned to bed with it.

The phone rang.

He thought about not picking up, then did.

"I'm sick of studying," Jen whined. "And all my roomies are doing is sitting around watching TV and waiting for the storm—hang on. What? Dawn says she's not watching TV, she's doing a sociological study of the enemy."

Jake laughed. "Tell Dawn I said hi."

"Jake says hi," she yelled to her friend, then returned to Jake. "Anyway, I need to get the hell out of here, take a walk or something."

"And you're calling me why?"

"I'm going to hike out by Wissahickon Creek, and just in case the storm swallows me up, I thought you'd want a last chance to say you love me."

It hadn't even been a year since Jen had moved away from home, but she'd changed so much. She laughed more easily and spoke with newfound confidence.

"Then again, you could offer to join me," she said. "That way you won't feel guilty when they find me next spring frozen beneath a snowdrift."

Jake looked out the window at the white sky.

"Come on. We've still got plenty of time."

He pulled a wilted piece of lettuce from his hoagie. Hiking in Fairmount Park beat the hell out of hanging around waiting for Tina's call. "Pick me up at the train station," he said. "I'll take the twelve twenty-five."

Jen met him at the Carpenter Street station in her beat-up silver Camaro. From there they drove to the creek, parked the car by the historic Valley Green Inn with its smoke spiraling from both chimneys, and walked past it to the trail by the gushing water. Icicles hung from the huge slabs of Wissahickon schist making the rocks sparkle more than usual. Jen broke off an icicle from a ledge and sucked it like a Popsicle, occasionally biting off bits to melt in her mouth. Jake tried not to watch. It made him shiver, even if she was wearing mittens.

"You know what I think," she said.

"That I should dump her."

"It just seems like she's the one who gets to make all the rules."

"This coming from someone whose relationships never last past a few dates."

"You asked."

"I did not."

Jen chuckled. "You should have. Who has your best interests at heart more than me?"

They hiked about a half-mile farther, sometimes in silence, sometimes speaking their thoughts, then they stopped to toss a few rocks into the churning water. The pools that were once soft and green with algae were now covered in spidery ice.

Jake looked at the darkening sky and rewrapped his scarf around his neck to seal out the blustery air. "Maybe we should turn back."

"But it's so nice to have the place to ourselves." Bundled in her pea coat, her turtleneck sweater pulled up over her chin, Jen begged him with her eyes.

Jake sighed. "Okay. If you're up for it, I am."

"What do you say we go for the Indian?"

"Now I know you're nuts."

"Come on," she said, climbing up the shallow embankment to the path.

Before long, they were scrambling up the steep trail to the giant white marble Indian, a popular destination honoring the Lenape tribe that once hunted and fished the area. Jen lodged her hiking boot against an exposed root and used a branch to pull herself up the steep path. Jake used the same branch to pull himself up.

"So what about you?" he asked. "You seeing anyone?"

She looked over her shoulder. "Don't ask."

"I'm asking."

She turned and looked right at him. "I've decided to stay single for the rest of my life."

"Right."

"I have. Now, let's get a move on. We've got to touch the Indian before turning back."

Jake left the narrow trial, crunching through piles of frozen leaves and forest debris to pass her. "Last one up buys dinner!"

Jen stopped. "Oh my God."

Jake spun around. "What?"

"I think it's an owl."

Jake returned to the trail. Sure enough, huddled by a log in a pile of crispy leaves, was a lump of feathers with feet and a beak.

Jen knelt down. "It's hurt."

Jake knelt next to her. There was sticky looking black stuff on the owl's back. "Blood."

"We need to get it help."

"Jen…"

"I'm serious."

"It's barely breathing. Just let it die in peace."

"We don't know for sure that it's going to die."

A big flat snowflake landed on Jake's jacket. He stood. "We should go."

Jen pulled off her pea coat and wrapped the limp owl in it. "We need to find a ranger."

Jake kicked at a pile of dead leaves.

"I'm not leaving it here, Jake."

The downhill path was slippery now that the snow was starting to pick up. Jake worried about Jen getting cold. "Aren't you freezing?"

"I'm fine," she said trudging forward.

"Come on. At least take my coat."

"What, and have *you* freeze to death over an owl you don't even care about?"

"I didn't say I didn't care about it. I said we should let it die peacefully."

When they reached the flat part of the path, Jen was shivering. "Just take my coat, for God's sake. We can switch back later." Jen turned to face him. "Would it ease your conscience?" "Yeah. It would."

He gave her the coat to wear, meaning he had to hold the owl while she put it on. The owl was lighter than he expected, and small. "It's young," he said, readjusting the pea coat to give the suffering owl more warmth. The only evidence that it was still even alive was its fluttering heart. "I wonder what happened to it?"

Jen slipped her hands underneath the coat-wrapped owl in his arms and took it from him. "It just seems young because it's hurt."

By the time they got back to the inn, the snow had changed from big fluffy flakes to swirls of small ones. Jen stood just inside the door while Jake asked the hostess at the restaurant if she knew how he could get in touch with a ranger. The hostess, focused on getting the customers served, paid up, and gone before the storm fully kicked in, let him use the phone and phone book, but told him to "take that mangy owl outside" when he was done. He called the SPCA. The guy who answered said they'd send a van.

Out on the porch, he and Jen settled onto a bench and watched the world get covered in white; she wearing his coat, the owl wearing hers, and he freezing his butt off. "You want your jacket back?" she asked. He said no and asked her how long she thought it would take the SPCA to arrive. "How should I know?" she said.

Jake was used to her getting snappish when she was upset so he asked her if she'd like a hot chocolate. She said she would. He went back inside and drained his wallet to buy them both a cup. The trip back was starting to worry him. The tires on Jen's car were bald.

He stepped back out into the cold. Jen was fussing with the owl. "It's panting," she said. "Like it can't get enough air."

"That's because it can't."

The SPCA van pulled into the parking lot and into an empty slot. A bundle of colorful winter garments with two legs and blond shoulder-length curls peeking from the sides of a pink and green knit hat stepped out. "You the ones with the owl?" the bundle called, puffing out little clouds as she spoke. As she trudged through the snow toward them, Jake made out rosy cheeks, sparkling eyes, and a feisty walk. He felt an immediate attraction.

"Yeah," he called back.

She took the steps up to the porch two at a time, her winter boots leaving tracks in the fresh snow behind her. "My name's Maye." One of her front teeth slightly overlapped the other, which Jake thought was cute.

Jake and Jen introduced themselves then Jen opened up the coat for Maye to see the owl. "It's wounded."

Maye pulled the coat back a bit to get a better look. "Hey, little fella. You don't look too good." She glanced at Jake. "Screech owl, a young one."

He shot a smug look at Jen. "I thought it looked young."

Jen wrapped the owl back up. "What do you think happened to it?"

"Hard to say, but we've had some slingshot incidents. I'll get a better look back at the shelter."

Jake was annoyed that the only thing he could think of to say was, "Slingshot. Wow."

"Well, let's get him to the van." Maye pressed her gloves against her cheeks for warmth. "This snow is coming down pretty hard, and I want to make sure I can get back. I've got someone cooking me dinner tonight. You all driving?"

Jake and Jen both nodded, Jake wondering who was lucky enough to be cooking her dinner.

"Well let's do it then," Maye said.

The three of them trekked to the van, Jen still holding the owl and Jake the two hot chocolates. The women spoke in gentle voices as they maneuvered the owl from coat to blanket and then into a small cage. It bothered Jake that the hot chocolates kept him from helping.

Maye slammed the van door and took Jen's mittened hand into her two gloved ones. "Thank you. A lot of people wouldn't have bothered. Especially in this weather." She reached for Jake's hand next. But he still had the damn hot chocolates. He thrust one forward.

"How about a hot chocolate for the ride?"

"Really?"

"Sure."

She took it from him, her glove brushing his, and smiled, revealing once again the slight overlap of the tooth. "That is so sweet." A snowflake landed on her eyelash and hung on when she blinked.

"Don't want you getting cold on the ride back," he said, feeling gallant.

"Speaking of cold," Jen said.

Jake wrenched his eyes from Maye's. Jen was peeling off his coat. "Here, take this. You're shivering."

Jen's observation embarrassed him, especially since, once she'd taken the coat off, she had to help him put it on due to the hot chocolate in his hand. "My sister," he said, not wanting Maye to misinterpret this bit of intimacy.

Jen shook her head. "Like she cares," she said then surveyed the damage to her pea coat.

Maye laughed, revealing dimples.

"Do you think it will make it?" Jake asked, trying to prolong their encounter. "The owl?"

Maye scrunched up her nose. "To be honest, he doesn't look too good."

Jake glanced at Jen. She was picking feathers off her jacket. Something was bothering her.

Maye set her hot chocolate on the dashboard of the van. "Call me tomorrow and I'll give you the scoop." She slipped off her glove to pull a card from her inside pocket. Her hand was small with neatly trimmed nails. "Use this number."

Still buttoning his jacket, Jake was about to take the card with his teeth when Jen took it instead.

Maye laughed again and Jake felt ridiculously happy.

"Thanks for the hot chocolate," she said. "That's the nicest thing that's happened to me today."

"No problem," he said.

As the van drove off, Jen scrutinized the card.

Jake plucked it from her grasp. "I'll call."

"Hey, *I'm* the one who found the owl."

"Yeah, but she was handing *me* the card."

Jen yanked his hat down over his eyes. "That was awfully nice of you to give her a hot chocolate." She took the remaining paper cup from him. "Guess we're going to have to share."

*

Aunt Jen and I sit on the deck watching Dad attempt to annihilate a stand of Scotch broom on the far side of the garden. He's going at it furiously, driving his shovel into the ground, using his boot to thrust it deep. He's sweating and cursing, or at least I assume he's cursing. It *looks* like he's cursing. For all I know, he's passionately reciting a grocery list. The slight breeze is blowing his words away from the house.

"Could he be any more pent up?" Aunt Jen asks.

While it does look like he's engaging in some primal Gestalt therapy, I can't get myself to poke fun at him. He really is struggling. "This has been pretty hard on all of us."

She grumbles something under her breath. I choose not to ask what. She rolls her neck, and lets out a long, low exhale. I know she wants me to bring up the whole secret thing, but I'm sick of playing mediator. Or should I say instigator.

She stretches out her tanned legs and waggles her boots.

I shut my eyes and turn my face to the sun.

"What's this thing Maye wants him to tell me?" she finally asks.

I open my eyes, take a slow sip of iced tea. "It's something he knows about Bates that you don't."

"Probably about Bates's affair with our mom. It really messed with his head."

I consider letting it drop then think of Mom and how much whatever this is seems to matter to her. "She blames herself that the two of you have grown so distant."

"Maye…" She sighs. "She's always thought she was the wedge between me and Jake. But he hated me long before she and I got together. He freaked when I came out as a lesbian."

We watch him wrestle with a root. He puts his whole body weight behind trying to yank it out.

"I guess I should go help," she says. "Maybe he'll talk to me."

"You going to be hungry anytime soon? There's a lot of lettuce in the garden and I found a can of tuna in the pantry. I could make a killer salad."

"Sounds good." She gets up and grabs a shovel. "Wish me luck."

I watch her walk out to him. Is this what you want, Mom? Is this going to make you better?

I pull my cell from my pocket and dial ICU. Some nurse I don't recognize picks up. I ask for Samantha. She puts me on hold, giving me plenty of time to dwell on how much I hate that she saw Dad storm from the hospital with me chasing after him like some pathetic little dog. She probably thinks we're all psycho.

"Samantha here."

"Samantha, it's Bean. How's Mom?"

There's a slight pause before she speaks. "She's starting to vocalize a little. No words yet, but she's trying."

Gratitude washes through me. "That's great."

"She's a tough one," she says. "She's really fighting this thing. And now, if there's nothing else you need, I've got other patients to attend to."

"Yeah, sure. And, uh, thanks."

I hang up the phone and am about to call out the good news to Aunt Jen and Dad when Aunt Jen yells, "Bean! Come here!" She's beckoning wildly.

My stomach tightens. What now? I stow my phone and start trotting over.

"We found a skull," Aunt Jen calls out.

You've got to be kidding me. That's what all the drama is about? "I've found a lot of those around here," I say, stepping around Dad's pile of branches. "Mostly rodents and other small critters, but I found a coyote once too."

Dad, his face pale, points to the spot where they've been digging. "It's human."

I look down. There's half a skull poking out of the dirt. It's got mud stuck to it and is partially eroded, but there's no mistaking what it is.

My first impulse is to laugh. Not because finding a skull is funny, but because this is so Bell. Here my dad and Aunt Jen are finally on the verge of dealing with whatever this secret is between them, and instead they dig up a fucking skull.

I kneel down to get a closer look.

"Don't touch it," Aunt Jen says.

"She's right," Dad says. "It's a crime scene, now."

They sound urgent as they issue these warnings, but I know deep inside they're both thrilled to have an excuse not to talk to each other.

## CHAPTER FOURTEEN

I'm sitting on the deck watching the sheriff and a bunch of other official-looking people crawling around taking pictures, talking into hand-held recorders, scrawling notes in their flipbooks, and forming little discussion huddles. They've got the area cordoned off with crime scene tape. One jerk is trampling Mom's oregano.

Dad's raking the gravel paths between the back raised beds. Not because it needs it; he wants the police to know he's watching. He reminds me of a janitor casting a suspicious eye over a group of after school punks.

I walk over and ask if I can take the rental down to see Mom.

"How long are you going to be?"

"I was thinking of spending the night."

He pries his eyes from the action to scrutinize me. "Maye said she wants to be left alone."

I cross my arms, realizing too late how defensive it makes me appear. "She wanted us to be together so we could bond, but now, with this"—I gesture at the police—"I don't think that's going to happen. A least not for a while." What's more, I could use the hour drive to clear my head. But I don't tell him this.

"Fair enough." He glances at the cops. "But check with Jen before you take the car, just in case she needs it for something. Otherwise, we'll expect you back in the morning. Or sooner."

One down.

I locate Aunt Jen on the front porch. She's talking on her cell phone, pacing back and forth and on complete overload. It's opening night at the theater and there's some crisis. From what I gather, the sound system has gone kaput, the sound designer is unreachable, and she's trying to talk the stage manager through the process of hooking a new CD player up to the soundboard. She gestures she'll be just another minute.

I saunter out to the flowerbed where Mrs. Simpkins is crouched warily beneath the Cosmos. "Everything is going to be fine," I say, giving her a scratch, but she's no dummy.

Aunt Jen comes up behind us. "You wanted me?"

"Yeah. If it's okay with you, I'm going to take the rental car and spend the night with Mom."

A flash of panic crosses her face. "So we'll be without a car until tomorrow?"

"Yeah. Did you need to go somewhere?"

"I might. Why don't I drive you?"

No Internet access is killing her. "You know, some people go for days on end without checking their e-mail."

She laughs. "Some people aren't trying to open a show from three hundred miles away. My new box office volunteer lost the reservation list. If I don't e-mail it to her, tonight will be chaos." She blows air through her lips. "Give me ten minutes and I'll be ready."

"Okay, but I'm driving."

She looks taken aback. "Fine."

❖

At the hospital, Todd, a young physical therapist, who could easily be Richard Simmons's twin, is manipulating Mom's legs, lifting them up and down and bending them at the knee. "Lift. Lift. Lift," he says with high-pitched enthusiasm. I stand in the doorway unsure if we should enter. Aunt Jen walks right in.

Mom's eyes are squinting in agony. Aunt Jen looks like she wants to deck Todd.

I go to my spot by the window. Dr. Reneaux told us that physical contact would be extremely painful for Mom, but I wasn't ready for this. It's excruciating.

I soften my gaze into a blurry stare. Maybe I could slip out and call Serena? Then again, I've called her twice. She should call me next.

"It won't be long before they'll be moving you out of ICU." Todd punches the "you" and "U" like a cheerleader. He picks up Mom's chart and makes some notes. "She's making great progress. A real can-do gal."

Aunt Jen and I wince at his wink, but at least it's followed by his departure.

I take his place next to Mom's bed. "You okay?"

She flicks her eyes downward toward her hand. It moves a few inches across the bed.

"Wow," Aunt Jen says. "That's great."

Mom inhales deeply then utters, "Ai eeee ooo." Her eye movement clues us in to her meaning—my feet too. Which she moves, ever so slightly.

"Way to go, Mom. You're on the mend."

She attempts to smile, but it's not much more that a stretch of the lips.

Neither one of us tells her about the skull. I'm sure Aunt Jen's thinking what I am: no need to worry her. But it's hard to think of other things to talk about. Aunt Jen tells her about the drama happening with her opening night; I give her an update on the garden. "The salad I made was awesome. The butter lettuce is so velvety and crisp. Oh, and the parsley is getting ready to bolt so I was thinking about pulling it and putting in some new."

We fall into a comfortable silence. Mom closes her eyes, Aunt Jen pulls out her phone to check for messages, while I let myself drift to the past when, like now, it was just the three of us, and there was no need for talking. It's one from my collection of Perfect Family memories. I covet them like jewels, each one precious because it's so deliciously mundane.

*I was on the floor of the living room working on a paper about the Chinese Revolution.* Mom was on the papasan chair altering a vintage dress she'd picked up at the thrift store, and Aunt Jen was stretched out on the couch reading a technical journal. I was in tenth grade. Christmas was just three weeks away. We had a fire going in the wood burner.

"How about some popcorn?" Aunt Jen said.

Mom looked up from her sewing. "Yum."

"Bean?"

"Sure."

Aunt Jen swung her legs off the couch and padded into the kitchen. She was wearing sweats, big wool socks, and her hair was in two long braids, Indian style.

Popcorn was a favorite at our house. Our method for making it was to put the kernels in a paper bag with just a splash of olive oil and a dash of Lawry's Seasoned Salt then throw it in the microwave. I listened as Aunt Jen went through these familiar steps. I noticed the fire was getting low and crawled over to add another log.

"Thanks," Mom said without looking.

I crawled back to my spot and opened the biography of Mao Tse-tung to check a quote, the sound of mini corn explosions in the background.

Aunt Jen returned with three small bowls of popcorn. She put one on the couch, one next to me on the floor, and one on the windowsill by Mom. When she started back to the couch, Mom grabbed the hem of her sweatshirt.

Aunt Jen turned to face her. "What?"

"Nothing," Mom said. "Just want to look at you."

From the corner of my eye, I could see the two of them gazing at each other for a couple of seconds. Then Aunt Jen bent to kiss her on the forehead and returned to the couch to read.

*I finished the paper to the sound of popcorn being munched, pages being turned, the occasional sigh.*

These are the memories I cherish the most, the ones where we acted like a normal family, where the love didn't need to be spoken. It was just there.

I look at Mom whose eyes are now open. "You doing okay?"

She blinks Yes, then No, then Yes, which I take to mean, "Hell no, but I'm doing the best I can."

I pick up the *People* magazine I nabbed from the waiting room. "Want to hear about the saucy lives of the stars?"

She blinks a definitive Yes. Anything to get her mind off her current situation.

Aunt Jen flips her phone shut. "Sounds like my cue to go find a latte." She bends to hug Mom then me. "Call if you need anything."

"Will do."

I open the magazine and find an article about Holly Hunter, one of Mom's favorites. As I read, she practices moving her fingers and toes.

It's two a.m. Mom and I are both awake. I've pulled in a second chair to prop up my feet, but it's damned uncomfortable. Mom looks anxious. Being trapped in her head must be horrible. I can't imagine how I'd be with all my diversions taken away. I'd probably go insane.

I shut the door and pull out my harmonica. Mom looks grateful. It's difficult to play softly, but I manage. I start with "Amazing Grace." Mom closes her eyes. I draw out the song, trying to pour as much emotion into it as I can. If only love had the power to heal.

Maye sat wrapped in a beach towel, her hair dripping with seawater. The day was warm for late April, but hardly beach weather. Which was what made the day so wonderful. They had the beach to themselves.

It was the Bell twins' twenty-first birthday and Jen had convinced Jake to take the day off and drive to the Jersey Shore, a place their dad used to take them when they were kids. Then Jake had invited Maye. At first, she was reluctant to go, not wanting to interfere with brother and sister spending the day together, but he'd been so insistent she'd finally given in. Now she was glad she had.

She stretched out her legs to warm them in the sun. They'd chosen a spot set back from the ocean's edge with the dunes as a wind block, but every now and then a chilly gust would blow through. She was still a little buzzed from all the champagne—two whole bottles they drank—but it was a yummy buzzed.

She looked at Jake and Jen out in the water. They were laughing and splashing; they were even crazier than she was. It had been her idea to strip down to their undies and jump in the ocean, but she never thought for a second they'd actually go for it. People were always intimidated by her impulsiveness. Not Jake and Jen.

"A birthday baptism," Jen said, ripping off her sweater.

"A washing away of our sins," Jake said, unzipping his jeans.

Dipping their toes into the frigid water, Jen and Jake sang a hymn, mimicking some weird pastor they'd grown up around.

"And noow I baptize yooou," Jen said using a scary preacher voice, "into the Church of Redemption." She tried to dunk her brother, but he dodged out of the way.

"No way," he said, "You're getting baptized into *my* church—the Church of Frozen-assed Water!"

"Church of Mermaids!" she countered, going after him.

"Church of Swimming with the Fishies!"

Maye wiggled her toes in the warm sand and tipped her head back to let the sun thaw her face. She could barely believe she was going to be a Bell. She'd accepted Jake's proposal of marriage just two days before. They'd yet to tell Jen, but planned to do so today. Maye felt Jake should make the first move, and expected him to do it over their picnic—knishes, dill pickles, German chocolate cake, and champagne. But Jen had spent the whole meal entertaining them with stories of her crazy roommates. Jake laughed so hard champagne squirted out his nose, which got the two of them laughing about some incident with the weird pastor and "meatloafs in heaven."

It must be amazing to be a twin, she thought. Brought up an only child, Maye envied their closeness. But now she was going to be a part of it. She was almost as excited about having Jen as a sister-in-law as she was having Jake as a husband. She and Jen had been hanging out quite a bit since the owl. They went to the Philadelphia Art Museum, to several plays on campus. Jen loved light—in paintings, on stage, in nature. She'd point out interesting reflections in puddles, shadow patterns the sun made when it filtered through trees.

And sweet Jake. He was quieter than Jen, more introverted, but when they got to talking, he had the most amazing ideas about things. He could figure out how anything worked. It was like he could intuit a gadget's inner mechanism. And in bed he was so gentle and always made sure to please her.

Maye looked out to the water. Jen was heading back toward their enclave, a red and yellow towel billowing around her shoulders like a cape. Her underwear was plastered to her lean body. She was a handsome woman, long-legged and tall, her skin olive against the white of her bra and panties.

Jake was crouched over by the water's edge, his green towel wrapped around his waist. He was no doubt looking for treasures. He was always bringing her wonderful things he found on his walks. The ring he'd picked out for her was an antique—a basket ring he called it. The diamond wasn't large, but the filigree setting was exquisite and looked perfect on her hand. She couldn't wait until it was back from the jeweler's where it was being sized.

Jen, breathing heavily, strode up to their spot nestled into the dunes. She was sopping wet and dripped water on Maye's exposed legs. "You haven't showered yet."

"There's a shower?"

"Used to be. And it had hot water." Jen scooped up her clothes. "Come on."

Maye grabbed her clothes to follow, but when she stood she realized she was a bit more buzzed than she realized. She placed a hand on Jen's shoulder for balance. It felt ice cold beneath her warm palm.

"You okay?" Jen asked.

"Just a head rush." Embarrassed, Maye removed her hand. "Too much champagne, I guess."

"Well, the shower's just up here over the dune. Think you can make it?"

"I'll be fine. But won't Jake wonder where we are?"

"He'll know. We always used this shower when we were kids."

The shower turned out to be a cement room with a shower on one side and a bench with some hooks above it on the other. A skylight provided what little light there was.

"Pray," Jen said, turning the knob, "that it still works." A thin stream of water sputtered out. "Yes. Now let's hope it gets hot." Which it did. "After you, m'lady," Jen said, acting the humble servant.

Maye stripped off her cold, wet underwear and stepped into the stream of hot water. "Oh, this is glorious. Yum. Yum. Yum. Yum." She noticed Jen shivering by the bench. "Come on in; there's room for two."

Jen peeled off her panties and bra and stepped into the gush of hot water. Tall Jen with her long, wet, chestnut hair spidering over her collarbone. She tipped her head back to let the water cascade over her muscular body and groaned, "God, this is good." Her small sandy breasts upturned and dimpled from the cold were just inches from Maye's face. A piece of seaweed was stuck to a nipple. Maye reached to peel it off.

Jen, startled by Maye's touch, stared at her through the stream of water. Mortified that she'd assumed such intimacy, Maye removed her hand and was about to apologize when Jen took up Maye's hand and pressed it to her breast. Maye's breathing quickened. She'd never touched another woman's breast and was surprised when she felt Jen's nipple stiffen. It was an extraordinary sensation. Insistent. Longing. Raw. She gazed into Jen's eyes. Strong, beautiful, Jen. Instinctively, Maye stepped toward her, rising up on her tippy-toes, to kiss her. If she had a thought at all, it was to let Jen know how much she cared for her, and that she would be her friend forever. But when her lips touched Jen's, everything changed. Maye wanted to dive into the kiss, into Jen. She wanted to press her naked body—

Flustered, she stepped back. What was she doing? She'd just agreed to marry Jen's brother two days ago! "Um..." she said. "I think I'm good. You can...um...have the rest of the shower."

"Maye..." Jen said, but didn't finish her sentence. Or if she did, Maye didn't hear her. She just swiped the towel over her aroused body, not even bothering to shake the sand out first, and pulled on her jeans, which was almost impossible. She kept tipping over.

Outside, someone was approaching.

"You two almost done in there?" she heard Jake say. "I'm freezing my fucking nuts off out here!"

When she stepped out of the hut she was still buttoning her shirt. It felt strange to wear her jeans with no underwear. The inseam pressed against her swollen skin.

"Aren't you beautiful," he said.

She made herself smile. "Jen's still in there."

"Well then, let me give you a token on my love." He opened his hand to reveal a palm full of brightly colored sea glass. "Jewels for my mermaid queen."

Her eyes began to burn. She was so undeserving. "They're beautiful." Behind her, she was aware of Jen stepping out of the hut.

"That was some shower," Jen said.

Maye knew the words were meant for her, meant to mark what had happened between them. But what *had* happened exactly? Weren't they just two friends goofing around? Two friends who loved one another? Who'd had a bit too much champagne?

She leaned her back into Jake and wrapped his arms around her waist, barely daring a glance at Jen. But all it took was that one glance to see that Jen was staring at her and Jake, a single accusatory eyebrow raised.

"Am I interrupting something?" Jen asked.

"Nope." Jake squeezed Maye so tightly that her feet left the ground. "Just me bestowing gifts on my fiancée."

Jen looked as if she'd been punched in the gut. "Fiancée?"

"Yup." Jake lowered Maye to the ground but kept his arms locked around her. "Can you believe it? This fine woman said she'd marry me."

✳

It's three a.m. I'm wide-awake. The sounds of the hospital are hushed but not gone—the swish of scrubs as a nurse walks down the hall, the single squeaky wheel of a cart, the electronic pinging of a neighboring heart monitor. Mom's sleeping. I've put my feet up on the other chair, but the makeshift bed is killing me.

I can't stop thinking about that skull, the way the dirt clung to it, trying to suck it back to some primeval place. The bone was broken around one of the eyes, making it look ghoulish. Is this really all we leave behind? Bony scaffolding?

I tiptoe to the vertical strip of a window, my body stiff and cranky. The parking lot with its smattering of cars glows a sickly golden from the sodium lamps. A single pigeon perches on an arched lamppost, its feathers fluffed out making it seem twice its size. A van pulls into an open space, but no one gets out. Who did the skull belong to?

I consider heading to the lobby where I could probably have a whole polyester-covered couch to myself, or do some quiet yoga stretches to work the kinks out. I return to my two-chair bed instead, then notice Mom's eyes are open. How long has she been awake?

"You okay?"

"Eh," she says, making it clear she's had better nights.

"Can I get you anything?"

"Nuh."

I should do something, say something. I'm the healthy one. "We had a little excitement today." Why am I telling her this? "While we were pulling up Scotch broom, we came across somebody's skull." I can't tell if the look she gives me is an upset or curious one. I analyze my motives for telling her.

Mom closes her eyes.

I watch her breathing. In. Out. In. Out. In. Out. My eyelids start drooping. I tuck my jacket under my head. Please make morning come quickly.

❖

I wake to the sound of someone entering the room. It's Bullfrog Barbara. She's surprised to see me.

"You spent the night?" she asks. Obviously, if she'd been on duty this never would have happened.

"Yup." I blink back the bright florescent light. "She wanted me to."

She gives me a once over, says, "I see," then proceeds to ignore me. "How are you doing today, Maye?"

Mom sighs. "Ohay."

Bullfrog Barbara begins fiddling with the IVs. "It's nice to hear your voice coming back."

"Woooo," Mom says.

I lower my feet to the floor and attempt to straighten my back. I feel like a roller derby queen the day after a brutal match. I run my fingers through my hair. "Morning, Mom." My mouth is gummy and tastes fermented.

Mom glances at me. She's getting some mobility back in her neck.

"Look at you," I say. "You're going to be up and dancing in no time."

"Kull," she says emphatically.

"Sorry, Mom. I don't understand."

"Kull," she says again. "I noh."

"You know whose skull it is?"

Bullfrog Barbara arches a thin eyebrow.

"We found a skull on her land," I say making our conversation sound even more suspect. I add, "It was buried," like this might help.

"Ailah," Mom says.

"Ailah?" I repeat.

She tries again, but I still can't make out what she's trying to say. She flicks her eyes to the alphabet board. I pick it up. We spell out TWYLA.

"I'm sorry, Mom, but I don't know what that means."

Mom glances at Barbara as if maybe she can help with this dense daughter of hers. Bullfrog Barbara doesn't notice. Mom looks back at the board. This time we spell out TAITE.

Barbara flicks the IV tube three times. "She's talking about Bear Woman."

I try not to feel annoyed. "Is that what you mean, Mom? Are you talking about someone named Bear Woman?"

With great effort, she lifts her head and attempts to nod. "Es!"

Bullfrog Barbara is writing something on Mom's clipboard.

"Who's Bear Woman?" I ask, although I hate to acknowledge that this smug woman might hold any information important to me.

She slides the board back in its pocket, looks at the small delicate watch around her chubby wrist, then deigns to answer me. "She's probably only a legend. Lived up the mountain sometime in the early eighteen hundreds. They called her Bear Woman because she could talk to bears. If you want to know more go to the McCloud Museum; talk to my sister. She volunteers there two days a week. Now you need to leave and let your mother rest. Dr. Reneaux will be here soon."

"If I could just—"

"Out," she says pointing toward the door.

Would it kill her to be nice?

Dad and Aunt Jen saunter into the waiting room just as I'm about to force down a second cup of burnt coffee. Aunt Jen thrusts forward a Starbucks Grande. "Here."

I take the cup and peel back the lid. She put in plenty of half-and-half. "Bless you."

Dad hands me a small paper bag. "Cream cheese on a sesame bagel."

"You guys rock."

They seem more relaxed around each other. Have they talked?

Aunt Jen tells me they've been to check on her car. Translation: she tried to see if the mechanic could turn it around any faster.

"The guy's swamped," Dad says.

"Or says he is," Aunt Jen says.

"Jesus, Jen. We saw the cars."

"You think those clunkers are going to get fixed?"

So much for hoping.

Dr. Reneaux strides in, her no-nonsense attitude putting an end to Aunt Jen and Dad's bickering. "I thought you'd like to know, we're moving Maye from ICU."

"What does that mean?" Dad asks.

Dr. Reneaux sits on the arm of one of the couches. We huddle around.

"She's on the upswing." She goes on to tell us that the next phase of Mom's treatment will include aggressive physical therapy, and that some people fully recover while others never regain full muscle function. She doesn't spare the details, citing examples of people who struggle with balance for the rest of their lives, break bones easily, or are greatly weakened.

My head spins with insinuations. Is my capable Mom gone forever?

"Anything we can do to help?" Aunt Jen asks.

"Depending on how she responds to the therapy, you all may have a *lot* to do once she gets home." Her implication that we all live together is a conversation stopper. "Any more questions?" When we have none she says, "If you think of any, you know how to reach me."

Once she's left, we sit there, dumbfounded. I'm not sure whether it's that she assumed we're one big happy family, or the possibility that Mom might spend the rest of her life feeble and leaning on a cane. Either scenario is hard to swallow.

"So." Aunt Jen claps slaps her hands on her knees. "I say we cross that bridge when—*if*—we get there."

"What do you mean *if*?" I shoot back defensively.

"She might recover effortlessly and not need much help."

I flop my head into my hands and groan. "I told her about the skull."

Aunt Jen draws out my name on a descending sigh, "Beeeeean," like she's talking to a two-year-old who's flung her food on the floor for the zillionth time.

I shoot her a defiant look. I will not apologize for speaking the truth. "No. It was good. She got excited about it. In fact, she thinks she knows whose it is."

Dad and Aunt Jen both get worried looks on their faces, as if Mom might be involved in some unsavory deed.

"Not like *that*. She thinks it's this Bear Woman who lived a long time ago."

"Bear Woman?" Dad asks.

"She's sort of legendary around here. The nurse told me we can find out about her at the McCloud Museum."

"Huh," Dad says, and I can tell he's about to blow it off.

"We should check it out."

He tosses his empty paper cup in the trash. "Don't you need sleep?"

"We'll be passing right by it on our way back to the house. And McCloud's just one main street. It won't be hard to find a museum."

He does his dad thing of just standing there, immovable, hoping I'll back down.

"For Mom," I say.

He checks in with the clock as if this has anything to do with anything, then with his feet, then with me. "All right. We'll give it a look."

Aunt Jen picks up a *People* magazine. "Sure, leave me here with Britney Spears while you two go out and have yourselves an adventure."

Historic downtown McCloud is basically a strip of buildings that sprang up next to a railroad in the mid-eighteen hundreds to shelter the flood of loggers that stripped huge patches of land of its lush pine forests. Or so I read in a *Via* magazine I picked up at the hospital. Now it's all quaint bed-and-breakfasts, one big hotel, and a few cute shops with stuff no one really needs. Mom says its Shasta's conservative cousin.

Dad and I find the museum right away. It's tiny. And closed. A handwritten sign posts its hours of operation. They seem random and scant.

"What day is it?" I ask Dad.

He looks at his watch. "Sunday."

"We're in luck. They open in an hour."

The fact that neither of us knew what day it is blows my mind. Well, not that *I* didn't know (it happens), but that Dad didn't know. That's unheard of.

We stroll down the wide main street toward the commercial center, about five businesses connected by an old-fashioned plank sidewalk and slanted overhang. We pass a few tourists reading about the old steam train.

Dad's got something on his mind. His hands are in his pockets and he's looking at the ground in front of him, his lips pinched tight. I suppose I could ask him, but decide not to. I've had enough of stirring things up. If he wants to say something, let him—

"Bean?"

"Yeah?"

"I'm sorry you're caught in the middle of all this."

I find his generalization annoying. "All this?"

He looks at the sky, genuinely pained. "I know I owe you an explanation, but I'm asking you to give me time."

Again? "Whatever you need to do," I say. What else can I say? No? Tell me everything now?

He inhales a lungful of air through his nose. I gather he's relieved.

At least one of us is.

"So what's happening with the skull?" I ask.

"They found a piece of a femur, so they've taken that to the lab too. When we left, they'd pretty much dug up that whole plot by the garden."

A lone shudder scoots up my spine. It's strange to think of being dug back up. "I hope they're at least pulling up some of the Scotch broom while they're at it."

He laughs.

We reach the commercial center and step up on the plank sidewalk where the shops are. "How about an ice cream?" he asks. The fact that it's not even noon doesn't faze him.

"Sure."

We enter a soda shop and ring the bell on the counter. We're the only customers. Still, it takes a whole minute for a surly teenager to emerge from the back. She's in such contrast to the whole Norman Rockwell décor that I almost laugh. I order a double scoop with rocky road and coffee on a waffle cone; Dad goes straight-up vanilla, sugar cone. We nab one of the two booths by the window. The teenager returns to her cave.

Much as this father/daughter expedition feels pleasant and almost normal—the two of us sitting at a booth in an old-fashioned ice cream shop, the little paper placemats on the Formica tabletop, the pleasantness of the day—it's not. We barely know each other. He doesn't accept my choices. "We've got to talk about the gay thing," I say.

He pinches off a mouthful of ice cream with his lips as if he hasn't heard me.

"You've got to quit hoping I'm going to go straight," I continue. "I know it must be hard for you considering what happened to your marriage, but you've got to find a way to separate my gayness from Mom's and Aunt Jen's. They are in no way related. It's a random fluke. Or maybe it's not. Maybe there really is such a thing as a gay gene, but if that's the case, you're the carrier, because Mom doesn't have it. She's bisexual, or should I just say she's sexual-sexual, to the world, to life. Women like Mom don't let a little thing like gender get in the way of their loving…" As my mouth rambles on, I become super conscious of looking like Mom, of the rocky road dripping down my fingers, the earnest expression on Dad's face, and I think, *Stop talking,* but I can't. "I'm not like Mom," I hear myself say. "I love girls. I always have. Even back in junior high and high school when I was going out with boys, which I was doing basically to spite Mom and Aunt Jen, I didn't feel about my boyfriends the way other girls felt about theirs. I liked them. Sure. And the kissing was okay. But I never wanted to go further. Ever. But I didn't want to be like Mom and Aunt Jen, either. It seemed too predictable. Not that they expected it, but I felt everyone else did. Isn't that what everyone's so afraid of? That gay parents produce gay children? Which of course is bullshit. I have lots of friends with gay parents who are straight. But that's a whole other issue. What I'm saying is, when I kissed a girl for the first time, it was like Yes! Here are the pinwheels, the fireworks, the electricity. This is who I am." Mercifully, with this remark, my mouth stops yammering. I lick the ice cream from my fingers.

Dad doesn't say a word. He's down one ice cream scoop and gazing at me.

My cheeks grow hot.

"So," he finally gets out. "Are you seeing anyone right now?" To my astonishment, he's not judging me. He really wants to know.

"Um…sort of."

"Sort of?"

"Well, Serena and I were kind of hooking up right when this all happened."

"In Sayulita."

I nod.

As he considers this, my mind shoots off on its own journey. Am I putting too much stock in Serena's and my…relationship? Is it a relationship? Why hasn't she called? I've called twice. It would be just like me to screw this up. It's what we Bells do. The moment we start caring about someone we begin sabotaging. Our most common tactic is to deem the person not good enough for us. I've seen both Dad and Aunt Jen scare off wonderful people this way. As for Mom, her sabotaging technique is different. I guess it's because she's a Parfrey. Her dates (women and men) ultimately all want to be considered family, which is reasonable. But she can't go there. The twins and I are her family, even though she broke up with the twins.

Please may I not screw this up with Serena. Please may I not screw—

I realize Dad is talking to me. "Sorry, Dad, I missed what you said."

"I asked, is she good to you?"

"We're good friends, but, um, now that things have changed, well, it's kind of hard to know how it's going to go from here."

"I hope it works out for you."

I get the feeling he thinks my odds are about as good as winning the lottery. "Thanks."

We both spend a little quality time with our ice cream.

"Wanna walk?" I finally say.

"Good idea," he says.

We reach the museum just as an elderly woman unlocks the door. She's dressed in cowboy boots, a vest with silver conchos, and a denim skirt. "Our first visitors of the day," she says with much enthusiasm "Where you from?"

Her perkiness catches me off guard. I guess I expected her to be like her sister. "Different places. I'm, uh, from Santa Cruz and my dad's from Philadelphia. We were actually looking for something specific. We were told you have some information on Bear Woman."

She places her hands on her ample hips. Her nails are fire engine red. "We certainly do. There's a display in the back in our pioneers section."

We thank her and make our way through the tiny cluttered museum crammed with junk people have pulled from their attics and barns—old farming and logging tools, sewing mannequins dressed in period clothes, train paraphernalia. Each has a typed three-by-five card explaining its importance. But mostly what the museum has are old photos.

It doesn't take long to find Bear Woman. She's trapped in an eight-by-ten frame, and looks unhappy about it. A tall woman, dressed in leather and furs with unruly black hair, she holds a shotgun.

Dad reads her name off the card. "Twyla Taite. That's the name on one of Maye's sculptures."

"What?" How could he know this when I don't?

"The one out front, to the right of the shed, with the hair made of twigs?"

Suddenly, it all clicks into place. All of Mom's sculpted women are based on real people. I've just never paid much attention to who. I lean in to read the commentary.

*Twyla Carmella Taite, aka Bear Woman or Mountain Woman 1841–????? An early settler of Mt. Shasta, Twyla Taite was said to have remarkable powers. Legend has it she could "talk the fur off a bear" and "plant a pebble and grow a tree." She was also known for her intolerance of logging. It's been said she would shoot at loggers encroaching on her property. Her disappearance is a mystery, but some claim her brother, a timber man, was involved.*

Dad whistles. "Sounds like quite a woman."

A vague memory of Mom talking about her niggles its way in. "Mom thinks she once owned her property."

"Oh good," the curator says, joining us. "You found her."

"In more ways than one," I say.

She gives me a quizzical look. I don't expound.

"Do they know where her property was?" Dad asks.

"Isn't it on there?" the curator asks, peering over my shoulder to the short biography. She emits a dismissive grunt. "I'll have to have one of the girls add it. She owned a lot of the property up Squaw Valley Road."

I give Dad a look. It's possible she owned Mom's land.

"My granddaddy used to talk about Bear Woman," she says. "Said he saw her and her brother having an awful fistfight in town once. Their feud was notorious."

"He wanted to log the property?"

"That's what they say. When she disappeared, he inherited the land. He made a lot of money off that lumber."

"You think he offed her?" I ask.

"My granddaddy did. He was sure of it."

We thank her again and walk outside into the bright afternoon.

"Wouldn't it be crazy if it was her?" I say.

Dad nods. "Maye would love it."

## CHAPTER FIFTEEN

When Dad and I get to the house, Ari's on the front porch watering Mom's potted plants. He's wearing his cutoff overalls with no shirt, pink high-top Converse sneakers with no socks, his usual stack of bead bracelets, and his hair in a high ponytail. What will Dad think of this walking cliché gay boy?

Ari sets the watering can down and watches us get out of the car. "What's with all the crime tape?"

"Are the cops gone?" I ask.

"I guess. I haven't seen anyone since I got here."

Dad walks a beeline to Mom's sculpture by the greenhouse. "This is the Bear Woman sculpture."

I trot over. It's a sculpture I've seen zillions of times. Surrounded by Shasta daisies and about six feet tall, it's one of Mom's earlier sculptures, when she first started mixing mediums. The torso is carved from a pine trunk and the head is ceramic. The hair (created by poking holes in the skull, then, once it's glazed and fired, gluing in twigs and sticks) is wild and covered in spider webs. But it's the expression on the figure's face that's most striking. Her eyes look through you, and her parted lips are so realistic you can almost hear the warrior cry. I bend down to read what's carved at the bottom. Sure enough, it says *Twyla Carmella Taite, A Goddess Among Us.* How could I have not noticed this before?

Ari prances over. "Would somebody please tell me what's going on? Is everything okay with Maye?" His voice is panicky.

"Everything's fine," I say. "Or not *fine*. She still can't move much, but she's getting better, and she's able to talk a little." I glance at Dad to see what he's making of Ari. But why should I care? "Ari, this is my dad. Dad, Ari."

Dad reaches out his hand. Ari blushes and takes it. Such a kid.

"I found a human skull out by the garden," Dad says. "That's why the police were here." Either he's ultra preoccupied with the skull or Ari's gayness has flown past his radar. Which is hard to fathom.

Ari's eyes grow wide and he presses his hands to his chest, the bitten fingernails painted alternately lavender, black, lavender, black. "A skull?"

We fill him in on the whole skull deal and Mom's idea that it belongs to Twyla.

"Finding Twyla would be da bomb!"

"You know who she is?" I ask.

"Sure. Maye only talks about her all the time. She used to live around here—a total Amazon. She could communicate with animals and stuff. Then she mysteriously disappeared," he says wafting his fingers through the air like vapors. "Maye says she can still feel her energy, says she made this sculpture to put her spirit to rest."

"Did it work?" Dad asks.

I scrutinize his expression to see if he's joking. I can't tell.

Ari just shrugs.

The whole exchange makes me feel like a bad daughter. I know Mom's talked about Twyla before, but I tend to tune her out when she gets too woo-woo.

"So where's Twyla's skull now?" Ari asks.

"We don't know it's hers," I say.

"Whatever. Where is it?"

"The police sent it to the lab."

Ari brandishes his finger. "Maye's not going to like that."

"We didn't have much of a choice."

He flips a strand of hair from his face. "You didn't *have* to call the cops."

I'm just about to tell him where he can shove his fucking attitude when my phone rings. I riffle through my backpack and check the readout—Serena Hall. No way am I going to have this conversation with stoic Dad and judgmental Ari listening in. I flip my phone open and head back toward the house. "Serena."

"Hey," she says, her voice soft, sexy.

My skin prickles in anticipation; the energy between us is that strong. "Hey," I finally get out.

"How's your mom?"

All it takes is the sound of her voice to remind me that I'm above squabbling with Ari and kowtowing to parents. "Doing better. They're moving her out of the ICU today."

"So she's getting some mobility back?"

"Some, yeah, but it's still pretty minimal." As I fill her in on Mom's progress, I'm aware that I act differently with her than other women I've dated. Which springboards my brain to a whole other train of thought. *Are* we dating? And if so, why aren't I acting all aloof and standoffish like usual?

"I want to be there," she says. "Helping you go through this."

I take the steps up to the porch, my mind doing a triple gainer. Is she saying what I think she's saying? That she wants to come here? Are we ready for this? Or is she just making conversation, saying she wishes she could be here the way people end postcards with, *Wish you were here!*

"I would love that," I hear myself say.

"Really?"

"Really." Shit! What am I saying? What will she think of my family? What if they scare her off? "I'd love for you to be anywhere that I am." Now you've done it! You dolt!

"I'm going to come then."

I dive into logistics. They're safe. Concrete. "What about the palapa?" Surely, she can't renege on that agreement.

"I met this surfer who's looking for a place. I bet I could get him to take over the rent."

"Will the agency let us do that?"

"If I told them it was a family emergency."

Serena. Family. Wow.

✳

Jake gazed at his and Maye's wedding gift to themselves—a brand new king-size bed. It was a belated gift because there had been so many expenses with getting married and moving into their new apartment, but here it was, at last, their wedding bed. It dwarfed the tiny bedroom and had milk crates for bedside tables, but this didn't worry Jake. He was moving up at his job, the foreman had even let him run the grader once. And Maye had her job at the SPCA. Before long they'd be able to afford a bigger apartment, or maybe a house, and it was there that they'd start their family. Maye was going to make a wonderful mother. So different from his own. She would be attentive to their children's needs, protective. And he would stick around. A father who cared. Who'd kick the shit out of anyone who tried to harm his child.

The shower turned off in the bathroom. Jake snuck into the kitchen and pulled out the bottle of Korbel Brut he'd hidden in a bag at the back of the refrigerator. He stood it on a tray with two regular wine glasses and a bud vase with a single red rose. He'd wanted to buy real champagne glasses for the occasion, but the ones he'd liked had been too expensive. One thing at a time, he told himself, and once he had everything on the tray, he thought it looked damned good. He carried it into the bedroom and placed it at the foot of the bed then stripped down to his pajama pants and threw a hand towel over his arm.

Maye stepped out of the bathroom in her fluffy pink robe, her hair still damp, and beamed when she saw him standing there like a butler. "Great minds think alike."

"Do they?"

"Let's just say I have a little surprise too."

He cocked an eyebrow.

"Patience," she said with a coy smile. "I want tonight to last."

He bowed at the waist. "Whatever you say, madam."

She giggled, then, with an impish look in her eye, walked to the bed, catlike, lowered herself onto it, and purred. He'd never seen this side of her. But then, what was new about that? She was always surprising him.

They made many toasts as they drank the champagne—to their love, to their home, to the poor little puppy who'd pulled through at the SPCA, and Jake couldn't stop thinking about how lucky he was. His heart was filled with his beautiful wife, and tonight he would show her. He tried several times to reach beneath her bathrobe, but each time she playfully slapped him away, saying, "Sloooow, Jake. Slooooow."

After filling the last two glasses with bubbly, he plucked the red bud from the vase and slid it down the front of her bathrobe into her cleavage. This time, instead of slapping him away, she nipped at his finger. She was ready.

He moved the tray from the end of the bed to the milk crate end table, placing his own glass on it, then leaned in to kiss her. He caressed the swell of her breast through the pink robe, all the while coaching himself to go *slooow, slooooow*. They explored one another's mouths, prodding, sucking, and nibbling. Once again, he tried to get under her robe, but she wouldn't let him. He felt himself swelling beneath his pajama pants. This teasing side of her was so new, so sexy. After a bit more kissing, she finally leaned across him to put her own glass on the milk crate. He had a strong urge to lift her robe up and take her from behind. They'd never tried that. Not tonight, he told himself. *Tonight I want her to feel cherished.* But this new openly seductive behavior made him wonder if there was a side to his Maye that was unknown to him.

Once the glass was safely stowed, he gently rolled her onto her back. She looked delicious against the cream-colored sheets, her blond hair framing her face. "I want you so much," he said propping himself up on one hand while reaching to open her robe with the other.

"Hang on. You're pulling my hair."

Could he be any clumsier? He raised up to release her hair. The look on her face changed. She had tricked him. She gave him a playful shove, flipping him onto his back, then straddling him, she slipped off her robe to reveal black lace lingerie. The rose dropped from between her breasts and onto the bed by his face.

"I thought it would be a shame not to christen our new purchase," she said in a smooth, deep voice.

His breath began to quicken. He wasn't quite sure what to make of this new side of Maye. She leaned down and ran her fingers through his hair, tugging slightly. "What do you say we baptize the hell out of this bed," she said teasingly, flaunting her breasts. "Cleanse out all our dirty little sins."

He took a shallow breath. *Dirty little sins.* Then another. *Dirty boy. Dirty, dirty boy.* His chest began to tighten. He was beginning to feel lightheaded. Trapped. Part of him wanted to push her off. Get away. Another part screamed, *What the fuck is wrong with you? Why are you panicking?*

Maye pulled back. "Are you all right?"

Whatever the hell was going on, he didn't want Maye to see it. "No. I'm not. I need to—Hang on." He slid from beneath her and bolted toward the bathroom.

"Jake?" she called after him.

Inside the small bathroom, images and sounds flashed through his mind—the cross that hung above Ernest's toilet, the clicking of the church water heater. He braced himself against the sink. Made himself breathe. Was he going crazy? Why was he thinking of Ernest?

Slowly, the details came back to him—Ernest showing him the magazines, Ernest counseling him about his sinful ways, the tiny church bathroom where Ernest exposed himself, made young Jake touch himself while he watched.

Maye knocked gently on the door. "Honey?"

He turned on the faucet and splashed cold water on his face.

"Is everything all right?" he heard her asking.

His chest was so tight; was he having a heart attack?

She eased the door open. She was back in the pink fluffy robe. "Are you crying?"

He realized that he *was* crying and fell to his knees, burrowing his head in her belly. She held him as he trembled and sobbed. And then somehow they were both sitting on the speckled bathroom floor that was peeling up around the edges, holding each other.

"Wanna go back to the bedroom?" she asked, her voice a flower petal landing on roiling water. He nodded yes and she helped him up. Wordlessly, they made their way back to the bed. She propped pillows behind his back, drew the blanket up over his legs. "What's going on?" Tenderly, she peeled a lock of hair from his damp brow.

And so he slit open his past and dumped on her what he'd barred from his memory. Everything. Disjointed as specifics came back to him. He spared her nothing.

Listening to him, her eyes filled with tears. "Didn't your mom wonder why he always wanted to be alone with you?"

He wrung his hands until his knuckles were raw. "Who knows?"

"How about Jen?"

"Not a clue. And I don't want her to know. Ever."

"But she might be able to help you sort—"

"No!" He picked up his champagne glass, downed the flat champagne, and swung his legs out of bed.

"Where are you going?"

"I need some space."

Already, he hated himself for what he'd told her.

As the apartment door clicked shut behind him, Jake felt another door close as well. Only this one was deep inside him. And he never wanted it to open again.

*

I find Dad in the backyard, leaning on a shovel and peering over the yellow crime tape to the dug-up ground where the skull once was.

"They sure made a mess of things," I say.

He kicks at a clod of dirt. "Amazing no one's come across it till now."

I consider telling him that Serena could be showing up in a few days, but I want the possibility to be mine alone, at least for a while. "I think I'm going to take a nap," I say. "Then I'm going to get serious about this Scotch broom."

"Sounds good. Think I'll tackle a little myself."

I start to walk off. His vulnerable-sounding, "Bean?" stops me. I turn around. He's standing there holding his shovel like a microphone stand. If it were intentional it would be comical.

"Yeah, Dad?"

He takes a deep breath. "Sorry about missing your first soccer goal, and when you played an Indian in *Annie Get Your Gun.* I love that musical and would have loved to see you in it."

"Dad—"

He raises his hand to shush me. "And I'm sorry I missed you getting the tenth grade English award, and your prom, and your high school graduation, and all those little moments of you growing into the wonderful woman you are."

While I'm touched by Dad's intention, I have no idea how to respond. I glance around, wondering where Ari is. Typically, when I need him, he's nowhere to be found.

Dad continues. "I know I've been a disappointment to you as a father, and that there are things you'll never be able to forgive me for. The times you visited, I didn't take time off from work. That was stupid. I was scared. I didn't want to mess things up. But you are what matters to me now." He drives the shovel into the dirt and lets it stand on its own. "The thing is, well, I know that this whole deal with Maye wanting me to tell Jen something must seem confusing to you, but it's difficult. Some things are hard to come to terms with."

The look in his eye scares me. Is he going to start drinking again? No, I tell myself, he's past that. But after a childhood of him coming home drunk most nights, there's still part of me that…"Dad, are you okay?"

He covers his eyes with his giant paw—is he crying?—but when he lifts his head there are no tears. "I just don't know how to make this up to you, Bean."

"You can't," I say. "It happened. It sucked. Now we have to move on." I know it sounds harsh, but if this is the big moment for making amends, I want it to be honest. "We just have to make it better. Now. It's all we can do."

He pulls the shovel from the dirt. I know he's hurting, but I hurt for years because of him. I walk over and attempt to hug him, but the shovel gets in the way making the hug awkward and unsatisfying. "I'm going to go take that nap now, okay?"

"Of course," he says. "I'm sorry I—"

"It's *fine*. I'm glad you said something."

As I walk off I hear his shovel plunge into the earth. *Chunk.*

For the next two hours, as I try to sleep, it doesn't stop. *Chunk. Chunk. Chunk.* Silence. *Chunk. Chunk. Chunk. Chunk. Chunk. Chunk.* Silence. The sound seems to arc up and crash through my window. *Chunk. Chunk. Chunk.* I get up once to watch him from the window. He looks like he's fighting with the earth. I return to bed, roll over, and pull the pillow over my head. It's hot.

*Chunk. Chunk.* Silence. *Chunk. Chunk. Chunk.* Like Morse code. If only I could decode it, then maybe I could decode my dad.

## CHAPTER SIXTEEN

My mind is thick with dreams I can't remember. I stare at the wide plank ceiling of my bedroom. How many days have I been here? Three? Four? The wall opposite the window glows with late afternoon light. Or is it early evening? Could I have slept that long?

Yawning, I prop myself up. Sleep hasn't quite let go of me yet; the world looks soft. I stare at the quilt covering my legs. Mom gave it to me on my sixteenth birthday. She'd been collecting fabric for it since I was a baby. There are patches from my first pair of denim overalls, my favorite shirt in second grade with the florescent palm trees, the snowflake pajamas that I got from Santa, the groovy purple curtains from my first real room in Santa Cruz, a tie-dyed skirt I wore just about every day in seventh grade. I can't imagine the discipline it took to cut three-by-three inch squares out of all my outgrown and discarded clothes, stow them away until there were enough, and then hand-stitch them together into this queen-sized quilt. It's so unlike Mom to follow through on this kind of long-term project. And I was such a punk about it. She gave me the quilt when I'd wanted UGG boots. I didn't even take the quilt to college with me.

I press it against my face and breathe in its clean scent.

I'm taking it with me this time when I go...where? Home? I don't have a home. When Serena and I took off for Mexico, I gave up my rented room in Santa Cruz.

Unlike my friends who get all disjointed when, years after they've moved out, their mother turns their room into a guestroom or home office, I have no sense of home. "But it's *my* room," my friends whine. "How could she do that?" Like they have some right to it. Like they'd ever move back.

My home memories of Philadelphia are vague—Mom and I eating dinner alone, Dad occasionally taking me to the park so I could ride my bike without having to worry about traffic, having to be super quiet when I was playing inside because the scary witch in the apartment next door would pound on the wall and yell, "Keep it down!" My room was blue.

My home memories of Santa Cruz are jumbled. Everything was temporary. I didn't even *have* a room when Mom and I first moved in with Aunt Jen. My bed was where the washer and dryer should have been. Then the three of us moved. Then we moved again. And again. There was something about each place that "didn't sit right" with Mom or Aunt Jen. It felt too claustrophobic, was too far from my school, from work, the Laundromat. The truth is, their guilt about Dad always moved in with us, and once that happened, there was no staying.

I roll out of bed and walk to the window. Dad's car is gone. So is Ari's truck. I drag my body downstairs, glad to have some time alone, but also feeling lonely. Mrs. Simpkins meets me at the bottom step and yowls, demanding to be fed. I stop to pet her. She indulges me briefly then head butts me toward the kitchen. Sighing, I go to feed her. There's a note from Dad on the table.

> *Bean,*
> *Went into Redding to take the next shift with Maye.*
> *Didn't want to wake you.*
> > *Love,*
> > *Dad*
> *P.S. I got Maye's van running. Keys are in it.*

I should feel happy. Mom's getting better, Serena's probably coming, and now Dad has provided me with wheels. But I can't shake this melancholy. I feed Mrs. Simpkins and saunter outside. Mom's van is parked by the side of the house. It's a Volkswagen that she painted herself with green palm fronds and tropical birds. The bumper sticker *Keep Santa Cruz Weird* is centered on the back bumper. To the left of it is one that says *Keep Santa Cruz Queer.* I stuck that one on when I was thirteen. I was making a statement. I wanted Mom and Aunt Jen to quit being so secretive about their relationship. To this day, neither one of them has ever mentioned the sticker. But my rebellious act worked. They started being more open with their relationship, actually referred to themselves as a couple.

I open the driver's side door, hoist myself in, and twist the key. It starts. I motor around the circular driveway several times then park by the walkway. I love this van. It's been my home more than any house or apartment. Every time Mom and Aunt Jen would decide to move, we'd pack it up and haul our stuff to the new place. More than once we had to sleep in it. I smooth out the feathers on the dream catcher hanging from the rearview mirror. I feel like crying.

✻

It was Sunday morning and Jen was sipping coffee at the large oak dining room table in her communal house in Mt. Airy. Carved into the worn top of the heavy oak table were names, poems, and doodles from previous residents. A student house for years, it was built from stone and had a solid feel and lots of cool built-ins. From where Jen sat in the dining room she could see into the lavender-painted kitchen where her roommate, Shannon, a salt of the earth type, was preparing Sunday brunch, the one meal all five women, and whoever else happened to have spent the night, ate together. They took turns cooking. Jen loved her roomies, especially the bohemian Shannon. She was the first out lesbian Jen had ever met.

"How's it going with Dawn?" Shannon asked, cracking an egg on the rim of a large ceramic bowl.

Jen ran her fingers over someone's carved initials, JEH, pondering how to answer the question about the woman she was seeing. Dawn's black-and-white judgments made her difficult to talk to. She was a political science major who thought there were right ways to think and wrong ways to think, good people and bad people. She was always harping at Jen about "siding with The Man." But making love with her was amazing. Dawn knew all kinds of ways to please her. Jen didn't like thinking of herself as a lesbian, though. It was frustrating to feel marginalized, confusing to have politics mixed up with your love. "It's going good," she finally answered then got up to pour herself another cup of coffee.

Shannon hiked one of her thick eyebrows. "Just good? It sounded more than good the other night when she slept over."

"Sorry about that."

"Why? It kept my mind off Tara being away."

Mortified, Jen spoke the next words into her coffee mug. "I didn't know we were being that loud."

"Shit, girl. You had Mary wondering if she shouldn't try out dyke love."

Mercifully, the doorbell rang. Jen went to answer it.

Maye was standing on the doorstep with Bean in a hand-held baby carrier. "Am I interrupting anything?"

Still flustered, Jen ushered her into the living room. "No. Come on in." She stopped at the newel post at the bottom of the stairs where the roommates tacked phone messages. She knew there would be no messages for her, but looked anyway. "Can I get you something to drink? Milk? Herbal tea?"

Maye shook her head. "No, I'm good."

"Everything okay?"

Maye gently placed the baby carrier on the floor then flopped onto the worn couch. "Jake didn't come home until past two."

"Again?"

Maye nodded.

Jen slid into the rocker across from Maye. "You want me to talk to him?" Not that she thought it would do any good. He was acting squirrelly again, and when he got that way there was no getting through to him.

"No. He hates it when I come crying to you." Maye tucked a curl behind her ear. "He's just got some stuff to work out."

"Stuff?" Jen mentally kicked herself for asking. Last time Maye had intimated that she and Jake were having some trouble in the bedroom, and that was more than she wanted to know.

Maye hesitated, as if deciding what to share, then settled on, "I keep trying to get him to see a therapist, but he won't."

Relieved that Maye had spared her the bedroom details, Jen found herself sympathizing with Jake on the therapist thing. She couldn't imagine telling a stranger about their bizarre family. What if the therapist suggested that Jake's troubles were genetic? That he'd inherited Evelyn's condition? An uneasy feeling crept up her spine. "Does he ever act...strange?"

"Not like your mom if that's what you're asking."

Jen noticed a sandwich wrapper that had slid partway under the couch, picked it up, and placed it on the coffee table. One of her roommates was a total slob. "Still, not coming home is bullshit."

Shannon poked her head in. "Maye, you and Bean staying for breakfast?"

Maye glanced at Jen.

"She's staying," Jen said.

Shannon retreated to the kitchen.

Maye kicked off her clogs and folded her legs beneath her flared skirt. "Thanks. I always feel so welcome here. So at home." Bean made a snuffling noise and Maye leaned over to check on her. "She didn't sleep well last night. She could tell I was upset."

Jen found it difficult to be this close to Maye without reaching out to hold her. "You can always call."

Trish the artist came down the stairs wearing a vintage satin slip and heavy wool socks. "You guys better have left me some coffee."

Shannon set a platter of pancakes on the table. "Will Greg be joining us for breakfast?"

"Nope. Had to leave early. His mom's in town."

"Does somebody need to go wake Frieda and Donna?"

"I'm up," Frieda said sauntering down the stairs in shorts and a T-shirt. "And Donna's on her way. She was moving furniture around in her room."

Jen asked what they were all wondering. "Furniture?"

"Sounded like it. Or else she was building a rocket for her astrophysics exam. It was hard to tell with my pillow over my head."

"Well, breakfast is on." Shannon pulled open the curtains. Sunlight streamed into the room. "Everybody grab a plate."

Jen got up to get one for her and Maye.

"Jesus," Trish said. "You and Dawn were sure going at it the other night."

Jen glared at Trish hoping to shut her up. She hadn't told Maye about Dawn.

"What?" Trish said. "I think it's great. I was hoping you could get Dawn to give Greg a few pointers."

Maye came up behind her. "Dawn?"

"Jen hasn't told you about Dawn Jaun?" Frieda said teasingly. "Her Latin lover?"

Jen handed Maye a plate. "It's just someone I've been seeing."

"I'd say you've been doing a bit more than 'seeing' her," Trish said. "The two of you have been going at it like alley cats."

Jen took a place at the table. "Can we just eat?" Why hadn't she told Maye about Dawn? About being a…lesbian? Maye was her best friend, her family. The answer was unwelcome. She was in love with Maye, always had been.

Shannon thrust a large wooden bowl at her. "Fruit salad?"

Once breakfast was over and cleaned up, Maye and Jen returned to the table with Bean who'd woken up hungry. Jen watched Maye lift her blouse. Her breast was swollen with milk. Bean latched on.

"Nervous about graduation?" Maye asked.

Jen cleared her throat. "Not really. I've done the hard part. Now I've just got to pay back my loan." It was a struggle not to look at Maye's breast with Bean's tiny mouth wrapped around the nipple. "You hiring at the SPCA?" she joked.

"You'd hate it. Too much politicking."

"Yeah." Jen wondered if Maye ever thought about that kiss they'd shared out at the beach. She watched her trace a lily carved deep into the table. She loved Maye's hands, her sturdy fingers and blunt nails...She wrenched her eyes away. What was she doing? Maye was off limits.

"So you've found someone to love," Maye said.

"I don't know about love..."

"Dawn? Is that her name?"

Jen rubbed her eyes. She wished she could just disappear. "Yeah."

"Have you told Jake?"

Jen pulled her socked feet up on the chair and wrapped her arms around her knees. She needed something between her and Maye. "You know how he is about gays. The guy's a total homophobe."

"But you'll have to tell him at some point."

"I guess. If I, well, you know, get serious."

"It must be lovely to be with a woman. You'd know what to do when you're—"

"Every woman is different."

"Oh?"

Jen felt her temperature rise. "Or I assume that to be true."

Bean made a little sucking sound.

"So you don't love her then?"

Jen pulled at a loose thread on the hem of her jeans, an uneasy thought worming its way into her mind. She could not stay in Philadelphia.

\*

Still melancholy, I wander out to Mom's garden, shovel in hand, to do my Scotch broom duty. She has eight raised beds as well as a bigger ground-level bed for corn, pole beans, peas, tomatoes, and okra. The growing season in the mountains is short, so she gets things started in the greenhouse then puts them in the ground as soon as the soil warms up. Every winter she says she's going to work on creating a customer base to deliver weekly bags of fresh produce. She never gets around to organizing it though and winds up giving away veggies and composting a lot. One more of her unfinished goals.

Dad's piles of uprooted Scotch broom are on the outskirts of the garden. Looking at them exhausts me. I sit on the edge of one of the raised lettuce beds. I need to either cry or get over it. I notice a weed sprouting up between two lettuce heads. I yank it. I notice another and yank it. Before I know it, I'm hosing aphids off the kale, securing rogue peas to their stakes, checking the broccoli for caterpillars, and thinning carrots and beets.

I coo reassurances to the plants. "Mom will be able to care for you when she gets back. She's going to be so happy when she sees you all so well taken care of."

Finally the tears come—not a downpour, more like intermittent showers. I have to keep wiping my eyes to see what I'm doing.

By the time twilight darkens to dusk, I'm feeling better and take in my basket of harvested veggies. I steam the sugar snap peas and broccoli, throw them over newly washed red lettuce, sprinkle with sunflower seeds and water chestnuts, then drench the whole salad in seasoned rice vinegar, toasted sesame oil, and plum sauce. Adding to this a slice of whole-wheat toast slathered in hummus and a cup of hot licorice tea, I head up to Mom's office. On her desk is a jar stuffed with the names and addresses of people who've shown interest in purchasing veggies in the past. They're written on everything from old store receipts to movie ticket stubs.

I sort them into two piles—legible and not legible. The legible pile has close to forty slips. I log on to Mom's ancient Mac and enter in the names, phone numbers, and any miscellaneous notes she has written about people's specific requests.

The phone rings.

"Hello?"

"Guess who?"

She's speaking slowly and with a raspy voice, but it's clearly Mom. "You're talking!"

"More or less," she says, slurring the "less."

"How are you feeling?"

"Nerves are screeeeaming." There's a slight pause before she adds, "They say will go away."

Aunt Jen comes on the line. "Pretty amazing, huh?"

"I'll say."

"She's been practicing all day for this phone call. Of course, I have to hold the phone for her, but she's on her way back to us."

"Tell her I'm setting up a program so she can organize her potential veggie customers."

I listen as Aunt Jen relays the news. She comes back on the line. "She's thrilled."

"Has Dad showed up yet? He left a while ago."

"He has, but he's been sort of preoccupied by Nurse Nice."

I hear Mom laughing in the background.

"Preoccupied?" I ask.

"He got here early to take her out on her break."

"Dad's making a play for Samantha?"

"Apparently, they hit it off the other night."

Mom says something in the background.

Aunt Jen laughs. "Your mom is sooo naughty. Anyway, once he's back I'll head up the hill. Can I get you anything?"

"Actually, I'm good. Dad fixed Mom's van, so I've got wheels if I need them."

Jen relays this to Mom, who comes back on the line. "Love you, Bean."

"I love you too, Mom. See you in the morning. And welcome back."

After hanging up, I take the last few bites of my salad. I should have told her about the work I did in her garden.

## CHAPTER SEVENTEEN

What the hell am I doing? I don't want to run Mom's veggie business. I want my own life. How am I going to get out of this?

I sit up in bed and gaze at the giant ponderosa pine outside my window. Creating a veggie spreadsheet kept me up late last night. Mom's computer just wasn't up to the task, so I used my own, then spent hours trying to find a way to transfer it to hers, which I never could figure out. A white-headed woodpecker digs its tiny talons into the puzzle-piece bark and begins pounding at it with its beak. *Tat tat tat! Tat tat tat!* The bird reminds me of myself, the way I hammer at a thought until my head hurts.

Alongside the *Tat tat tat tat tat!* I hear the *Chunk! Chunk!* of a shovel at work, only the rhythm is much more erratic than Dad's. Must be Aunt Jen getting an early start. I check the clock. Seven thirty a.m. No doubt she saw Dad's Scotch broom piles and felt she had to do her share. Or more.

My bladder finally convinces me to drag myself out of bed. In the bathroom I brush my teeth and splash water on my face, but still don't feel ready to face my life. I return to my room and unroll my yoga mat to do some basic stretches—triangle, warrior one and two, tree pose—then I move into the complicated poses. In the middle of half moon pose, balanced on one foot and one hand, my other foot and hand stretching out into mid air, I have a brilliant idea. Ari! He can run Mom's business. Mind spinning, I topple out of half moon. The veggies wouldn't bring in much more than his paycheck at first, but once people tasted what Mom had to offer, sales would surely pick up. And even a few sales would beat composting. I abandon my yoga practice, throw on a T-shirt, jeans, my flops, and trot downstairs.

I make myself a cup of French roast then head out to feed the chickens and collect eggs. Once that's done, I take my coffee and wander over to Aunt Jen. She's putting all her body weight into wrestling a stalk of Scotch broom from the earth. "Son of a cocksucker."

"Morning," I say brightly.

She releases the plant and tips back onto her butt. "Jesus Christ, these motherfuckers are stubborn."

"Takes stubborn to know stubborn."

"Don't you get started on me too."

"Too?"

She reaches over to a rock for her coffee mug and slugs a mouthful. "Your dad and I got into it last night."

"Really?" Maybe they finally had "the talk."

She wipes the back of her wrist across her sweat-soaked forehead causing the dirt to streak. She looks at me dead on. "Am I condescending?"

I pause. I know a trick question when I hear one. "Um, sometimes?"

"Of course I am *sometimes*. Everyone is *sometimes*. But would you consider me a condescending person in general?"

I decide not to mention that she's acting condescending now. The bog of accusation looks too thick to be safe. "Why are you asking?"

"Jake said I was condescending."

"Were you?"

She scratches the back of her head. "I might have been, briefly, but—"

"What did you say?"

"I was just asking about his nurse—"

"You called her Nurse Nice, didn't you?"

"No," she says sounding affronted. "Like I said, I called her 'his nurse.'"

"I hear a 'Nurse Nice' underneath the way you say that."

My observation elicits from her a sharp exhale. "You have to admit it's kind of weird that he's—"

"Oh. And now you're going to defend yourself so you don't have to face up to your condescending…ness."

She knocks one boot against the other to loosen the dirt. "It's just—"

I hold up my palm to silence her, then quote the guy who wrote Jonathan Livingston Seagull. "Argue for your limitations and they are yours." I'm not exactly sure this applies, but it shuts her up. "Think about it," I say, before walking off. "I'm going to go do my shift with Mom. I'm taking her van."

"She's out of ICU," she calls after me. "In room 2248."

Finally, some good news.

✳

Maye sat at the small table off the kitchen, which she wished was a dining room. Bean was scarfing down spinach lasagna that Maye had spent much of the day preparing. The tomato sauce was made from scratch. But Maye wasn't hungry. She was angry.

Today had been Bean's first day of fourth grade at her new school. She'd had trouble in her last school, being generally antisocial and withdrawn, so they were giving this new smaller school a try. Jake had promised to make it home for dinner, agreeing it would mean a lot to Bean. Now, once again, he was late, which could mean only one thing; he'd gone out with the guys after work. He'd probably planned on it being a "quick one," but there were no "quick ones" for Jake anymore.

Maye massaged her temples trying to ease her throbbing headache. She was so stupid! In their last argument when he'd admitted his drinking was hurting not just her but Bean too, she'd believed he was making progress.

"So what else did the teacher have you do?" she forced herself to ask Bean.

Bean, just about to shove another humongous bite of her "favorite meal ever" into her small mouth, let the fork hover in front of her. "Worked on sentences. Each table got a bunch of cards with words and we had to put together one declarative, one interrogative, and one imperative."

Maye rested her head on her fist. "I bet you were good."

Bean shoved in the bite of lasagna and tried to talk around it.

"Swallow your food, Bean."

Bean chewed a bit then swallowed. "I made up the sentence, 'Get that tractor out of the bedroom.'"

Maye made herself smile. "Good one." Then she got up to get some aspirin.

❖

Maye was kissing Bean goodnight when she heard the front door click open.

"Is that Daddy?" Bean asked through a yawn. "I wanna tell him about school."

"It's kind of late, honey." Maye ran her fingers through Bean's blond curls hoping it would relax her, but Bean had already started squirming.

"Mom, he'd want to know."

Maye had to bite her tongue to keep from saying, *If he wanted to know that much he'd have been here.* "You can tell him at breakfast."

"But I want to tell him *now*."

Jake stuck his head in the door. "How's my little princess?" He stunk of alcohol.

Maye fought back the urge to pick up Bean's twirling galaxy lamp and hurl it at him. "It was her first day at school." She hoped this would be enough to jog his pickled memory. "She wanted to tell you about it, but since it's so late she's going to have to tell you in the morning."

"Meanie," Jake said then came around the other side of the bed and sat down. He was a smooth drunk, never betraying his inebriation by wobbling or knocking things over. "I want to hear about it now. It's a big day for our girl."

Maye started the silent count to ten—she would not blow—but by the time she reached three she'd blurted, "And you missed it."

"Mom!" Bean cried.

Jake gave Maye an icy stare. "So that's how you're going to be."

"I just meant…"

Jake shook his head. They had promised not to fight in front of Bean. But why could he break a promise and not her? Why was it always her having to make things right?

"Jake…"

"I'm real proud of you, princess." Jake leaned down and gave Bean a kiss on the head. "But we're going to have to talk about this later. *Mommy* doesn't want you staying up."

"Dad!" Bean called after him as he got up and left the room.

The apartment door clicked open then shut.

Maye tucked the blanket in around Bean. "Sorry, honey. I know you're disappointed."

Bean glared at her. "You hurt his feelings."

Maye took a deep breath. "I can understand why you're mad."

"No, you can't!" Bean kicked at the blankets. "I hate you!"

It took Maye a whole twenty minutes to calm Bean down after that. When she was finally sleeping, Maye slipped out of the room. She was drinking a cup of herbal tea on the couch when the door finally clicked open again.

Jake stopped when he saw her. "I wasn't drinking. I was walking."

"Jake. I smelled the—"

"I'm not talking about before. I'm talking about now."

She nodded as if this made a difference to her, as if this argument was just about tonight, as if his coming home late had nothing to do with his withdrawal from the relationship. When was the last time they'd made love? Maye couldn't even remember.

Jake ran his fingers through his mussed hair. "I just don't get why you're always pushing me to be what I'm not."

"I am *not* pushing you. I happen to believe there's more to you—"

"This is who I am. I've accepted it. Why can't you?"

Maye was stunned. He'd accepted it? He wasn't even going to try to quit drinking? She stared at him for a few moments trying to figure out how to respond to this new low then simply said, "I'm going to bed."

Sometime in the night, she woke to him snoring beside her.

❖

Sunday morning, Maye stood at the back door looking out. Bean was sitting by herself in the only spot of sunshine in the walled-in communal weed patch shared by all six units. She was practicing tying the knots she'd learned in Girl Scouts.

Maye still needed to tell her they were going away for a while. She'd bought the plane tickets, called in all her vacation time, arranged with Jen in California to stay for an "undetermined" amount of time, but still, the trip slated to take place in two days seemed unthinkable. Was she leaving Jake? For good? Jen said they could stay as long as they needed, but what about school for Bean? And what would happen when Maye's vacation time ran out? She reminded herself she only had to know the next step; the rest would come.

She hadn't told Jake yet, either. The right moment hadn't presented itself.

Outside, Bean cinched a shoelace noose around a doll's neck. Maye strode out the back door toward her. This was too much. Jake's and her arguments were taking too big a toll on Bean.

✳

Figuring out this new wing of the hospital takes a while. I find Dad before I find Mom. He's at the nurses' station with Samantha. They're talking to a competent-looking nurse behind the desk. Dad's elbow is touching Samantha's. I walk up to the desk. "Hey, Dad. What's the news?"

He steps back, flustered. Shy about Samantha? "We were just discussing Maye's release date. It could be as soon as Monday."

I have to think for a second. Today is Wednesday; that's only five days away.

The elderly nurse adds, "Of course it's Dr. Reneaux's call, but your mother's progressing very quickly. She has quite the spirit." She smiles as if she expects me to say something, but all I do is smile back. I'm sick of talking about Mom like she's some invalid.

The nurse picks up a chart. "Well, then. If you don't have any more questions?"

Dad shakes his head. "Thank you, Eleanor."

Samantha elbows Dad playfully. "Told you."

He blushes and tries to pretend nothing is going on between them.

She gives me a look as if to say, *Can you believe your Dad*, then actually does say, "Nice to see you again, Bean."

"You too." I fall a tad short of her cheerful tone. She's clearly smitten with Dad, but women always fall for Dad. What's surprising is he seems just as doe-eyed. "Is Mom awake?"

"Todd's in with her now," he says.

Samantha adds, "I'm sure you can go in," and gestures down the hall.

I fake a smile then follow the room numbers to 2248, the whole way trying to shake the vision of Dad acting all infatuated. But it's hard. He seems so…adolescent.

Todd, the perky spa-instructor-wannabe, is leaving as I enter Mom's new room. "See you this afternoon, Maye!" He flashes me a Crest toothpaste smile.

The room is bigger, has a real window, a TV, a phone, a bathroom, and a remote-controlled bed that's currently propping her up. Mom's scowling after Todd—a welcome sight. She's regaining control of her facial muscles.

"Check you out," I say, "and your fancy new digs."

"Look." She raises her arm to shoulder level, trying not to wince.

"Wow. That's great."

She carefully lowers her arm, exhaling a long breath. "Oof."

We both tear up. "Welcome back," I say.

"Sorry I scare you," she croaks.

Speaking is still tough for her, causing her words to come out clipped.

We hold our gaze a few seconds longer then I start to hug her. She stiffens at the prospect of being touched but then reaches her arms up as far as they will go to return the hug. It's heartbreaking. I sit on one of the two chairs. "Your nerves still going bonkers?"

"A li'le."

Typical Mom response. She could be hit in the head with a baseball bat and she'd mention a headache.

"Sorry about you trip," she adds.

"Will you stop? You're way more important than Mexico." But I have to admit, even as I say this, I feel a bit resentful. Why couldn't this one thing have worked out for me? I make a mental note to call Serena. Maybe the palapa is still ours. Maybe I can still salvage a bit of Bean's Mexican Adventure. "I've got to tell you this idea I had about your veggie business." I say this to keep her from bringing up Dad and Aunt Jen.

She listens intently to my thoughts about her garden then asks, "You talk to Ari?"

"You want me to?"

She nods, and I can see she's trying to act enthused, but there's something else…

"Skull?" she says.

"No news yet. They sent it to the lab."

She closes her eyes. "She came to me."

"Bear Woman?"

"Twyla."

I say nothing.

"Dream," she says, her brow furrowed. "Beautiful. Wrapped in furs. Bear behind. Hawk on shoulder." The effort it's taking for her to speak is huge. "Told me I had strength to pull through."

"That's amazing."

"That's why I knew. Her."

I'm never quite sure what to make of Mom's "prophetic" dreams. I suppose it doesn't matter. If she thinks Twyla's helping her get better, so be it.

An elegant dancer of a woman wearing a skirt covered in tiny mirrors swooshes into the room bearing a large bouquet of proteas. "Maye dear, I just heard!" She places the flowers on a shelf. "You poor dear."

"Sylvia." Mom looks truly happy to see her and introduces us. "Has restaurant in town. Yummy salads."

Sylvia runs her hands through a mane of blue gypsy hair. "Your mother is one of my biggest fans." I notice that Sylvia has a lazy eye, making it hard to tell what she's actually looking at.

"She knows her food," I say.

Mom tells her about the skull and how she's sure it's Twyla's. Clearly a believer, Sylvia offers to walk around the spot where the skull was found to see if she can "pick up any energy."

Mom gestures to Sylvia and says somberly, "Psychic."

I smile. No doubt Sylvia considers herself to be part Lemurian, the mysterious race of aliens whom, myth has it, live inside secret tunnels laced through Mt. Shasta. "Cool," I say, then switch to my own thoughts while Sylvia blathers on about some global healing event she attended.

Does Mom even remember what she asked me to do? Maybe her request was fever-induced and has dissolved into brain ether. I get up and peer down the hallway. Where *is* Dad? Is it possible that Mom talked to him directly? Maybe the whole secret deal is already settled. Maybe I don't have to worry about it anymore…

I return my focus to Mom. She looks tired. Should I say something to nudge oblivious Sylvia into leaving? But Sylvia's psychic powers finally kick in. "I should let you rest," she says, gathering up her large purse. "Let me know if you need anything. And if you want visitors. Everyone's been asking for you, dear."

"Can I ask you something?" I say.

Sylvia cocks her head and fixes her gray-blue eyes directly on me, or as directly as she can. "Of course, dear."

"Where do you get your produce?"

## CHAPTER EIGHTEEN

Ari shows up at the hospital around noon. "How's she doing?" he whispers so as not to wake Mom who's zonked after her second round of physical therapy today.

The session was tough to watch. Todd manipulated her arms and legs like she was a Barbie doll, the whole time coaxing her on in that obnoxious, high-on-life voice. Mom was in obvious pain. She even cried out once.

I left. I couldn't stand it.

I don't tell Ari this, though. I don't want to freak him out.

"She's great," I whisper. "She's starting to move her arms and legs a little. And she can talk. Her voice is hoarse, and she's using short sentences, but hell, she's communicating. The physical therapist thinks she might try standing as soon as tomorrow."

Ari leans over the bed so he and Mom are face-to-face, and flutters his fingers, the tips of which are now painted in multi-color nail polish. "Hi, Maye," he says softly then turns toward me. "It's funny to watch someone sleep."

"She needs it. She worked hard today."

He quietly lowers himself in the other chair and picks up a *Fortune* magazine from the pile I stole from the waiting room. He begins flipping through it, stopping on a photo of somebody's gaudy mansion. "People with no taste shouldn't be allowed to be rich," he whispers.

"Which reminds me…"

He looks up from the magazine. "What did I do now?" Like I'm his mom.

"It's not something you did; it's something I hope you're going to do."

In a hushed tone, I explain my idea for Mom's veggie business, emphasizing the part I can see him playing. "I've already started a file of potential clients."

He snaps his finger and points, all cool-like. "I'm so in."

"I'm thinking only ten or fifteen hours a week at first. Then we'll see how it goes."

"We need to come up with a name."

"Yeah."

"Oh! Oh! Oh!" He bounces on the chair, unable to contain himself. "How about Bear Woman Organics? Our logo could be"— he swooshes his hand in an arc creating an imaginary banner—"a bear holding a bunch of veggies."

My finger jumps to my lips in a shushing motion. I glance at Mom. She's still out cold. "I like it," I whisper. "But Mom gets the last say."

He stretches out his bony legs and clasps his colorful fingers behind his head. "What's not to like?" he whispers. "It's perf."

"Mr. Cocky."

"When you're good, you're good."

I stand. My hamstrings feel like iron girders from all this sitting. "What do you say I walk down to the cafeteria and bring us back something to eat?"

Ari snaps his fingers and points. "Fabolicious."

Mom makes a little grunting noise as if she's about to wake up. I glare at Ari. Mom resumes her steady breathing.

Ari cups his hands around his mouth and whispers, "All we had in the house this morning was cold sausage pizza."

I kick his outstretched legs aside and leave.

Half an hour later, I return with two tuna fish sandwiches, a bag of chips, and a couple of bottles of water. Mom is sitting up awake and has two more visitors—a young mother and her two-or-three-year-old daughter with matching blond honky dreads and matching Guatemalan-print dresses with loose-fitting slacks underneath.

Ari, who has somehow procured a pen and pad, asks the mother, "So, Crystal, can I put you down for weekly pick-ups?"

"Absolutely." She ties her dreadlocks into a knot. "I've been after Maye to get this going since last summer. Nobody's tomatoes come close to hers, and her butter lettuce is to die for. We'll live on it all summer." She tousles her daughter's dreads. "Won't we, Sierra?"

Sierra wags her head like a good little Rastafarian.

"I'll let you know when we get our pricing figured out," Ari says.

Mom looks delighted. "My manager," she explains to Crystal.

Ari, now the total businessman, slides the pen behind his ear. "To get Bear Woman Organics up and running before the big summer harvest, we've got to move."

"Move!" echoes Sierra.

*

Jen rinsed the wok with hot water and placed it on the lit burner of the gas stove to dry. She was burping up red peppers from the stir-fry that Maye made for dinner. She pulled the dishtowel off the handle of the oven door and began hand drying the rest of the dishes, hoping that all was going well with Maye and Bean. They were at Bean's fourth grade play. Bean was playing a Yankee soldier.

The two of them had been staying with Jen for almost three months. Actually, Maye had been going in on rent and groceries, so really it was more than "staying with her," although that's what they both called it. Maye had even scored a landscaping job once she let go of the SPCA job in Philly. The extra income was welcome. Jen's job, running sound at a local jazz club, didn't pay enough to support all three.

Jen leaned back against the sink and looked at the laundry nook she'd converted into a room for Bean. The foam mat on the floor left just enough room for the back door to swing open, and not even all the way. On a shoebox by the bed was a tin of lip balm, a piece of quartz, three tiny Pegasus figurines, and a Liberty Bell pencil sharpener. Bean was fanatical about their placement and would scream when anybody touched them. "Moving was hard on her," Maye said. Maye made her own bed on the futon in the living room, every morning stowing her sheets and blankets underneath so as not to "completely take over your life." This touched Jen. The house *was* tiny.

At first she'd been a little nervous about having a kid in the house. It was strange to have to act the responsible adult. But Bean was cool. Precocious. Not two days ago, she'd decided they needed to start recycling plastic bags and made a drying rack out of a hanger and clothespins. Ingenious. And she'd figured out a solution to the ant problem. She'd methodically searched out their point of entry through a crack in the bathroom floor behind the sink then poured cayenne pepper into the crack. On several occasions she'd even accompanied Jen to sound checks at the club. She was too young to attend during working hours, but she loved getting to meet the bands and learn about the sound system.

So why was Jen feeling so restless? Tense?

Bean had invited her to go to the school play, but Jen had declined using the ultra-adult excuse, "I have some work to do." It wasn't that she didn't want to see Bean. That would be great. But spending all that time with Maye would be tricky.

She switched off the burner, put up the last of the dishes, and grabbed a light bulb from underneath the sink. One of the lamps had gone out during dinner. She pulled a chair to the center of the room and stepped up.

The phone rang.

She stepped back off the chair and went to answer it in the living room. "Hello?"

"How's the happy homo family?" Jake slurred.

Jen flipped the receiver up so the mouthpiece was above her head. Why had she picked up? She flipped it back. "Jake. You're wasted."

"So what if I am? My lesbo twin is fucking my wife—or wait, you can't fuck her can you? What is it exactly that you lesbos do anyway?"

Jen cursed herself for a slip she'd made a month ago in a phone call where she was trying to talk some sense into Jake. "If I was lucky enough to have a woman like Maye, I'd never let her go," she'd said. Jake had hung on to those words and twisted their meaning to suit his deluded pity party.

"Jake, I'm going to hang up."

"I want to talk to Maye."

"She's not here."

"Bean?"

"She's not here either."

"Liar."

She was so sick of these weekly—sometimes hourly—calls. She closed her eyes, willing herself not to snap. "They're at a school play." She was careful to keep her tone clear, neutral. "You need help, Jake."

"*I* need help? Coming from you that's priceless." His breathing was thick, raspy. "So tell me, Jen, do you go after all women, or just the ones that are already married?"

"Jake, I'm going to say this one more time and then I really am hanging up. I did not steal Maye from you. She and I are not lovers. You fucked up your marriage all by yourself."

"You lie!" he yelled. "You lie!"

She hung up the phone, took a few deep breaths, and rubbed the back of her neck. What right did he have to judge her life? He was a drunk. She collapsed on the futon next to the open window and lay back on what she called the Quaalude pillow. Its insane softness melted her tense muscles. A warm breeze fluttered the light cotton curtains. She stared at her bare feet while a wave of sadness swept through her. How had her brother gotten so screwed up?

A group of neighbor kids ran by the house shouting and laughing. It made her want to cry.

She'd been so careful not to cross the line with Maye. And it wasn't like there hadn't been plenty of opportunities. When Maye and Bean stepped off the plane, Maye'd been so vulnerable, so needy. And there were all the intimate moments that came from living in tight quarters—the flash of skin as a towel-wrapped Maye emerged from the shower, Maye's sleeveless nightgown revealing the swell of her breast as she lay sprawled on the living room futon asleep. Even more tempting was the fact that Maye was starting to act like she wanted more from their relationship, acting coy, flirtatious. Or was Jen just imagining it? No. Last night, after Bean went to bed, the two of them were sharing a glass of wine in the living room. Maye lifted one of Jen's socked feet into her lap and began massaging. Jen tried to accept it for what it was, a simple foot massage given by a sister-in-law, but Maye began working her way up Jen's calf, then the back of her knee. Jen excused herself and went to bed. It wasn't easy. She wanted to make love to Maye right there on the futon, to press her back against the cushions and—

Jen shook her head. What would it take for her to quit fantasizing about Maye? A good night's sleep? She sure hadn't had that since Maye and Bean moved in. Each night, she lay there thinking about what it would be like to sneak into the living room and wake Maye one kiss at a time.

But she hadn't. That was the point. She hadn't.

Did it matter? Jake already believed the worst. He hated her. Hated them both.

She pushed herself up from the couch and grabbed the light bulb she'd left on the windowsill. Fuck him. Just fuck him.

After two hours, she'd finally shaken the phone call and was stretched out on the futon with her second glass of wine and a Nevada Barr novel.

Bean burst through the door and raced for her "room."

"Whoa!" Jen said. "Where's the fire?"

"Gotta get my stuff," Bean gasped. "Mom said I could spend the night at Becca's."

"Where *is* your mom?"

A frazzled Maye stepped inside the door. "Here." She dropped her purse to the floor then yelled out to Bean, "Don't forget your toothbrush!"

Bean, her arms full of overnight gear, raced back through the living room. "I didn't."

"Hold on," Maye said.

Bean stopped in her tracks. "*Mom*, they're *waiting*."

"Aren't you going to kiss me good-bye?"

Bean pecked her on the cheek. "Bye, Mom." She ran over and kissed Jen too. "Bye, Aunt Jen." The door slammed shut behind her.

"Wow," Jen said, "that girl has some energy."

Maye flopped down on the futon next to Jen's feet. "I'm just glad she's making friends. And Becca's parents seem very nice."

Maye wore a short, light pink, spaghetti-strap dress over black leggings. An oversized sweatshirt with the neck cut out hung off one shoulder. Gold dangly earrings brushed the top of her smooth shoulder.

Jen averted her eyes, a familiar ache budding between her legs. "How was the play?"

"Awful. Bean was great, though. Held that rifle like a pro."

"The reception?"

"Fine. Except the father of one of the kids kept putting the make on me." She sighed. "Do we have any of that wine left? I could use a glass."

A flash of jealousy shot through Jen. She put her novel aside. "I'll get it."

"Oh no, you don't," Maye said, getting up. "You look way too cozy. Want a refill?"

"Sure."

When Maye returned she headed for the faded papasan chair by the window then changed her mind and returned to the end of the futon by Jen's feet.

Jen sat up, head rushing from the wine, and slipped her naked feet beneath her. No need to tempt the situation.

"Sorry to bust in on your quiet night alone." Maye held the wine bottle between her thighs and pulled out the cork.

Jen tried to ignore the desire that was roiling inside her, but was finding it difficult. The wine wasn't helping. "No, no. It's fine."

Maye refilled Jen's glass. "You're probably wondering will they *ever* leave? And I promise we will, it's just—"

Jen leaned over and pressed her finger to Maye's lips.

What had she just done? And, more importantly, what was she going to do now? This was so inappropriate. So…so…

Maye nipped her fingertip. The sensation exploded in Jen's body. Her mind screamed, *Stop! You can't do this!* Then another message, this one more subtle, more furtive, began whispering to her. *Who are you protecting? Jake? Maye? They're both grownups. They've made their own choices.* Trembling, she let her finger travel the soft rise of Maye's cheek, curl around a blond tendril of hair. She wanted to say, *I love having you here,* but couldn't get the words from her brain to her lips.

Maye smiled a wicked smile, tipped her head back slightly, and parted her lips.

Jen leaned in.

Maye leaned in.

They were so close one's exhale became the other's inhale. Yet still, Jen was unsure. She needed Maye to make the choice. If they were going to cross this line, betray Jen's twin brother, Maye's husband, she needed to be sure it was conscious, consensual. "Want to move to the bedroom?" she asked, her lips almost brushing Maye's.

"This *is* my bedroom," Maye said.

Jen tried to make sense of Maye's answer, but her heart was pounding so loud in her head it was scaring off the thoughts. "I mean, do you want to move into *my* bedroom."

Maye slowly grazed her lips over Jen's. "What do you think?"

Before Jen had the wits to respond, Maye pulled her off the couch and into the bedroom.

*

Aunt Jen breezes into the room an hour earlier than we'd arranged. Two fifteen p.m. "How's everybody?" she says, interrupting my animated reading to Mom about a woman's camel trek across the Sahara. I try not to let the disruption bother me, but between the visitors, orderlies, and physical therapy, this is my first time alone with Mom today.

I put the *National Geographic* aside. "You're early."

Aunt Jen sits on the edge of the bed and gazes at Mom. "How're you feeling?"

Mom tips her head to the side. "Tired."

"You have the energy for that sponge bath we talked about?"

Mom looks as if Aunt Jen has just offered her an all-day session at a swanky spa. "Yesssss."

So much for the spitting camels and sweltering sun. "Need help?" I ask, before thoroughly thinking it through. Will I have to... interact...with Mom's privates?

"It wouldn't hurt if you stuck around." Aunt Jen sets the paper bag of things she's going to need next to the bed. "I spoke with the nurse on duty and she said this would be an excellent window of time."

"Okay then."

Aunt Jen tucks a stray curl of hair behind Mom's ear. "I watched a YouTube video on how to wash a person's hair while they're lying in bed. You want to try it? It doesn't look too hard."

"Ahh," Mom says. "Would love."

We decide to do the hair first. Jen plugs up Mom's ears so they don't fill with water and tucks a towel underneath Mom's head. Next, she pulls out a plastic garbage bag and tears it partway so she can tie it around Mom's head like a hood to catch the water. Once Mom is comfortable, Aunt Jen wets her head and gently massages in the shampoo.

"All good?" she asks Mom.

Mom, eyes shut, replies, "Mmm."

Aunt Jen uses a spray bottle to rinse. I hold a washcloth over Mom's face to keep the water from dripping down. Her breathing starts to get shallow, quick, and I ask again if everything is okay.

"Fine," she says, but I can tell she doesn't like the washcloth over her face.

I take a deep breath for her. "It'll just be a few more seconds."

"Yup," Aunt Jen says. "Almost there." She sprays the final bits of suds from Mom's hair. "There."

I remove the washcloth. Mom looks über relieved.

Aunt Jen towels off her head. "So far so good." She pulls out a comb and starts gently dragging it through Mom's hair.

Mom's beaming as much as her face will let her. "Feels good. Clean."

"You look beautiful," Aunt Jen says and damned if Mom doesn't blush.

"Ready for the sponge bath?" Aunt Jen asks.

Mom nods, but I can see she's bracing herself. Being touched is obviously still really painful. Aunt Jen fills a bowl of warm soapy water and one of warm clear water. She adds a washcloth to each.

"Let's start with your face and work our way down."

"Yes," Mom says and closes her eyes.

Aunt Jen runs the soapy washcloth around Mom's face, careful not to get anything in her eyes. Then she moves to her neck and arms, tenderly raising each arm to sponge her pits. Their intimacy is palpable. And makes me damned uncomfortable. I feel like I'm some kind of voyeur, only with my mother, which is beyond creepy. I excuse myself with the lame-o pretext of needing to stretch my legs.

I stroll around the parking lot. The sky is cloudless and it's getting hot. I pass Cell Phone Dude getting out of a silver Maserati. We nod awkwardly at one another. Is his loved one still up in ICU? I watch a few small brown birds shuffling around in the dirt of one of the planters, then head back.

Mom's dry and changed into her favorite fluffy robe from home. But something else has changed. She's gazing at Aunt Jen with an almost embarrassing amount of devotion, and Aunt Jen, hell, she looks downright tranquil—a state almost unknown to her.

"Feeling good?" I ask Mom.

Her eyes flit briefly to mine, "Uh huh," then return to Aunt Jen's.

Okay then. Fine. I get it. My shift is over. I've been replaced. I say my farewells and prepare to depart. Aunt Jen says to tell Dad that she'll stay the rest of the day, so he doesn't need to come down.

Sure. Make me the messenger. That way it'll be my head that gets lopped off. I kiss Mom on the cheek. It's nice to have her smelling like herself instead of hospital. "Love you," I say, boring into her eyes with mine. My hope is to shoot some sense into her. This is no time to be stirring things up between Dad and Aunt Jen.

"You too." She smiles like there's nothing going on, even though we both know there is.

I wander through the maze of halls to the parking lot. Couldn't they at least have the decency to wait until Dad's gone? I forget where I parked and have to walk around awhile before I spot the van. Once in, I can't get out of that parking lot fast enough.

Partway up the mountain, I decide that the only thing that's going to mellow me out is a glass of wine, which is odd. I don't usually drink. I stop at the more bohemian of Shasta's two health food stores and pick up a bottle of organic Pinot Grigio, some cheese and crackers, a small tub of hummus, a loaf of bread, yogurt, and some eggs. It's great to have my own set of wheels, to be able to do my own shopping, and be among people doing regular chores in their regular lives. I'm extra chatty with the hippie cashier, talking about the weather, the produce, any mundane thing I can think of.

I get home feeling rejuvenated by my foray into the world beyond my dysfunctional family, and whistle as I unload the groceries. Then I search out Dad. I want to pretend like everything's okay. Or as okay as it can be under the circumstances.

He's on the deck and looking intently out onto the garden. He points to the area where the skull was. Mom's cockeyed friend Sylvia is beating a Native American drum. Another young woman is chanting what sounds like mumbo jumbo, although it's hard to tell from the deck. For all I know she could be singing the national anthem. But I doubt it.

"They've been at it close to forty-five minutes," he says incredulously.

I settle onto the step. "Mom says she's psychic."

"Which one?"

"The one with the drum."

"Good to know." He drains a Dr Pepper.

I think about the loving way Mom looked at Aunt Jen. Would it be okay to pour myself a glass of wine and have it out here on the deck? Would that be weird for Dad?

"How's your mom?" he asks.

I rip a splinter of wood from the step. "I barely got two minutes alone with her. She's had tons of visitors."

He smiles. "People love to love Maye."

If only he knew. We sit in silence for a few minutes. What's there to say? I remember what Aunt Jen told me to tell him. I take a deep breath and spit it out. "Aunt Jen says she'll finish out the day with Mom, so you don't need to go down." I wait for him to go ballistic, to start ranting about how pushy she is. He just sits there staring out at Sylvia and her chanting friend.

"What do you suppose they're hoping to accomplish?" he asks.

Before I have a chance to answer, his phone rings. He flicks it open, checks the number, and takes it out to the garden.

I watch Sylvia and her protégé doing wiggly fingers at the sky then decide to get that glass of wine after all. I mean, why not? Dad's an adult. Surely he's used to being around alcohol. Still, once I open the bottle, I head up to my room with it and a glass. Why rub his face in it?

Passing Mom's room, I'm drawn inside, just like I always used to be as a kid. I walk over to her dresser. It's covered in antique perfume bottles, pinecones, jewelry, and bottles of various healing tinctures. Photos are tucked into the mirror frame, including ones of Aunt Jen and Dad. I look nothing like them. Maybe that's why I always feel it's me and Mom against them, the short blondes against the tall brunettes. Aunt Jen used to say Mom was the antidote for being a Bell.

What's going to happen if she and Mom fall back in love?

One of Mom's dresser drawers is open. And there's a laundry basket on the end of the bed with a few piles of folded laundry next to it. The unfinished nature of the task reminds me of Miss Havisham's disturbing room from *Great Expectations* where time has stopped. I shut the drawer with my hip and put the wine bottle and glass on the nightstand. Then I clear the bed and stuff a few pillows behind my back so I can sit comfortably. When Mom gets home we're going to have to move her bed downstairs, or put her in the guest room. At least for a while.

I pour myself a glass of wine, take a sip. It's almost too sweet.

I grab Mom's bedside phone and dial Serena. I need the antidote for being me.

# CHAPTER NINETEEN

Serena picks up on the first ring. "I was just going to call you."

"You were?"

"Yeah. I grabbed my cell and it rang."

I spread my toes, pinching back a smile. "Yay."

"How's it going?" Her voice brims with concern.

Suddenly, I'm a popped champagne bottle, gushing forth the events of the last few days—Dad fixing the van so I have wheels, the perky physical therapist that reminds me of Richard Simmons, Bear Woman, the veggie business we want to get started for Mom, Aunt Jen asking if I thought she was condescending to Dad and Samantha, Aunt Jen and Mom acting like they're falling back in love, my fears about Dad's reaction when he gets wind of it. "I mean, he's going to go ballistic. Who wouldn't? Mom asks him to come, presumably because she cares about him, and then she reopens the old wound. Like it's nothing. I swear, her impulsiveness is just a mask for self-centeredness. She'll be all like, 'What do you know? Your sister and I are falling back in love. Isn't that just cosmic?' She doesn't even think about what it might do to Dad. Not that he's perfect. I'm not saying that. But he's been trying. He really has—"

"Um, Brianna?"

"Yeah?"

"Save something for tomorrow."

"Why?"

"Because I'm flying into Redding at twelve forty-eight. Can you pick me up?"

At first I'm not sure I've heard her correctly. "You're what? You're coming?" Adrenaline shoots through me.

"Do you still want me to?"

"Yes! Totally! I would love it!" Did I just use the word love?

"Oh good. I want to be there for you…with you."

We go over the logistics—airline, flight number, where we're going to meet, but before we hang up she says she's had an experience earlier in the day that she's got to tell me about. Her saying this makes me feel like a total dweeb. I just dominated the whole conversation with my wah-wahing. I'm just like my mom. Self-indulgent. "Do tell," I say, leaning forward to show my concern—like she can see me.

"I was heading out to that great beach we found, on that forest path…"

I immediately know the one she means. The path takes you through a patch of rainforest where a bunch of grave markers are planted among the tropical foliage, some quite elaborate with giant marble crosses or virgins, while others are little more than a flat stone with a name, but every one of them, big or small, is decorated with a huge gaudy wreath of plastic flowers still in its original plastic wrapping.

"Well, on the way out there I passed what I guess was a funeral, only it wasn't like an Anglo funeral. It was like a party. The men were drinking beer while passing around the shovel to dig the grave, and the women were dishing out beans, rice, and tortillas from the back of a beat-up station wagon. Kids were running around playing. It was so cool. Such an amazing way to honor death. And family."

It's hard not to compare this to my family—uptight, white, and fractured by our various neuroses. I think about how I wasn't allowed to go to my grandmother's funeral, and that I had a grandfather I never even knew. Oops. I've slipped back into self-indulgence. "Wish I could have been there."

"You're right where you're supposed to be, Brianna. And tomorrow I'm going to be with you."

My heart goes all mushy. She's leaving a Mexican paradise for me. This kind of devotion normally causes me to squirm out of a relationship, but so far I haven't had that urge with Serena. I just want more. Am I in love? Is Serena my antidote?

Through the window I see a wispy cloud splinter into blue sky.

"I can't wait to see you tomorrow," she says softly.

*

Jake knew her only as Violet Dream, but he was sure it wasn't her real name. She was tall, even taller in her fuck-me pumps. She had a different colored pair for every outfit, but always, no matter what, she wore that violet ribbon tied in a bow around her left ankle. It meant open for business.

At a corner table back by the restrooms, Jake sucked down his malt whiskey on the rocks. Was it his fifth? Sixth? He didn't know, didn't care. His eyes were on Violet Dream as she worked the smattering of men sitting at the bar. A pudgy accountant with fat red cheeks couldn't tear his beady eyes from Violet's tits, which were barely held back by the hot pink sequined tube dress that crawled up her ass. She wore a cropped, white lace, short-sleeved jackety thing that had no purpose but to accentuate her voluptuous cleavage. Tonight the fuck-me pumps were white. And the ribbon was tied. Oh yes, it was.

Jake had come to hate that little ribbon, had even told her that to her face. What had she said? "It's my trademark." He hated the thought of a person having a trademark like a product. He also hated the way she was making the moves on the pig-faced accountant.

He scrutinized his glass, blinking several times to bring it into focus. Empty. He signaled Rosie the barmaid.

She sidled up to his table. "Jake, don't you think you've had enough?"

"One more," he slurred. "Been a rough day." He could feel her cocking that painted-on eyebrow. He cleared his throat, sat up a little straighter. "Come on, you know I can hold it."

She sighed. "Oh, all right, one more. But after this, I'm cutting you off, mister. I want you getting home tonight."

He was filled with gratitude, affection even. Rosie understood him. Why couldn't Maye? The thought of his wife—ex-wife as of today's legal action—brought with it the suffocating feeling of being sucked into a mire of muck.

A new drink appeared before him. He slammed it back, his head swimming with disgust.

Violet Dream was playing with the pig's tie. It wouldn't be long now before she coaxed him out of the bar and into that dingy hotel room with its beaded lampshade. There she would debase herself for the pig's pleasure.

Jake pushed himself up from the table and lurched across the room. "Temptress!" he yelled. "Let the pig be! Let him wallow in his own stink!"

Violet Dream glanced at the bartender. The next thing Jake knew, his arm was being wrenched from its socket, cranked behind his back, and he was being thrust out into the cold night air.

He lay in front of the bar with his face squashed against the rough cement.

Then there was nothing.

Then someone going through his pockets.

Then his face pressed against the cool window of a moving vehicle.

He woke on his own couch. It was light. Too light. His head was screaming; blood was pounding in his brain. Inches from his face, on the coffee table, was a business card propped up against his wallet. He powered an arm out and pinched the card between his fingers. He had to squint to read it. YOU NEED HELP. YOU CAN FIND IT HERE. There was an address for something called STRAIGHT POOL. There was also an arrow scrawled on the card. It made no sense to him until he put the card back on the table. The arrow pointed to a photo that had been taken from his wallet. Bean at her sixth birthday party.

Jake snatched up his wallet. All the cash was there. He glanced around the apartment. Nothing seemed to be missing or out of place.

He flipped the card over. Nothing. It was probably just some AA bullshit with its crock of God shit. He heaved himself up to see if he had any beer to chase off his mother of a hangover.

Sometime later, he woke up in his empty bathtub. He had to call the operator to find out what day it was. Two days since he was thrown out of the bar. He hit the answering machine. His boss asking where he was. One of his coworkers calling to see if he was okay.

This was a first. He'd never let his drinking get in the way of work. He collapsed onto the couch and ran his fingers through his greasy hair. There was dried puke on his slacks. Only one foot had a sock on it. What the fuck was he doing? What kind of loser intentionally destroyed his own life? After berating himself this way for a half hour or so, he finally got to his feet and began rifling through his house for that damn card. He found it stuck to his refrigerator with a magnet Bean had sent him years ago for Christmas. The magnet was a bunny holding a heart in its big fluffy paws that said LOVE. How the fuck had the card gotten there? Did he do it? He must have. He clawed at his stubbly face. He was out of control.

An hour and a half later, he was standing outside a well-lit poolroom in Germantown. Through the plate glass window he made out a dozen or so guys hanging around three pool tables. The energy was boisterous. Bruce Springsteen's "Born to Run" was rocketing out of a portable CD player. He walked in anyway. A couple of guys looked up then went back to their game. He thought about leaving, but a barrel-chested longhair in a leather jacket came over to talk to him. "You found us," he said, his tone familiar, like he knew Jake.

Jake squinted at the guy.

"My name's Leo. I gave you a ride home the other night. You were in a pretty bad way."

Uneasy that this biker knew so much about him, Jake said, "What is this? Some kind of AA?"

"No, no, my friend. That it is not. We're just a bunch of guys helping each other keep straight. You play pool?"

"Not well." Jake glanced at the door.

"Good." Leo laughed. "The guys will appreciate that." He clapped his hand on Jake's shoulder. "Let me introduce you around. Then we can go over the do's and don'ts—oh, and sorry for going through your wallet the other night, but I had to find your address. Cute little girl you got."

Jake walked over to the pool tables, his heart hammering in his chest.

*

After Serena and I hang up, I hold the phone to my heart. Did I really almost say, "I love you?" I feel my mouth stretch into a silly grin. She's wonderful. Gorgeous. Insightful. And she cares about me me me!

I put the phone on the nightstand and, flat on my back, pull my knees into my chest. I feel like laughing and crying and shouting all at once. I straighten my legs so the soles of my feet face the ceiling. The late afternoon sun splinters through cut crystals hanging in Mom's bedroom windows making sprays of rainbows across the walls. I reach over to the bottle of wine and my glass, rest the glass on my belly, and, with my legs still stretched up to the ceiling, attempt to fill the glass. Serena's coming back to see m—

"There you are."

I jerk my glass and bottle of wine away, trying to hide it from Dad, which is impossible. I slosh Pinot Grigio everywhere. How did I miss hearing him come up the stairs?

A look of disappointment flashes across his face. "Bean," he says gently. "I've been sober for over thirteen years."

Using my elbows, I scoot up to sitting. "Sorry…" My T-shirt and cargo shorts are drenched.

He sits at the foot of the bed. A rainbow sliver alights on the center of his forehead. "No. I'm the one who should be saying sorry to have put you through all that."

All what? The alcoholic years? The gay-hating ones? I set the glass and bottle by the phone and grab a tissue to blot up some of the wine. "It's okay," I say. "I got over it."

He smiles, but his face is tight, closed. Is he mad at me?

"Serena's coming tomorrow," I say. And I can't help feeling that I've used her as a shield.

Dad tips his head to the side, and the rainbow moves from his forehead to his temple. "That's great. I look forward to meeting her." But something's still bothering him, and it's not the wine. Does he know about Mom and Aunt Jen? Is that it?

"Are you all right, Dad?"

He rubs his hands on his trousers. The rainbow disappears then reappears, disappears then reappears. "You okay doing dinner on your own?"

"Sure. Why?"

"Samantha and I are going to meet up in Dunsmuir. Apparently, there's a nice Thai restaurant there."

*That's* what this is about? A dinner date? "Thai twice in one week. Dad, you're getting wild."

He chuckles but doesn't mean it.

"That's great you're going out with Samantha," I say cautiously. "She seems like a nice lady."

He massages his knuckles. "Yeah. She is."

I wait a few seconds then decide to be forthright. What have I got to lose? "So why do you look all stressed?"

"Do I?"

"Your knee is doing the jitterbug; you look like you're trying to rub the skin off your knuckles." It's the Pinot Grigio talking now. "So yeah, I'd say definitely a little stressed."

The rainbow has moved to right beneath his right eye, making him look like one of those sad clowns.

"Guess you know me pretty well, Miss Bean."

"So what's up? What's got you in such a snit?" I have never before used the word snit. Where did that come from?

He takes a deep breath. "Oh, I'm just a little nervous is all." He picks a thread off his pant leg. "About my date."

God. Could he be any cuter? "You like her that much, huh?"

A single "ha" bursts out of his mouth. "Yeah. I guess I do. She seems like a really special lady."

"You're a great catch, Dad. Good-looking, employed, intelligent..."

"Yeah, yeah." He looks up from fussing with his trousers, his eyes glinting with the last of the day's sun. "I'm sorry, Bean. I didn't mean to lay this on you."

"Dad. That's what family is for. To be there for each other when things get tough."

He nods. "I guess I'm still learning that."

I crawl across the bed and rest my hands on his shoulders. "Just be yourself. You're a good person."

He smiles. "Thanks, daughter. You're pretty smart."

We hug. And for the first time ever, I'm not itching to let go.

## CHAPTER TWENTY

It's a little after nine in the morning and Dad's already out digging Scotch broom. I stare at the burbling empty Mr. Coffee waiting for it to fill and wondering if the "watched pot" warning applies. The phone rings. I follow the sound of Mom's phone to the living room. "Hello?"

"Bean, I need you to pick up a wheelchair," Aunt Jen says. "Maye's coming home today."

My pre-caffeine brain makes it difficult for me to fully comprehend what she's saying. Today? Yesterday's wine isn't helping either. "Didn't Dr. Reneaux say Monday?"

"You know your Mom. She charmed the good doctor into releasing her early."

Mom says something in the background.

"What did she say?" I ask.

"She's telling you she pooped. She's been crowing about it all morning."

I walk back to the coffee pot. A quarter full. "Isn't she supposed to get a bunch more physical therapy?"

"I promised Dr. Reneaux that one of us would drive her down every day. Now, I've got a wheelchair rented, but we need to have it here by the time they release her this afternoon."

"Shall we put her in the guestroom?"

"That's what I was thinking. I'll move up to her room. She can't do stairs."

I consider telling her that Serena's coming then don't. I'm not ready for Serena's visit to become a family happening. Not yet. Aunt Jen tells me the address of the rental place and Mom's approximate release time, one o'clock, while I go over logistics in my head. That's plenty of time to clean up, do my morning chores—maybe I'll even cook breakfast—then drive down the mountain, pick up the wheelchair, and meet Serena at the airport. She and I can deliver the wheelchair together. Talk about an entrance.

Three hours later and cranked on coffee and French toast, I've got the wheelchair in the van and am on my way to the airport. I'm nervous, and it's not the caffeine. What if when I see Serena I realize I've made a terrible mistake? Or she does? What if the sizzle has sizzled? Then what? The palms of my hands sweat against the faux-leather wrap on the steering wheel. This could be sooo awkward.

I flick on the radio. It's tuned to an oldies station that's playing a slew of love songs (yay), but when I pull into the Redding Municipal Airport parking lot, the station kicks into Paul Simon's "50 Ways to Leave Your Lover." I snap off the radio, praying it's not an omen.

Filled with a prickly mix of excitement and dread, I park and head to the terminal. I so want this to work. I want my antidote. But standing with the small crowd in the passenger greeting area, I start feeling discouraged. Serena is too healthy for me, too well adjusted. And she likes me. Which must mean there's something wrong with her.

I spot her coming down the hallway in a loose-fitting yellow sundress, huaraches, and those big gold hoops that accentuate her long neck. Her curly black hair is knotted on top of her head, her red backpack slung over one shoulder. In other words, she looks like the woman I'd like to spend the rest of my life with. She's talking with some guy in a business suit. Something he says makes her laugh.

What do I do when she reaches me? Kiss her? Hug her?

She sees me and breaks into a radiant smile.

Kiss? Hug? Kiss? Hug?

I go for the hug, then, ever the Casanova, manage to mutter, "Hey."

"Hey," she says back, but she sounds hurt. Or I think she does. Should I have gone for the kiss?

An elderly woman rolling a suitcase nearly mows us down.

"Shall we, um, get your bags?" I wish I'd thought to wear something besides my cargo shorts and Club Bed T-shirt.

"Sure." She slings her arm around my shoulder. "I can't tell you how good it is to see you."

We step into the stream of humans. Why am I acting like such a dweeb?

❖

Standing next to Serena as bags orbit around the carousel, my self-consciousness escalates. I'm reminded of those times when I've had a super sexual dream about a casual friend then run into her the next day. Only this is worse. Much worse.

She slips her hand into mine; it's cool compared to my sweating palms. "You doing okay?"

I see her bag tumble out the chute. "Isn't that yours?"

Her second bag follows. "Yup." She lets go of my hand and steps forward.

I cut her off. "Got 'em."

I heave the first bag off the track, chase after the second and heave it off, then get ridiculously macho and insist on rolling them both to the car.

She looks at me like I'm a total case. "I'm not helpless, Brianna."

"I know," I say, extending the handle on the bigger bag, "but you've had a long flight." I try to hook the second bag on the bigger one but the clip is broken.

She reaches for the smaller bag. "Brianna, let me—"

"No way." I flash what I hope is a debonair smile. "I'm all over it."

Steering the bags separately is harder than I expected, especially going over the outside curb where one of them almost topples over, but I act like everything's cool, asking about her flight, about

Sayulita. I barely hear a word she's saying. All I can think is: What is my problem? What's making me act like such a total geeber? When we finally reach the van, my arm sockets feel dislocated. I unlock the back door and load her bags in next to the wheelchair. Then, with the slam of the door, it comes to me, an insight so obvious I laugh out loud. I'm bracing myself for the moment I screw things up.

She cocks a dark eyebrow and rests her hands on her slender hips. "Brianna, you sure you want me here? Because if not—"

I take her gorgeous face in my hands and plant a kiss right on her lips. The kiss takes a bit longer to execute than I'd planned, because the moment our lips touch they don't want to stop. What's more, our tongues want in on the action too. She falls back against the van to brace herself. I press my whole body against hers. It feels so good, so right, her hands running slowly up and down my back, grabbing at my butt, our tongues probing, exploring. But we're in a damn airport parking lot. I force myself to pull back, struggling to catch my breath. "Does that answer your question?"

Her chest, with the insanely sexy collarbones, is rising and falling, rising and falling. "I'll say."

I can barely make my legs walk over to unlock her door. We kiss one more time before she gets in. Then I get in on my side. I have to focus to line up the key with the ignition.

She rolls down her window. "I'm so glad I came."

On the ride to the hospital, I fill her in on Mom's pronouncement that she's coming home today. Listening intently (something I love about her), she lets her hand drag in the wind. So sexy.

"Good for her," she says. "Hospitals are great places to get fixed, but no place to get well."

The two of them are going to love each other.

*

Jen lined up eleven metallic seed beads—two navy blue, one silver, two turquoise, one red, two more turquoise, one more silver, and two more navy blue—on a hair-thin needle, positioned them next to the other lines of beads on the loom, and secured them in place with a second pass of the needle. She was in the final stages of the belt she was making for Bean's sixteenth birthday. Maye, on the bed next to her, was writing in her journal. The door was shut, but was doing little to stifle the pulsing music and raucous noise of thirteen partying teenagers crowded in their living room. Bean's birthday bash was being held four days early because her birthday fell on a Wednesday.

"Think I could sneak out there and nab us a plate of guacamole and chips without being noticed?" Jen asked Maye.

"If there's any left."

Bean had petitioned that she was old enough to have a party without chaperones, but neither Jen nor Maye agreed. Especially since the bungalow they were staying in was a sublet. It had shown up right when their condo lease expired, and Maye couldn't resist. "It's only for the summer, but wouldn't it be great to be so close to the beach?" Reluctant as Jen had been, she had to admit the place had been great. Only two blocks from a secluded beach and nestled next to a grove of eucalyptus trees, it was the perfect summer beach house.

"You going to get that done in time?" Maye asked.

"After this, all I have to do is get it tacked to the leather, which I should get to tomorrow. Then the buckle and voilà."

"Bean's going to love it."

Something crashed in the kitchen.

Maye put down her journal and swung her legs off the bed. "My turn."

"Check the guac scene while you're out there with the savages."

"Will do." She closed the door behind her.

Jen put her beads aside and stretched her legs, numb from sitting cross-legged. Something poked her in the thigh. She reached into her jeans pocket and pulled out a glass marble painted to look like Earth. She'd forgotten all about it.

Beyond the door, Bean was berating Maye for butting in. "Mo-*om*. We've got it under control."

Maye slipped back into the room, closing the door on the blasting music.

"What broke?"

"That ugly blue glass bowl you picked up at the flea market."

"Hey. I like that bowl."

Maye flopped back onto the bed. "Better make that statement past tense."

Jen laughed. "Speaking of the flea market, I picked this up for you today." She tossed the marble up in the air for Maye to catch. "I give you the world."

Maye held the tiny Earth in the palm of her hand. "It's so perfectly painted."

"That's what I thought."

Maye kissed Jen's cheek. "You sweetie. Thank you." She reached over to the nightstand to set the marble on the stump of a burned down taper then went back to writing.

"I take it there was no guac left."

"There was before the bowl went crashing to the floor."

"Ouch. A double whammy."

"Want me to make us some sandwiches?"

"You would?"

"Yes. Even though it's officially your turn."

"No way. This one doesn't count. It's for us."

"I still have to face a room full of hormonally-pumped teenagers." She rested her finger on her chin. "Then again, you did just give me the world."

"Yeah. That counts for something, doesn't it?"

Bean stuck her head in the door and yelled over the music. "Mom, can we order a pizza?"

"What happened to all those wraps I made?"

"Gone. Can we?"

Sighing, Maye swung her legs off the bed.

"Good luck," Jen called as she was swept into the belly of the party.

Jen lined up the last row of beads, secured them in place, and tied off the project. If affixing it to the leather went as smoothly, she could have it ready with a day to spare. She scooped the beads off the tray and returned them to their individual containers, careful to keep the colors sorted, then put loom, bead containers, and tray into the large Tupperware bead box. Once that was stowed under the bed, she did a few stretches and returned to her spot on the bed. She felt trapped. She began looking around for what to do next and noticed that Maye had been writing a letter, not in her journal. She'd just been using the journal as a hard surface. The letter began, "Dear Jake."

Jen's impulse was to read on. She resisted. That would be stooping too low. But she couldn't stay on the bed and *not* read it. She got off the bed and stood by the closet, far enough away that she couldn't make out the rest of the words then just stared at the letter. She stayed this way until Maye returned with the sandwiches.

Maye set a tray with sandwiches and milk on the bed. "What's up?"

"You're writing to Jake."

Maye's eyes flicked to the letter. "You read it?"

"Should I have?"

Maye shrugged. "I was just keeping him informed of his daughter's activities."

"I thought you'd given up writing him because he never acknowledged receiving them."

"I did."

"So why are you writing now?"

Maye sat on the bed and picked up a cheese and avocado sandwich. "He's her father."

"Don't patronize me."

"I'm not. I'm just speaking the truth." Maye put her sandwich down and picked up the letter. "You want to read it?"

"No."

"Yes, you do."

"No, I don't."

Maye tossed the letter onto the tray with the sandwiches. "You're making too big a deal of this."

"Am I?"

"Read it. There's nothing—"

"Can we just forget it?"

Maye held Jen's gaze. "I can. Can you?"

*

I push through the hospital door and hold it open for Serena. I'm excited for Mom to meet her, which is amazing. I never like bringing my girlfriends home. Mostly because they always love Mom, making the imminent break-up that much harder. But for the first time ever, I'm not planning an escape route. I want me and Serena to last.

We take the stairs because Serena wants the exercise after her long day of travel.

"You told her I'm coming?" she asks.

"Nope. We're going to surprise her."

Serena does not look happy. "Doesn't she have enough going on without you springing me on her?"

"Trust me. Mom thrives on over-stimulation. She'll be thrilled."

Then again, maybe I should have warned Mom.

I take Serena's hand at the top of the stairs and we start down the hallway, passing the competent elderly nurse I met earlier. "Oh good," the nurse says. "Your mom's all clear to go. She and her... friend are in there waiting for you."

I thank her and we continue on, stopping just shy of Mom's room. I stop and take both of Serena's hands in mine. "Just so you know," I say quietly, "this mom you're about to meet isn't my real mom. I mean, she is my mom, but she's really different than she usually is."

Serena looks like she wants to laugh.

"What?"

"You're nervous."

"No, I'm not."

"Yes, you are."

"No, I'm not."

She gives my hands a squeeze. "Don't worry. It's cute."

I shake my head and pull her into the room, nearly falling over backward when I see what I see—Mom and Aunt Jen spooning on the hospital bed, both of them sound asleep, but looking every bit the picture of true love.

"I thought you said they weren't together anymore," Serena whispers.

"I did."

The following seconds are filled with my inner primal scream. What the hell kind of game is Mom playing?

Serena slips her arm around me and speaks softly into my ear. "You didn't tell me you looked so much like your mom."

"Yeah, well, I do." I'm trying to figure out what to do next. Leave and come back, pretending we never saw this? Pitiful as it sounds, this would probably be my course of action if I didn't have Serena by my side. But since she's here, I have to at least appear to have some integrity. "I should wake them and tell them we're here," I whisper.

"But they look so sweet."

"I'm just glad we're not my dad. Him seeing this could set off World War Three."

"Brianna, don't jump to assumptions. Your aunt might have fallen asleep comforting her."

But after a lifetime of dealing with these people, I know what I see is real. I can feel it in my bones. I reach across Mom and gently shake Aunt Jen's shoulder.

She blinks awake. "Bean." She clears her throat. "You're here."

"Sorry to get you up from your...nap." I have to work to keep the anger from my voice. "But I brought the chair."

She pushes up to sitting, waking Mom.

"Hey, Mom."

She smiles dreamily, and without a trace of guilt in her voice, says, "My sweet Bean."

Couldn't they have waited?

I take Serena's hand. "I have Serena with me. She flew back from Sayulita to give me moral support."

Mom starts to struggle up to sitting. I step forward to help her, but Aunt Jen stops me. "She can do it herself. Can't you, Maye?"

Mom makes a grunting sound and squirm-pushes her way up. Once sitting, she lets out a long exhale, "Whoooo." She attempts to pat her hair into place, clearly painful for her. "Serena. Nice to meet you. Bean has talked a lot about you."

Hearing Mom sound like herself is such a relief, I almost forget all about her and Aunt Jen's budding romance. Almost.

Serena steps up to the bed. "It's nice to meet you too. Brianna says you're making amazing progress."

"So they say," Mom says, managing a chuckle.

Try as I might to be happy about Mom and Serena meeting, my anger gets the better of me. "So what's going on with you two?"

Aunt Jen and Mom look at each other, as if neither one of them has given it the slightest thought.

"Who knows?" Mom says.

Aunt Jen laughs. "I plead the fifth."

I wait a few seconds for a more thorough answer. When it's not forthcoming, I say, "We've got the wheelchair in the van."

## CHAPTER TWENTY-ONE

Mom wants to ride up the mountain in the van with me. Aunt Jen needs to pick up her Subaru, which is now fixed. Serena offers to go with Aunt Jen in the rental eggplant to get her car. From there they'll split up and drive the two vehicles up the mountain. I call Dad to warn him that he's going to have to help me unload Mom. He doesn't pick up. I leave a message.

Mom doesn't have the muscle power to hoist herself into the van.

"Are you sure you wouldn't rather ride in Dad's rental?" I ask.

"I'm sure."

Aunt Jen and I exchange looks. Okay then.

Aunt Jen grabs Mom under the armpits, I grab under her knees, and we lift her into the passenger seat in front.

I fasten Mom's seatbelt. "Comfortable?"

She tips her head back and looks at the small prayer flags hung across the ceiling. "I love this van."

Aunt Jen kisses her cheek. "See you at the top."

I pull Serena aside. "You sure you're okay with this?"

"It's fine. She needs to get her car."

"But you've had this long day."

"Brianna, it's no big deal. I'm happy to help."

We do a quick kiss and go our separate ways, me praying my family doesn't scare her off.

I climb into the van. "Need anything in Redding before we head up?"

"Just take me home," Mom says.

As I negotiate the congested Redding traffic, Mom natters on about people she met at the hospital. A green Jetta fails to stop at a four-way, and I have to slam on the brake. She tells me about the nurse's granddaughter whose 4-H sheep took a gold medal. An SUV swerves in front of us on the on-ramp. She goes on about one of the orderly's marital problems. The fervor with which she's imparting all this trivial information to me makes me think she's trying to make up for lost time.

"You know," Mom says, as I merge onto the interstate, "this experience hasn't been all bad."

I brace myself for her trying to convince me that coming down with Guillain-Barré syndrome was a gift. I flick on my blinker to change lanes. I know I should be more understanding. She's been through this horrible ordeal. Hell, she's still going through it, but this part of Mom that always has to find the cosmic silver lining can drive me nutso.

"It's made me realize," she continues, "what's really important."

"About that," I say. "I don't think Dad and Aunt Jen have had their little talk yet."

She gestures out the window, her movement still jerky and unrefined. "Look at the new growth on that pine. Isn't the color glorious?"

"Mom. Did you hear me?"

She lets her hand fall into her lap. "Of course I did. It's just that it doesn't matter."

I tighten my grip on the steering wheel. "Oh no, you don't. When you were at your worst, when you thought you were dying—Christ, when we *all* thought you were dying—that seemed to be the only thing that did matter to you."

"Well, I was wrong."

"Wrong?"

"All that matters is that they both came."

The lake comes into view. She takes a sharp inhale. "Look at that blue!"

I wish I could dive into her bliss bubble where everything happens for a reason, and the reasons are always good, but prickly me just has to pop it. "Mom, what's Dad going to think when he finds out you and Aunt Jen are…doing whatever it is you're doing?"

"Guess we'll find out tonight," she says dreamily. "Jen's going to tell him."

My stomach lurches. Not with Serena here! But I should have known. Grand finales always include fireworks.

\*

Maye drained the water from the pasta into the sink. The steam was so thick and hot she had to turn her face away to keep from being burned. "We have to invite him."

Jen looked up from the guest list she was working on. "Why? He won't come."

"That's not the point. He's her father. He should be invited to her high school graduation."

"We're not talking about her graduation; that's public. He can come or not. Who cares? But her graduation dinner—at *our* home— is a whole different matter."

Maye dumped the linguini from the colander back into the pot. "He's your brother, Jen. And he's Bean's father—"

"And he blames me for the divorce. Why would I want to be around that? Why would you?"

"It's not a question of what we want," Maye said, scraping pesto out of the blender and into the pot of noodles. "It's a question of what Bean wants."

Jen shoved the pad with the guest list across the table. "You think Bean wants him here? Want me to go ask? She's in the backyard."

"Well, maybe she doesn't want him, but she should."

"We *all* should, Maye, but we all *don't*. And there's a reason for that—"

"He's been sober for years."

"He's a homophobic—"

"You know how I feel about labels being used in this house."

"Sometimes they apply."

"Us being together can't be easy for him."

"We've given him plenty of opportunities to—"

"Stop." Maye had no intention of listening to Jen rehash all of Jake's shortcomings. It was pointless. And misguided. There was so much Jen didn't know.

Jen tossed her pencil onto the table. "What now?"

Maye walked into the living room to gather her thoughts but knew exactly what she had to do, even though just the thought of it caused tears to prick the corners of her eyes. She returned to the kitchen, held her hand over her heart. "I can't do this argument anymore."

"Then don't," Jen shot back, her voice hard, flat.

"No. I really can't. We've been having it for nine years, and I'm sick of it."

"Maye—"

"Listen to me. Maybe you can live with estrangement from your brother, from Bean's father, but I can't. It's like kryptonite in our relationship."

"Kryptonite?" Jen's tone was biting, cruel. "What, we're a comic strip now?"

Maye dug her hands into her hips. "You know what I mean. It's killing us."

"What are you saying?"

Maye could tell by the cross of Jen's arms, the closed expression on her face, that she didn't want an honest answer, but she steeled herself nonetheless. She had to do this, not just for herself and Bean, but also for Jen and Jake. "I can't keep doing this…us." The tears she'd been fighting off ambushed her eyes, but she would not look away.

Jen stared at her. "Maye—"

"I can't fully love you with this…I don't know…heartbreak? Betrayal? Between us."

Jen groaned. "Maye. When are you going to let it go?"

"When you and he sort things out. But I can't—won't—be between you two anymore."

Jen pushed back her chair. "Is this about the graduation dinner? Because if it is—"

"It's not about the stupid dinner!" Maye held a trembling hand to her brow. "It's not working between us. Our love for each other isn't enough. You know it, even though you won't admit it. I know it…" Maye waited for Jen to say something, disagree with her, anything. When she didn't, she spoke the plan that had been circling in her mind for months. "I'll leave after Bean's graduation. I'll take the money Mom left me and get a place of my own. Or travel. I don't know. But I can't keep—"

"What about Bean?" Jen asked, as if Maye hadn't remembered she had a daughter. "What are you going to tell her?"

"She's not stupid. She knows we've been struggling."

Jen slammed the table. "Would you quit? You're talking crazy! We love each other. We're a family."

"I've made up my mind."

"Just now? Just like that?"

"No. Not just like that."

"Then why didn't you say something earlier?"

"I have. And you always blow it off, like it shouldn't bother me that I broke up your family."

"I keep telling you, you didn't. He and I—"

"Jen. Get real. Until you work this out with your brother, come clean to him—and yourself—about your guilt, we'll never be able to have a healthy relationship."

Jen reached for her wrist. Maye jerked it away, her eyes so full of tears that the world had gone blurry.

Jen shifted into her "rational" mode, which Maye hated. "What can I do to get you to change your mind?"

"Work it out with Jake."

Jen swept her arms out wide. "There's no way. He hates me. He won't even pick up the phone when I call."

"When was the last time you tried?"

Bean pushed through the back door, stopping to take in the scene. "Am I, like, interrupting something?"

Maye turned to the refrigerator to wipe her eyes. "Jen and I were having a discussion. What's up?" She hated for Bean to see them fighting. It broke her heart.

Bean looked down at her ratty Vans sneaker held together with duct tape. "I was just wondering when dinner's going to be. A bunch of us are meeting outside of the Rio at six forty-five."

Maye collected herself and faced Bean. "A couple more minutes, sweetie. I still need to dress the salad."

Bean walked slowly, deliberately, to the table, grabbed a piece of garlic bread, and retreated to her room, letting the door slam behind her.

Maye felt Jen glaring at her, but refused to meet her eyes, choosing instead to reach into the cabinet above the stove for the olive oil. It was no surprise when she heard Jen's Doc Martens storm across the floor and out of the house.

✳

It's early evening and the sun is hovering above the tips of the tallest ponderosas. Mom, in her wheelchair, is gazing contentedly at her garden from the back deck. Across from her, Serena and I sit sideways on the glider, she nestled between my legs. The warmth of her back pressed against my chest, belly, and nether regions, is both stimulating and soothing. I twirl my finger through a curl that's come loose then give the glider a gentle push with my foot.

"The kale needs to be harvested," Mom says.

In the few hours she's been here, her coloring has gone from pallid to rosy, and she seems more confident, more herself. She even stood on her own for a few seconds while Aunt Jen helped her into her favorite pajamas.

"We'll get to it," I say. "We've been a little preoccupied around here."

"Do you need a blanket over your legs?" Serena asks Mom. "It's starting to get a little cool."

As expected, the two are getting along famously.

Mom raises her arm slightly, wincing. "I'm fine."

I turn my attention to Dad and Aunt Jen furiously digging up Scotch broom on the far side of the garden. Aunt Jen strode purposefully out to join him as soon as she got back with her newly repaired car. They've been at it ever since. I keep waiting for them to blow.

Serena runs her thumb over my knuckles, bringing me back to what's good in my life. A yellow and black butterfly lands briefly on the rail before zigzagging off. A raven high up in a ponderosa flaps its wings and calls *AWK!*

I hear Ari's truck pull up out front.

"Back here!" I yell.

We listen to him tramp around on the gravel path. "Check this out." He thrusts a drawing in front of Mom. "Dad drew us a logo."

Mom looks thrilled. "I love it."

I reach out a hand. "I wanna see."

He brings it over to show me and Serena. The drawing is great. A portrait of a bear, which looks weirdly like Mom, in front of a cornucopia of veggies. Underneath, it says Bear Woman Organics.

"Ari's dad is a tattoo artist," I tell Serena then introduce them.

Ari places his arm across his waist and executes a flamboyant bow. "Mah-velous to meet you."

"You too," Serena says and flashes him that gorgeous smile.

He holds up a fan of glittery sticker-filled three-by-five cards. "Oh, and I made up some postcards about the project. Mom said she'd hand them out to her friends. And I can put stacks all over town."

"Ari, you are an angel," Mom says.

He flaps the postcards like wings. "Don't you mean a fairy?"

We all laugh, and I think to myself, maybe everything will work out. Mom's getting better. Her business is coming together. I'm holding a woman in my arms that I'm pretty sure I love. Hell, I do love. A lot. And I'm going to tell her so tonight. Then I notice that Dad and Aunt Jen have stopped digging and seem to be in an argument. While it's too far away to make out what they're saying, it's clear that Dad is pointing his finger not two inches from Aunt Jen's chest, while she, standing firm with her fists clenched, holds her ground. I glance at Mom. She sees it too. My gut tenses up. Our blissful nirvana is about to come to a screeching halt.

Serena removes my hand from her belly. "What do you say I throw together that corn salsa?"

"Good idea," I say, making it clear I want to go with her.

"Oh no, you don't. You're staying out here with your Mom." She looks at Ari. "But I could use some help."

He dons his gentleman persona. "Delighted."

I have no interest in watching Dad and Aunt Jen rip each other to bits, and almost say so, but Mom says, "Yes. Stay, Bean."

Serena heads inside, Ari at her heels. A chilly emptiness replaces her.

Dad's finger has gone from pointing to jabbing.

"I told you he'd go ballistic," I say.

"It's more than that," Mom says, squinting. "He's about to do what I asked him to."

"And how would you know that?"

"I can see it in his eyes."

I don't bother to mention that from here there's no way in hell she can see his eyes. "It doesn't look like he's confiding any secret, Mom. It looks like he's yelling."

"He hasn't gotten to it yet. He's still battling the trolls around his heart."

We watch for a while longer, Mom's expression annoyingly serene. "It's so easy to lose sight of the big picture," she says.

"Big picture?"

"Twyla's gift to me."

Ah. That big picture. The one where her illness was all part of some dead bear whisperer's plan. "We don't even know if the skull is hers, Mom."

"It's hers," she says knowingly.

Dad turns his back on Aunt Jen and walks over to the crime tape. He squeezes the bridge of his nose. His shoulders begin shaking.

"Is Dad crying?"

Aunt Jen walks over and places her hands on his shoulders, dropping her forehead onto his back. Dad keeps talking without looking at her.

"Mom, you've got to tell me what's going on."

"It's not my secret to share, Bean. But I suspect sometime soon your father will tell you himself." She gives the arms of her wheelchair a tap. "What do you say you wheel me back inside and I get to know this girlfriend of yours."

Her use of the word girlfriend sends a little shockwave through my body. Are we girlfriends? We haven't really talked about it. "I think it's a little premature to call her my girlfriend."

Mom gives me that annoying look that says she knows me better than I know myself. "Whatever you say, Bean."

In the kitchen, Serena sets me up as her sous-chef, grating cheese, chopping lettuce, tomatoes, and garlic. I sneak over to the window to see what's going on outside. I even use Mom's bird-watching binoculars to get a better look. What I see shocks me. Aunt Jen and Dad sitting cross-legged on the ground facing each other. Aunt Jen, looking tortured, appears to be bearing her soul to Dad.

"Bean," Mom says. "Think you could tear yourself away from the window to set the table?"

I hang the binoculars on the hook. "I just want to make sure they're not killing each other."

Ari pours corn chips into a bowl. "You should see Mom and Dad's fights. One time Mom says she pulled a gun on Dad."

"That's horrible," Mom says.

Ari shrugs. "Mom says that was the night I was conceived."

By the time the table is set and Serena's vegetable enchiladas have come out of the oven, we've given up on them for dinner.

"They'll come in when they're ready," Mom says.

Serena wipes her hands on a dishtowel. "Shall we just serve ourselves?"

I push Mom up to the table. "Sounds good."

Ari sets the corn salsa on the table and also a platter of baked winter squash and a huge green salad.

I take one last look out to the garden. They're gone. I turn around to tell everyone, but right then they walk into the kitchen, their arms thrown over each other's shoulders. Both their faces are splotched and puffy.

"Something smells good," Aunt Jen says.

Serena puts the enchiladas on the table. "You're just in time."

"Dad, this is Serena," I say.

His eyes graze over her, but I can tell he barely sees her. "Nice to meet you."

"Nice to meet you too," she says.

He walks over to Mom and squats so his face is level with hers. "Thank you, Maye," he says. "For everything."

I glance at Aunt Jen, but she doesn't notice, just puts her hand on Dad's shoulder and adds, "That's from both of us."

"Okay. Somebody's got to tell me what's going on," I say. "You guys are totally freaking me out."

Dad, Mom, and Aunt Jen laugh. Then Dad does something he hasn't done since I was a tot. He picks me up off the ground to hug me. "I promise to tell you, Bean. Just not tonight. I'm wiped."

I wiggle free. I mean, Serena's watching. "Fine. Leave me in the dark."

This causes another round of laughter, which I find totally annoying. I pick up my glass of water and take a sip, trying to appear older than I feel, only my mouth seems to have a hole in it and a little dribbles out the side.

There's a loud rapping on the door.

"Allow me," Ari says.

I walk over to the stove where Serena has begun wiping a bit of tomato sauce from one of the burners. My family's drama has got to be weird for her. I put my arm around her. "Thanks for cooking."

She kisses me on the cheek. "You're welcome."

Aunt Jen wheels Mom to the head of the table.

"Hang in there," Serena whispers.

I swear, she's the only thing keeping me from floating into outer space.

Sylvia swooshes into the kitchen. "Maye! Love! I called the hospital to tell you about my incredible visitation with Bear Woman, and they told me you'd been released."

"We're about to eat," Mom says. "Want to join us?"

"That would be divine." She holds up a plastic milk bottle that's full of something orange. "I just happen to have some fresh-pressed carrot juice from the restaurant. We over-juiced, you might say."

Dad's cell rings; he checks the number.

Ari goes out to the deck for a chair.

"I'm going to take this outside," Dad says. As he walks out we hear him say, "Samantha…"

Once he's out of earshot, Mom asks, "Do you think Jake's serious about her?"

"Oh, yes." Aunt Jen pulls a chair next to Mom. "He seems quite smitten."

Could it be that I've been wrong all this time about Dad wanting to get back with Mom? Is that possible? Or has he simply given up? Ari returns with the chair for Sylvia. "For you, madam."

"Such a gentleman." She spreads out her colorful tiered skirt to deposit her large derrière.

I quietly suggest to Serena that we sit across from each other.

"Perfect," she says and pulls out the chair closest to us. I circle the table and claim my spot across from her, which unfortunately is also next to Sylvia.

Dad returns from his phone call and places his hands on the back of the chair next to Serena. "May I?" he asks.

She looks up at him and smiles. "Sure." It's so strange to have the two of them in the same movie.

Settled into the head of the table with Aunt Jen, Mom says, "Everything okay, Jake?"

"With what?" he asks.

"Your phone call."

He can tell she's fishing, but isn't going to give her the satisfaction. "None of your business." He almost pulls off the attitude too, until he goes to sit down, then he bonks the table making everyone's water glasses slosh.

"Shall we eat?" Mom asks, obviously delighted that she can still get a rise out of him. I swear, she's like a butterfly, flitting from person to person, spreading the love. I just hope Dad doesn't take her flirtations too seriously.

I serve myself some salad and pass the bowl to Sylvia.

"I must tell you…" Sylvia helps herself to a whopping portion of salad. "The vibrations I felt out in the garden were powerful. I'm quite certain it was Bear Woman. I could feel her history in the soil. It's as if she were pulsing through me."

Serena finds my foot on the plank support under the table and rests her foot on it. I hand her the bowl of corn salsa and we let our fingers brush. Are we girlfriends?

Sylvia passes me the enchiladas, her kimono sleeve dragging over my food. I scoop one out. The cheese makes strings to my plate that I have to cut with the edge of the spatula. This morning's French toast seems like days ago.

Halfway listening to the conversation noodle along about the skull, my primary focus remains on what's *not* said. There's the moment that Aunt Jen places her arm around Mom's wheelchair. It's a cautious move, but also deliberate. Dad, of course, notices. He was supposed to. And he and Aunt Jen hold each other's gaze for a few seconds, making it clear they've discussed Mom and Aunt Jen's new status, then Dad goes on with his meal. Aunt Jen relaxes and takes a big gulp of carrot juice.

It hurts Dad to see Mom and Aunt Jen so happy. I can tell by the way he keeps glancing at them. But he also looks oddly content, as if sitting around this table with his family is something he's dreamed about for a long time. Maybe his trip wasn't about getting back with Mom. Maybe he just wants love. As I watch him push enchiladas around on the plate (as if a porterhouse or Big Mac might magically appear), I wish for him that things work out with Samantha. He could use a good snuggle.

Sylvia reaches across the table, once again dragging her sleeve through my dinner. "Is there more of that delicious corn salsa?"

By the time we move on to dessert—Coconut Bliss, dark chocolate, and strawberries—the conversation has moved away from the skull and into the past. Aunt Jen is talking about a skateboard that she and Dad made when they were kids.

"We used to take turns roaring down the street on that thing," she says.

"Right past Tommy Delario's house," he says.

"God, that kid was a knob."

The two of them start laughing hysterically as if remembering the same incident at the same moment.

"When he—" she sputters.

"Got his pants caught—" he says between heaves of laughter.

"On that bush!" they say together.

"Oh. My. God," she says, making an effort to explain to the rest of us. "He was running after Jake—"

"When his pants got caught on a bush and ripped right off him."

"They were those little"—she snorts back a laugh—"elastic waist ones his mom used to make him wear."

"And his underwear. They had Friday embroidered on the front!"

They erupt into another round of hysteria, while the rest of us look on amused, but not really getting it. It seems like they're laughing about more than the skateboard. Something deep. Something buried beneath piles of pain.

It's so amazing to see them get along, and at the same time so…tenuous. Will it last?

Serena rubs her foot against mine, sending a shock wave of arousal up my leg. We gaze into each other's eyes. *Be in the now*, her eyes seem to say to me. I look around the table. I'm surrounded by people I love. And all of us have full bellies. Outside on the windowsill, a jungle-wild Mrs. Simpkins watches over her humans.

"Ari," Aunt Jen says. "Tell Jake what you told me Maye said."

Ari furrow his brow. "Huh?"

"You know, when we first met, about Jake and I being her favorite examples of good people—"

"Who came from a supremely fucked-up family!" Ari finishes.

Everyone laughs.

"It's amazing what we survive," Sylvia says.

Mom, in an effort we all recognize as momentous, lifts her glass of carrot juice above her head and says, "To life."

I raise my glass. "To love."

Aunt Jen raises hers. "To family."

This is followed by some serious clinking of glasses.

## CHAPTER TWENTY-TWO

I'm watching Serena sleep. Her expression is peaceful, her breathing rhythmic. I wish I could jump into her dreams and surprise her. I would make love to her—an encore of last night's quiet passion. The memory of her biting down on the pillow to keep from crying out makes me wet. My girlfriend. The thought fills my heart. I consider kissing her cheek and working my way down, but hear creaking floors and clinking dishes downstairs. Everybody must be up. Serena makes a sweet snuffling noise and pulls the pillow over her head. She needs sleep. She was already exhausted when she arrived yesterday, then she had to deal with Aunt Jen's car, and went on to make that amazing dinner. I mouth, "I love you," and slip out of bed. I throw on pajama pants and a T-shirt before tiptoeing into the hall. I'm careful not to let the door latch click behind me.

Eager to see what my family is up to, I pass Mom's room and notice the bed hasn't been slept in. A clue. Aunt Jen must have slept in the guestroom. With Mom. An uneasiness tries to move in, but I don't let it. Everything got worked out last night. Everything is fine. Still. Serena and I made such an effort to be quiet and now it turns out no one was on the other side of the wall.

There's a half pot of coffee in the kitchen but no one around. Odd. I imagined a trio of congenial parents sitting around the table drinking coffee. I peek out the window. Not a soul. I pour myself a cup and notice we're getting low on half-and-half. I start a grocery list and stick it on the fridge.

Mrs. Simpkins gets up from the nap she was taking in a spot of sunshine and yowls.

I bend down to give her a pat. "Where is everyone?"

She arches her back and rubs against my shin, purring loudly.

I fill her bowl with kibble, refresh her water bowl, and put new water in the ant moat then, mug in hand, I head out to the back deck.

I stop on the screened-in porch. Dad and Aunt Jen are standing on either side of the burn barrel by the chicken coop burning Scotch broom. Aunt Jen is dressed in black sweats, flip-flops, and a ball cap, while Dad's in khakis, a crisp white button-down, and Top-Siders. Flames lick the top of the barrel; billows of black smoke spiral upward. There's a book in Dad's hand. He rips out a fistful of pages and tosses it into the flames. Aunt Jen adds a branch of Scotch broom from the wheelbarrow. They stand back and watch the flames grow. Aunt Jen grips her coffee cup with two hands. Dad takes his cup from the nearby stump, takes a sip, then rips out more pages for the fire.

I inch close to the screen, but can't make out their murmurings. I do, however, recognize the book. It's the Bible from Aunt Jen's car. Dad's Bible. The one Reverend Bates gave him.

The secret. It must be.

Aunt Jen stokes the fire with more Scotch broom. Dad drops the gutted cover into the flames. Sparks shoot up like mini fireworks. Aunt Jen raises her hand above her head like a Baptist testifying. Dad keeps his eyes on the flames. She walks around and drapes an arm over his shoulder and the two of them stand that way for some time. Aunt Jen says something to Dad. He laughs. They do a high five. She throws more branches in the barrel and they both pick up their coffees.

Figuring this is as good a time as any, I push through the screen door.

They hear the crunching gravel and turn toward me.

"Bean," Aunt Jen says, her face soft but guarded.

"Morning," I say nonchalantly. "Kind of early to be doing the chores, isn't it?"

The two of them make eye contact. Are they going to tell me?

"Not that early," Aunt Jen says. "Your dad's already been to Redding and back."

"I met Samantha for breakfast," he adds.

"Tell me you did *not* take her to IHOP."

He laughs, but doesn't say one way or the other.

I take a long sip of coffee, giving them ample opportunity to tell me they just burned a Bible. They don't.

"How's Mom?" I ask Aunt Jen.

"She had a rough night, but seems to be sleeping peacefully now. I put a bell beside the bed for when she wakes up."

Mrs. Simpkins pushes through the cat door. It flaps in her wake. The chickens scratch at the dirt and make burbling chicken noises.

"That Serena of yours seems like a keeper," Dad says.

Aunt Jen nods.

Is this the Dad that just days ago was trying to talk me out of being gay? "She's pretty special," I say.

"And she can cook," Aunt Jen says. "That's something worth sticking around for."

I think about Serena biting down on the pillow. *That's* something worth sticking around for.

We're all now looking at the barrel. A curl of black smoke twists its way up and disperses into blue sky. There's not a trace of the Bible. Aunt Jen tosses on another branch.

"Here's something you'll be interested to know," Dad says.

"Yeah?"

"I stopped by the police station on the way back from Redding."

Not exactly what I was expecting. "And?"

"And the skull isn't Bear Woman."

Aunt Jen snickers for reasons I don't understand. I choose to ignore her.

"How do they know?"

Dad looks like he wants to laugh too. "It's a man's skull for starters."

Aunt Jen slaps her hand over her mouth to keep from cracking up.

"Mom's going to be disappointed," I say, hoping to remind them of the seriousness of the situation. "It could affect her recovery."

Aunt Jen coughs into her fist. "We're not telling her."

"At least not right away." Dad uses an overly solemn voice to act like he doesn't think this is funny. "Sooner or later, it will come out in the news—"

"Or not," Aunt Jen interjects.

Have they not thought this out at all? "Hel-*lo*? Mom gets the local rag. It's bound to get a mention there."

Aunt Jen folds her hands around her mug, trying to behave. "We'll make sure she doesn't see it."

"Yes, we will," Dad says, sounding every bit the Boy Scout.

I go on, "Well, someone's going to have to give Sylvia a heads up. Make sure she doesn't say anything."

Dad chuckles. "Oh, I've *got* to be there for that."

Aunt Jen whacks his arm. "Jake!"

"What? That woman needs to be taken down a notch or two."

"You guys!" I glare at both of them. "Mom is going to be heartbroken."

Aunt Jen puts her hand on my shoulder. "That's why we're not going to tell her."

"Exactly." Dad pours out the dregs of his coffee. "But you have to admit, Bean, it is kind of funny."

"Especially after all Maye's hoopla about Bear Woman's spirit 'emerging from the earth to heal her,'" Aunt Jen tacks on.

"Mom said that? About emerging from the earth?"

"Oh yeah," Aunt Jen says. "Last night after you and Serena went to bed, she went on and on about Bear Woman 'rising up' to heal our entire family."

I kick a clod of dirt. "Just because the skull isn't Bear Woman's doesn't mean her spirit didn't show up."

Aunt Jen shoots me an incredulous look from beneath the brim of her ball cap. "You really believe that?"

I realize, of course, that I don't. I've taken up Mom's cause because that's what I always do. Us against them. But the family geometry is changing. I just wish I knew into what. "It is a tad woo-woo," I concede.

"Just a tad," Dad says.

Aunt Jen takes a swig of coffee. "The skull probably belongs to some old logger."

"Or a drunk," Dad says, "who lost his way back from the tavern."

"Could be an outlaw," I say.

Aunt Jen puts her coffee down and sticks her hand out, palm-side down. "So. Are we agreed then? We keep this from Maye as long as possible? Or at least until she's walking?"

Dad places his hand over hers. "Agreed."

I look from one expectant face to the other. They're asking me to finish off this pancake stack of hands with my own. But the recasting of alliances is short-circuiting my ability to move. The Bell twins have reconciled. I no longer have to choose between them. They're both mine. I'm not just my mother's child anymore. I'm Brianna Sheridan Bell, a girl with a mom, a dad, and another mom who just happens to be my dad's twin.

I place my hand on top of theirs. "I'm in."

# About the Author

Award-winning author Clifford Henderson lives and plays in Santa Cruz, California, where she and her partner of nineteen years run The Fun Institute, a school of improv and solo performance. In their classes and workshops, people learn to access and express the myriad characters itching to get out. Her other passions include gardening and twisting herself into weird yoga poses. Her first novel, *The Middle of Somewhere,* was ForeWord Magazine's Gold Medal Book of the Year and took the Lesbian Fiction Readers Choice Award for both comedy and general fiction.

Contact Clifford at www.cliffordhenderson.net

# Books Available From Bold Strokes Books

**Breaker's Passion** by Julie Cannon. Leaving a trail of broken hearts scattered across the Hawaiian Islands, surf instructor Colby Taylor is running full speed away from her selfish actions years earlier until she collides with Elizabeth Collins, a stuffy, judgmental college professor who changes everything. (978-1-60282-196-5)

**Justifiable Risk** by V.K. Powell. Work is the only thing that interests homicide detective Greer Ellis until internationally renowned journalist Eva Saldana comes to town looking for answers in her brother's death—then attraction threatens to override duty. (978-1-60282-197-2)

**Nothing But the Truth** by Carsen Taite. Sparks fly when two top-notch attorneys battle each other in the high-risk arena of the courtroom, but when a strange turn of events turns one of them from advocate to witness, prosecutor Ryan Foster and defense attorney Brett Logan join forces in their search for the truth. (978-1-60282-198-9)

**Maye's Request** by Clifford Henderson. When Brianna Bell promises her ailing mother she'll heal the rift between her "other two" parents, she discovers how little she knows about those closest to her and the impact family has on the fabric of our lives. (978-1-60282-199-6) **Chasing Love** by Ronica Black. Adrian Edwards is looking for love—at girl bars, shady chat rooms, and women's sporting events—but love remains elusive until she looks closer to home. (978-1-60282-192-7)

**Rum Spring** by Yolanda Wallace. Rebecca Lapp is a devout follower of her Amish faith and a firm believer in the Ordnung, the set of rules that govern her life in the tiny Pennsylvania town she calls home. When she falls in love with a young "English" woman, however, the rules go out the window. (978-1-60282-193-4)

**Indelible** by Jove Belle. A single mother committed to shielding her son from the parade of transient relationships she endured as a child tries to resist the allure of a tattoo artist who already has a sometimes girlfriend. (978-1-60282-194-1)

**The Straight Shooter** by Paul Faraday. With the help of his good pals Beso Tangelo and Jorge Ramirez, Nate Dainty tackles the Case of the Missing Porn Star, none other than his latest heartthrob—Myles Long! (978-1-60282-195-8)

**Head Trip** by D.L. Line. Shelby Hutchinson, a young computer professional, can't wait to take a virtual trip. She soon learns that chasing spies through Cold War Europe might be a great adventure, but nothing is ever as easy as it seems—especially love. (978-1-60282-187-3)

**Desire by Starlight** by Radclyffe. The only thing that might possibly save romance author Jenna Hardy from dying of boredom during a summer of forced R&R is a dalliance with Gardner Davis, the local vet—even if Gard is as unimpressed with Jenna's charms as she appears to be with Jenna's fame. (978-1-60282-188-0)

**River Walker** by Cate Culpepper. Grady Wrenn, a cultural anthropologist, and Elena Montalvo, a spiritual healer, must find a way to end the River Walker's murderous vendetta—and overcome a maze of cultural barriers to find each other. (978-1-60282-189-7)

**Blood Sacraments**, edited by Todd Gregory. In these tales of the gay vampire, some of today's top erotic writers explore the duality of blood lust coupled with passion and sensuality. (978-1-60282-190-3)

**Mesmerized** by David-Matthew Barnes. Through her close friendship with Brodie and Lance, Serena Albright learns about the many forms of love and finds comfort for the grief and guilt she feels over the brutal death of her older brother, the victim of a hate crime. (978-1-60282-191-0)

**Whatever Gods May Be** by Sophia Kell Hagin. Army sniper Jamie Gwynmorgan expects to fight hard for her country and her future. What she never expects is to find love. (978-1-60282-183-5)

**nevermore** by Nell Stark and Trinity Tam. In this sequel to *everafter*, Vampire Valentine Darrow and Were Alexa Newland confront a mysterious disease that ravages the shifter population of New York City. (978-1-60282-184-2)

**Playing the Player** by Lea Santos. Grace Obregon is beautiful, vulnerable, and exactly the kind of woman Madeira Pacias usually avoids, but when Madeira rescues Grace from a traffic accident, escape is impossible. (978-1-60282-185-9)

**Midnight Whispers: The Blake Danzig Chronicles** by Curtis Christopher Comer. Paranormal investigator Blake Danzig, star of the syndicated show Haunted California and owner of Danzig Paranormal Investigations, has been able to see and talk to the dead since he was a small boy, but when he gets too close to a psychotic spirit, all hell breaks loose. (978-1-60282-186-6)

**The Long Way Home** by Rachel Spangler. They say you can't go home again, but Raine St. James doesn't know why anyone would want to. When she is forced to accept a job in the town she's been publicly bashing for the last decade, she has to face down old hurts and the woman she left behind. (978-1-60282-178-1)

**Water Mark** by J.M. Redmann. PI Micky Knight's professional and personal lives are torn asunder by Katrina and its aftermath. She needs to solve a murder and recapture the woman she lost—while struggling to simply survive in a world gone mad. (978-1-60282-179-8)

**Picture Imperfect** by Lea Santos. Young love doesn't always stand the test of time, but Deanne is determined to get her marriage to childhood sweetheart Paloma back on the road to happily ever after, by way of Memory Lane—and Lover's Lane. (978-1-60282-180-4)

**The Perfect Family** by Kathryn Shay. A mother and her gay son stand hand in hand as the storms of change engulf their perfect family and the life they knew. (978-1-60282-181-1)